NILE

by

T. Lidd

authorHOUSE®

AuthorHouse™
1663 Liberty Drive, Suite 200
Bloomington, IN 47403
www.authorhouse.com
Phone: 1-800-839-8640

First published by AuthorHouse 12/11/2008

ISBN: 978-1-4389-0044-5 (sc)

Library of Congress Control Number: 2008906514

Printed in the United States of America
Bloomington, Indiana

This book is printed on acid-free paper.

PROLOGUE

Prior to World War II, college football's substitution rule stated that once a player came out of a game, he was not allowed to return to the field until the next quarter. As a result, footballers played both offense and defense as teams exchanged possessions through punts, turnovers, or scores. Key players on a team often came out of the game shortly before a quarter ended, so they could get an extended rest – the last two or three minutes of the quarter, plus the break while the teams exchanged ends of the field – before re-entering the game to start the next quarter. The game required more aerobic endurance than today's modern game. There was also less scoring, lending even greater significance to punting and field position. Sometimes the offense punted prior to fourth down, trying to catch the defense off-guard without having a player deep to receive the punt, and return it.

In the early 1940s, due to World War II, fewer men were playing college football, so the substitution rule was changed to allow players to exit and enter the game between plays. This, in turn, resulted in coaches not only substituting freely since they had fewer players, but they began coaching some players to specialize at offensive positions and others at defensive positions. Eventually, when teams traded possessions, eleven offensive players came out and were replaced by eleven defensive players, and vice versa for the opponent.

Nile is a historical novel about young men, one in particular, who played the game in the late 1930s prior to the substitution rule changes. Having grown up while the effects of The Great Depression were still influencing the nation, these young men played the game without feelings of entitlement. The games, scores, key plays, scoring drives, and injuries depicted in this book are factual. The characters are real.

Freshmen were not allowed to play on the varsity, but liberty was taken to introduce Al Couppee early, and playing as a freshman, because he was a colorful character and an integral part of the story. Many of the personal accounts in *Nile* are based on information from a book written by Al Couppee, the quarterback of the 1939 Iowa Hawkeyes.

Four parts of the novel are written verbatim. Nile Kinnick's senior class commencement speech, his famous Heisman speech, the letter from the Navy to Nile's parents, and various paragraphs from newspaper articles are presented word for word.

I owe a very special thank you to my 'personal' editor, Jane Kelly. Thank you, Jane, for the idea, the encouragement, the editing, and most of all, happiness.

Left End	Left Tackle	Left Guard	Center	Right Guard	Right Tackle	Right End
Prasse	Walker	Tollefson	Diehl	Luebcke	Enich	Evans
Smith	Bergstrom	Pettit	Andruska	Hawkins		Norgaard
			Frye	Snider		

Quarterback
Couppee
Gallagher
Ankeny

Left Halfback	Fullback	Right Halfback
Kinnick	Murphy	Dean
	Green	McLain
	Vollenweider	Busk
		Gilleard

The right shift from the T-formation into the Notre Dame box. The ball is hiked directly to the left halfback.

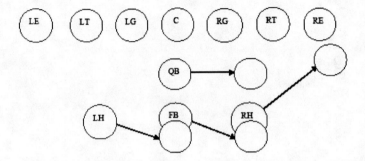

CHAPTER ONE

Sunday nights on North 15th Street were a family ritual. Dinner was a special event with all four grandparents in attendance, his parents, his brothers Ben and George, and Uncle Charles' family. Grandma Clarke's food was delicious and plentiful in this Norman Rockwell-esque setting in Adel, a small rural town in Iowa.

Dessert followed in the parlor. His grandmother, Arletta Clarke, often played a classical composition on the piano following dinner. April through September, when weather offered warmer sunsets to the west, everyone gathered outside for dinner's final course. Magnificent tall white pillars lined the wrap-around porch, giving a sense of antebellum grandeur and charm to those sitting in the wicker chairs. The scene belied the economic times. Many, throughout the nation, didn't enjoy such prosperous settings. The Great Depression of 1929 was seven years ago. Even those on this beautiful porch, on this warm August evening, had been experiencing better circumstances not long ago. Those good times were becoming a distant memory to an eighteen year old. Almost half his life had been lived since then.

The conversations were topical and educational. Oftentimes politics were discussed. It was a common theme, especially considering Nile Clarke Kinnick's maternal grandfather was the governor of Iowa years ago. George Washington Clarke, the host of these Sunday gatherings, was a two-term governor of Iowa from 1913 to 1917. His rise to the governorship took a path common to many with political aspirations. Small accomplishments slowly and steadily stair-stepped to larger dreams. A successful small town attorney, he later became Speaker of the State Assembly, where he gained vast support because of his honorable and forthright approach to political issues confronting both parties. This preceded his rise to Lieutenant Governor, and, finally, Governor. He more recently served as Dean of the Drake University Law School in Des Moines before retiring.

Sunday nights were for family. It was a time when grandchildren were challenged to read a few pages from a book, or a poem, followed by an engaging dialogue of interpretation. Everyone participated. Tonight, Nile read Longfellow's poem, "Excelsior." The former Governor had asked Nile two days prior if he would read this poem. The importance of this family setting was indescribable to a grandfather so accomplished in the past, and so understanding of life's fleeting moments. Grandpa Clarke's health was failing. His neck curved backwards in an attempt to hold his head upright, compensating for his forward slouching shoulders. A cane was always nearby.

Young Nile started to read:

> *The shades of night were falling fast*
> *As through an Alpine village passed*
> *A youth, who bore, mid snow and ice*
> *A banner with strange device, - Excelsior!*

He read with all the passion he could assemble. He had practiced it several times since his grandfather's request. Nile, too, felt these fleeting moments. He understood, unlike his younger brothers and cousins, his grandfather's illness. He also knew his own participation in these Sunday evenings would soon end, and, instead, he would be walking the sidewalks and hallways of the University of Iowa campus. His high school graduation was two months ago. Nile knew, engrained into him from these Sunday nights, the power of well-thought written or spoken words. So he continued, trying to give the poem life, telling the story of a young boy wanting to scale a mountain, determined to let nothing stand in his way of accomplishing his quest.

A traveler, by the faithful hound,
Half buried in the snow was found,
Still grasping in his hand of ice
That banner with the strange device,
-Excelsior!

Nile looked up from the page and saw his mother beaming because of his delivery. A strong voice projected out while he frequently made eye contact with his familiar audience. Frances Clarke Kinnick had prepared her eldest son well.

There in the twilight cold and gray,
Lifeless, but beautiful, he lay
And from the sky, serene and far,
A voice fell, like a falling star, - Excelsior!

It was tradition to let the younger children go first. Nile was the last of the cousins to read. Soon, Nile's younger brother, Ben, would undertake the role of final reader with Nile away at college

Applause followed from the fifteen people on the porch. It was more than an obligatory applause. It was an applause honoring not only tonight's well-read passage, but acknowledging years of Sundays, and this young man's continual growth. All knew there was something special about

Nile. All knew these evenings would have great effect. His confident and calm demeanor showed in his easy smile and superb stature. His eyes took in life.

He attained celebrity status not only in Iowa, but also while living his senior year in Nebraska. He experienced tremendous success in high school football, basketball, and baseball in both states. After three stellar years for Adel High School, his family had moved to Omaha, Nebraska. His abilities were quickly noticed by the sportswriters in Omaha as he collected first team all-state honors. He had decided he would try to play all three sports at the University.

Moving to Omaha his senior year was due to his father, Nile Kinnick Sr., struggling financially with farming. He had amassed a fair amount of land, but Nile Sr. struggled with the cash flow after the Depression. He finally sold the land after Nile's junior year and became a land appraiser for the Federal Land Bank of Omaha. At the time, Nile, Ben, and George didn't realize how great their father really was. Nile Sr.'s dignity and honor never wavered as he faced unwanted changes, and financial hardship. He remained the pillar of the family, always loving and kind to his wife and children, always helpful and friendly to those he knew.

William Butler Kinnick, Nile's paternal grandfather, was a successful banker and landowner. He and his wife were always invited guests at George Washington Clarke's home. Nile's two grandfathers had become close friends through the years. Nile had great admiration and respect for both grandfathers as they stood, side by side, giving their own ovation for Nile. It was also their vote of approval for the parental skills of Nile Sr. and Frances.

Sunday night rituals at Grandfather Clarke's home were now a monthly, rather than weekly, event for Nile's family since moving to Omaha, giving each gathering more significance. The ex-Governor had asked Nile to read this particular poem tonight. The other grandchildren were unaware how special this moment was for a grandfather after receiving his most recent diagnosis. While Grandpa Clarke wasn't the type to share the details of his health concerns, he was astute enough to know he needed to savor every moment with his family. His voice had a slight quiver as he spoke with moistened eyes. "For all such ambitions, all such resolves, all such persistent efforts; even against the most difficult of times, the whole world will shout 'Excelsior.' So may it be with you, Nile. We all wait to witness the triumphs as they come to you. We know you will hold your head high and never vacillate from what is 'right.' I believe someday you will experience the feeling of leadership, knowing many will anticipate and cling to your thoughts and words. And your decisions will be wise. Excelsior, my dear Nile. Excelsior."

Nile gazed out the rear window on the ride back to Omaha that evening. The warm humid days would soon be replaced by cool autumn evenings. The bright green fields would slowly lose their color and fade to browns, signaling harvest time. The tree leaves would change from bright yellows and oranges to deeper reds and maroons before drifting from their branches, leaving the dark skeletal trees to stand bare against the harsh winter winds. The farm chores would intensify, trying to crowd two days of work into one before the sky darkened every night. His father had farmed from morning to night during those hectic October weeks. Nile remembered how he helped his dad after school and football practices. He missed the purity of farming and the contented feeling of knowing the crops were in and the work done. There was a tremendous sense of pride in being a steward of the land. Riding a tractor in the middle of a field, no one in sight or within hearing distance, was a spiritual experience almost inexpressible to someone from the city. So many times he had experienced that feeling of tranquility. There was serenity knowing that everything in sight, from horizon to horizon, belonged to the family.

He knew those days were memories. Everything was different now. The thought of going to Iowa City and not seeing his parents or brothers daily caused him to pause. Yet, the unknown journey seemed adventurous. He experienced sadness and exhilaration simultaneously. He knew his feelings were no different than those of any other incoming freshman. It was time to move on and reach the top of his 'Alpine mountain.'

As he was thinking about the poem he read earlier that night, his thoughts were interrupted by his brother, Ben. "I think you should have gone to Minnesota. Iowa isn't any good. Wouldn't you rather be on one of the best teams in the country?"

Ben was asking a question Nile had already asked himself many times. Playing high school football in a larger city this past year might be the reason his notoriety caught the eye of Bernie Bierman, one of the most successful coaches in the country. The University of Minnesota Golden Gophers' coach was a perennial Big Ten champion and led one of two football programs vying annually for the number one ranking in the country. Notre Dame was the other team. Coach Bierman was riding a wave of success enabling him to recruit almost any high school player he chose. Bierman liked Kinnick's affability and eloquence. He thought Kinnick could be a natural leader, so Nile was asked to visit Minneapolis in June for a team tryout. But at 5'8" and 165 pounds, Coach Bierman didn't think Kinnick had the size, or speed, to make a contribution to his dynasty. Kinnick wasn't sure he wanted to join Minnesota anyway, especially after Bierman's lack of enthusiasm following the tryout. Nile wanted to play where he could make a difference. And Iowa, still reeling from a recruiting scandal in 1930 over allegations of a slush fund to pay athletes, had become the doormat of the Big Ten. The challenge at Iowa was apparent. But what Kinnick desired most was an education and possibly the opportunity to attend his grandfather's law school alma mater.

"Ask me that same question in another year, Ben. It'll be a great challenge to help Iowa's fledgling program rise above to respectability. What would I prove by going to Minnesota - just that I was good enough to be recruited? The challenge will be immense at Iowa, and if the program turns around, the reward will be so much sweeter. Anyway, ask me again after I've had my head beaten in a few times with the Hawkeyes."

Nile Sr. spoke. "Frankly, I'd much rather cheer for Iowa. Who could relish the thought of their son being a Gopher?" Ben and George both chuckled. Frances merely shook her head at her husband's attempt at humor.

The decision had been made. Nile was headed for the worst football team in the Big Ten.

CHAPTER TWO

Two years later, Friday, June 10, 1938. A young man in Council Bluffs packed his clothes into a small suitcase, a recent high school graduation gift from his parents. When he was done compressing his entire wardrobe into his suitcase, there was still room for more clothes if he had owned more. Mary Couppee watched. Her son was headed to college, an accomplishment no one except young Al Couppee thought possible.

The '30s saw most families still reeling from the Great Depression. It affected everyone living in this economically impoverished area surrounding Thomas Jefferson High School. The dilapidated houses were small and in need of repairs. Most were rental properties with tenants who cared little about the unpainted siding, and even if they did care, they were unable to spend money for paint and brushes. Mature weeds grew in the jagged cracks along the uneven sidewalks. The dirt-packed lawns possessed only an occasional tuft of grass.

"Al, I'm worried about you hitchhiking to Iowa City. I know Mr. Jennings has promised you a job when you get there but I worry about you not eating right and being lonely in an unfamiliar city."

"Mom, I've dreamt of this day ever since they talked to me about playing for the Hawks. It's not Notre Dame, but it's better than Creighton. I know you'll worry; you're my mom. But I've got to do this. The idea of trying this is so exciting. We can always write each other every week."

Mary stared at the floor while Al Couppee continued soothing his mom's uneasiness. "I'll be okay. I can always come home if it doesn't work out. But the thrill of it has me feeling butterflies in my stomach, Mom. I can't wait to see what happens next, from the first driver that picks me up, to where I'll sleep tonight, who I'll meet, who will be my friends, how I'll compare to college football players, how I'll do in the classroom."

"We are proud of you," Mary said. His mom looked up at him with that rare but beautiful dichotomy of tearful eyes on a smiling face. "Remember when people were making fun of you taking college prep classes? We thought you might be wasting your time, too. There was no way your dad could pay for college. But you always thought something would change, and you made it happen." Mary let out a huge sigh before continuing. "We often have a tendency to think something in our future will enrich our lives beyond expectations, and change everything. But the reality is, it's our efforts that alter our destinies. And you, my darling son, seem to have realized this better than anyone."

A few minutes later Al set his suitcase next to the street so he could give his mom and sister final hugs. His brother was somewhere in the neighborhood unaware his older brother wouldn't be home for awhile. He extended his right hand to his father. "Dad, promise me you'll be at my first college game."

His father was a good and decent man, but like so many others, he had fallen on hard times. He lost his job five years ago at the meat packing plant and was now delivering cattle feed and hardware to local farmers six days a week, ten hours a day. His father's grip was strong, his eyes soft, and his smile beaming with pride, even though he felt the failure of his financial inability to contribute to his Son's college education. Young Al sensed his dad's sadness.

"That will be worth saving some money, son. Your mom, sister, brother, and I will all be there. I promise you that."

Al walked towards the 25th Street and Avenue A intersection. He hopped on a street car that would take him through the downtown area of Council Bluffs to U. S. Highway 6. Fourteen hours later, involving 6 different rides from strangers he would never see again, he arrived in Iowa City. The final driver dropped him off at "The Academy," an Iowa City pool hall/restaurant where many of the University's athletes spent time. A young man with a suitcase and appearing lost in a new environment was a common sight this time of year.

He watched two students play a nickel-dime Kelly pool game. He was tired, hungry, and thirsty, but adrenalin kept him going. He was finally here, the beginning of his dream.

"Your shot, Pettit."

Al Couppee looked over at the well-muscled student-athlete busy talking to a coed, suspending his turn at the pool table. Pettit came back and contemplated his next shot.

"Are you Ken Pettit?" interrupted Al.

"Yes, I am. Who's asking?"

"I'm Al Couppee from Council Bluffs. I remember watching you play some games in high school."

"I know who you are, Couppee, the next high school star anxious to showcase his talents on a bigger stage. Glad to meet you, Couppee. And good luck with the showcasing. By the looks of your suitcase, I'd guess you just got here and don't have any idea what to do next."

"You're right. When I took off this morning, I didn't know when I'd get here. There aren't a lot of places to be dropped off at nine o'clock at night."

"Consider this your lucky night, Couppee. First, go order some food." The billiards game temporarily stopped while Pettit talked. "Are you supposed to see Hi Jennings about where you're staying and working this summer?" Ken Pettit knew the answer before he asked. Hi Jennings was in charge of all student-athlete housing and jobs. Academic scholarships were available for some of the luckier players, but athletic scholarships, other than free tuition, didn't exist. A promise of a part-time job during the school year and summer employment was the best the University could do, especially in these economic times and with the athletic budget still reeling from the recruiting scandal.

"Yes. But it's too late to contact him tonight."

"No, it isn't," Pettit replied. "As soon as you're done eating, we'll walk over to his house. He won't care. In fact, he'll be happy he has another recruit on campus. It's not as if we're a Big Ten powerhouse with players waiting to be recruited. Some back out at the last minute."

Hi Jennings just lived six blocks east of downtown. Ken Pettit knocked on Jennings' front door at ten p.m. Jennings was surprised to see them but was cordial and invited them in. He was on the phone immediately and, within one hour, contacted Al's new landlord, verified a job he had previously arranged for Al with the University's grounds maintenance crew, and secured a board job that would provide meals.

By eleven p.m., on the same day he stepped onto the street car in his hometown, Al Couppee was set to begin his journey.

Six a.m. came early for an excited and anxious freshman. He was to join some other athletes at "The Academy" where they would each receive instructions about their job duties for the week. Al was told he would be building the rock wall buttressing the hill along Westlawn, the nursing school dormitory.

Couppee took off walking in the direction he was told. As he approached the jobsite, he encountered his first look at Big Ten football. A college student was carrying a full bucket of wet cement to be poured over the twenty and thirty pound rocks. The football player was as tan as anyone Al had ever seen in his life. His coal black hair atop a chiseled jaw and crooked nose was imposing to an eighteen year old away from home for the first time. His physique was extraordinary. Al Couppee had never seen someone so large and physically sculpted. His massive biceps and triceps bulged from the weight of the bucket. His barrel chest protruded above well-conditioned abdominal muscles.

Couppee stood in silence looking at this mammoth specimen. But it was only for a short moment that this hulk was the most astonishing body Couppee had seen because, just then, a blonde Greek-like god reached up from the trench with even bigger arms to grab the cement.

"Are you Couppee?" asked the dark-haired, tanned twenty-one year old, wiping the sweat from his forehead.

"Yes, Al Couppee." He felt inadequate addressing this guy from his one hundred eighty pound frame.

"We've been expecting you. I'm Mike Enich. That's Wilbur Nead down there. We're in charge of you this week. All you've got to do is what we tell you to do. Are you ready?"

In time, Couppee would realize Mike Enich, the best lineman on the Hawkeyes, was a gentle giant. "Yes. What do I do?"

"Kinnick can't make it today, so you can do his job. I'm sure I don't have to tell you who he is." Enich gave a wry smile.

Nile Kinnick had practically become a legend in one year at Iowa. He was All-Big Ten in football as a sophomore. He also was a starting catcher for the baseball team. And, this past winter, he was the second leading scorer on the Hawkeye basketball team. But Couppee also remembered Nile Kinnick passing to Kinnick's younger brother, Ben, at Benson High in Omaha, a pass that beat Couppee's Thomas Jefferson High team. Couppee had been chasing Nile Kinnick when Kinnick let go of the thirty-five yard pass.

"I thought he'd be on an academic scholarship, not working here, anyway," responded Couppee. "But I guess everyone needs money."

"You never know about Kinnick," Enich said. "One day he's speaking to the Rotary Club about his view of college athletics, or even politics. The next day he's out here in the trench. He's something else. But I'll tell you what, Couppee, Nile Kinnick is the most impressive guy you'll meet all year. He's got that leadership thing going. He just has total belief in his abilities. But he never talks about his accomplishments. He just makes things happen.

"I remember last winter, Bob Hobbs and he had just pledged the Phi Kappa Psi frat house. There was this big party. So at the party he meets this Delta Gamma girl, Era Haupert, who was a beauty queen in the Hawkeye yearbook. They start talking and he invites her to meet him at the Ohio State basketball game in the Fieldhouse that Saturday. He gives her two tickets. He tells her he will meet her there. So, she brings a girlfriend, I suppose thinking he would show up in the seat next to her. Well, the tickets are right behind the Hawkeye bench and Kinnick is on the court warming up for the game because he's a starting guard. He says 'hello' to her just before the game begins. Then, at halftime, he's awarded a scholarship out at half court for his academic achievements of the past year as a student-athlete. He scores fifteen points, but the Buckeyes win. Anyway, she didn't know he was on the basketball team. Just another day for Kinnick."

"I heard he was quitting baseball and basketball this year," Couppee added.

"He wants to focus on his studies. In fact, I think he's planning on applying for a Rhodes Scholarship. Frankly, I'm glad he chose to quit those sports and continue football. He's our main man. We almost turned the program around last season but injuries killed us. Think about it. How often does a team with a 1-7 record have an All-Big Ten player who is also third team All-American? He's one of the reasons we're hoping for a good season this fall."

Al changed the subject. "By the way, no one ever said how much we make."

"Either the athletic team has high hopes for you, Couppee, or you come from the poor side of town like the rest of us," Wilbur Nead added. "Everyone here gets $40 a month. That's as good as you can do."

The players were bigger than Al imagined - big enough to scare him. And the money was three times more than he anticipated! His thoughts flashed to his dad. Forty dollars was almost what his dad was making, but he knew this kind of paycheck would only last for the summer. He'd send some money home to his parents, he thought. Football, a job, college; it was happening fast, but he liked it. His adventure was no longer waiting in the future; his adventure was occurring now. "What do you want me to do?"

Enich smiled again. "Help us get a couple of victories this fall."

During the summer evenings, the football players gathered at "The Academy" for fried snacks and billiards. After perspiring for eight hours in the summer heat and humidity, they looked forward to collapsing into the booths under the large fans hanging from the ceilings. The fast-moving wooden blades created a cooling breeze, helping them forget the tiring daytime work. Camaraderie quickly trickled down from the upper classmen, embracing the incoming freshmen, who also had to take their turns being the brunt of good-natured hazing. When Mike Enich wanted another Coca-Cola, Al Couppee was quick to get it. Enich and the others happily allowed the younger players to serve them, just as they had done when they were wide-eyed, apprehensive freshmen. It was a ritual passed down every year to the future heirs of the gridiron. It was part of the process to become a member of a Big Ten football team. Major sports consisted of ten professional baseball teams, all in the east, and Big Ten football. Boxing and horse racing had its followers. Professional football was beginning to stake its claim in the sports world. But once the World Series ended, attention shifted to the young men of the Big Ten. These Iowa players, even though last season was a failure, knew their autumn experiences momentarily captured the nation on Saturday afternoons.

"Erv and I have the next game against you, Enich; that is, if you win." Nile Kinnick entered the backroom with Erv Prasse at his side.

"Alright, boys. Intellect and quickness against beauty and brawn," responded Mike Enich. "Of course, I'm always concerned taking on a Chicago boy in billiards. I just feel like I'm getting hustled before the game even begins." Enich was referring to Erwin Prasse who, like Nile Kinnick, was also a starter for the Hawkeye football, basketball, and baseball teams. Many thought Prasse was the better athlete even though Kinnick garnered the football honors. Both displayed abundant talent to play professionally in either baseball or basketball. But Kinnick had dropped baseball for academics, and was now doing the same with basketball. People were surprised because the Chicago Tribune wrote last year that sophomore Nile Kinnick "was one of the best, and quickest guards to play Big Ten basketball in the last three years."

Kinnick's interests went beyond sports. Even though he loved the games, he knew glory would someday be fleeting. He wanted to be an attorney, and maybe enter politics. He had recently finished reading Sandburg's *Prairie Years* and Steinbeck's *Grapes of Wrath*. He was just beginning Tolstoy's *War and Peace*, and would later tell his parents that it "was possibly the greatest novel ever written, all 1,350 pages." He was considered a serious intellectual by some. His engaging dialogue often elicited long conversations, a time in which others would feel his intensity. Even with his unassuming presence, he was, without question, the leader.

Erv Prasse was always smiling. Having grown up in Chicago, he loved being in the openness and beauty of this small university town. It was a breath of fresh air every time he came back to campus from the fast-paced Chicago lifestyle, where busy highways were lined with manufacturing plants and exhaling smokestacks. At first, Prasse thought the pace was too slow in this Iowa town, but, once here, it seemed a better pace. In two years, he had more friends, probably life-long friends, than he ever had in the city. In Chicago, he knew the neighborhood. Here, he knew people from all across the country. The diversity, he realized, caused him to grow in ways his old buddies back home would never experience. "Well, guys, you should all do what I just did. I spent the day with Kinnick while he talked to a church group and a summer camp for boys. After Nile got done talking to these twelve year olds, one boy said, 'My dad said you once memorized and recited the Gettysburg address when you were our age for school, or something.' Kinnick said that's true. He said he did it for a seventh grade speech contest. So this boy asked Nile if he remembered it. Kinnick stood up and recited it word for word. Then he told the boys the importance of that speech on that particular day, and why it's important to be kind to everyone. You should have seen the looks on the parents' faces."

"It was a rougher crowd than the church group," Kinnick quipped, as he glanced towards the new member of the group. "Who's the new errand boy?"

"Couppee. Al Couppee." Al reached out his hand just as he had done two days ago to his father before heading for the street car. He was shocked by Kinnick's firm grasp.

Nile Kinnick sensed the freshman's eagerness. "It's a pleasure to finally meet you, Al. My brother, Ben, said you had a great game against him last year. And I also remember some nice plays you had against me two years ago." Nile spoke loud enough to ensure the recognition was heard by the group. The kind gesture gave Al a sense of pride, something Kinnick's empathy knew would bring ease to Couppee, away from home for the first time. Nile remembered the feeling. "So I suppose Enich worked you pretty hard today. Don't worry, I'll be there tomorrow to keep him in line. Besides, we need to make sure he's lifting those buckets for his conditioning because I don't think billiards qualifies as training."

"I'm Erv Prasse." Prasse smiled, shaking the freshman's hand. "Rack 'em up, Couppee." Racking the billiard balls was also a freshman's job.

Al Couppee was playing his first game of pool with Nile Kinnick, Mike Enich, and Erv Prasse. He was a member of the team.

CHAPTER THREE

Monday, July 18, 1938. Fall practice began. Though the players enjoyed gathering again with the annual ritual of hopes for a great season ahead, everyone knew two-a-day practices in the July humidity were overbearing at times. But it was as much a part of the game as the game itself. Toughness was learned during those excruciating practices. The eight a.m. practices were too early. Muscles were still tight from the previous afternoon. And the two p.m. practices were worse. The afternoon summer heat often crushed egos and energy levels. The gray cotton sweats, along with the warm helmets and pads, caused even the fittest athletes to lose a few pounds of water weight each day. When a player was hit and fell to the ground in the late afternoon, he often had to find inner strength to get up and do it again. But it was done on the practice field within eyesight of Iowa Stadium, possibly the grandest football stadium in the country. The brick stadium, with its domed entrances, served as a constant reminder of why they were there. Hearing thousands of fans rising in unison to get a better glimpse of a critical play, hearing the joyous thunder when the home team ran or passed the football across the goal line - those moments of glory were the motivators, helping everyone through the two-a-day workouts. No one enjoyed the grueling practices, but life-long relationships were evolving. These comrades, growing up in the hard times of the 1930s, were experiencing life lessons in their own unique ways. The sweating and exertion for a common goal, making stellar efforts every day that few understood, brought them closer together.

It wasn't just Iowa football that had stumbled on hard times. The economic status of the state of Iowa was in a downward spiral, as was the nation's. The stifling economy had taken its toll. It seemed no one escaped the harshness of the times. But heroes sometimes rose up and lifted others along the way. So it was as a Big Ten athlete, even on a team desperate for a victory. Opportunity was there on the Midwestern collegiate gridiron every Saturday afternoon, stretching from warm Septembers to oftentimes frigid, snowy Novembers.

Irl Tubbs was beginning his second year as coach of the Hawkeyes. He came to Iowa the prior year from the University of Miami. He took over following Coach Ossie Solem who carried the Hawkeyes through difficult times following the 1930 scandal. Coach Solem brought integrity back to the program, and he did it with dignity, but wins were lacking. Recruiting against the powers of the Midwest was an incomprehensible task. The consummate athletes turned a deaf ear towards Iowa. They naturally chose other football dynasties, most notably in Minneapolis or South Bend, Indiana.

Irl Tubbs was soft-spoken, though slightly aloof. He was a small man, physically unimpressive. But he had built a winning program at Miami. He successfully hired two exceptional assistant coaches while at Miami and they followed him to Iowa. Pat Boland had starred at Minnesota and had been Tubbs' linemen coach. Ernie Nevers had been an All-American fullback at Stanford.

Even after finishing with six straight defeats for a 1-7 record in 1937, hopes were high with the talent assembled for the upcoming season. And, unlike last year, the returning players now had one year of familiarity with Coach Tubbs' offensive schemes. Enthusiasm infiltrated the team, as it did most teams during preseason. But this year seemed different. Kinnick, Prasse, and Enich were back after each had enjoyed great personal seasons last year. Couppee, though two years younger, was demonstrating a great understanding of the offense and an ability to do the play calling at quarterback. Mike Enich was arguably the best tackle in the country. He would lead Kinnick's halfback runs to the right; and when Kinnick passed, Erv Prasse would be on the receiving end with a basketball player's gifted hands.

Monday, August 29, 1938. "Okay, gentlemen, let's review what we've been doing." Irl Tubbs' voice bellowed out across the field. Seventy-four players quickly ran to his side. Tubbs was standing in the middle of the practice field as everyone gladly planted one knee on the ground. One head coach, two assistant coaches, and seventy-four players would be putting their reputations on the line again in just four weeks.

"Last year didn't play out the way we planned," he continued. "Some of that was due to injuries. Some was due to being out-manned in a couple of games. Some of it was my fault. But, gentlemen, the losses started accumulating when we started expecting to lose. Our greatest obstacle is ourselves. We've got to change our expectations. We cannot accept defeat.

"As I look out at you right now, I see some fine personnel. In my opinion, we've got as much talent as there has ever been at this institution. Obviously, there are three teams on our schedule that are very imposing. And they'll probably be stronger this year than last. It will take our greatest effort to stand tall on those three afternoons. And I believe, with the proper preparation and attitude, we'll still be looking them straight in the eye in the fourth quarter.

"We'll prepare for the games, one at a time. One week at a time. We'll always prepare for the next game as if it's our last.

We've got to always focus on the next game, gentlemen. That is the only game that ever matters.

"Coach Nevers has our offense looking good with Couppee and Kinnick getting a feel for each other. Prasse is looking as good as ever. Coach Boland tells me the line is improving every day, especially on the right side with Enich, Hawkins, and Evans. Tollefson, Diehl, Pettit, Walker, and Bergstrom are also looking good on the line.

"I believe we can match up against anyone. But do we win or lose when we hit the gridiron? It's not just what you do for those two and a half hours on a Saturday afternoon; it's also what you do everyday on this practice field. We've got to push each other. Playing our very best every play of every practice not only makes you better, but it makes the guy across the line from you better." Irl Tubbs was believable. He was a man of civility and courtesy. He cared about his players. But could he convince them to leave last year's one victory season in the past?

Nile Kinnick believed they could turn the misfortunes of last year into a year to remember, but he also experienced an honest anxiety wondering whether or not they could really do it.

"Coach Nevers, run them through the defensive schemes we're adding for the UCLA game. Gentlemen, it's the first game of the season. UCLA possesses a lot of quickness at the running positions. And they have great strength at the ends. We must play our greatest football right from the first snap of the season. Otherwise, it's a long trip back from Los Angeles. Now is the time to make sure we are ready. "

Coach Nevers grabbed a ball and chose the line of scrimmage by placing the ball on the ground, signaling the beginning of practice. "Okay, boys. First team defense. Kinnick, Dean, Prasse, and McLain deep. Enich, Hawkins, Tollefson, and Walker up-front. Couppee, Pettit, and Andruska in the middle. Second team on offense." He put the whistle up to his lips and gave one hard blow, telling everyone 'it's time to get serious.' Players jumped to their respective positions. Adrenalin took over. Hearts beat faster. Muscles tightened. They were ready to fight.

The second string offense ran four UCLA plays that the Bruins regularly used the previous year. Scouting didn't involve sending an assistant coach to the opponent's previous game, especially when the opponent's previous game was last autumn. Scouting the opposition in the 1930s usually involved a zealous alumnus living in the opponent's area. And so it was with Iowa. A three year football letterman that graduated from Iowa in 1933 lived in Pasadena. He was the mole supplying the information about UCLA's offense.

Iowa knew UCLA would run their All-American halfback, Richard Green, off right and left tackle, depending on where Iowa's defense seemed weakest. Enich had earned a badge of honor with his play from the right tackle position the previous year, so most likely, the Bruins would run to the opposite side of Iowa's line.

Then, the second team ran a fifth play, a play that drew unexpected gasps. Even though it was a play run in practice, it was a season-altering play for the Hawkeyes, a coach's worst nightmare.

As Nile Kinnick came up to make the tackle from his backfield position, Ham Snider attempted to block the defensive tackle, Mike Enich. James Murphy, a solidly built fullback from Great Neck, New York, cut to his left in an effort to avoid Enich, but Enich lunged to his right trying to tackle Murphy. Snider went sprawling to the ground from Enich's shove. Kinnick's left leg buckled under Snider's weight. A cracking sound was heard by the twenty-two players involved in the scrimmage and the others standing alongside watching. Kinnick's contorted expression acknowledged the pain, and the seriousness. He fell to the practice field's threadbare grass. The hopes of a promising season may have fallen with him. He was the anointed leader on both defense and offense. He was the Big Ten's top returning punter. The players stood in silence as the coaches rushed to Nile's side.

Irl Tubbs shouted to the team managers, "Get a stretcher over here. I don't want him walking on that leg." Fortunately, the practice field was bordered on the east by the University of Iowa Hospitals, no further away than the Iowa Stadium's dark and intimidating shadow to the west.

"Coach, I'll be okay. Just let me walk on it for a minute." Kinnick grimaced as he spoke.

"I can't let you do that, Nile. You could injure it more."

"Honest, Coach, I'll be okay. I don't want to go to the hospital. I can't." Nile didn't elaborate as he stood and limped slowly to the dressing room with one team manager under each arm.

Coach Tubbs watched with concern to see if Kinnick could put weight on the foot. He knew it was instinctive for every injured athlete to try to walk before acknowledging the seriousness. But Kinnick's foot barely touched the ground before he lifted it up in pain. In a split second, the aspirations of a team that had waited nine long months to redeem its reputation and pride from the '37 season received a blow that may have snatched the one player they absolutely needed for every game. Coach Tubbs didn't know what to say. "That's all for tonight, gentlemen. Let's get some rest."

Inside the locker room, two intern doctors from the University Hospitals approached Kinnick and told him they needed to examine his ankle.

"No thanks, boys, I'll be alright. I just need to get in my bed and rest. Can you give me a ride to the Phi Psi house?" Nile was pale and aching.

"I'll get some crutches," responded one of the interns. "We can probably use one of the coach's cars. But we really should take a look at it."

"Not tonight," Kinnick retorted. "I'll be ready in ten minutes."

Coach Tubbs walked in. "Nile, we really need to have it examined to see the extent of damage. You'll be fine, son."

"Coach, I just need a few days off. I know what I need."

Irl Tubbs had known Nile Kinnick for less than two years. But in those two years he had come to know Nile as the most well-mannered, polite college student he had ever been associated with in twenty-three years of coaching. His bravery was matched by no one. The sudden behavior change concerned the coach almost as much as having his star player injured. He knew the next twenty-four hours were crucial to the team, and maybe eye-opening to his prized student athlete.

Nile's indifference to medical treatment was bewildering. Coach Tubbs wondered if Kinnick was frightened at the possibility of hearing he had a season-ending injury; or was he not acknowledging the seriousness, hoping it might go away if just left in the past?

The next day, a warm autumn morning greeted the upper Midwest. Coach Tubbs stared out his office window watching the students walk to their next classes. Life seemed so perfect for these young kids, he thought. Their lives are ahead of them. He watched them walk with a swift pace portraying an eagerness to discover what awaited them; whether it was five years from now, or just around the next corner, the future was theirs. The enthusiasm was visible in their zealous steps.

Coach Tubbs just got off the phone with Frances Kinnick. He let out a deep sigh, set his coffee down, and picked up his car keys. The Phi Psi fraternity was a half mile north on Riverside Drive.

Irl Tubbs pulled into the parking lot next to the limestone fraternity. It sat high on a bluff overlooking the Iowa River. White pillars supported a roof that extended out from the two story building, providing afternoon shade all along the front porch. It was a majestic structure housing thirty-five young men, half of them athletes in various sports. The fraternity had frequent visitors, but it wasn't often they received a guest of such stature.

"Hello, Coach, can I help you?" exclaimed a student just exiting the front door.

"Yes, I stopped by to see Nile Kinnick. I thought he might still be here this morning."

"Yes, sir, I just saw him. He's upstairs in his room. I'll show you where it is."

The student led Coach Tubbs up the grand stairway with the polished oak banisters. They walked down the second floor hallway to the last room on the end.

"Nile, you've got a visitor. See you later, Coach."

Coach Tubbs gave his escort a gracious smile. Then he turned towards Nile and did the same. "How's the ankle?"

"It feels a little better. I kept some warm wraps on it when I got back last night."

Kinnick's eyes looked reddish and puffy underneath. His hair was uncombed and he hadn't shaven. It was obvious Kinnick hadn't left his room all morning.

"It looks like you stayed up half the night doing it, Son. You look like you haven't slept."

"I'll be honest with you, Coach, it hurts. But it is feeling a little better."

Coach Tubbs cared a great deal about his players. They were, just as he often addressed them in one-on-one dialogue, 'sons' to him, all seventy-four players. The feeling was reciprocated by the athletes. They gave him the respect he was due because that was the way he always treated them, even after a 1-7 season.

Coach Tubbs looked at Nile for awhile, searching for the right words before continuing. "I was concerned about the way you didn't want any x-rays or medical treatment yesterday.

So I called your mother this morning. She said you refused medical treatment because you're a Christian Scientist. I told her I was sorry that I didn't know more about your religious beliefs. I told her I was planning on seeing you this morning.

"Son, one of the great things about our country, even though we've had some trying times lately, is that we are free to choose our religion. We have several different denominations, and religions, represented right on our football squad. And I respect every player and whatever course their faith might take them. So I want you to know, Nile, I support you in whatever you feel is right. In fact, your mother used that word, 'right,' a few times in our conversation. She said you would think 'right' and do 'right' and I think she said you would make it 'right.' I understood her to be referring to a metaphysical belief of some sort that you'll somehow will your way to health. Anyway, I told her I would support you in whatever decisions you make."

"That's very honorable of you, Coach." Nile's eyes expressed relief. "I just didn't know if people would understand. And you're correct, or should I say right, in what you said. Our belief is that the mind and body are very strongly linked, and an injury or illness goes beyond physical, so your 'metaphysical' description is accurate."

Nile Kinnick had the good fortune of being in the presence of great people all his life. This moment, he realized, was no different. And he would do everything he could to help Irl Tubbs turn the misfortunes of the Hawkeyes around. This is why he chose Iowa. He wanted to help change something, not just be a part of a program that was already doing well.

"Son, I want you to do whatever you feel is right. And, obviously, you shouldn't be at practice for awhile. Let me know what I can do for you, and let me know when you're ready."

"Thanks, Coach."

"By the way, your mother wanted me to let you know, and I wrote this down." Coach Tubbs pulled a piece of paper from his jacket pocket to read his scribbled note. "She would be working with you by 'absent treatment to create a fine demonstration.' She also said, 'Good work would be done.' Anyway, that's your mother's message."

"Coach, we believe an error most likely occurred because of using 'mortal mind.' And we believe that with right thinking, the power of transcendent mind, or truth, will correct the situation."

"Nile, I'm behind your decisions." Coach Tubbs stood up to leave. "As I said, everyone has a right to practice their own religion. But I do have some apprehension about not, at least, looking into the extent of the injury. For instance, if a doctor looked at your ankle, would that violate your beliefs if he doesn't perform any treatments, but just looks at it? I don't want to lose you for the season, Son, and I also don't want you to suffer any permanent injury."

"I'll be ready for UCLA," Nile said. "It's too important for the team. And I believe we're going to turn this thing around, Coach."

Coach Tubbs walked down the stairway hoping the injury wasn't serious. But he remembered the dreadful cracking sound he heard as Nile fell to the ground. It was a season-ending sound, he thought. Coach Tubbs also knew Kinnick was different than most. As he drove down Riverside Drive back to his office, no one wanted to believe in the Christian Scientists' beliefs of self-healing more than Irl Tubbs.

CHAPTER FOUR

Friday, September 23, 1938. The Hawkeyes stepped off the bus and walked into massive UCLA Stadium. It was a beautiful sunny afternoon. Forty-three thousand suntanned fans were ready to cheer on the Bruins against the visiting Big Ten team. Excitement and tension permeated the air. The Hawkeyes were feeling good. Nile Kinnick's presence, after missing practice for three weeks, gave the entire squad hope. Offensively, most plays were designed to use Kinnick's passing and running ability from the left halfback position. That's the way the team had practiced the offense until Nile's injury. But with Kinnick's left ankle still sore, Coach Tubbs decided to use him sparingly at right halfback. Buzz Dean would take over at left halfback, swapping positions with Kinnick. On defense, Kinnick could play his usual safety position where there was less chance of falling awkwardly and causing further injury.

Last year, Nile showed he was one of the best punters in the nation. Today, the substitution rule would be a nightmare for Coach Tubbs. The rule stated, 'once a player leaves the playing field by substitution, he cannot return until the following quarter'; so Tubbs needed Kinnick on the field, if only for his right-footed punting. There was too great a chance of taking Kinnick out of the game to rest, only to have a punting situation develop, and Kinnick unable to re-enter the game.

Coach Tubbs wished Iowa hadn't scheduled UCLA for the first game of the season. Usually, a large university took on a smaller school for the opening game, allowing players to get a feel for the game while a victory was all but guaranteed. But instead, the Hawkeyes' character would be tested today, especially with Kinnick unable to give one hundred percent.

The Bruins drove deep into Iowa territory on their second possession. A hobbled Kinnick, playing deep in the backfield, seemed easy prey for UCLA's passing attack. On a second down from Iowa's thirteen yard line, UCLA ran their left end on a post pattern across the middle of Iowa's secondary. Kinnick, though unable to move with his usual quickness, still had the sense of a predator stalking its prey. He cut in front of the UCLA player and fell into the end zone cradling the ball in his arms. Interception and touchback! The attack was thwarted. It was Iowa's ball on their twenty yard line.

Iowa outplayed UCLA for the first half. It was a stellar defensive performance for two quarters by two teams, both desperately wanting to begin the season with a victory, and to justify all the practices since July. Too much effort had gone into the preparation for this opening game. One win could make it all worthwhile. For two quarters Iowa shed the frustrations of last year, and, instead, experienced the euphoria of winning, or at least competing well. Suddenly, they felt cleansed of the burdens from a year ago.

Mike Enich, Chuck Tollefson, Max Hawkins, Ham Snider, Jens Norgaard, Wilbur Nead, and Erv Prasse gave all they had to give. The seniors - Jack Eicherly, Glen Olson, Al Schenk, Frank Balazs, Chuck Brady and Bob Allen - played with their hearts, hoping to avoid the same fate that struck the players that preceded them. The seniors sensed the release of this heavy weight more than anyone as the Hawkeyes battled. The season's eight games were the seniors' final stage performances. One good season could replace years of disappointment.

Everyone in black and gold had made the decision in the last one, two, or three years, including the coaches, to place their hopes of success in Iowa City. So far, the commitments to attend Iowa, and be Hawkeyes, had brought feelings of frustration. Everyone wanted to move beyond the failures of the past, but UCLA was an enormous test. Today, a victory was everything - a loss, a continuation of their experiences.

Happiness and energy returned. The Iowa football team was basking in a novel radiance of accomplishment.

The defense, the part of the game that's played with instinct, was flawless for the first two quarters. But the offense, with Kinnick out of position and unable to make a difference, never found its rhythm. Nile punted four times in the first half. Four times his face grimaced with pain.

With all the effort and exhilaration Iowa exhibited, UCLA ran off the field at halftime to a thunderous roar of approval from the home crowd, and a 7-3 lead.

Slowly UCLA claimed victory in the third and fourth quarters while Iowa sank sluggishly from their earlier emotional high. The Hawkeyes felt jubilation only once last year, beating Bradley 14-0 in the second game. Now, a year later, they were forced to wait at least another week for the elusive victory.

Nile Kinnick was hit hard twice in the second half. Both times he got up from the turf after those problematic collisions. The second, a block from a pulling guard, connected directly on Kinnick's right side, causing him to lose his breath for fifteen long, exhausting seconds. A constant moan accompanied the passage of air leaving his lungs. The second impact also caused him to roll on his weakened ankle as he hit the ground.

When the UCLA lead reached 27-3, Coach Tubbs replaced Kinnick. The warrior was no longer needed.

The long train ride back from California was quiet, until Nile Kinnick stood up and walked towards Mike Enich, Irv

Prasse, and Al Couppee, all three sitting in seats facing each other. Prasse and Couppee sat near the windows. Enich stretched his legs down the aisle. Losing was never fun. To leave all your energy, strength, and emotion on the gridiron, and then walk away a failure, was too much sometimes. Young Al Couppee realized college glory, in front of a large crowd, involved physical pain he hadn't experienced at Thomas Jefferson High School. The ferociousness of big time college football left its marks. He wasn't sure if his throbbing right elbow or tender left hamstring was more painful. Mike Enich, one of the toughest and strongest players in the Big Ten, hurt his neck when he fell in the second quarter. His lower back had been twisted in a pile-up while going for a loose ball. His right knee was injured by an illegal block from a UCLA lineman. Kinnick's limp was his battle scar. Yet no alliance compared to the camaraderie of men having fought in a battle together, whether won or lost. Victory brought ecstasy; defeat brought quiet attachment. Both were better shared.

"I have never felt more pride being a Hawkeye than during that first half," Kinnick said. "We were a team. We believed in ourselves. We felt the game and what we needed to do. We're all disappointed. But there was a silver lining in all of this today. UCLA is one of the best teams in the west. They played well. For the first thirty minutes of the game we were their equal.

"I believe the tide, when taken at the flood, will lead to great fortune. I believe in every one of you.

"I know I didn't do my part today. I feel I let the team down, and I don't know if I can bounce back by next week." Kinnick looked directly at each of the three teammates. "You are the leaders. Everyone looks up to you, especially you, Mike. You are the meanest player any of us has ever known. Erv, you're the best athlete on the team. People pick up on your cues. Al, you may not feel like a leader, yet, but you are the man making the calls in the huddle. Today, the players looked at you and listened. They believed in you.

"We're going to get it done. I know we are." Nile stood up and returned to his seat, put his leg up, and fell asleep. Prasse, Enich, and Couppee gazed out the windows and reflected on Kinnick's words. Without talking, they knew they were sharing the same thoughts. One game wasn't a season, but one game did serve as a reminder of last year. No one wanted to experience that again. 27 to 3. The Hawkeyes were 0-1 to start the season.

CHAPTER FIVE

Saturday, October 8, 1938. Iowa Stadium was almost full for the warm afternoon game against the Wisconsin Badgers. Forty-nine thousand people were in attendance for the first home game of the season. The coaching staff decided to move Nile Kinnick back to his old position at left halfback where he could run to his right following Enich and Luebcke. Sometimes he would play the tailback position, lined up directly behind the center and quarterback. From this position he would not only take on the running and passing duties, but he would call the signals as well.

The disheartening emotions from the UCLA defeat a week earlier were immediately erased when the Hawkeyes ran out of the tunnel and into the heartfelt embrace of their loyal fans.

Less than five minutes had elapsed when Kinnick intercepted a Wisconsin pass at midfield and ran it back eight yards to the Wisconsin forty-three yard line. But the offense was halted by Wisconsin's surging defensive line that wouldn't allow Iowa to advance the ball. Shortly after, Wisconsin scored the first touchdown of the game.

As the scoreboard ticked off the final seconds of the first half, the scoreboard read Wisconsin 13, Iowa 0.

Midway through the third quarter, Nile Kinnick found senior Al Schenk in the corner of the end zone for Iowa's first score. It was the Hawkeyes' first touchdown of the season. For a moment, with the Hawkeyes trailing 13-7, an energy erupted on the sideline. If only they could stop the Badgers quickly and get good field position, so Kinnick, Prasse, and Couppee could take over, then the Hawkeyes could celebrate.

Kinnick intercepted his second pass of the game. The crowd grew louder. The Hawkeyes ran three unsuccessful plays, however, and Kinnick was forced to punt. The punt sailed forty-six yards. Erv Prasse, with great quickness and finesse, managed to get to the punt receiver without being blocked, and nailed the Badger at the Wisconsin fifteen yard line. The stadium burst with even louder cheers. On Wisconsin's first play from scrimmage, Mike Enich exploded off the line of scrimmage and not only pushed the Wisconsin lineman straight backwards, but he knocked the lineman into the runner, grabbed the runner with one arm, and fell on both. The Iowa Stadium detonated with sound for the third time in less than two minutes: Kinnick's interception, Prasse's tackle on the punt returner, and now Enich showing why he was one of the best in the country at defensive and offensive tackle. The crowd was exuberant but it was nothing in comparison to the fervor and passion on the Iowa sideline. Their moment finally seemed to arrive. They sensed newness to the game they all loved.

Despite the Hawkeyes' zeal, Wisconsin started to regain control. Field position started favoring Wisconsin as Iowa, losing ground on the 'tug-of-war' battle, successively began their first downs closer and closer to their own end zone. On a second down play from their own twenty-nine yard line, Couppee handed off to Kinnick, then turned and lead Nile behind Enich and Luebcke. What started out as a routine running play around Norgaard, playing right end, ended with Kinnick re-injuring his ankle, falling awkwardly under two Badger players. Coach Tubbs immediately took Nile out of the game. If they were going to rely on Kinnick's Christian

Science beliefs of self-healing, Tubbs thought, he couldn't leave Kinnick in any longer and possibly worsen whatever injury already existed.

Slowly reality set in. The Hawkeyes, for all the desire they showed entering the Iowa Stadium two hours earlier, were not ready for the elite teams of the Big Ten. Though they had athletic players like Prasse, and Kinnick when healthy - and gifted players on the line with Enich, Luebcke, Walker, Hawkins, Tollefson, and Diehl - the talent pool was short compared to other schools. The better teams in the league went three deep at most positions.

Iowa couldn't withstand Wisconsin's constant substitutions. Fresh Badgers in the second half continually swarmed the Hawkeye ball carriers after first hitting the tiring Iowa linemen. The Hawkeyes slowly wore down physically.

As the clock slowly ticked off the final minutes, a lifeless cloud seemed to hang over Iowa Stadium. The scoreboard again showed the home team trailing, something that was too customary for the alumni, university, and season ticket holders. They were concerned it might be a repeat of last season. Old memories started surfacing. Coach Irl Tubbs and his two assistants would not be spoken about kindly in the parking lots after the game. The newspapers would again have few compliments in tomorrow morning's sports pages. The players in black and gold felt the frustrations as they solemnly walked off the field. It was quiet. Many in the stands had already exited after the scoring deficit reached 31 to 13.

The following Monday, the team and coaches gathered in the locker room before practice. Mike Enich was sitting next to Kinnick. "Nile, are you going to practice today?"

"I can't, Mike. The ankle isn't getting better." Enich didn't respond. Kinnick continued. "I know what you're thinking. 'Why can't he just have his ankle, at a minimum, examined to see what's wrong?' It's my conviction. My faith won't allow it. Up until now, I've always gotten over these injuries quickly.

"I've thought about it all weekend. I even called my parents. My mother is convinced my healing will take place with proper thinking."

"We all know about your beliefs, and I can tell you, no one has questioned what you have or haven't done for the ankle." Enich's words were comforting to Kinnick. "One thing we have on this team is respect for each other. We may not understand everything about your faith, and the actions you choose to take. And it may not be the decision I'd make, but the guys accept it."

"Thanks, Mike. It means a great deal to know the team is behind me. Hopefully, the ankle improves and we start doing what we're supposed to do. Win."

Coach Tubbs addressed the team. "This past weekend, gentlemen, we let ourselves down. And this coming weekend, we can make it right. The University of Chicago may not be in the Big Ten much longer. Their struggles have been noted. This will be our opportunity to get on the winning track. With a victory, we can be .500, one win and one loss in league play. And that's a start. That's our start. One game at a time, gentlemen. We haven't started the season the way any of us wanted. But I can tell you, I've never been prouder of a group of guys than the ones in this room. There is nothing I want more than to turn this program around for the school, the fans, and especially, ourselves. These past two weeks, these last two seasons, we have learned to savor wins. And starting this week, we are going to revel in our wins. Now let's go hit the practice field! Let's begin right now, gentlemen!"

The team responded with an enthusiastic yell from everyone as they rose excitedly from the long benches running parallel to the lockers. Many life lessons were learned on these wooden benches. Unfortunately, it had often been about dealing with defeat. But learning even from a loss could shape a young man into a successful and honorable person, teaching him what to avoid and why to work hard toward goals.

The Hawkeyes didn't have the talent and depth of some teams they would face, but it wasn't the coach's fault. The school's football reputation wasn't attractive to the elite athletes coming out of high school. But the Hawkeyes in this room would do anything for this coaching staff. And they sensed an urgency to act before the naysayers became too vocal.

Smiles returned as they spontaneously met in the center of the room, pushing and shoving each other with renewed enthusiasm. It was time for practice but the reaction seemed as if it was game time. There was a buoyancy in everyone's stride as they ran to the field, except for Kinnick.

"Coach, a lot of people are concentrating on my healing. I'm hoping I'll be ready for Saturday."

"I know you are, Mr. Kinnick. And I'm hoping, too."

Saturday, October 15, 1938. The Iowa Hawkeyes traveled to Chicago and beat the University of Chicago 27-14. It was the Hawkeyes' first Big Ten victory since 1935. Even though the opponent was also immersed in losses, a victory was a victory. Happiness was happiness.

The Morrison Hotel, in downtown Chicago, was a great place to celebrate their Big Ten victory and .500 record in the conference. There wasn't a better place than the "World's Tallest Hotel" at the corner of Madison and Clark for a group of young men from Iowa to spend one night of celebration. The lobby of the forty-six story hotel was taken over by the young vibrant athletes in black sport coats with gold ties and khaki pants. Their delight kept them milling around the lobby, with its two story ceiling and surrounding mezzanine. Green carpet ran down the centers of the gray marble floors. The pillars and ceiling beams were also green, with gold gilding. Dark wood paneling surrounded much of the area. Two Roman statues, and brightly colored urns with palms, were situated on both sides of a large white marble fireplace. It was an unfamiliar setting for these footballers.

Though the players ate together at the hotel's casual-dining Grill Restaurant, it was the Terrace Garden Restaurant that caught their interest. The ballroom had an immense dining area curving in a semi-circle around a dance floor and stage. Each row of tables was one tier higher than the row in front so everyone could view the stage. None of the Hawkeyes could afford the three dollar cover charge, let alone the dinner. So they strolled back and forth by the entrance in order to get a glimpse of the well-dressed Chicagoans, but in particular, to get a glimpse of Tommy Dorsey and his band. Hearing the music from a distance as it floated through the hallways was enough to create life-long memories. The place was alive, and so were these animated young men. Tomorrow morning they would be on "The Rocket" train back to Iowa City, but tonight they were in the big city soaking up the energy.

It was a night they didn't want to end.

On Sunday morning, Erv Prasse, Al Couppee, and Nile Kinnick walked down the hallway towards the elevator. The team was meeting in the lobby before heading to the train station.

"Well, Coup, did you get to bed at a decent hour?" asked Prasse.

"The band quit playing around one o'clock. Tollefson and I were the only ones left in the hallway. It was fun watching the women, but they were all on dates."

"That's probably just as well for you," said Prasse. "I mean, you're probably a few dollars richer this morning since you didn't spend it on someone you'd never see again."

As they neared the elevator, Kinnick stopped and asked a maid, "Ma'am, do you have the time?"

The woman looked at him and bellowed back, "Oh, I've got the time, honey. I just don't have the desire."

For all of Kinnick's sophistication, he was also an innocent and naive youngster with a small town background. Couppee and Prasse buckled over laughing, almost unable to stand when the elevator door shut. Kinnick had thought the woman to be rude, even though he politely smiled back at her. His two roommates had to explain the old lady's humor. An impish grin came over his face as there was nothing else he could do but chuckle at his own naiveté.

"And to think, she reminded me of my grandmother," Kinnick quipped.

Heart wrenching laughter, by all three, proved contagious to everyone joining them on the elevator ride. By the time they got to the lobby, they couldn't speak. Tears of laughter rolled down their cheeks.

At the expense of the stalwart leader, no one could resist some good fun on the train ride home. Soon, everyone was asking Kinnick if he 'had the time.'

CHAPTER SIX

Saturday, October 22, 1938. The Colgate game couldn't have come at a better time. Kinnick was continuing the self-healing of his sore ankle and was not expected to play much. Still, the Hawkeyes were anticipating a win. With the victory over the University of Chicago last week, their Big Ten record stood at 1-1. The school hadn't felt this good about the football program in a long time. They only had one win so far this season, but it was a Big Ten win and still early in the season. The 1930 slush fund scandal was eight years ago. Maybe this season could put that controversy to rest and mark the start of a new era.

Though Colgate University was not a Big Ten opponent, playing the team from Hamilton, New York, was an opportunity to improve the season's record to 2-2. The losses to UCLA and Wisconsin stung, but two victories in a row could inspire the team and change its course. It was the second home game of the season. There was a slight buzz around the campus, on the streets, and in the downtown restaurants.

The players gathered at the Memorial Union next to the Iowa River for the Saturday morning team breakfast. Family and friends met in the hallway outside the large University cafeteria waiting for the players. Parents reintroduced themselves to each other and exchanged pleasantries, waiting for Coach

Tubbs to finish his post-breakfast talk with the players. It was a common ritual acted out before each home game. The players and coaches changed over the years, but the Saturday morning breakfast at the Memorial Union was a tradition that started over twenty years ago.

Nile Kinnick Sr. and Frances Kinnick graciously made introductions between parents that hadn't met before. Nile Sr., who had a stoic presence just like his son, wore a fine woolen gray suit. The vest hung perfectly to his belt, covering a white shirt with a well-starched collar. He held his brimmed Fedora in his left hand so he was free to shake hands with the other parents. Frances broke from her traditional well-dressed but conservative look. Today, she wore a black skirt to her heels with a gold jacket, showing her support for the team. A white carnation was pinned to her lapel, a present from the athletic director, signifying her as a Hawkeye mother. Nile Sr. often came to the games with Ben and George, but today Frances accompanied him. As much as she loved watching her son play, staying at home and listening to the radio broadcast was just as enjoyable. She wasn't fond of the drive from Omaha and back the same day. And, with Nile Sr. and the younger boys on their way to Iowa City, Saturday mornings provided an opportunity to read or volunteer at the Church in the morning before the one o'clock radio broadcast.

The players could be heard in the cafeteria on the other side of the wall singing the Iowa Fight Song. The sound signaled to the parents that Coach Tubbs had finished addressing the team with his motivational morning talk. It also meant Reverend James, from the Presbyterian Church, was done with his closing prayer for everyone's safety.

The cafeteria's double doors burst open. The players, who had parents waiting, quickly glanced across the crowd searching for familiar faces, then respectively joined their families until the team bus was ready to leave. Most hadn't seen their parents Friday night so there were many hugs with mothers and handshakes with fathers.

"Hi, Mom. I'm glad you made it." Nile gave Frances a hug. "Unfortunately, you'll only see me punt today. I just can't shift my weight. It's probably best that I take it easy for awhile."

"Everything will be alright, Nile. I knew you might not be playing but I wanted to come and let you know how much we are thinking of you." Frances Kinnick was delighted to see Nile smiling, even though so many hopes were being dashed by his very swollen ankle. "We'd like to take you to dinner after the game before we leave. Can you join us?"

Just then Erv Prasse and Wally Bergstrom walked by and stopped to say hello to Kinnick's parents. As they walked away, Prasse turned and said, "Hey, Nile, do you have the time?"

Nile just shook his head as they kept walking away laughing. The ribbing from the Morrison Hotel incident continued and, of course, thoroughly entertained Prasse and Bergstrom. They knew Kinnick would awkwardly ignore the comment to avoid having to explain it to his mother.

Erv Prasse was clearly the most amusing comic on the team. He was always in the midst of playful banter with someone, usually at the other person's expense. The circumstances never mattered to Prasse. He distinctly believed humor was not sacred. If he could make you laugh, no matter what it involved, he would.

Nile Sr. spoke up. "I have a feeling we don't need to know what's behind that quip."

"You're right, Dad. It's an old joke. Maybe I'll explain when we're not graced by Mother's presence." He smiled again. Frances shook her head and knew not to ask.

A few feet away Al Couppee talked with his father, sister, and brother. Mary Couppee was not feeling well enough to make the all day trek across Iowa. She had been feeling weak, and no one knew why.

The day Al hitchhiked to Iowa City, his father promised they would all be there for the first game against Wisconsin, but an emergency came up at work and he couldn't break away. So he made sure he had today off in order to deliver on his promise of bringing the family, even if it wasn't the first home game, and even if it was without Mary. Couppee's father had taken an extra job delivering newspapers to pay for the Iowa City trip. Al was glad to see them, but saddened that his father's circumstances required extra work to pay for the weekend.

Mr. Couppee and the two children were thrilled to be in Iowa City. Their style of dress was less fashionable than some of the other people in the room. The cut of their clothes was outdated, but the clothes were the best they had, and it didn't matter.

Nile Sr. and Frances Kinnick both had a strong sense of empathy. They knew the Couppees were from Council Bluffs, just across the river from Omaha. And they knew this was a new venture for them. "Mr. Couppee, I'm Nile Kinnick and this is my wife, Frances." The three parents engaged in dialogue while Nile Jr. and Al Couppee talked to Couppee's younger brother and sister.

"Why don't you and your children join us," Nile Sr. said. "We'll teach you how to survive a day in Iowa City. Some streets are easier than others when trying to get to the stadium or around downtown. This town gets a little crowded on game days."

Mr. Couppee and the Kinnicks said goodbye and good luck to their sons before they headed to the team bus. As Al Couppee shook Nile Sr.'s hand, he said, "Thank you, Mr. Kinnick, for showing them around." Then Al Couppee turned to Nile Jr. adding, "Hey, Nile, got the time?"

Nile Sr. enjoyed the ribbing his son was graciously taking today. He understood the bonds that grew between team members because he had played college football at Iowa State

University. He was glad, and even relieved, to see the positive temperament of the players.

Nile Jr. quickly replied, "Yes, it's time for you to make some big plays."

The players gathered outside the Union to board the bus for the short ride across the Iowa River. The bus passed the gold domed Old Capitol building, the original capitol of Iowa before it was moved to centrally located Des Moines. Now the symbol of the University of Iowa, it sat high on the Pentacrest hill overlooking the campus. The bus turned onto Iowa Avenue at the foot of the Old Capitol and headed across the river to the stadium. It was another beautiful autumn football Saturday in the heartland. Today, the Iowa Hawkeyes could even the season's record at two wins and two losses. After only one win all of last year, two wins halfway through the season would be sweet redemption.

Colgate University was located in the countryside near the village of Hamilton in upstate New York. Playing one Big Ten opponent on the road was an annual challenge for the small university. Each year the Big Ten rotated who would play Colgate. For Colgate, being the visiting team against a larger school meant sharing the gate revenue produced from the larger stadium. One game, even though it probably meant a loss on the season record, was worth it. It meant more revenue to Colgate's athletic budget than all their home games would generate for the entire year in Hamilton. The Big Ten commissioner and the President of Colgate were old college friends at Michigan State years earlier. That friendship now paid dividends to a remote, beautiful campus in New York state.

Colgate proudly faced the bigger players. They didn't back down. They always were prepared and fought the Goliaths hard. That's why the Big Ten universities, knowing wins were almost assured, enjoyed scheduling an early season game with this lesser foe. Today, Colgate more than accepted the challenge. For two and a half hours, Colgate forgot they weren't supposed to win.

The fourth quarter ended far too soon, or maybe not soon enough for Iowa. The scoreboard showed 14 to 0 in favor of the visitors. The Hawkeyes never came close to scoring. Kinnick's only action involved three punts. Coach Tubbs gambled with the substitution rule, trying to give Kinnick time to heal. He would immediately take Kinnick out of the game after each of his three punts, hoping the team wouldn't need to punt again until the next quarter, when Kinnick could re-enter. Four times Buzz Dean had to punt when Kinnick was not allowed to come back in the game. Dean had never punted before; and field position never favored the Hawkeyes.

Colgate was supposed to be a sure win. Today, disappointment flooded the state of Iowa. It was a devastating loss to everyone involved. Losing to Colgate was not acceptable to the fans, particularly the alumni. The coaching staff now walked closer to the firing line. The players were speechless, not even knowing where Hamilton, New York, was on the map.

Nile Kinnick's ankle was now so swollen many thought it was broken. Planting his injured left foot solidly, so he could punt with his right leg, had become increasingly painful. Still, he refused medical treatment and desperately continued his self-healing. Coach Tubbs had stated he would stand behind Kinnick's beliefs, and he remained true to that promise, even though Tubbs felt he was shirking his responsibility by allowing an injury to go untreated.

Of greater concern to Coach Tubbs was the team. Defeatism hadn't been removed, yet, from the players' indelible psyches. Iowa had now won only one game in its last ten going back to the 1937 season. And that win, on the road in Chicago last week, wasn't witnessed by the local fans. Many were becoming restless with the current football program. The newspapers and radio shows soon began to call for change.

Nile hobbled out of the locker room and met Nile Sr. and Frances. His ankle was not improving. It was obvious he needed time off from football.

Still playing host to the Couppees, the Kinnicks took them to The Lark, a well-known steakhouse eight miles west of Iowa City. Nile and Al invited Erv Prasse and Mike Enich to join them since their parents weren't in town for the game. They gladly accepted because a steak dinner was too inviting to turn down. But even the ever-jovial Erv Prasse was solemn at dinner. The Hawkeyes' record was one win and three losses with four very tough opponents remaining on the schedule. Minnesota, the national champions three of the last four years, and Purdue were almost sure losses. Indiana and Nebraska would also be formidable foes.

Mike Enich, Erv Prasse, Al Couppee, and Nile Kinnick couldn't celebrate as they had last week at the Morrison Hotel. One loss to lowly Colgate and they all felt the season slipping away.

Mr. Couppee drove Al back to the Boars' Nest dorm room in the Fieldhouse. Nile Sr. and Frances dropped Mike Enich and Erv Prasse off downtown before driving Nile to the Phi Psi house.

Frances ended the silence of the ride. "Nile, I know this is a difficult time but I also believe that whatever is wrong and causing this injury will change." She had been his main source of spiritualism all his life. He knew that would never change. And he knew how important the Christian Science religion was to her. She continued, "We have to keep believing and eventually everything will be alright."

Nile smiled from the backseat of his parents' 1935 Buick. "I know, Mom. I also believe circumstances are not always what they seem, and maybe what is happening is very possibly occurring for a reason far greater than we know. We just need to wait, and learn what is right.

"Thank you both for coming today. It meant a lot to me."

"Son," Nile Sr. spoke, "football, in the greater scheme, is of diminutive importance. In the end, it is just a game. But all the peripheral lessons that come with this game are what turn boys into men.

"I'm very proud of your development. Sure, we wish the lessons were accompanied with wins, but maybe the greatest lessons are disguised in the loss column. You'll figure it out. And in the meantime, know that your mother and I are very proud of you, not to mention your two younger brothers."

Nile Sr. reached back over the front seat and the two firmly shook hands. Then Nile Jr. leaned forward, put his hands on his mother's shoulders, and kissed her on the cheek as she turned her head toward him.

Nile Jr. watched his parents drive away from the fraternity's front lawn. The car's rear lights grew smaller until finally vanishing over a hill. He loved and respected his parents, but his ankle was stinging. He started to question his values and why the medical world was supposed to be unneeded, and even avoided. Other players had sprained ankles this year and were back playing at full strength. He knew his teammates, even though they respected him, had to be questioning his logic as well.

CHAPTER SEVEN

Saturday. October 29, 1938. The Purdue Boilermakers were in Iowa City to face the Hawkeyes. Following the Colgate loss, the Iowa fans' enthusiasm had diminished, resulting in only nineteen thousand fans filling one-third of the stadium.

Midway through the afternoon, following four quarters of hard-fought football, the scoreboard read 0 to 0, a scoreless tie with Purdue, one of the Big Ten powers. The Hawkeyes were experiencing perplexing states of emotion. They ran off the field to a standing ovation from their home crowd. It felt like a victory, yet it wasn't. The season's won-loss record was 1-3-1.

After the euphoria of an exciting game lessened, the realization of not winning eventually surfaced. Including last season, the Hawkeyes accounted for only one win in the last eleven games. Some of the players didn't know how to process their situation, or what to feel. They had all known the thrill of victory from bygone high school days, but college football threw them a giant curve, something they weren't accustomed to experiencing. The disheartening emotions were only magnified by the newspaper reporters and radio broadcasters who were losing patience with the Iowa coaching staff. Tying Purdue was a shallow victory but, more importantly, another failure. Frustrations heightened.

Coach Tubbs walked into the silent locker room. "Today, gentleman, I don't give a hoot about what anyone outside this room thinks or feels about this team. I just know what I feel. And as I've said before, I have never been prouder to be associated with a group of young men. Personally, I feel good about the performance I just witnessed. Purdue was contending with Minnesota for the championship before you changed all of that today.

"I don't care what the newspapers or radio stations want to say about not winning today. In my mind, we gave a stellar performance I will never forget the rest of my life. I hope, gentlemen, you can feel the same way I do. I know when you look back on this game, whether it's this winter or thirty years from now, you'll feel great pride. Purdue came here entertaining great thoughts about their season. Today, they left saddened, but also with a respect for the Iowa Hawkeyes.

"But I don't care about their season. I care about this team and every single person on this team. That was one terrific ballgame. I shall never forget it."

Coach Tubbs slowly walked around the room shaking hands with every player in the room. The players knew he meant every word because he embodied truthfulness. Irl Tubbs also knew his time as the head coach of the Iowa Hawkeyes was coming to an end.

That evening Nile, as he always did following a game his parents didn't attend, wrote them a letter.

> *Dear Family,*
> *Today, Iowa played a ball game – a REAL*
> *ball game. We fought hard, played hard for*
> *sixty minutes, and had a great time. We*
> *tackled and blocked the way this game is*
> *meant to be played. Our line whipped*
> *their line...the same Purdue line that kept*

*Minnesota's offense from scoring four times
from the one foot line, and three out of four
times held Minnesota once the Gophers got
inside the ten yard line.*

*Today, we did everything but win.
Regardless of our record, I am proud to
be a Hawkeye. We reached down within
ourselves, individually and collectively as a
team, and found that desire to win. It was
the greatest effort I have ever witnessed as a
member of any team.*

*Much was learned today by all of us,
regarding football and life.*

*Sincerely and happily,
Nile*

The following weekend Iowa traveled to Minneapolis to take on a team focused on the Big Ten title and another national championship. Minnesota's Coach Bernie Bierman clearly had one of the greatest programs in the country, winning three national championships in the past four years. And this year, they had the personnel to do it again.

It was a cold afternoon. The gray sky sporadically unleashed rainfall on the already dampened Hawkeye spirits. The field was slippery, providing an advantage to the much larger Minnesota linemen. Runners couldn't get their footing when making their cuts. Neither team played particularly well, but Minnesota was successful in advancing the ball on four drives, twice in the first half and twice in the second half. The final score was 28 to 0 in favor of the highly touted home team.

Though two games remained on the schedule, the season was over. Dreams had vanished. Defeating Minnesota would have been possibly the greatest upset in Iowa's history, but no one realistically anticipated a victory. But, also, no one expected a lackluster effort and a third game in a row without scoring a single point. The loss to Colgate still soured many, but now, the bubble was officially burst.

Oftentimes people come close to achieving life goals, Kinnick thought, only to fall short. The 1938 Iowa Hawkeyes chose to attend Iowa to earn degrees and rebuild a football program. Nile knew the education would come from classroom effort. He hadn't fully accepted, or appreciated, what his father had told him in the car after the Colgate loss, that "maybe the greatest lesssons are disguised in the loss column." He was growing impatient with thinking these Saturday afternoon lessons, or defeats, were a great teacher, though he did realize they were the ultimate motivator. If it's true one must feel the depths of depression before being able to soar with the eagles, he thought, then he and the other Hawkeyes were ready to soar; but now was too late for this season.

Nile Kinnick was done for the year. His self-healing failed. The ankle became too swollen to walk, let alone run and compete. He felt he failed the team, too, and he continued questioning why this was happening. His faith had taught him that there was a reason for injury, and 'right' thinking and living would improve conditions. He couldn't help but question his beliefs and values that had been engrained early in childhood. Even so, he remained steadfast to his family's principles and values.

The following Saturday Indiana visited Iowa City for the second to last game of the season. The Hoosiers left town with a 7 to 3 victory. The three point field goal would be the only points the Hawkeyes would score in the last five games of the season.

Iowa traveled to Lincoln, Nebraska, for the final game. The Hawkeyes lost 14 to 0. Irl Tubbs resigned the following week.

The next coach would promise new life and direction. The university, alumni, and state would believe; but most importantly, a group of young men that hadn't attained their goals would also need to believe.

CHAPTER EIGHT

Erv Prasse, Al Couppee, and Nile Kinnick walked out of the Iowa Theatre. It was five o'clock in the afternoon and they had each spent fifteen cents once again on their Saturday afternoon ritual now that the season was over. *Jezebel*, starring Bette Davis and Henry Fonda, told a story of an antebellum southern woman causing problems for the people around her. There was talk of Bette Davis winning an Oscar for her role, so Kinnick convinced the others to join him. Motion pictures were a main source of entertainment for these college students. Hollywood was impacting the nation's conscience as the rapidly improving medium captured America's culture, and history, on the big screen.

"Enich said a few guys are meeting at The Academy tonight. Let's head over there." Al Couppee, the youngest of the group, was confident in suggesting activities to the upperclassmen.

"Coup's still calling the Saturday afternoon plays," Prasse said with his always constant grin. "What do think, Nile? Should we still listen to him?"

"Maybe this is the start of him calling the right plays. Anyway, we might as well all try to deduce who's the next coach. And we can let Coup call a few runs through traffic to get Coca-Colas at the counter." Kinnick wasn't about to let Couppee forget he was still the underclassman.

It was colder than normal for late November. The temperature was well below freezing. Two inches of snowfall were predicted to blanket the ground through the night. As they walked toward The Academy, they passed one of the city's most well known businesses. Harry Bremer, the owner of Bremer's Clothing Store, was annually one of the biggest donors to the athletic department. He knew the players well and they knew him. Every year he always hired a football player to work part-time in his clothing store. It was good for business. Many of Harry's customers stopped by just to talk football with the employee. This year Ken Pettit was the beneficiary of the clothier's job.

The threesome walked by Bremer's Clothing Store just as Ken Pettit walked out the front door. Harry stood behind Pettit, ready to lock the door after the workday ended.

"Come on, Pettit. You might as well join us." Al Couppee again called the play.

"Hello, boys. Headed out for something to eat?" Harry Bremer projected success, always dressed in a suit and tie. He lived and breathed Hawkeye sports.

"Yes, sir," Kinnick responded. "We're headed over to The Academy to discuss the coaching situation."

"Well, I've heard an announcement should come this week," said Harry. "It's too bad about Irl. I liked the guy a lot. Anyway, I guess we'll see what happens.

"Al, don't you have a warmer coat than that?" Harry Bremer always noticed how others dressed.

Couppee was wearing a dark-brown, waist-length leather jacket, too thin to get him through the Iowa winter, especially walking back and forth across the river to classes and downtown. Despite his recent celebrity, new clothes weren't an immediate priority, or possibility. "This is all I've got, Mr. Bremer. But it gets me through."

"Boys, why don't you all come inside for a minute. We can't have our quarterback freezing all winter."

Couppee felt a little embarrassed, but Kinnick, Prasse, and Pettit all urged him to go on in.

"Let's see. I think this should fit you. Try it on." Harry Bremer had an avuncular presence around the players. He was genuine. He cared about these young men who chose to come to Iowa City, and was always willing to help the program whenever he could.

Nile Kinnick sat on the edge of the table next to the three sided mirror as Al tried on the long, dark-green overcoat. Kinnick was aware of Bremer's philanthropy. Couppee pulled the large collar up around his ears, momentarily shielding his eyes from the other three players. He was hiding the moistness in his eyes. He had never owned a coat like this.

"It looks perfect, Mr. Bremer," Kinnick said.

"Nobody's wearing it when it's just hanging on the store rack. Take it, Al," said Harry.

Couppee turned and looked at Harry. "It's great, Mr. Bremer. But I don't feel right letting you do this."

"Son, I tell you what. I want you to have the coat. Someday, you'll see someone that needs a little help, and when you do, you can return the favor to them. And this is just between us, boys. No one needs to know a booster gave a player a coat. Okay?"

"Your gesture will never be mentioned by us, Mr. Bremer," said Erv Prasse, speaking for the group.

"Good," said Harry. "Have a good evening, gentlemen."

"Thank you, Mr. Bremer." Couppee reached out to shake the kind man's hand.

"You are very welcome, Son."

The four walked out of the store and continued to The Academy. They were all touched by the generosity they had witnessed.

"You know, things like that make me glad I left Chicago to come to Iowa City," Prasse said, "because now I bet you can get our Coca-Colas and hamburgers all in one trip with those big pockets."

Al Couppee was feeling the warmth: the warmth of his new wool coat, the warmth of generosity, and the warmth of these guys walking down the street. "I even have some room for fries with these inside pockets." Humor was a good deflection for Couppee. He didn't quite know how to express his emotions. He was happy about his new coat, but it also made him sad, remembering his family's plight and inability to afford such luxuries.

The Academy was full. Twenty-five players were in the booths and tables surrounding the billiard tables. Word spread yesterday about the informal team meeting in the back room.

Kinnick couldn't help but think how successful Irl Tubbs had been putting this team together because a real team wins together, loses together, and stays together. Obviously, the guys in this room were close to each other. Coach Tubbs had certainly united a group of fine people, he thought.

"I'm hoping maybe Ernie Nevers or Pat Boland gets promoted to head coach." Mike Enich's left hand was on the billiards table steadying his cue stick behind the cue ball as he lined up his next shot. "But I have a feeling the athletic department wants a fresh start."

Kinnick responded, "I think it could possibly be a Notre Dame man. They want to make a big splash, and that would certainly make a ripple around here."

"Do you think a Notre Dame man would take us on? I mean, with our record, we would certainly be a risk to some coach's career," responded Chuck Tollefson. He was Enich's pool partner against Ray Murphy and Bill Diehl.

"Well, the radio reports are saying there is a strong likelihood Buck Shaw at Santa Clara could end up here. He played at Notre Dame. An upward move from Santa Clara's conference to the Big Ten would be worth the risk." Kinnick smiled. "No matter the coach, next year will be different. I know it will. Frankly, I don't know if the coach is as important as our attitudes. We've taken a bruising lately, but maybe our desire can outweigh our lack of success. Bottom line, winning is something we must learn to do.

"Prass and I have the winners." Kinnick studied the balls on the table. "And right now it looks like that's Enich and Tollefson; skill players against the linemen, again."

"Big guys against the little guys," added Mike Enich.

Sitting in a booth along the hallway leading to the back room, barely within hearing distance of the conversations surrounding the billiards tables, two gentlemen sat in suits and ties. Neither was talking. They were too intent on listening.

Eugene Gilmore, the President of the University of Iowa, interrupted their silence. "This is why I brought you to this pool hall and eating establishment, Doctor. You wanted to see the players from a distance. I had a hunch they would be here. It's a well known hangout for them."

"Tonight, Mr. Gilmore, you have convinced me of what I need to do. Hearing young Mr. Kinnick speak, I realize the team does have one of those required intangibles, a leader.

"I accept your offer, Mr. Gilmore." The person speaking was a Notre Dame man. But he wasn't Buck Shaw. Instead, this gentleman was one of the most successful disciples of the legendary Knute Rockne. He was a college star on Notre Dame's unbeaten national championship teams in 1919 and 1920. He was a teammate of the legendary George Gipp, the 'Gipper,' and in 1921 was voted team captain. He had played a major role in the development of Notre Dame's reputation. And here he sat in his gray suit in a booth at The Academy listening to, and getting a feel for, the team he would take over. The announcement of Dr. Eddie Anderson as the University's new head football coach would be in two days.

"Hey, Coup, I think our food's ready and it's time you broke in your new pockets." Prasse never missed an opportunity to haze underclassmen.

Kinnick stood up and turned to Couppee. "Come on, Coup, I'll help you carry the food. We don't want you getting greasy stains on that coat the first night you wear it."

Dr. Eddie Anderson's eyes connected with Nile Kinnick's as the two Hawkeyes walked by Anderson's booth. Kinnick and Anderson smiled towards each other. Neither yet knew the other person, but that would soon change.

Later that night, Nile was in his upstairs bedroom at the Phi Kappa Psi fraternity. He decided to write a letter before going to bed.

> *Dear Family,*
> *I'm sure you have heard the reports that a Notre Dame man might be taking over the reins here. I don't know how you feel about me playing for a Roman Catholic, but I want you to know my values are strongly against all forms of prejudice. The only bigotry I hold in my heart is that I cannot tolerate intolerance. Whether it is the plight of the black man in this country, or the poor souls in northern Europe fighting for their freedoms, I believe we must learn to accept each other as equals, no matter our skin color, our heritage, or religion. We must grow together and learn to appreciate our differences. Those differences must be woven into the fabric of our quilt. How boring would it be if we were all the same? However, it would be interesting to have the entire world possessing the same values and beliefs of human decency.*

I don't understand the tyrannies thriving in Europe right now. Why do some oppress others? It seems like such a waste of how to spend one's life because of someone's corrupt, immoral, and selfish agenda. The loss of life is intolerable, especially when linked to something so unethical.

Tonight, several of the players got together. We appear to have collectively rebounded from our dismal season. There is a new attitude emerging already. I can feel it. Helping my comrades experience the heights of success will be my only endeavor other than to get my grades back up.

I have also decided that maybe fraternity life isn't conducive to good study habits. It is a fine group of guys, but it sometimes is difficult to find the proper studying time. The Rhodes Scholarship is still very much on my mind.

> *Love,*
> *Nile*

Hundreds gathered November 28, 1938, on the front lawn of the Old Capitol building to hear President Gilmore announce the next Iowa Hawkeye football coach. Speculation was rampant following Irl Tubbs' forced resignation.

The Old Capitol, sitting on the crest of a hill overlooking the Iowa River and the origins of this town, was a symbol of the past when it served as the center of Iowa politics. Constructed with limestone blocks weighing four tons each, it was built in 1840, six years before Iowa received statehood. It served as the state capitol when the first governor of Iowa was inaugurated and the First Iowa General Assembly adopted the state's constitution. When the capitol was shifted to Des Moines in 1857, the Old Capitol housed nearly the entire University of Iowa. Military men had been trained for the Civil War on the lawns of this grand building. The gold helmets of the Hawkeye football team symbolized this landmark's gold leaf dome.

In 1921 and 1922, many recognized the Hawkeyes as the best team in college football. Harry Bremer remembered those glory years as did some of the older professors standing on the lawn. And so did one man standing at the top of the Old Capitol steps, about to be introduced.

"Ladies and gentlemen, thank you for attending this grand moment in Hawkeye sports," President Gilmore began. "I have the privilege of introducing the University's next head football coach. But before I do, let me share with you a little about the man that will lead the Hawkeyes.

"I know it has been rumored that it might be a Notre Dame man. Well, that is true. He played for Knute Rockne from 1918 to 1921. He was an All-American end and team captain his senior year. But what he has done since then is even more impressive."

The Hawkeyes were standing in small groups blending into the throng of hundreds, their letter jackets visibly standing out among the crowd. The athletic director had asked them to attend, but even if he hadn't made the request, the footballers would have been there, anyway. No one was more interested than these young men.

President Gilmore continued. "After beginning his coaching career at Columbia College – now Loras College - in Dubuque, Iowa, he took the coaching position at DePaul University in Chicago. While he was coaching at DePaul he also attended Rush Medical School and graduated with a specialization in otolaryngology. And if coaching college football while attending medical school wasn't enough, he was also the player/coach for the National Football League Chicago Cardinals."

Nile Kinnick started smiling. He recognized the man standing next to President Gilmore. He had seen him two nights ago in a booth at the Academy.

"He comes to us from Worcester, Massachusetts, where he guided one of the eastern powers, Holy Cross, to forty-seven wins during the past six years while also practicing medicine. In that time, he also had two undefeated seasons. In a sense, he's coming home. Born in Oskaloosa, he later played at Mason City High School before heading off to Notre Dame.

"It is my great honor to introduce to you the next University of Iowa head football coach, Dr. Eddie Anderson."

The crowd was excited. The applause was more than cordial. After hearing his accomplishments - coaching, medical school, playing and coaching in the National Football League, all at the same time - the crowd instantly embraced the man and his credentials. Doing any one of those things was impressive, Nile thought, but to do all three at the same time was unbelievable. And, he also thought, the Holy Cross success was equally impressive.

After the long applause ended, Dr. Eddie Anderson looked out at the people gathered. "Thank you. Thank you very much. Mr. Gilmore, everyone here, and especially the football players I see among the crowd, I am truly grateful for this opportunity. This is a great institution. I am honored to be chosen as the next Hawkeye football coach.

"I have spent a great deal of time assessing the personnel on this team. I believe we have the core of something that can be great. There is no lack of talent on the line or at the skill positions. Being the fittest team on the field, no matter who the opponent, will be a focus of my coaching staff from the very beginning. Endurance will be tantamount to our success. And we will begin in three months. February will be the beginning of a new era. There is football, and there is championship football. We will endeavor to bring the latter to Iowa City as soon as possible, and that means next year."

Erv Prasse and Mike Enich looked at each other and smiled. Of course a new coach wants exuberance from the start, but there was something about his presentation that was believable. Anderson's voice was confident and strong, his posture tall. As he spoke, his eyes would settle, for brief moments, on the people in letter jackets.

"Three gentlemen will be helping me accomplish our goals. Two of them are standing here with me today. The first gentleman is Frank Carideo."

Al Couppee's jaw dropped as Frank Carideo stepped forward and waved to the crowd. Carideo, considered by many to be the greatest quarterback that ever played at Notre Dame, had been Couppee's football hero. Al stood in disbelief thinking that this would be the backfield coach he would be working with every day. The long hitchhike ride from Council Bluffs to Iowa City suddenly crossed his mind. The long season the Hawkeyes had just experienced, he thought, was quickly vanishing into the abandoned past. Everything seemed new.

Eddie Anderson continued. "Frank is one of the most successful quarterbacks to play at Notre Dame. He will be working with the backfield. He also has an amazing gift of kicking that will be useful in his teachings."

Nile was also aware of Coach Carideo's punting abilities. He was impressed by the choice of Anderson, but also the addition of Carideo.

"And next, I'd like to introduce a man that helped me tremendously at Holy Cross with his stellar work with the linemen, Jim Harris. I must share with you a distinction Jim will always carry with him. He will always be known as the last substitute Coach Knute Rockne sent into a game." The audience collectively smiled and laughed. They also realized the entire coaching staff would be ex-Notre Dame people. "Jim

Harris was the last substitute to enter the game on the 1930 national championship team at Notre Dame.

"And the third gentleman, who couldn't be here today, is Bill Hofer. He will be working with the freshman team."

Harry Bremer and the other downtown businessmen, standing under a large oak tree, nodded and gestured approvingly to each other. The Notre Dame legend appeared to have moved westward across the Mississippi, and settled in Iowa City, Harry thought. It was only November and his hopes for next year were already rising.

Coach Eddie Anderson cordially brought his comments to an end, thanking everyone for coming and hoping they would be at Iowa Stadium next fall to help in this "great transition." And then he concluded, "And I'd like to invite all the footballers to a team get-together at the Memorial Union, right after this. I hope all of you can make it. Thank you."

As the crowd mingled in the lawn, and chatted about the news, the players moved towards the Union two blocks away. The players sensed an emotional release having heard their new leader speak, and they were impressed. Sometimes it's difficult to move from a known to an unknown, Kinnick thought as he walked along the sidewalk with his teammates, but it appeared to be a good move. He felt the others were experiencing the same sentiments.

CHAPTER NINE

The Hawkeyes filled the small ballroom in the Union. Most stood around the buffet table eating hors d'oeuvres awaiting Dr Eddie Anderson. Radio and newspaper journalists gathered outside the entrance door. It was to be strictly a team meeting. No one else was allowed in the room.

Flashbulbs started lighting up the hallway as a wave of commotion moved towards the players. Reporters could be heard hollering out questions as a contingent of people slowly moved along the tiled hallway toward the ballroom. He never slowed for the cameras or the questions. He walked with purpose to the people he would be spending hundreds of hours with over the next few months. As he entered, the players en masse began to applaud. Dr Eddie Anderson came to a complete stop. With hands on his hips, he smiled with a confidence everyone felt. And then he started clapping his hands together, returning the applause as he looked around at every player in the room. A mutual respect had begun.

Mike Enich was the closest to the doorway. "Hello, Dr. Anderson. My name is Mike Enich."

"I know who you are, Mr. Enich. It's a pleasure to meet you." Dr Eddie Anderson started walking down the line that formed. "Mr. Hawkins, it's nice to meet you also. Mr. Prasse, I understand you are one of the toughest ends in the Big Ten. We will be working on making you one of the best in the country, if not the best. That was my position at Notre Dame."

As he walked along, each player cordially said it was nice to meet him, or have him in Iowa City. Maybe it was an unconscious appreciation for Irl Tubbs, but there was a slight reserve in the young men's greetings. "You must be Hank Luebcke. I heard you were the largest man on the team, and I can't image anyone being larger.

"Mr. Evans. Mr. Diehl. Mr. Tollefson. Mr. Pettit." He continued down the line demonstrating a tremendous memory from having earlier studied the football program which displayed every player's picture, and also demonstrating an ability to take charge because of his preparation.

"Nile Kinnick, how's that ankle coming?" His handshake was the firmest Nile had ever felt. All the players would soon learn his crushing grip was a well-known trait of their new coach.

"It's doing well now, Dr. Anderson. Welcome back to Iowa."

Coach Anderson continued moving to his right. "Mr. Andruska. Mr. Norgaard. Mr. Walker." The lesson of preparation continued. They instantly realized the new coach paid attention to detail. He seemed to know every player by name.

"And Mr Couppee. I understand you did very well on the entrance exams."

Al Couppee was surprised he knew that. "Yes, sir, I did okay."

"Okay, young man? I heard it was the second best test score ever by anyone at this university. That's more than okay. I'm going to need that mind when it comes to calling the plays." None of the other players knew Coup had done so well. It was a side to Couppee they had never known. His brash, bold style was antithetical to his intellectual side. Everyone naturally thought Kinnick was the team's scholar.

"Gentlemen, first I want to tell you that I've known Irl Tubbs a long time. He's a great man. For whatever reasons, I'm here now but I want you to know I have the deepest respect for him just as I know you do. Sometimes life takes unexpected twists and turns, but I know Coach Tubbs is still moving straight ahead towards greater things. I know you'll miss him. And that's understandable.

"All of you have been given a great opportunity to attend this University. I want to do my part to ensure that your experiences here, in addition to being members of this team, will make you greater individuals."

Coach Anderson's presence was captivating. His confidence reverberated through the tonality in his words. The players appreciated the kindness demonstrated to Coach Tubbs. Irl Tubbs was a father figure, especially to those not from the immediate area. Transportation home, or even parents coming to visit the campus from long distances, wasn't always easy, or affordable; so Irl Tubbs took on a higher role for those players. Now came someone new and some, unsurprisingly, wondered if he would be as kindhearted. "Gentlemen, as I said on the steps of the Old Capitol, there is football and there is championship football. Pardon what may at first seem like arrogance, but I only know the latter. And you will, too.

"You all know by now that I had some good years under Knute Rockne. Part of the reason for our success was that we simply didn't know any other way. Coach Rockne was famous for saying 'you can't just have the will to win, you must have the will to prepare.' That advice has always stayed with me. Being more prepared than the opponent on the other side of the line of scrimmage gives you a tremendous advantage. And the other great advantage is being in greater physical shape than the opposition."

Dr. Eddie Anderson was connecting with the very fiber of their souls. It was a connection no one could quite explain other than to say Coach Anderson exuded leadership. The players believed his message. Nile Kinnick was mesmerized by his delivery. Anderson was aggressive, positive, and enthusiastic. His command of the language, thought Kinnick, must be one of the reasons for his success. Explicit. Direct. While Anderson spoke, Kinnick took mental notes of his hand gestures, his rotating gaze, and the solid stance on both feet.

"I took this job because my research told me this team has character. You stuck together against the odds. There is no greater sign of character than a person who puts the needs of the group ahead of his own. It's a selfless act. I know this team has that selflessness. And I know this team has talent.

"Spring practice won't start until February." Dr. Eddie Anderson noticed a collective look of bewilderment among the players. February seemed extremely early for the September 30th opener against South Dakota. Anderson continued. "But I do want all of you to stop by my office next week, between eight o'clock and eleven o'clock to get a playbook. You'll find it a little different than what you've seen before. Everyone must familiarize themselves with the play calling before February. Al Couppee and Nile Kinnick, I want to talk with both of you when you stop by, so please come together, and plan on scheduling a good hour at my office."

Al Couppee looked at Kinnick. They both gave each other an approving half smile. It seemed like the 1939 season had begun.

"Thank you all for being here. I hope you perceive the same shared consciousness I feel at this moment. We don't know each other, yet, but we have very common goals. And we have an opportunity to achieve those goals together. The sum is truly much greater than the individual parts. Coach Carideo, Coach Harris, and Coach Hofer are all committed to giving their best. I really believe we are on the cusp of greatness.

"And I don't mean to come across as the new coach coming into town that speaks of the grand achievements about to transpire. I don't mean to be patronizing in any way. I look around the room and see talent, heart, and I know there is not a campus across the country that can produce a greater team than us.

"Please enjoy the food. Tonight is a night to celebrate."

The players smiled while applauding. That was followed by some loud 'yeahs!' that were heard by the reporters anxiously waiting outside in the hallway. Mike Enich walked towards Nile Kinnick. "I'm already feeling our senior season will be a good one. No more ankle injuries, okay?"

"Okay," Kinnick responded. "I have played this game for a long time, waiting for that one stellar season. We've got to make it happen, Mike. I'll make you this promise: you lead the line, I'll lead the backs."

"It's a deal," Enich said as the two footballers shook hands, staring squarely at each other. "It seems like Dr. Eddie Anderson wiped out two seasons of frustrations in three hours."

"I hope so, Mike. I hope so."

Al Couppee joined them.

"Keep eating, Al," Kinnick said. "I want you to bulk up so you can lead me a little better alongside Enich on those sweeps."

"Let's go meet the coaches," Couppee said in between mouthfuls.

When Enich, Prasse, Kinnick, and Couppee finally made it up to Dr. Anderson, Kinnick spoke first. "Dr. Anderson, what was Knute Rockne like?"

Coach Anderson responded, "Once I get to know my players, they usually call me 'Dr. Eddie.' It's a little less formal. A little easier to say, don't you think?"

"Yes, Dr. Eddie," Nile answered with a smile.

"He was the greatest influence in my life. He is the reason I went to medical school. Few know this, but Coach Rockne always wanted to attend medical school. He knew I was contemplating it. So he told me how much he regretted not chasing his dreams. He made me believe I could do it."

"What kind of seasons did you have when you played, Dr. Eddie?" Bruno Andruska spoke from the other side of the huddled group.

"Well, you might all find this interesting, men." Dr. Eddie was engaging his future. He detected their unabridged youthful enthusiasm, and they detected his overpowering zest. "In my senior year we had a twenty-two game winning streak going. We went 9 and 0 my sophomore year. We went 9 and 0 my junior year. And we started off my senior year in 1921 at 4 and 0. Then we played a Big Ten opponent that would later be considered by many as the national champions. This was before the Associated Press picked a national champion. Different news agencies and publications all had their own polls. Well, that Big Ten team ended our win streak. That team, gentlemen, was the Iowa Hawkeyes." Everyone laughed at the irony of the situation. Here he was now at the school that delivered that one unforgettable blemish to Dr. Eddie's college career. "And, as I'm sure you know, we will have an opportunity to beat Notre Dame this fall. It's November eleventh. I bought a 1939 calendar already just so I could circle the date. It's just before Minnesota, which I also circled.

"Oh, how great November can be for us. And the preparation for that greatness starts now."

More questions followed. Most were about Notre Dame. Some were about his family and medical practice.

Nile Kinnick thought how different this man was from himself: a Roman Catholic, a medical doctor. Kinnick wondered if he would be as open as Irl Tubbs to Nile's religious beliefs. And, yet, Kinnick couldn't help but admire the new coach. Nile had always been fascinated by the written word, but he was even more fascinated by the spoken word. Winston Churchill, in Kinnick's mind, was the best at being able to speak and lead with his delivery and phraseology. Anderson, too, had demonstrated a lot of 'right' thinking, Nile thought.

After the players slowly strolled out through the ballroom doorway, the reporters quickly stepped in to ask Coach Anderson a few more questions. The media allowed the players to walk by without inquiring about their thoughts on the new coach. They respected the feelings of these young students experiencing some major changes in their lives.

Couppee and his roommates walked with Kinnick across the river before heading to their room in the Fieldhouse. Kinnick then walked alone on North Riverside Drive to the Phi Psi fraternity. Enich strolled up the hill to Washington Street where he had a one room apartment above a shoe store. Erv Prasse, Max Hawkins, and Ray Murphy headed for The Academy to see who could win a couple of dollars at the pool table before bed.

They went their separate ways but all recognized a change in their teammates and themselves. It felt good. Two wins in the past two seasons was wrong. They knew they were better than that. Dr. Eddie quickly distinguished himself as being in charge. He gave them new hope. Sometimes hope felt as good as success, especially when success was elusive.

Kinnick's roommate, Bob Hobbs, was asleep when Nile got back to his room. He reached for a pen and began to write in the darkened room with only a bed lamp providing light.

> *Dear Family,*
> *The new coach is a Notre Dame man. He is Dr. Eddie Anderson from Holy Cross. He has experienced some great success as a coach and as a player under Knute Rockne. At least three hundred people were at the Old Capitol to greet him. He has a tremendous command of the language. He seemed to say all the right things. I saw a glimpse of why he has been so successful. You are*

automatically drawn to his every word. Maybe I was spellbound because I have one more year, and I am desperate for any ray of hope. More likely, I was enthralled because I sensed he can turn it around for the Hawkeyes. I have waited my whole life for this one moment.

This past football season was difficult emotionally. But in the process, I have learned a great deal in defeat. The season was not without its fruits, even though they may be unseen. I am now willing to acquire new and greater lessons from Dr. Anderson.

Such irony isn't it? Everything I've done in athletics has led me to this final hour, and I will be led by a Roman Catholic who is also a medical doctor. But again, he seems like a very good man.

One last item before bed. As you know, I've been helping clean the Fieldhouse for my board job. The pay matches the work. Last week I was approached by Mr. Frank Williams, the President of First Capitol National Bank. I am leery the job will pay quite handsomely while requiring little effort. Mr. Williams was a Phi Psi. I don't believe it would be right to accept such a position. It may cause guilt and I have no desire for such an emotion. I will stay true to rightful thinking and actions. I cannot afford another injury brought on by poor thought. But should the position be legitimate, requiring real effort and productivity, then I will seriously consider it.

Thank you, Mom and Dad, for your constant support this past season. Pray that next season is without injury.

Love,

Nile

CHAPTER TEN

The massive Iowa Fieldhouse accommodated the university's basketball arena, swimming pool, wrestling rooms, and handball courts. It was well-known as a raucous, ear-piercing decibel advantage for the Hawkeye basketball team. On the third floor of the Fieldhouse was an old classroom recently converted into living quarters for six football players. It was nicknamed the "Boars' Nest." It consisted of six bunk beds, six large clothes lockers, and some desk space. It possessed a cold, barren atmosphere which was further enhanced by its immaculate cleanliness. The six players received a free place to stay and they were also paid board money for keeping the place clean, but not just their room, the entire Fieldhouse. It was a lot of work. Nile Kinnick, Mike Enich, and Jim Walker also performed some of the janitorial duties with the six Boars' Nest roommates, though the three lived at other locations. Kinnick was at the Phi Psi fraternity. Mike Enich had a one-room apartment downtown he shared with a hometown friend. And Jim Walker lived at the Quadrangle dormitory across the street from the Fieldhouse.

The six inhabitants of the Boars' Nest were a very special, tight group. They lived together, kept the Fieldhouse clean together, and on autumn Saturdays, fought on the gridiron together. Their bond was strong. Their fusion was, in part, due to the destinies that brought them together.

Burdell "Oops" Gilleard was an orphan from New London, Iowa. George "Red" Frye grew up in Albia, Iowa, with his mother. Bob Otto, from Fort Dodge, also had a single mother who was now raising his younger brothers and sisters. Willie Gallagher grew up in a home constantly under financial constraints where chili soup, according to him, was always watered down to feed his large family, and water was often the only beverage.

Chuck "Tollie" Tollefson was trying for a second time at Iowa. He first came to the University in 1934. The football, and his college experience, didn't work out and he ended up riding the rails for three years. Tollie was a hobo, but Tollie gave the term an air of distinction. He went from farm to farm to follow the harvesting of crops, starting in the southern Midwest and working his way north as the crops matured. Each week he moved a little farther north in a passing train's boxcar without knowing his next destination. When he saw golden crops ready for harvest, he would hop off the train and end up being housed in a barn that served as his temporary home. He would get up early every morning before anyone else, go to the chicken coop, and get some fresh eggs to eat before anyone else noticed him. Eating raw eggs every morning, he said, got old fast. He could rationalize stealing a few eggs, because it was survival. During the day, he ate ears of corn while out in the fields. He rarely ate any other vegetables because they were usually planted in gardens nearer the farm houses, and he didn't want to risk detection. In 1938, he walked into Irl Tubbs' office, and without any explanation needed, Coach Tubbs accepted him back on the team.

Al Couppee was the sixth man. The board job was enough for his tuition, books, and an occasional night downtown. With his high grade on the college entrance exam, he was offered an academic scholarship, but he refused it because the academicians didn't want him spending time playing football. He never told any of his teammates about his scholarship offer.

Couppee was lying on his bed studying for a history test in two days. His mind drifted to Nile Kinnick. Kinnick was a superstar athlete his sophomore year in basketball and football before his ankle problems this past year. He quit basketball so he could study, feeling it was much more important to make Phi Beta Kappa than All Big Ten in basketball. So, tonight, after the basketball game, Nile Kinnick, Mike Enich, Jim Walker, and the six Boars' Nest residents were cleaning the Fieldhouse after the Iowa basketball team beat Indiana 35 to 29. Couppee wondered if Nile ever felt he made the wrong decision. Kinnick could have been playing on the court tonight; instead, Nile was sweeping up discarded popcorn bags and soda cups. Al's epiphany, while studying for his history test, was that everyone makes decisions and sacrifices. He passed on the academic scholarship. Kinnick chose to give up both basketball and baseball.

Al Couppee's parents still struggled financially. He knew some months his parents were strapped with mounting bills, so he continued sending money home whenever he could. He pondered his parents' future as he also wondered about his own.

It was time for sleep. Al looked around at his five roommates. The six drew strength from each other, he thought, knowing they were fighting, surviving, and dreaming together.

The ringing phone in the administration office could be heard from the Boars' Nest. The athletic director only had one rule concerning the group using the phone at night: no long distance phone calls. Tollie ran down to answer it. A few moments later he walked back in. "Dr. Eddie wants to talk to you, Coup."

Al ran downstairs and grabbed the phone. "This is Couppee."

"Al, I'd like Nile and you to stop by my office around noon tomorrow. Can you make it?"

"Sure, Coach Anderson, I can make it."

"Have you spent much time looking at the playbook?" Coach Anderson asked.

"Yes, sir. And I have to admit, it's a little overwhelming. I'm used to about twenty-five or thirty offensive plays. What you've got is overwhelming. I'm not sure I can figure it out."

The coach responded, "It will make sense sooner than you can imagine. You're right though. There are over two hundred different formations and plays. I'm counting on Kinnick and you to be the leaders in familiarizing yourselves with the book. The others will follow your lead.

"See you tomorrow at noon," Dr. Eddie concluded.

"Okay, Coach Anderson."

"Call me Dr. Eddie. Good night."

"Nile, Al, come on in. Spring practice starts this afternoon, or should I say winter practice since it's February 1st. I know it seems early, but since there are no rules governing spring practice, I want to get in as much time as possible before our opening game. I'm counting on the two of you to call the plays next fall. I'm sure what you've been looking at seems 'overwhelming.' Isn't that the word you used, Al? But it will become natural. I want two players that know the playbook inside and out. The two of you will be out there together and you can consult with each other, but there won't be much time."

Nile spoke first. "Do you mean there won't be much time between plays, Dr. Eddie?"

"Precisely. Gentlemen, you will be doing something I don't believe has been tried in the Big Ten."

Al spoke. "You mean calling the huge assortment of plays?"

"I mean no huddles!" Dr. Eddie stood up and briskly walked around his desk.

"No huddles, Dr. Eddie?" Coup exclaimed in disbelief. "How?"

Nile sat smiling, chin resting on his hand. He could see the possibilities. He felt a twinge of excitement thinking about the surprise to other teams. And even once the Hawkeyes are scouted by upcoming opponents, he thought, the defenses will still have little time to react. It was an extremely innovative idea. The Hawkeyes might lack depth, but maybe they can make up for it with deception. Last year it appeared as if waves of new, fresh players kept entering every game to battle the weary, short-handed Hawkeyes. And next year wouldn't be any different.

This sounded fun and different, and Kinnick thought that sounded good. "Just like you always do, Coup," Kinnick responded. "It's just that you'll do it from your position. Now I understand why you gave us playbooks two months ago, Dr. Eddie. But I have to say, I think many of the players are a little lost looking at it, and are wondering how they can pass fifteen hours of academics while also studying this."

Dr. Eddie Anderson laughed. He knew there would be an instant shock in response to the playbook. "That's why the two of you are here now. I'm counting on the two of you to lead this offense with a positive attitude, never doubting for a moment how it all makes sense.

"I believe the others will follow your lead. If you demonstrate a total belief in the playbook and what we want to accomplish, the others will respond in the same way. I'm also meeting with Prasse and Enich in another hour about how their attitudes will be absorbed by the other linemen. I have spent a great deal of time determining that the four of you will be my coaches on the field."

"You've gotten my attention, Dr. Eddie," Nile said.

"I'll see the two of you at practice this afternoon at 3:30. Bring your smiles, enthusiasm, and attitude," Dr. Eddie said. "I'll have our first chalk talk after the training table at the Union tonight."

The two players walked out of the office. Al looked at Nile. "What do you think?"

"I think we just might be verging on greatness, Coup. I'm intrigued. And it will be interesting to see what a Knute Rockne practice is like this afternoon."

Eighty players were in gray sweatshirts and pants with 'Iowa' written across the chest. They met in the west end of the Fieldhouse, the opposite end from the basketball court. It was an open, indoor arena, wider than a football field and nearly as long. They wore canvas running shoes because the west side of the Fieldhouse had a dirt floor. They quickly learned running shoes were the proper attire because Dr. Eddie Anderson didn't even have footballs at the first practice. He didn't even talk about football. They just ran, and ran, and ran.

After a ten minute run around the inside of the enormous building, they would do five sprints the length of the indoor field. Then another ten minute run and five more sprints. The run and sprints were repeated a third time. The last run was for thirty minutes and, finally, five sprints sideways, interchanging their right foot in front of the left and then the left in front of the right.

Thirty-three players never made it to the final run. There was complete exhaustion. The other forty-seven players slumped, their hands braced against their knees, staring down at the ground, trying to catch their breaths.

Then Coach Carideo took over. Everyone was on the ground doing ten push-ups, then turning over to do twenty sit-ups. They continued this for twenty minutes.

One player stood smiling, looking at the others. He hardly seemed winded. Nile Kinnick had started increasing his workouts the day after Dr Eddie Anderson was named the head coach in November. Every morning he hopped out of bed before anyone else was awake and did one hundred push-ups and two hundred sit-ups. Then he would get in some handball or do some running. Finally, he would head to the Fieldhouse for a few punts. He had heard of Rockne's workouts and he anticipated Dr. Eddie would be following the same regime. He had one season left, and then it would be over.

Al Couppee, although not conditioned quite as well, noticed how Kinnick was better than the rest. He vowed to get his own conditioning up to Kinnick's.

Erv Prasse was always in good shape, but he wasn't quite ready for this much running. He looked over at Mike Enich. Enich had been suffering in the early aerobic portion of the workout, but he came back strong during the strength exercises. No one, except maybe Kinnick, was as solid as Enich. And Enich outweighed Kinnick by sixty-five pounds. Mike Enich smiled back at Prasse.

One practice and they were being tested. Kinnick walked by, and without saying a word, stuck his hand out for Enich to give an approving slap. They were both simultaneously remembering their conversation the night Dr. Eddie Anderson became coach. "I'll make you this promise: you lead the line," Kinnick said that November day, "and I'll lead the backs."

Erv Prasse, Mike Enich, Al Couppee, and Nile Kinnick. Coach Eddie hand-picked these four to be his leaders. He didn't have to, though, because they were already the leaders.

The training table at the Iowa Memorial Union allotted the players one meal a day. One of the smaller rooms off the main banquet room was a place where stories grew from players eating legendary amounts of food. Once, the Iowa City Press

Citizen had a column dedicated to the large quantities of food consumed by Luebcke and Enich.

Solidarity was rampant in this room after practices. Conversations were about the usual topics confronting young men: football practice just completed, studies, parties that were being planned, coeds. Everyone enjoyed these meals. This was their Iowa City family.

After dinner, the team walked in small groups up the hill to the Commerce Building. They gathered in the third floor lecture hall where several had been earlier in the day listening to professors talk about Business Law, Money and Banking, Economics, or Accounting.

Tonight, Dr. Eddie Anderson, Frank Carideo, and Jim Harris were standing at the front of the lecture hall. The room had elevated seating with each row one step higher than the preceding row in front. The seating capacity was two hundred. All eighty players were there after the first practice. The lower ten rows were nearly full.

A blackboard stretched the length of the room behind Dr. Anderson.

"Good evening, gentlemen. We have begun. We will take action every day toward our goals from now on. And as you may have noticed, I want my team to be in greater shape than any team we face all season. I want you to be in such superb condition that we win two or three games based on endurance alone, and I want you still going strong long after the other teams have tired, even the teams that go three deep at each position.

"Our talent will also carry us through, but our endurance will mean that we will be as fresh in the fourth quarter as in the first. And this will require tremendous effort on your part. I'm not asking you to give one hundred and ten percent, but one hundred percent times ten! If you do, no one will beat us. Frank, Jim, and Bill Hofer will be there to help me push you, but it's up to you to respond."

At that moment, Dr. Eddie spotted a player slouched in a chair. The coach stepped around from behind the teacher's podium and walked over toward the player. The student had also turned a desk sideways in the row ahead so he could put his feet up. "Get your feet off that desk and get out of here! You don't belong on this team with that lethargic look." The coach stood staring at the player. The player never said a word. He just gave a bewildered and disapproving glance towards the head coach and walked out. Coach Anderson knew he was not one of the key players and would eventually be released, anyway; so he used the situation to teach his team a lesson. Dr. Eddie also calculated that the slouched player, even though he would have a negative attitude about the confrontation, would most likely learn a life lesson from the moment as well.

As the exchange occurred between coach and player, many other players slowly straightened up in their chairs, hoping no one noticed their sudden improved posture. The coach made it clear he wanted complete attention and effort at all times. He was serious and expected the same from everyone. The room's tension increased dramatically. At the expense of one player, the team took a major step forward.

Coach Anderson went back to the teacher's stand and scanned the room. "First, I am going to improve the conditioning of the team. Then, we will focus on learning the system and running plays. Every other day we will have a hard scrimmage. Today is February 1st and we will continue until June 1st. I want everyone going hard even though it's spring. In the fall, our contact drills will decline a little because we won't have the luxury of an entire summer to overcome injuries. So, get ready for some spring contact."

Silence continued over the seventy-nine players in the room. Collectively, they were stunned that practices would continue until the first of June.

The coach continued. "We will be teaching you the Notre Dame system and the Rockne system. And you'll also learn my system. And it starts with conditioning to make sure no opponent ever out-lasts us, or out-hustles us.

"I'm sure you've all looked at the playbooks and been somewhat intrigued with the formations and shifts. What the playbook doesn't say is that it's done without a huddle."

Couppee looked at Kinnick and grinned. The two looked over their shoulders to take in the bewildered looks.

"After you run the plays enough times, probably several hundred times, and find yourself dreaming about them at night, it will come naturally," Dr. Eddie assured them. "For tonight, men, I have a rules book for each one of you. I want you to study it all week. We'll have a test one week from tonight. You might be asking yourself, 'why?' Let me ask you a question. Mr. Pettit, can either team advance a blocked kick?"

Ken Pettit paused to think about game situations of the past.

"It was a rhetorical question for the group, Mr. Pettit. But let me tell all of you this right now. In a game, you don't have the comfort, or time, to wonder what the answer is. No matter what the situation, I want my players to always know what to do. And, by the way, that question will be on the test. I want all of you to know the rules so well you can officiate a high school game. That's all for tonight, gentlemen. We'll see you tomorrow."

Coaches Carideo and Harris passed out the rule books at the back doors as everyone exited. The players were tired, but they were also excited about the glimpse of Anderson's organization and detail. It seemed like a military boot camp, but they were all open to change if it meant victories later, seven months later.

The team experienced the same practice the next day. There were sore muscles, but only from running, sit-ups, and push-ups. No one was sore from contact drills, yet. Dr. Eddie knew his depth was short. Most good players throughout the nation played offense and defense because of the substitution rules. Once a player came out of the game, he couldn't re-enter until the next quarter. When the game situation allowed it, top players would exit the game just before a quarter ended. With the additional few minutes rest, coupled with the game's stoppage while teams traded end zones, the best athletes could always start the next quarter.

Dr. Eddie knew, from the beginning, he didn't have as many pure athletes as the established perennial powers Iowa would be facing. He wouldn't have the luxury of resting his key players as quarters ended. He knew he had to turn his starters into "ironmen." The linemen as well as the backs would need increased endurance. So the team continued the drills. No football was practiced. There wasn't even talk of football. Fitness was the one key goal in the early practices. Running would become a trademark of Dr. Eddie's practices. Sheer size of the players, and there were some big linemen, wouldn't be enough. Endurance and quickness would be tantamount.

Routines developed immediately. After practice, everyone walked across the river to the training table in the Iowa Memorial Union, and then up to the Commerce Building for the chalk talk.

Tonight, the players initially thought Dr. Eddie was attempting to be humorous, but they weren't sure. "The game is played on a rectangular field three hundred sixty feet in length and one hundred sixty feet in width," he began. "The lines at the end of the field are called end lines; those at the side of the field are termed sidelines. This is where the battle takes place. I never want a ball carrier for the Iowa Hawkeyes to run out of bounds. I want to repeat what I just said so I never need to repeat it again. I never, ever, want to see a ball carrier for the Iowa Hawkeyes run out of bounds. Halfbacks, fullbacks, quarterbacks, ends, kick and punt returners will always remain in bounds. We will always attack and move forward. We will always keep the game moving, never stopping the game clock and allowing the other team to rest because one of us went out of bounds. The only exception will be if we are behind at the end of a quarter, or at the end of the game, and it's to our benefit to stop the clock. That is the way we will play. Three hundred sixty feet by one hundred sixty feet. Any questions so far?"

Everyone sat in amazement. Few even knew the width of the field. None had ever heard a coach say his team will never run out of bounds. No questions followed.

"Then I'll continue. The ball shall be made of pebble grained leather without corrugation of any kind, enclosing a rubber bladder. It shall be inflated with a pressure of not less than twelve and a half pounds and no more than thirteen and a half pounds, and shall have the shape of a prolate spheroid, the entire surface to be convex.

"Mr. Prasse and Mr. Evans, it will be up to you, when you sense a weakness in a particular defender and feel you can beat him to the goal line on a pass play, to politely ask Mr. Kinnick to please pass you the prolate spheroid."

The room erupted. No one laughed harder than Dr. Eddie. The Hawkeyes were seeing a different side of the man who, just yesterday, kicked a player off the team for the way he sat.

Dr Eddie wanted the players to see and experience the game in ways they had not known before. Every person in the room grew up playing football. No one had the game explained as if from an encyclopedia. The coach felt knowing this information would prove invaluable, if only for one or two plays all season. Coach Eddie knew one or two plays could change a season.

"Mr. Kinnick, imagine you are calling the play from your left halfback position. We want to start out in the T-formation, shift to the Notre Dame box, you're now lined up at tailback four yards behind the center, and wanting a pass play to the number three receiver. What do you call?"

Nile Kinnick always sat in the front row as did the other designated leaders from those two private meetings with Dr. Eddie. Al Couppee was sitting to his right, Mike Enich to his left, and Erv Prasse to Enich's left. Nile scarcely hesitated. He knew immediately what the coach wanted. "Six, eight, three, forty-three, seventy-five, thirty- two."

Anderson looked approvingly at Kinnick after writing the six numbers on the blackboard. "And Couppee, on that call, what is the snap count?"

"The ball is hiked on the count of four." Couppee was following right along with Kinnick.

"And how do you know that Couppee?" the coach asked.

"Anytime the third digit is four or less, in this case Nile called 'three,' then the count is four. If the third digit is anything higher than four, the count is five."

"Very good Mr. Couppee. Mr. Enich, which way do you shift on Mr. Kinnick's play call?"

Mike Enich likewise knew the answer and elaborated. His large sculpted frame contradicted the intellectual hidden within. "The shift is to the right. We would shift right from the T-formation into the Notre Dame box. Anytime the first digit of the first two digit number is even, we go to the right. Nile called forty-three."

"My front row has been studying. Well, I can't leave Mr. Prasse out of this discussion. Mr. Prasse, what do you do on this play call?"

"I hold a block for one second, cut at an angle across the field, holler politely at Mr. Kinnick to please throw me the prolate spheroid, and then race across the goal line for six points."

The room exploded again at Prasse's humor. They also smiled because they had just heard the front row give all the right answers. These four would be the ones making decisions on the field. No one in the room doubted that for a moment.

Dr. Eddie looked at Prasse. "Exactly!"

"My stellar students were all correct. Tomorrow we will start reviewing the offensive play calls. Everyone will learn this inside and out. Believe me, it will all make sense when you see it. Good night, gentlemen."

February 3, 1939. The third practice was a repeat of the first two. There wasn't a football in the Fieldhouse. Running was the primary focus. It was painful. They would continue these drills until it started feeling comfortable.

Running, push-ups, and sit-ups. They were preparing to play a player's game. The Hawkeyes started to believe the new style, once autumn arrived, would be fun. Their endurance would keep them going stronger than the opponents, even if the opponents used more personnel. And once the formations and shifts were learned, they would take pride and delight in confusing the defenses on the other side of the line of scrimmage. The defenses would be out of position and confused by the shifts and the quickness of the center snaps. At least, this was Dr. Eddie's plan. It had worked at small Catholic colleges and universities: Loras in Dubuque, DePaul in Chicago, and Holy Cross in Massachusetts. Athletics was an afterthought at the scholarly Holy Cross, yet Dr. Eddie turned the school's football program into one of the best in the nation. Though he was also the head of Otolaryngology at Boston's Veterans Hospital, and he and his wife were enjoying the Boston area, the lure of the Big Ten was too much. He had to know if he could incorporate his own brand of football, with hints of Rockne and Notre Dame, at the highest level.

He also knew he would rely on twenty or twenty-five players to prove his coaching ability on the larger, more visible stage. His new footballers hadn't fully grasped his plan, but when autumn arrived, they would be in the greatest shape of any team in the country. The pain would be worth the reward, he thought. He knew his players would someday thank him.

The chalk talk was always precisely at seven o'clock after dinner. Tonight, he would give everyone some insight into the play calling so there wouldn't be so many stunned faces when Kinnick or Couppee called a play from their desk in the front of the lecture room.

"We're working on the offensive play calling tonight. The individual calling the play will call a series of six numbers. The first three numbers will be single digit numbers. "For instance, 'five, seven, three,' what do you pay attention to in this sequence?" Dr. Eddie asked the group.

"The last digit, Coach," chimed Ray Murphy.

"Correct. And what does the number 'three' signify, Murphy?"

"The ball will be hiked on a four count because the number is four or less. With any number four or below, the ball is snapped on the fourth count. Anything above a four and the ball is snapped on a five count."

"Correct again, " Anderson responded. "If the first three numbers are 'five, seven, six,' then it's a five count snap because 'six,' the third digit, is higher than four.

"What do the first two digits mean?" Anderson scanned the room.

This time Bruno Andruska spoke. "Nothing, Coach."

"That, too, is correct. So, the man from New York and the man from Chicago understand the first three digits called. The first two numbers mean nothing. You only need to pay attention to the third digit. Ninety percent of the time, we will hike the ball on a four count. But those few times when we go to the five count, everybody's got to be paying attention. That's when we keep the defense honest so they aren't trying to time the snap. They will be lulled into 'hike, one, two, three, four.' But those few instances when we hike on 'five,' the play-caller will emphasize 'four' with his voice, and we catch them offside. If we have three yards to go for the first down, and we hike the ball after they're offside, then the Hawkeyes have a first down.

"Also it will be up to Diehl or Andruska to hike the ball *anytime* you see an opponent beyond the line of scrimmage. Again, five yards for us and maybe even a first down." Anderson knew they understood simple strategy, but he also knew it paid huge dividends to verbalize and remind everyone.

"Okay. So Kinnick is bellowing 'five, seven, three' and so we all know that means it's a four count on the hike," Dr. Eddie continued. "But it also means number three variation on the play. And you'll need to study the playbook in depth so you always know the variation. Just a reminder, there are only four variations on any play, and that's why 'five' or higher tells you it's a five count. It will never be confused with a four count hike with a variation. Anytime you hear 'five' or above, there's no variation."

Dr. Eddie sensed he was losing his audience but he moved on, anyway. "Again, gentlemen, I know this may sound confusing, but it will be second nature to you in time. So, let's talk about the next three numbers. Again, the first three numbers are always single digits. The last three numbers called are always double digits. 'Five, seven, three, sixty-three, seventy-four, twenty-two.' Kinnick, you explain the last three numbers." Dr. Eddie wrote all six numbers on the blackboard.

"Sixty-three, seventy-four, twenty-two. The first digit 'six,' because it's an even number, means we will shift to the right from the T-formation to the Notre Dame box. The second digit of the first number, 'three,' and the first digit of the second number, 'seven,' give us the play being called, play 'thirty-seven.' The third double digit number, 'twenty-two,' means nothing. It just gives us an extra second to think about the play."

Dr. Eddie again said, "Exactly! And there will be times when we will surprise the other team with a quick hike. In those instances, we won't call the three single digit numbers.

We'll just call three double digit numbers. No shifts. The ball is hiked immediately on 'hike.' Believe me, this will net yards most every time."

Anderson continued talking about the individual plays and variations. His audience was attentive because they desperately wanted to master this unique system. They had never witnessed no-huddle offenses with shifts. Slowly, the entire team became advocates, knowing the past successes of their coach, but some still wondered if it could work in the Big Ten.

Nile Kinnick became engrossed more and more with this man's leadership. His presentation and stature left little room for doubt. Anderson was similar to Churchill, Nile thought, getting people to believe and follow a cause. Nile felt there was something immensely captivating about Dr. Eddie. He was confident. His voice never wavered. As Nile was studying the coach's delivery as much as taking in the subject of the discourse, he suddenly became shocked, but intrigued, by what Dr. Eddie said next. "I have no doubt this team will win the Big Ten championship this fall. That's not just motivational rhetoric. I am absolutely sure of it. The element of surprise is on our side. We have a playbook put together with a great deal of input from Coach Carideo. Obviously, there's a lot of Notre Dame basics involved but Coach Carideo and myself have fine-tuned several schemes.

"I also know Mike Enich is one of the best linemen in the country and Nile Kinnick, if healthy, will have a season unlike anything seen at Iowa in the past. Nile, you were injured much of last year but you showed real talent as a sophomore. It's as if this playbook were designed for a player with your ability to run and pass, not to mention kick. Prasse was All Big Ten. And Couppee is another year older and, I think, ready to make a greater impact. I mention these names, but I know many others here are also very capable athletes. It will take a tremendous effort from all of us, but I truly believe the championship is ours if we want it.

"The next time you are completely spent from the running drills, I want you to remember I said we can win the Big Ten championship. Total effort and superb conditioning will be needed in order to have the results I envision. Effort, conditioning, and preparation are what Knute Rockne was talking about when he said 'you must be willing to prepare to win.' So, when you're lying in bed at night thinking about how grueling practice was earlier in the day, remember there is an end goal; the Big Ten championship is within our reach. No other Big Ten team is practicing this early in spring, so everyday we are closing the gap between the perennial powers and ourselves. We will do it, gentlemen, together."

"Coach, may I speak?" asked Nile Kinnick. The coach gestured for him to come up to the podium.

"I've played football, it seems, all my life. I've always found myself hoping the next season was the moment it would all come together. Because, quite frankly, I've only played on one team with a good record and that was my junior year in high school.

"I, for one, am completely committed to doing everything in my power to prepare for next season." Nile paused. "Why not? Why not reach for that one seemingly unattainable goal? I believe, in the next seven months, we can conquer the unimaginable by doing what the coach said: to out-prepare and out-perform our opponent.

"Somewhere right now, every player we will face next autumn is going about college life just as we are, with one exception. We are already preparing for next season. Think of the guy from Minnesota, or Notre Dame, or Michigan, or Wisconsin, or Indiana that you will be lining up against next year. Think of him looking you squarely in the eye. Will he have a smirk on his face because they are winning and our efforts are in vain? Or, will he have a confused, tired appearance? I believe, as the coach alluded to earlier, that the scoreboard can show Iowa victorious at the end of every game if we out-work, out-practice, out-condition, out-perform, and out-prepare every team every week next fall, and every week right now! But it won't just happen. We've got to make it happen. I want to remember, for the rest of my life, the guys in this room and how we turned the tables on the football world that one shining season in 1939!

"None of us are putting out this effort, hoping to accomplish mediocrity." Nile continued looking around the room, making eye contact with his teammates. "Let's do it for ourselves! Let's do it for ourselves because we can! We have this great opportunity, and for some of us, one last opportunity before we graduate. It's up to us. All of us."

As Nile finished, everyone stood and began yelling in agreement to what they had just heard, because he had expressed what they were thinking. In that moment, there was a universal commitment to give total effort. Dr. Eddie, Frank Carideo, and Jim Harris were also applauding.

Nile walked back to his chair as the others converged on him. Dr. Eddie knew no more words needed to be spoken. An unplanned team huddle formed at the front of the room around the student-athlete who verbalized their sentiments. Mike Enich shook Kinnick's hand and then gave him a bear hug lifting Kinnick off his feet. He had summarized their feelings, which in turn, caused their emotions to grow even stronger. And then in unison, following the lead of Erv Prasse, they broke out in their own impulsive and passionate version of the Iowa Fight Song. Though many voices were off key, none had ever sung with so much fervor.

CHAPTER ELEVEN

Though routines continued, the intensity of spring practices grew each day. The team continued learning the numerous options on offense. The training table always followed practice at the Memorial Union. And then they marched, in unison, up the hill to the Commerce Building for Dr. Eddie's seven o'clock classroom teaching.

Warmer days gradually eased into the Midwest during the final days of March. Practices were held outside whenever the weather permitted. Those outdoor practices on the larger field were accompanied with longer runs and more sprints, followed by the usual sit-ups and push-ups until arms and abdomens were fatigued. Dr. Eddie sensed they were approaching his target.

In early February, eighty young men came to the first practice. Only half that number remained as spring approached. Some players quit because the grind affected them too much. Some were injured because of Dr. Eddie's physical, full contact scrimmages every other day. And others were eliminated if Dr. Eddie didn't see the fire, the dedication, and the attitude vital for his plan to succeed. He wanted each player to be self-motivated, and yet, he knew they would also be influenced by the guy next to them. The rugged, motivated forty grew to believe in the system they were learning.

Anderson's practices were not for commonplace individuals. Every player had to earn the right to be there, and as a consequence, each survivor became prouder as the weeks went by. They were proud to be on that practice field. They didn't always want to attend the grueling workouts, but each witnessed their teammates doing it, and so they did it, too. Confidence and self-respect blossomed with the knowledge of having held on one more day. Nothing quite as exquisite as painful camaraderie, whether on a football field or battlefield, could create such closeness.

The linemen were particularly challenged by Coach Anderson's philosophy that aerobic endurance and quickness were far more important than strength. The linemen were losing the excess weight. Jim Walker, Chuck Tollefson, Bill Diehl, Bruno Andruska, Max Hawkins, and Ham Snider lost several pounds each and, consequently, were exhibiting tremendous improvements in speed. Henry Luebcke lost more weight than anyone, yet still remained the largest player on the team. Mike Enich was initially so solid his weight didn't decrease very much, but his quickness improved noticeably. The players were becoming who they wanted to be because they were changing who they were.

Al Couppee and Nile Kinnick had an Economics class together at one o'clock Mondays, Wednesdays, and Fridays. On this particular Friday, after class, they were walking toward the Iowa River, headed to practice. Most students were done with classes for the week. Many lounged on blankets or sat near the rocks lining the east river bank; some were fishing. A few college sweethearts drifted slowly along in canoes. Two fraternities were in an intense battle of touch football on the open courtyard next to the Memorial Union while girlfriends watched. A cloudless blue sky seemed to bring everyone outside on this early spring day. Green grass was starting to appear. Al and Nile stopped and sat on the stone wall running adjacent to the sidewalk to watch a few football plays by the fraternity teams. They had an hour to relax before another demanding practice. Today, a full contact scrimmage awaited.

Al Couppee was more interested in the coeds watching the touch football game than he was in the football game itself. "Nile, isn't that Era Haupert over there with some of her Delta Gamma sisters?"

Nile had already spotted her. She stood out among those standing along the sidelines. She was beautiful, he thought. Her dark hair was pulled to the side and held in place with a pin. She was wearing a letterman's sweater, probably belonging to one of the touch footballers, over her white blouse.

Era Haupert was the young lady Nile had invited to the basketball game last year while forgetting to mention he was on the team, or at least that's how Mike Enich told the story to Couppee. In the months after that basketball game, Era and Nile dated a few times but he was too busy with sports to continue pursuing a relationship, though he enjoyed her company. Her conversation was engaging, Nile thought, contrary to the popular sorority girl appearance she conveyed.

She spent last summer in her hometown, Marshalltown, Iowa, and when she returned for the fall semester, she was dating an old high school boyfriend now attending Iowa. The relationship with Nile never rekindled.

"I think you're right," responded Kinnick. "Yes, I'm sure that's her."

"I've got to tell you, Kinnick, I think she spotted you because she's talking to two friends, and now they're all looking over here. They're probably wondering 'who's the handsome dude with Kinnick?'" Couppee laughed.

Nile grinned as he continued gazing in her direction. "You might be right. Well, if they are asking that, I think we should go over there and meet them so they won't need to be curious any longer." Kinnick's sense of humor was almost as strong as

Couppee's interest in meeting new coeds. "In return for me introducing you to her friends, you'll need to call an extra play for me every game."

"Okay, it's a deal. You want the right end sweep with the option to pass?"

"I was thinking a little more about a five, seven, three, forty-three, seventy-four, twenty-two." Just as Kinnick said this, Era Haupert started walking down the sideline of the makeshift football field, ignoring the game's action. "Look at this, Coup. I think she's coming over here. Doesn't it look like she's got some guy's sweater on?"

Nile looked towards the two fraternity huddles. One player seemed particularly curious where Era Haupert was walking.

"Yeah, I'd say that's some guy's sweater. Could this be one of those 'Nile, see how much I'm over you' scenes?" Couppee laughed again.

Era Haupert waved to Nile, attempting to keep him from suddenly leaving. They hadn't spoken in almost a year. Three sorority sisters watched from the distance.

Her pace quickened as she approached. Nile kept watching. He remembered how her eyes conveyed not only beauty, but a certain serenity and happiness. Her father owned a manufacturing plant in Marshalltown. The plant produced a rolled metal used by the military in the production of weapons. The plant was doing quite well, a direct consequence of the military stockpiling inventories in the event Europe's and China's problems engulfed the United States.

"Hello, Era. It's great to see you. It looks like you are through with classes for the day." He had forgotten how captivating her smile was.

"It's great to see you, too." The two exchanged a short embrace. "One of my friends is dating one of the guys playing over there. So, it seemed like a good excuse to get outside."

"Era, this is my friend, Al Couppee. We were just on our way to practice."

"Nice to meet you, Era."

"You, too, Al." Era turned to Nile. "I've heard the new coach is working you pretty hard. I hope your ankle's okay. I was so disappointed watching you play injured last season."

Nile smiled. "It's fine now. And you're right. Dr. Eddie has us ready to play Notre Dame. We all feel we have something to prove next year."

"Oh, I just realized I'm still wearing someone's sweater. It belongs to the guy who is rooming with my girlfriend's boyfriend, if you can follow that. I'm not sure I did."

"I followed it," Nile said with a chuckle. "So, do you know your girlfriend's boyfriend's friend very well, or is it just a sweater-borrower type of relationship?"

Al Couppee interjected, "I followed that, too."

"I guess I would be classified as a one time sweater-borrower. The weather's a lot cooler than I thought it would be. Nile, a few of us are going to *Mr. Smith Goes to Washington* tonight. Then we're having a little party afterwards at the house. I know you may be busy and this is very short notice, but you're welcome to join us. It's just an informal gathering." Era realized she was being somewhat forward, but felt comfortable inviting Kinnick to a group activity.

"And Al, you're welcome to come, too."

"I think we can make some of it. Al and I have a team meeting at seven o'clock so we'd miss the movie, but we could stop by later. What do you think, Coup?"

"Sounds good to me." All of a sudden the chalk talk with Coach Anderson didn't seem so important to Couppee.

"Is that alright if we join the rest of you at the sorority house?" Kinnick asked.

"That would be fine. We probably won't be home until around 9:30. See you two later." Era smiled at Nile as she turned to walk away.

"Era, is it true Kinnick invited you to a basketball game but forgot to mention he was on the team?" Couppee was curious about the story.

Era turned back, still smiling. "I'm not sure he forgot to tell me. I guess you need to ask Nile. Personally, I think he was going for the melodramatic effect."

Kinnick only smiled. The story, he thought, took on a life of its own if he left it alone.

Era headed down the sidewalk to rejoin her friends.

"Okay, Couppee, how many plays is that you owe me?"

"Well, I think our deal was that you would introduce me to those other coeds, first. Introducing me to Miss Haupert, who seems to have her mind on someone other than me, doesn't count."

The two footballers started walking to the afternoon practice. Suddenly, their day was only half over. Couppee looked at Kinnick. "Now was that five, seven, three, forty-three, seventy-four, twenty-two?"

"That will work," responded Kinnick. "Several times it should work."

The practice was rugged. Dr. Eddie yelled at Al Couppee, in particular, the entire scrimmage because he knew Couppee could perfect the play calling. Mediocrity wouldn't be tolerated. He didn't want Kinnick or Couppee to relax for a single moment.

A train always passed by the stadium and practice field at six o'clock. The players habitually listened intently for the train's whistle, knowing it signified that the end of practice was nearing. A quick shower, a walk to the Memorial Union for dinner, and then the seven o'clock classroom with Dr. Eddie would follow. Tonight, it couldn't end soon enough for his two star backfield players.

As they exited the Commerce Building after Coach Anderson's meeting, Prasse suggested loudly that the team should meet at The Academy. It was Friday night and there was no better place to go for anyone without plans, especially since Dr. Eddie canceled Saturday's practice.

Kinnick looked at Prasse. "Sorry, Erv, Coup and I have plans tonight. But maybe we'll catch up with you later."

Prasse was slightly stunned at the rejection to a Friday night activity. "What do you mean you'll catch up with us later? You guys have big plans?"

"Yes, I'm going to watch Couppee in action tonight," replied Nile. "Apparently some women want to meet him." Kinnick looked at Couppee. "And I can't pass up the opportunity to observe his style."

"Sounds like you need me along, too." Prasse responded. "The Academy can always wait until later tonight."

The three proceeded to the Delta Gamma house. It was a long walk from the Commerce Building. They walked past the Old Capitol, seemingly protected by four stalwart buildings surrounding it, the center of the Iowa campus. They crossed the Old Capitol's front yard where Dr. Eddie had been introduced a few months ago. The journey continued down Iowa Avenue to Governor Street, went south on Governor, and then east on Burlington Street until reaching Summit Street. It was a long walk after a punishing practice, but somehow their spirits were lifted knowing they were attending a sorority party with fresh faces to meet, at least for Couppee and Prasse. Nile hoped he would be spending the evening talking to Era Haupert.

"I don't know if my left leg will hold up tonight." Couppee had been tackled hard from the side, bruising his left quadricep in practice earlier. "I've still got to retrace these steps back to the Boars' Nest."

"You know, Coup, it sounds like an excuse for why you should stay at the sorority tonight." Prasse surmised.

"Good thought, Erv," Couppee said. "But you know what? I can always hit Enich's couch. He's not far from here. But thanks for the idea."

The Delta Gamma front door was open so new arrivals didn't need to knock. Visitors were streaming in while people danced in the middle of the living room. News of the Delta Gamma party had spread quickly.

As the three Hawkeyes walked through the vaulted entry into the main room, Era Haupert moved towards them as others noticed the new guests. Nile Kinnick and Erv Prasse needed no introductions. Everyone recognized them. Even Al Couppee was recognized by most because of the status he had garnered in just one year as a Hawkeye. The team's won-loss record didn't tarnish their celebrity. On Saturday afternoons they had been thespian performers on the biggest stage in town.

"Al and I found one more person to join us tonight, Era. This is Erv Prasse," Nile said.

"It's nice to meet you, Erv. I'm glad you could join Nile and Al."

Couppee and Prasse headed straight for the kitchen where the majority congregated. Kinnick stayed with Era.

"Thanks for inviting us here," Nile said. "We get so focused on football that a moment like this is nice. Our days are very routine." Era and Nile locked into each other's eyes. Everyone standing nearby became momentarily invisible as they talked. The rest of the party slipped into a peripheral distance. Tonight, they were interested in learning about each other, their recent pasts, their hopes and plans. "Era, I feel like I should apologize for drifting away. I'm not sure why we quit seeing each other. I really enjoyed our time together. Somehow basketball became baseball which flowed into football. It was taking all my energy to just do those things and keep my grades up."

"No explanation necessary, Nile. I know you're busy. Maybe it was just the wrong time. I enjoyed our time together, too."

The conversation was kind and heartwarming, and continually interrupted by Era's friends walking by, wanting to meet Kinnick. Era and Nile were cordial to everyone, realizing privacy would not be part of tonight's design. Yet, even though it was not a time for profound conversation, the opportunity to reacquaint aroused old feelings.

Swing music played through the night. The 'jitterbug' was sweeping the nation and became the focal point of the party. The three footballers were finding amusement from discovering all three were fairly good dancers. Erv Prasse and Al Couppee were dancing with someone different every song while Era and Nile shared the time with each other. Couppee's sore thigh suddenly wasn't so sore. A beer he was handed in the kitchen, some music, and interesting people made him forget about the bruise. Prasse not only danced every song, but sang along with the popular hits, sometimes to the delight of his dance partner. Kinnick knew the steps. He occasionally even practiced them at night after his one hundred push-up ritual. The Shag, The Big Apple, Peelin' the Peach, Truckin,' Peckin,' and the Susy-Q were new and popular. By the end of the night, the willing participants had learned all six dances.

One o'clock in the morning came soon and everyone slowly departed. Many walked away with the hope and anticipation of later seeing, for a second time, someone they just met. It was a fundamental rite of passage for these young collegians, yet another reason to anxiously wait for tomorrow, and until then, dream about their futures. Erv Prasse, the wild guy from Chicago, Al Couppee, from the poor side of town, and Nile Kinnick, with his aristocratic upbringing, walked down the front porch steps together. They had danced most of the night. For the second time in the last twelve hours, perspiration glistened on their faces.

Kinnick turned and looked at Era Haupert one last time. "I hope we get together soon."

"That would be nice," Era responded. She watched as the three slowly faded to obscure figures in the faraway darkness.

CHAPTER TWELVE

Spring practice finally ended but not without Dr. Eddie receiving commitments from every player to continue running and strength training throughout the summer.

Kinnick took the job at First National Capitol Bank. Nile told Frank Williams, the President and a former Phi Psi, he would only accept the bank position if it required genuine effort. He wouldn't accept the job if it was merely an alumnus paying an athlete far more than deserved. Mr. Williams quickly learned to appreciate the young man's integrity, spending a few hours each week with Kinnick, teaching him the executive aspect of banking.

Erv Prasse worked at a boys' camp north of Iowa City during the week and bar-tended on weekends at The Academy. Helping kids and serving beer kept Prasse busy, and happy. Living in the camp's log cabin, so different from his childhood, was exhilarating for the Chicago native.

Mike Enich was offered a summer position at a law office. He had expressed interest in law, and his grade point average suggested he would perform well in the legal setting. But instead, he chose to work outdoors again for the University, doing the same laborious job, strengthening his body and getting tan.

Al Couppee found a job conducive to his lifestyle. He could sleep in as late as he wanted before doing his morning workouts at the Fieldhouse. He was hired by the University's Finkbine Golf Course, nestled into the hills and trees just west of Iowa Stadium. Every night he watered all the putting surfaces. About ten feet behind each green was a three-foot square hole protected by a white wooden manhole cover. Each storage hole contained a sixty-foot hose coiled around a water faucet. Couppee used a maintenance vehicle, an old rusted pickup truck, to get from one green to the next. The lights quit working years ago and the windshield and door windows were missing.

As soon as Al had gone around to all eighteen greens, he repeated his route, this time moving each sprinkler to a different area of each green. Then he traversed the course a third time to turn off the water, recoil the hoses, and put the wooden covers back in place. It was a job performed in the dark every night.

The peacefulness of being on the golf course all alone was often a time of self-reflection and self-talk for young Al Couppee, contemplating what was truly most important in his life. Occasionally, however, he did convince a young coed to join him in his three excursions around the course. Sometimes he brought a bottle of wine. Other times his night work was interrupted by his teammates, who used him as a taxi service. A handful of nightclubs stretched along the far side of the course. The clubs were a long walk from campus so some of the footballers would show up at the number one green, at the start of Coup's shift, so he could drive them to the bars. It usually resulted in moments of hilarity and bonding. The truck wasn't licensed for the road but that didn't stop Couppee from driving off the golf course and down the city streets the final quarter mile. Five times the city police stopped him that summer, but they always let him proceed with his chauffeuring duties after making sure he hadn't been drinking. Al got to know the nightshift officers by name, officers that never mentioned the sightings to the athletic department or the university.

The problem for Couppee was that his football comrades often expected a ride back to the campus. On occasion, he hid the pickup truck in an alley behind the bars, out of view of any university people that might recognize the dilapidated maintenance vehicle, and joined his teammates inside. One evening, in particular, Couppee stayed at the club too long so he employed five buddies to assist turning off the hoses. As they approached each green, it was clear they had left the sprinklers on far too long without re-positioning them. Some greens resembled small ponds after being drenched by water for hours.

The morning after this debacle the phone rang at the athletic office. The secretary who answered walked up to the Boars' Nest and knocked on the dorm room. She said a gentleman was on the phone and he insisted on talking to Couppee immediately.

Al hurried to the office and grabbed the phone. "This is Al Couppee."

"Hello, Al. This is Dr. Eddie."

"Hi, Coach."

"Al, I got a call from Finkbine Golf Course this morning. It seems a few golfers were complaining that several of the greens were extremely wet this morning, yet it didn't rain last night. In fact, every golfer that played this morning complained. Do you know what might have happened?"

"Yes, sir, I do. I left the sprinklers on a little too long last night," responded Couppee sheepishly.

"A little too long?" Dr Eddie repeated. "I heard the balls were plugging in the greens. I'm sure you won't let it happen again, right?"

"Yes, sir. I won't."

Al Couppee never heard another word about that night from Dr. Eddie or the manager at the golf course. The taxi service continued shuttling teammates - that night in fact - with a lot of laughter, but Al stayed in the truck the rest of the summer; no more parking in the alley.

> *Dear Mom & Dad,*
>
> *Summer has been fun. Considering how hard the new coaching staff worked us this spring, I'm surprised I miss the daily workouts. In another four weeks we'll be going at it again.*
>
> *I think we are on the threshold of a breakout season. The guys got into tremendous shape and we've all been working hard to maintain our conditioning.*
>
> *I'm sorry I can't make it home this summer. It would be so good to eat your food again, Mom. It would probably take four days to travel to Council Bluffs, visit with everyone, and get back to Iowa City. I can't be gone that long right now from my job at the golf course. But I am hoping you can make it to a game this fall. You would love it, Mom. The games are so exciting to play. There isn't a day I don't dream about the upcoming season.*
>
> *Our first game is Sept 30th against South Dakota. I hope all of you can make it. Take care.*
>
> *Love,*
> *Al*

Throughout Al's high school career, Mary Couppee cooked Friday nights at a local restaurant. Basketball games were occasionally on week nights and baseball was played in the afternoons, so she frequently attended the basketball and baseball games. But high school football occurred Friday nights when the restaurant was busy. Mary Couppee had never seen her oldest son play football.

Nile Kinnick walked along the river bank with Era Haupert after the movie. *Gone With The Wind* enthralled them so much they talked about it for an hour. Witnessing history on the big screen in technicolor rather than black and white footage, coupled with a romantic love story, was more than either expected. They felt the Southern struggles surrounding the Civil War, depicting a troubled time for the nation. They agreed it might be the best movie they had ever seen.

The two came upon a silvery-black wrought iron park bench and sat down. The moon was almost setting behind the trees on the west side of the Iowa River.

"Nile, something I have always admired about you is that you never talk about sports. You're probably the biggest athlete on campus, yet, it almost seems unimportant to you."

"It's important to me, but in a different sense. It's a means to an end." Nile's gaze shifted from the moon to Era. He put his left hand over her right hand. "I love sports. But wherever it takes me, I know it's short lived."

"Where do you want sports to take you?"

"It already has. I'm here studying at Iowa. But with one season of football remaining, I need to think about the next venture. It seems everything we do is a stepping stone to our next endeavor.

"What about you, Era? What will you be doing next year?"

"I'm thinking about graduate school. I'm not sure which school. But my parents are willing to help me out. So, I'm undecided and it bothers me a little that I can't make up my mind."

"It's great that you can think about it for awhile. You are very lucky, Era."

"You've always seemed destined for politics, Nile. Maybe it's because your grandfather was governor."

"I've thought about my future a great deal lately. It is very noble to live an honest, upright life. Sometimes I remember the days on the farm and how pure and wonderful it was to be a steward of the land. And at other times I feel a duty to serve my government and country. Philosophically, I feel we all need to leave our society a better place for the future.

"Most likely I'll attend law school. I've looked into Harvard, but I'll probably apply here at the University." Nile felt he had talked about himself too much.

"You once mentioned applying for a Rhodes Scholarship. Did you give up on that idea?" Era looked at his hand holding hers.

"I think getting away from the fraternity would probably serve me well if I want to make it to Oxford." Kinnick laughed. "I've learned fraternities are probably not the most advantageous lifestyle for studying. But I do enjoy the guys. And they just voted me to be the Phi Psi manager this coming year, which is great. It actually pays enough that I'll quit working at the bank."

After a long pause Era spoke. "What do you think is the most important aspect of all this, college I mean?"

"I think it's learning to think for ourselves and learning to enjoy learning. What if everyone was interested in gaining knowledge? I just think so many people get into the rhythms of their own lives and just exist day to day, never thinking about their own possibilities. And I think learning to express one's own ideas is a major experience of college. After all, what can we truly accomplish in life without expressing our views, and conveying our beliefs to others?"

The two sat in silence for several minutes holding hands. Kinnick appreciated Era's genuine and kind personality. There was an ease about her. The effortlessness of being in her presence, he thought, felt comfortable. Nile leaned over to kiss her. It was a short, but slow kiss. He pulled his head back just far enough to look in her eyes. They both smiled before kissing again, this time while embracing each other.

"I should probably walk you back to the sorority before it gets too late."

"That would be nice, Nile. But walking me home from here is a long way out of your way." Era rested her head against his shoulder.

Imitating tonight's movie, Kinnick said, "Frankly, my dear, I don't give a damn."

"Oh, Rhett!"

CHAPTER THIRTEEN

September 29, 1939. Nile Kinnick and Coach Carideo continued their daily ritual before practice. Frank Carideo, the greatest quarterback to play for Knute Rockne, also punted for the fabled Notre Dame coach; so every afternoon before practice started, Kinnick and Carideo punted to each other. Players often came to practice early just to watch the exhibition. Carideo and Kinnick, standing about fifty yards apart, kicked the ball back and forth. Neither had to move more than four or five yards to catch the other's punt. In addition to practicing accuracy, Coach Carideo taught Kinnick the art of making the ball bounce sideways and out-of-bounds, reducing the number of runbacks. Kinnick was beginning to perfect the sideways bounce, a skill that could be a great weapon in the Hawkeye arsenal.

Tomorrow was the first game of the season against the University of South Dakota. Dr. Eddie had an easy workout, running plays without shoulder pads and helmets, a final rehearsal while avoiding last minute injuries. February practices were a long time ago. Two-a-day practices in August were also in the past. Tonight, when the six o'clock train whistled while going by the practice field, the players weren't anxious to leave and shower. Tonight was different. Tonight was fun.

Dr. Eddie walked into the lecture hall at seven o'clock. "Gentlemen, when we started practice in February there were eighty people sitting in this room. Thirty-five of you are still here. I have pushed you harder than any players have been pushed in this country. You have worked harder than any college team in the country. Believe me, I know what Notre Dame does in practice and they fall a distant second to the effort and energy all thirty-five of you have expended over the course of these months.

"I am proud to be standing here in front of you. Someday you will look back on these grueling practices with pride. And I believe you will feel that pride for two reasons. First, you will look back on the terrific season you had in 1939. And, second, you will look back and know you gave your best. You never gave up. You came to every practice. You will remember those practices were the moments you realized preparation, dedication, and effort lead to success. And if you never learn anything from me other than that, then I've done my job.

"It isn't only about the victories. It is also about learning to thrive and rise above mediocrity. Many never know their true potential or abilities. But none of you will ever suffer from that commonplace reality because you now know the difference. You know that effort is an acquired skill.

"I became a medical doctor because Knute Rockne told me to go after my dreams. As great as he was, and with the legendary career he enjoyed, he always regretted that he didn't pursue his dream of being a medical doctor. When he discovered I had the same dream, he pushed me. He made me realize I could do it. Because of him, I realized I could coach, play football, and go to medical school all at the same time." Dr Eddie slowly looked around the room and into the eyes of each player. "I came here wanting to make an immediate impact. I wanted to make a difference for you, but quite selfishly, I wanted to prove to myself that I could turn a Big Ten program around.

"I learned a long time ago that you can't continue doing things the same way while expecting different and better results. That's why Coach Carideo, Coach Harris and I have pushed you to the brink of exhaustion every day. We wanted to change everything. And we wanted to raise your awareness of what real effort and determination mean. Now, after all these months, you have a better understanding of your threshold of tolerance, energy, and drive.

"The coaching staff has been extremely impressed by what you've shown us. Your efforts have been exemplary. We are indebted to you for having taught us." Applause interrupted Dr. Eddie. Then the applause grew louder as the thirty-five collectively stood to acknowledge their leader. "So, here we are on the brink of our season. South Dakota comes to Iowa City to face us tomorrow. South Dakota should be a formidable opponent, but I don't think they have any idea of what they are about to encounter. And I don't think the Big Ten knows either.

"We've been picked to finish last in the Big Ten and I'm sure you are aware from the newspapers last week, I predicted this team will win the Big Ten this year. A lot of people think I'm crazy. Many think I'm saying these things to fire up my troops. But I can tell you, I meant every word. I like what I see.

"Our depth isn't great. But our endurance will offset our lack of depth. Our team quickness and our no-huddle offense will create havoc for defenses and will catch teams off guard. You will look across the line of scrimmage at your opponents' bewildered stares and know you are winning. Believe me - we are on the cusp of something great.

"So, tonight, go home and get a good night's rest. I'll see you at breakfast."

Erv Prasse, the new team captain, stood up. "Coach, I know I can speak for everyone here when I say 'thank you' for putting us through hell." Laughter filled the lecture room.

"You are correct. We have higher thresholds of pain now."
Again laughter interrupted him. "We have learned what it
means to give everything. So, thank you, Coach, for teaching
us willpower and character."

Nile Kinnick looked over at Prasse and smiled. He couldn't
have said it better. It was great, he thought, to hear the captain
express the team's mood. Kinnick couldn't help wonder how
great the season would be.

It was Mike Enich's turn to speak before everyone exited.
"Dr. Eddie, Coach Carideo, and Coach Harris, we took up a
little collection for you. We wanted to give you something to
remember your first Iowa game and first Iowa victory." He
had three long narrow packages gift wrapped from Bremer's
Clothing Store. He handed one to each coach. The three
coaches opened their gift boxes and pulled out matching gold
and black striped ties.

"Thank you, men." Dr. Eddie said. "These should help
you spot us on the sidelines. Just remember, don't listen to
anything yelled at you from the sideline unless the person
hollering is wearing one of these ties."

Saturday, September 30, 1939. The players met at the Iowa
Memorial Union for breakfast. Some players were brought to
the front door by parents who traveled Friday night to Iowa
City. Others knew they would see their parents after the game.
Nile Kinnick's and Mike Enich's parents drove together. Erv
Prasse's parents were coming by train from Chicago with Henry
Luebcke's, Bruno Andruska's and Dick Evan's parents. Jens
Norgaard's and Ham Snider's parents lived in Iowa City. Bill
Diehl's parents had a short ride from Cedar Rapids. None
of the parents of the infamous Boars' Nest dorm room could
attend, though. Al Couppee's parents couldn't afford it. Red
Frye's and Bob Otto's mothers were busy at home with their
younger siblings. Oops Gilleard was an orphan.

Dr. Eddie spoke to the team after breakfast. After he was done, thirty-five young men got on the bus for the ride to the stadium. The quiet ride masked the nervous tension ready to explode. They weren't sure what to expect. The 1939 season was about to commence.

Mike Enich looked out the window and thought about all those walks across the river to and from practice. Erv Prasse was thinking about his new role as captain and what he might say to the team just before they ran onto the field. Nile Kinnick watched the Old Capitol disappear in the distance, hoping and praying this season would be injury-free. He had waited too long for this moment - to step on the gridiron with a healthy body. Dr Eddie Anderson clutched a rosary hidden in his jacket pocket. It was a good luck ritual he had started at DePaul. He wasn't about to change his superstition, not before his first game at a Big Ten school.

Sixteen thousand fans greeted the Hawkeyes as they ran into Iowa Stadium. The crowd was sparse. Still, for those thirty-five players, there wasn't a greater thrill than rushing onto the gridiron's manicured green grass, driven by new empowering hopes and aspirations. Last season was a long time ago. A new season and a new era were here. It was time to erase the old memories and begin new ones. It was time for the opening kickoff.

Erv Prasse and Dick Evans were the starting ends. Jim Walker, one of two blacks on the team, was starting at left tackle and Mike Enich was the right tackle. Chuck Tollefson and Henry Luebcke were the guards. Bill Diehl was at center. In the backfield, Al Couppee was the quarterback, Nile Kinnick was at left halfback with Russ Busk at right halfback. The fullback was Ray Murphy.

The Hawkeyes were writhing with anticipation. Last year they only scored three points during the last five games of the season, and forty-six points for the entire season. Hopefully, a new chapter would emerge over the next two and one-half hours. As badly as the Hawkeyes wanted a new and different outcome, nothing was guaranteed, except the opportunity.

The referee whistled and motioned for Erv Prasse to kick off. The game, and the season, began. The ball rolled out of bounds on the South Dakota thirty yard line. A penalty was assessed to Iowa for kicking the ball out of bounds, putting South Dakota to almost midfield. This was a North Central Conference team Iowa was expected to beat. South Dakota, at midfield, was not the beginning the team anticipated.

The nervous energy was expended quickly while both teams failed to move the ball. South Dakota and Iowa both settled for punts on their first possessions. A second punt by South Dakota only six minutes into the game gave the Hawkeyes the ball again. Kinnick took the punt on Iowa's thirty yard line and ran it to the Hawkeye forty-seven. But after three running attempts without advancing the ball, Kinnick had to punt again. This time, however, the training with Coach Carideo showed. The ball angled across the field, bounced on the twelve yard line, and rolled out of bounds at the nine. Unlike kickoffs, punts were not penalized for going out of bounds. For the first time, Iowa had good field position. And Iowa wasn't about to let the opportunity slip away.

The Hawkeye defense came alive. Enich shoved two South Dakota players to his side and brought the halfback down with a shoestring tackle. Tollefson stuffed the next run up the middle. Third down was an incomplete pass over the middle after Couppee knocked it to the ground. On fourth down, Kinnick took the punt again and ran to the South Dakota forty-three yard line, but a fumble on Iowa's first play - a handoff from Couppee to Ray Murphy - gave the ball back to South Dakota.

Again the Iowa defense stopped South Dakota on three consecutive plays, forcing another punt. Nile Kinnick fielded the punt, this time at the Iowa twenty yard line, and ran it back five yards. On the first play from scrimmage, Russ Busk took the ball ten yards around the left end with Couppee and Walker leading the blocking. The line of scrimmage was moved to the Hawkeyes' thirty-five yard line. Then Nile Kinnick heard Al Couppee call the play he had waited to hear. "Six, eight, two, forty-three, eighteen, sixty-three!" The 'two' meant Couppee wanted the ball hiked on a four count. The Hawkeyes got excited when Couppee hollered the 'three' in forty-three followed by eighteen, which meant 'one' because of the first digit in eighteen. The play call concealed that it was "thirty-one to the right" from everyone except the ten Hawkeyes listening for Couppee's signals.

From the T-formation, they shifted to the right into the famous Notre Dame box.

"Hike, one, two, three, four!" Diehl centered the ball directly to Kinnick who had shifted from left halfback to directly four yards behind the center. Right guard Henry Luebcke and right tackle Mike Enich cleared a path with Couppee behind them to take on the linebacker. Kinnick raced around the right end. Dick Evans blocked the defensive back to the outside and Kinnick cut back, heading down field. The crowd rose to their feet watching the play unfold. Dr. Eddie, with his black and gold stripped tie, started marching down the sideline in the direction of the flow. The Iowa players knew the outcome of the play. They had seen it numerous times in practice.

In the briefest of moments the play extended down the field. Each Hawkeye looked for a South Dakota player to take to the ground so Kinnick could do the rest. At five feet eight inches tall and one hundred seventy-five pounds, he was neither the biggest nor the fastest Hawkeye. But he showed something to all sixteen thousand in attendance. Maybe it was pure determination. Maybe it was a sense of understanding the play better than others. Maybe it was frustration from two losing seasons. But Kinnick knew he was headed for the end zone. He cut to his left, then right, then out ran the last two defensive backs.

It was the team's first touchdown since October 15, 1938, against the University of Chicago. It was Dr. Eddie Anderson's first score at Iowa. Nile's ankle was healed.

Erv Prasse kicked off following the touchdown. South Dakota showed some offense and moved the ball to midfield before Bill Green halted their drive, darting in front of an unsuspecting South Dakota receiver for an interception. Suddenly, results from all the efforts of the past seven months appeared. The Hawkeyes started getting stronger and more confident with every down.

The no-huddle offense was employed again as Couppee called for a pass play. The Iowa backfield started in the T-formation and again shifted right into the Notre Dame box. Kinnick took the snap from Diehl and passed to Green for a twelve yard gain. Again no huddle. Radio announcers in the press box, as well as the fans in attendance, were amazed, wondering how the Iowa players got organized at the line of scrimmage without a huddle.

Couppee called a shift to the left and Diehl centered the ball directly to Kinnick behind Jim Walker at left tackle. Walker and Tollefson lead the charge, this time around the left side, not wanting to be outdone by Luebcke and Enich on the runs to the right side of the line of scrimmage. A gaping hole opened. Couppee hit the middle linebacker again. Erv Prasse sealed the defensive back to the outside and everyone in the stands stood for a second time to watch Kinnick run down the field. Thirty-eight yards later Kinnick found himself mobbed by his exuberant teammates in the end zone. Kinnick drop kicked the extra point once more and the scoreboard showed Iowa 14, South Dakota 0. Frank Carideo and Dr. Eddie smiled while shaking hands.

The Hawkeye defense took over and exerted its will on South Dakota, forcing yet another punt. Kinnick followed the Hawkeyes' three unsuccessful downs with his punt to the corner and out of bounds on the South Dakota five yard line. This time, Iowa allowed South Dakota to advance the ball thirty yards before forcing another punt. South Dakota's punter kicked a beautiful punt, forcing Iowa back to its own thirty. Kinnick fielded the punt and ran it back to the opponent's forty-two yard line, dodging defenders as if they were in slow motion, unable to catch their prey. Three defenders closed in on Kinnick as he moved towards the sideline. Just as a defender grabbed Kinnick's left leg, Kinnick lateraled the ball to Russ Busk who gained an additional thirteen yards. The crowd loved the impromptu decision and let the team hear their appreciation.

Dr. Eddie sent Wally Bergstrom in for Jim Walker. Ken Pettit replaced Chuck Tollefson and Max Hawkins came in for Henry Luebcke.

Al Couppee wanted to get one more score before halftime. So he called 'the play.' The Hawkeyes knew what to do. South Dakota was helpless in trying to stop it. Kinnick raced around the right end again. Hawkins did just what Luebcke had done before, plowing through the line of scrimmage next to Enich. Kinnick crossed the goal line again.

Pandemonium filled both sides of the stadium. The fans sounded like a sellout of fifty-three thousand, not sixteen thousand.

Kinnick drop kicked the extra point for a 21-0 lead. The Hawkeyes were quickly discovering the reward for being well-conditioned. And now, adrenalin was adding to their superior conditioning. Dr. Eddie's constant running drills were paying off but no one was thinking about those arduous workouts now. The lack of a huddle continued to cause South Dakota problems, but the real reason for the Hawkeyes' sudden success was their physical energy.

Again Iowa stopped South Dakota's offense and took over the ball at midfield. The clock was running down and they had time for one more play before halftime. They shifted again into the Notre Dame box. This time Kinnick had the option to run or pass when he spotted Russ Busk streaking across the thirty yard line. Kinnick delivered a perfect pass into the arms of Busk who ran the rest of the way to the goal line. Suddenly, it was 28-0.

Mayhem filled the stands as the first half ended. Dr. Eddie was a savior.

The locker room at halftime was joyful as the athletes walked into the room with their four touchdown lead. It was more festive than if the game had just ended because they knew they had more football to play, and today, they didn't want to take off the helmets and pads. Winning made the afternoon too short. It wasn't a Big Ten opponent, but it was a new season.

Dr. Eddie walked into the locker room. "Everyone take a seat please.

"I am seeing things out there today that look very good. That was one of the best performances the Iowa fans have witnessed. And it wasn't just Nile scoring the touchdowns. I didn't know my linemen had that kind of speed. It's amazing how a little crowd noise can energize your weary legs, and heart.

"There are scouts from the Big Ten out there. Everyone wants to scout a new coach's offense, so we will tone down what we do in the second half. We will continue with the same handful of plays we ran in the first half." Coach Anderson walked through the middle of the group, contemplating his next words. "The second string will take the field when we go back out. And the third string needs to be ready. You are all playing the rest of the way.

"Gentlemen, you make me proud. I want everyone to go out and play with intensity and to play with respect for the opponent. You know what it's like to be on the losing end. Show the other team the respect you would want if you were losing.

"Vollenweider, I want you deep to receive the kickoff." Henry Vollenweider, from Dubuque, was the third string fullback behind Murphy and Green. He was stunned hearing the coach call his name. An underclassman, he hoped to get in the game, but never considered playing so soon.

South Dakota kicked off to start the second half. Vollenweider caught the ball at the ten yard line and started up the middle behind his blockers. He cut to the opening to his left. The defense swarmed toward the runner so Vollenweider cut back to his right. His teammates systematically blocked or knocked down one South Dakota defender after another. Suddenly, Vollenweider was at the fifty yard line with only one man to beat. Young Hank Vollenweider angled towards the corner of the end zone and out ran the lone defender. 34-0. Many of the sixteen thousand weren't back yet from the halftime socializing in the concourse when the roar of the crowd echoed down the tunnels after the Hawkeyes' fifth touchdown.

Suddenly, it all seemed too easy. Prasse and Kinnick were standing next to each other watching Vollenweider celebrate in the end zone.

"Can you believe this?" Prasse asked his teammate.

"I think so. It's been so long I've forgotten what this feels like," Kinnick responded. "Dr. Eddie has changed us. I'm starting to believe, Prass."

"Let's just make sure we keep it going," said Prasse. "We can't let anyone get too high. The new guys haven't experienced what we felt last year. Remember the celebration at the Morrison Hotel last year? That emotional high lasted one week before Colgate ruined it." The upper classmen knew jubilation could come tumbling down in a week's time, but today they didn't care; it felt too good.

South Dakota returned the kickoff to their forty yard line. Slowly they moved the ball to the Iowa nine. On second down and goal, their fullback plowed through the middle for a gain of three yards to the six. A quarterback sneak moved the line of scrimmage to the three. Iowa's second string was struggling, backed against its own end zone. On fourth down, the Hawkeyes' defensive linemen planted their feet on the goal line. Iowa's linebackers and defensive backs stood ready in the end zone waiting for the next play. Either South Dakota would score or, if the defense rose to the occasion, Iowa would get the ball back.

The fullback charged straight ahead after receiving the handoff. Eleven Hawkeyes converged to the middle of the line of scrimmage. The referee's whistle could barely be heard over the cheering crowd. The second string's goal line stand was magnificent. Iowa took possession of the ball at the one yard line.

Dr. Eddie turned to Couppee who was standing a few feet away. "Couppee, go in, and get that ball down the field." The coach wasn't concerned about the poor field position. He saw an opportunity to test his young quarterback in a tense predicament.

Couppee called running plays for Buzz Dean and then Ed McLain. Bruno Andruska, Ken Pettit, and Wally Bergstrom created havoc for South Dakota on the left side of the line. Max Hawkins and Ham Snider worked hard on the right side. Iowa advanced the ball but not enough. Buzz Dean punted with Kinnick on the sideline. The kick sailed to the Iowa forty-five yard line. Red Frye substituted for Bruno Andruska at center.

Neither team could score as they battled for field position. Finally, with less than a minute remaining in the game, Dr.

Eddie told Nile Kinnick to reenter the game along with John Maher. The coach wanted to end the game on a high note after a lackluster performance by the second and third teams. The reserves hadn't scored since Vollenweider's kickoff return at the beginning of the second half. Coach Anderson wanted the reserves to experience success advancing the ball on offense. The line of scrimmage was at the fifty yard line.

Dr. Eddie gave them final instructions before they ran onto the field. "Nile, Maher is one of the fastest guys we've got. Hit him deep. Maher, I want you to run a post pattern with everything you've got."

The rules of the game prohibited players entering the game to talk to any teammates until one play had been run. It prevented coaches from constantly sending in plays. So Kinnick and Maher couldn't tell Couppee what to call for the next play. Couppee thought about calling a simple running play up the middle; Kinnick could then give Dr. Eddie's instructions for the next play. But Couppee knew something was up if Dr. Eddie wanted Kinnick back in the game with less than a minute left. And with Maher coming in the game at the same time, Couppee instinctively knew Dr. Eddie wanted to use Maher's speed. So, instead of wasting a running play with so little time remaining, Couppee called a pass play for Kinnick to Maher.

Kinnick faded back with the ball, as Maher streaked to the end zone. He unleashed the pass. Maher caught it running at full speed and was immediately tackled on the fifteen yard line. There was time for one more play.

Couppee called the same play but to a different receiver. This time, Kinnick saw Robert Kelley alone in the corner of the end zone. A perfect spiral hit Kelley in the hands. In two plays, Kinnick took them half the length of the field for a touchdown.

Kinnick kicked his fifth drop kick for the extra point. Iowa 41, South Dakota 0.

The defense had been stellar. The Hawkeye quickness stifled everything the opponent tried while a great player from two years ago was reborn on this September afternoon. Nile Kinnick had personally accounted for thirty-five of the Hawkeyes' forty-one points, running for three touchdowns and passing for two more. He kicked five consecutive extra points. He gained one hundred ten yards on eight carries. He punted beautifully to the corners. He returned punts and a kickoff, and made several tackles on defense. All this, playing the first half and the last minute of the game.

As Kinnick walked off the field with his teammates, he remembered his father telling him, "Fame rests well when it falls on someone not seeking it." His childhood trained him to never boast about accomplishments. "It's better to let achievements speak for themselves," his father also once said.

Up in the stands two very proud parents practiced what they preached. Many came up to Nile Sr. to congratulate him on his son's performance. But to everyone Nile Sr. responded the same way. "It's a team game. Eleven people made every play."

Nile Jr. sat in front of his locker with his elbows resting on his knees, looking around the room at his ecstatic teammates. He hoped rightful thinking and living would keep the ankle healthy. For now, he thought, indefinable momentum, that had been too elusive for too long, would help them prepare for the next opponent, Indiana. He wondered if Dr. Eddie's prediction could occur.

CHAPTER FOURTEEN

Thursday, October 5, 1939. Iowa City was still vibrating after the opening game against South Dakota. Everyone was talking about the forty-one points scored, which almost equaled the total points scored for the entire 1938 season. Dr. Eddie Anderson and his no-huddle offense were discussed as much as the performance of Nile Kinnick. Interest bloomed and speculation grew as fan support spread rampantly.

At the end of the post-dinner meeting in the Commerce Building, Dr. Eddie closed his talk addressing the players on the importance of focus. "Gentlemen, we played well Saturday. I know you have been stopped on the sidewalks and in the classrooms, asked about the team, the upcoming game, congratulating you on the South Dakota game.

"All the hype and enjoyment are gone in a moment if you lose sight of our goal. We want to keep improving, and winning. This is just the beginning and it's crucial that we never rest on our laurels. We have much to achieve and it will progressively become more intense, and fun, each week, as long as we win.

"Coach Carideo, Coach Harris, and I have worked you harder this past week than any week since we've been here. We worked on the pass defense because of Indiana's Hursh. He's a great passer and he has good receivers, especially Zimmer.

Frankly, the idea of running wind sprints backwards this week was Coach Carideo's idea." He smiled and looked over at Frank Carideo. "So you have him to thank for those sprints.

"Gentlemen, a few quick facts. Does anyone know the last time Iowa beat Indiana?"

Kinnick answered quickly, "1921, Coach."

"Correct. Anyone know the last time Iowa won its Big Ten opener?"

Red Frye fielded the question. "I think it was 1933, Coach."

"Correct again. And one more fact, and I'll just tell you this one: Iowa has won only two Big Ten openers since 1900.

"Saturday isn't just about beating Indiana. It's also the moment we change history. We begin a new course. From this moment on, people will look back on this game as the beginning of a new Hawkeye era.

"Indiana is very good. Hursh and Zimmer can be very explosive offensively. Archie Harris will be a definite problem if we let him get open. He's strong and quick. I think you all know he holds the world record in the discus throw. When a ball is thrown in his direction, he comes down with it. And Emil Uremovich is nearly as good as Enich and Walker at tackle." Dr. Eddie gazed around the room at the thirty-five players sitting in the desks facing the podium. Kinnick, Prasse, Enich, and Couppee sat in their usual front row seats. No one ever interrupted Coach Anderson when he silently scanned his troops; instead, they waited patiently. "I remember my playing days well. 1921 was a lifetime ago for you, but as you get older, eighteen years is not such a long time in relation to your entire life. Consequently, time seems to go faster as you get older because you compare a moment to an ever-lengthening lifetime of experiences and memories.

"We had a lot of big games at Notre Dame. I always found it difficult to sleep the night before a big game. And so I share with you what I learned. I made sure I got a good night sleep two nights before the game.

"So, make sure you get to bed early tonight. And, of course, eat well tomorrow. Friday might be a little more difficult to sleep, and as the season goes on, and the games become increasingly more important, you'll always need to be well rested going into Friday night." Dr. Eddie laughed. "And then you can hope the other team is sleeping worse than you on Friday night."

Dr Eddie had one more item to discuss. "Due to working at the hospital in the mornings, I know how busy the place is on any given weekend. Currently, it is not busy so I have arranged for the entire team to stay Friday night at the hospital. You will be staying on the fourth floor of the south wing. Coach Harris will be accompanying you. I want to keep you away from downtown, your friends, and any other distractions. You'll need to wait until Saturday night to see family and friends. So pack a duffle bag, and your books, and a team bus will take you there after our meeting tomorrow night."

Saturday arrived quickly. It was a sweltering, Indian summer afternoon. The temperature was predicted to reach ninety degrees. Thirty thousand people were attempting to stay cool in the stands as a strong wind blew from the south.

The Hawkeyes were dressing in the Iowa Stadium locker room. The coaches hadn't entered the locker room, yet. Nile Kinnick was lacing his shoes for the right firmness: tight enough for maximum ankle support, yet loose enough to change direction comfortably. It was a silent moment allowing the players introspective thoughts about what would unfold over the next few hours. Kinnick reflected on how quickly an ankle injury changed his entire season last year.

"I'm feeling good about this one, Nile," Mike Enich said. "I want to be sitting here after the game thinking about how sweet it is to be undefeated and with a Big Ten victory."

"That, my friend, would mean we are in a tie for first place." Kinnick grinned at his massive, dark haired friend sitting next to him. "I like the sound of that." Kinnick turned to Prasse and Evans. "Are you two ready to catch a few prolate spheroids thrown to you?"

Prasse was quick to respond. "Only if it's made of pebble grained leather without corrugation of any kind."

Dick Evans added, "And if the entire surface is convex."

None had forgotten that first practice with Dr. Eddie when the new coach described the football and the dimensions of the playing field, and later tested them on the rules of the game. At the time, they weren't sure if Dr. Eddie was serious, but they soon realized he wanted to start from the beginning and teach them the basic fundamentals they had never considered.

The intensity in the locker room grew. The air filled with anticipation, ready to burst through the locker room doors. As was the custom, the team captain led them to the field. Erwin Prasse took his position at the front of the team. With a loud and excited voice he yelled so everyone could hear. "Let's keep it going today! We are as ready as we can be. The coaches have prepared us for this game. Let's make sure we come back here to celebrate.

"I might be the captain, but we all know Nile is our leader. Nile, come up here with me. I want you leading us out, too." Kinnick joined Prasse at the front as the team clapped their hands in unison, starting slowly, then building to a crescendo.

The doors opened. The heat and humidity smacked them in their faces but their energy was too high for them to even notice. The weight and the thickness of their football armor didn't matter either. As they entered the stadium, the crowd reacted. It had only been one victory so far, but the fans were showing their enthusiasm. They were also very curious how Al Couppee was calling the plays without a huddle. The Hawkeye fans didn't understand how he did it, but they enjoyed watching how baffled South Dakota had appeared last week.

Indiana looked a lot bigger than last week's foe, and Coach Bo McMillin had his team ready to play. Both teams completed their warm up drills, trying not to expend too much energy in the scorching heat.

Prasse won the coin flip and elected to defend the south goal, giving the Hawkeyes the southerly wind at their backs. Indiana subsequently chose to receive the opening kickoff. The Big Ten season was about to commence.

Erwin Prasse, aided by the strong wind, kicked the ball beyond the north goal line. Following the touchback, Indiana started their first play from scrimmage on the twenty yard line. After a series of short runs up the middle, Indiana's Hursh handed off to Tofil for an end run. As he crossed the thirty-two yard line, in the grasp of Iowa's Dick Evans, he lateraled to Hal Zimmer. Zimmer gained another eight yards before being forced out of bounds. On the following play, Jim Walker slid off the Indiana blocker and tackled Zimmer for a one yard loss. Iowa's Walker hit Zimmer so hard that Zimmer had to call a timeout. The stands erupted. Zimmer groggily walked to the sideline for some water, but he didn't leave the game. Coach McMillin felt there was too much football remaining in the first quarter to be without his ace halfback.

A few plays later, after the timeout, Hursh passed to Zimmer at Iowa's thirty-three yard line and then Zimmer out ran Couppee to the eighteen. After four more plays, Indiana kicked a field goal for a 3-0 lead.

Emil "Moose" Uremovich was destined for the National Football League after his senior year at Indiana University. Uremovich taunted the Iowa team by running alongside them singing the Iowa 'Corn Song' as the Hawkeyes ran back to their sideline. He came up to Couppee's face with a big grin repeating the lyrics loudly. The fans sitting close to the field booed Uremovich's arrogant and unsportsmanlike conduct.

Kinnick fielded Indiana's kickoff and ran back to the Iowa forty yard line where, just as he had done last week, he lateraled to Russ Busk who maneuvered his way through a crowd of red and white Hoosiers. Everyone stood as the play developed, voicing their loud approval as Busk gained twelve additional yards.

The Hawkeyes ran three plays unsuccessfully without getting a first down before punting the ball back to Indiana.

Hal Hursh and Hal Zimmer slowly brought the ball down the field. Archie Harris caught a pass in front of Bill Green and Buzz Dean, spinning to his left and dragging both defenders five additional yards. Then Zimmer caught another pass for a twenty yard gain. On the following play, Indiana's Brooks took the ball around the left end following a fake pass. Brooks lunged across the goal line. Indiana led 10-0 after the extra point kick. Uremovich did his song and dance again, this time along the Hawkeye bench.

Couppee was upset. "Let's make him regret doing that!" He singled out the offensive linemen. "Walker, Tollefson, Diehl, Luebcke, and Enich. I want that guy on his back every play! You hit him and then I'm right behind. Every play!"

Kinnick's cooler head prevailed, wanting to calm his quarterback down. "Coup, let's make him regret it by winning the game. That will be the greatest humiliation for him. Okay? Concentrate on what we need to do. If we do that, you can have the final taunt. And we'll walk off beside him."

Couppee nodded without saying anything. He knew Kinnick was right. Decisions shouldn't be based on retaliation. Victory would be the sweetest revenge.

Again Kinnick received the kickoff. He caught it on the five yard line and advanced it to the twenty-five. On the first play from scrimmage, Couppee wanted to catch Indiana off guard. Couppee knew which game situations warranted certain trick plays because they had practiced them frequently. He called for Kinnick to punt on first down.

The play call was short. "Fifty-one, ninety-two, twenty-four!" Couppee eliminated the first three single digit calls. The 'one' meant a trick play. The 'nine' meant punt. The ball would be snapped as soon as he said 'hike.' From the T-formation, Kinnick shifted to the tailback position five yards behind Diehl. Couppee shifted to the left behind Tollefson and Walker. Buzz Dean moved forward, behind Luebcke and Enich, as Murphy moved from his fullback spot to right halfback. Kinnick was well protected, though only five yards behind the line of scrimmage. His ability to punt quickly would be far more important on the play than his ability to place the kick to either side of the field, and have it bounce across the sideline.

Indiana never suspected the punt, especially not on first down. Kinnick took the center snap and booted the ball. It sailed over fifty yards in the air before hitting the ground. With no Indiana player back to catch and return the punt, the ball bounced five times and rolled out of bounds on Indiana's three yard line. The crowd went from dismay, not understanding a punt on first down, to exhilaration as the ball rolled to the sideline. The seventy-three yard punt changed the momentum.

While the Iowa players jogged to the other end of the field, nine teammates smacked Couppee and Kinnick on their helmets in celebration of a brilliant play call, and a clutch performance.

Indiana, backed up against their own goal line, conservatively called three runs through the middle of the line of scrimmage. The Iowa defensive line anticipated all three plays, knowing it was risky to throw a pass from the end zone. Tollefson and Walker nailed Zimmer on the first two plays. Enich tackled Zimmer with shear brute force on the third play for a two yard loss. Indiana was forced to punt from their end zone.

Kinnick fielded the punt on the Indiana forty and advanced it to the thirty. On first down, Kinnick dropped back to pass. He saw Prasse near the fifteen yard line. A perfect pass landed softly in Erwin Prasse's hands, and without ever breaking stride, Prasse ran across the goal line. Delirium rang from the thirty thousand in the stadium. Couppee's assignment on the play was to provide the last line of protection for Kinnick in case any Hoosier rushed through the line. So when the play ended, Couppee was standing next to Kinnick.

"Not yet, Coup. We're still behind." Kinnick knew Couppee was looking for Uremovich. "By the way, Coup, do you know the words to 'Indiana, My Indiana?'"

Couppee grinned back at Kinnick. "I do, as a matter of fact."

Kinnick dropped kicked the extra point but the celebration was kept short. Though they had closed the gap, the Hawkeyes still trailed 10-7.

The first quarter came to an end.

The heat started flexing its muscle, taking a toll equally on the shorthanded Hawkeyes and their opponent. Luebcke was dehydrated and replaced by Max Hawkins at right guard between Diehl and Enich. Ray Murphy came off the bench for Bill Green at fullback.

Indiana couldn't move the ball on their possession, so Bringle set up to punt again. Nile Kinnick caught the punt on his thirty-three. He avoided the first two tacklers before being brought down on the Iowa forty-two.

Before the first play from scrimmage, Kinnick leaned into Couppee's ear. "I think this is the moment for you to pay me back for taking you to that sorority party."

Couppee smiled. He knew what Kinnick meant. As the Hawkeyes lined up, Couppee hollered, "Six, eight, two, forty-three, seventy-one, twenty-five."

The Hawkeye backfield shifted into the Notre Dame box.

"Hike, one, two, three, four."

Diehl snapped the hike directly to Kinnick who had repositioned from left halfback to tailback. Hawkins and Enich, the stalwart rocks on the right side of the line, blocked their defensive assignments towards the middle of the field. Walker and Tollefson likewise blocked to the left. Evans took out the Hoosier defensive end.

Kinnick ran patiently behind his blockers, waiting for the play to unfold. Instinctively, he followed Couppee through the gaping hole Enich and Evans created. Couppee slammed the linebacker to the turf. The field opened. Kinnick only saw green grass and the several white yardage markers he ran across, each signifying being five yards closer to the goal line. The forty-five. The fifty. The forty-five, forty, thirty-five, thirty, twenty-five. Fifty-five yards after the play started, Kinnick was tackled at the three yard line. Momentum increased for the Hawkeyes.

As Kinnick walked by Couppee, Al hollered over the bedlam, "So, are we even on the sorority party?"

"Get us across the goal line and we're even," Kinnick yelled back.

Only three yards stood in the way of a lead against a Big Ten opponent by this small group of hearty footballers. They were collectively attaining new heights Iowa was unfamiliar with through the 1930s.

Three yards separated the Hawkeyes from euphoria. Couppee knew what to do. He knew Nile Kinnick was the guy to get the job done.

"Thirty-seven, eighteen, fifty-four, hike."

Indiana was anticipating Iowa's shift. Instead, it was another quick play: no shifting, no four count before the ball was hiked. Kinnick took the centered snap and drilled the line of scrimmage behind big Jim Walker and Chuck Tollefson on the left side. Kinnick ran across the goal line before the Hoosiers could react. No defender touched him.

As Kinnick celebrated in the end zone with his teammates, he looked over at Dr. Eddie, remembering when the coach talked about deceiving the adversary and the puzzled looks that would appear on the opponents' faces, unable to guess what the sophisticated Hawkeye offense would do next. The Iowa Hawkeyes were becoming proficient at Dr. Eddie's game of deception, he thought. Iowa 14, Indiana 10.

Iowa kicked off following the touchdown. Enich and Hawkins took over on the defensive line. Hursh and Zimmer were respectively thrown to the ground by Iowa's right tackle and guard on successive plays. Third down. Enich again slammed Hursh to the ground as he released the ball. The pass fell incomplete.

As Kinnick ran back to receive the punt, the crowd sensed that maybe the transformation of this small group of Hawkeyes was more than a dream. If the Hawkeyes could hold on to the lead, they would be undefeated after two games, and more importantly, undefeated in the Big Ten after facing a highly regarded Hoosier team.

Kinnick caught the punt and returned it to midfield. On first down Ray Murphy, still in the game for Bill Green, gained six yards. Next, Kinnick retreated deep to pass but slipped and fell to the ground at midfield. Then, Couppee called the play Prasse was waiting to hear. "Four, eight, four, forty-three, forty-one, sixty-five!" It was known as play 'thirty-four, one.' Kinnick dropped back again, looked to his left, and saw Prasse racing past the defensive cornerback. Kinnick unleashed the pass.

Prasse looked back over his right shoulder, reached out with his soft basketball hands, and latched onto the ball as he stepped across the goal line. Kinnick missed his first extra point drop kick of the year, but at the moment, it didn't matter. Iowa was ahead 20-10.

The celebration was immediately spreading across the entire state, thanks to the radio broadcast. The announcers mentioned that the Hawkeyes looked smaller than their counterparts, but seemed quicker and stronger.

Indiana wasn't willing to run out the clock and end the first half. Following an excellent kickoff return by Tofil, Hursh completed five passes to various receivers. On the fifth pass, interference was called on Iowa's defensive secondary and the ball was placed on the Hawkeye twelve yard line. Another pass from Hursh to Dumke took the ball down to the six. Two incomplete passes followed before Hursh found a rarely used reserve, Tipmore, in the end zone. Iowa 20, Indiana 17.

Kinnick threw an interception to Indiana's Hursh on Iowa's first play following the kickoff. Indiana had one last chance before the end of the first half.

Hal Hursh went back one more time looking for his favorite receiver, Archie Harris. Nile Kinnick anticipated Hursh looking for his big receiver and darted in front of Harris just in time to return the favor to Hursh: an interception before falling to the ground. A brutal half of football came to an end.

The afternoon temperature had reached ninety degrees, but the players had been oblivious to the heat. Adrenalin pumped through their veins. The excitement and intensity begged their minds and bodies to keep pushing themselves: running, blocking, tackling - getting up off the ground and doing it again.

Everyone grabbed a large cup of water before sitting on the long bench in front of their respective lockers. Dr. Eddie stood in the middle. "Gentlemen, that was impressive. I can't imagine there is any place any of you would rather be than right here, right now. I'm not sure, but I think you are starting to believe in the system. It's getting fun, men. The magic is just beginning if you let it. But you can't let up, not for a moment. So we must be better, faster, stronger, and tougher in the second half. You've got to reach deep inside and find that something extra. The Hoosiers might have more players on their side of the field, but none are conditioned like the Iowa Hawkeyes. Now, if you look in your lockers, you'll see that everyone has a clean uniform. So, take off your equipment and rest a bit. I want everyone drinking plenty of water, then put the pads back on with the dry uniforms."

Prasse and Kinnick again lead the team down the hallway towards the battlefield. Dry clothes, hydrated bodies - they were ready to start over again. The doors opened and the intense heat of the afternoon sun instantly slowed them in their tracks, more than any hit from a Hoosier earlier. The temperature, combined with the humidity, felt like a July afternoon.

Indiana kicked off to start the second half. Kinnick ran it back thirty-three yards. After three unsuccessful running attempts, Kinnick punted away to Hursh. Ham Snider tackled Hursh at Indiana's thirty-four yard line. After a short run by Tofil, Hursh went back to pass, finding Archie Harris along the right sideline. It was a twenty-seven yard gain to Iowa's thirty-seven. Tempers began to flare along the line of scrimmage. Big Jim Walker wanted to take on Archie Harris, by himself, anytime Harris wasn't running downfield as a receiver. Scuffles broke out and continued after the referees' whistles were blown.

Hursh found Zimmer on the fifteen yard line. Kinnick and Murphy desperately tried to catch him, Murphy diving at the last second for his feet, but Zimmer scampered into the end zone for six points. The crowd grew silent, thinking maybe their hopes had been dashed. The extra point attempt failed, but Indiana had taken the lead back, 23-20.

Iowa accomplished very little on the next series. On second down, Couppee hollered the play call for a run by Russ Busk around left end. The team shifted left into the Notre Dame box, leaving Couppee lined up behind Tollefson and Walker. Busk took the snap directly from the center just as Kinnick did when this play was called to the right. Walker was blocked out of the play by the defensive end, putting Al Couppee on a collision course with the much larger Archie Harris. Couppee lowered his body and blocked his shoulder into the Hoosier. A popping sound was heard by everyone in the near vicinity.

Kinnick rushed to his fallen comrade. "Coup, are you alright?"

"No, I can't move my shoulder." Prasse signaled for a timeout to the referee.

Dr. Eddie came running onto the field with the team's trainer. "Al, where does it hurt?" the coach asked.

"My shoulder, Coach."

Dr. Eddie sensed the shoulder was out of alignment. "I'm proud of you, Al. That was one hell of a hit you put on Harris. You get to take the rest of the day off.

"Gallagher, you're in," hollered Dr. Eddie. "Nile, you're calling the plays."

Kinnick was ready. He had shared the play calling all preseason with Couppee. But facing third down, and with Gallagher fresh off the bench, he wanted to give the new quarterback a little time to get a feel for the game. So, Kinnick called for a shift into their quick punt formation. Before Indiana could get a man back to receive the punt, the ball was sailing down the field. The strategy worked well as Iowa gained field position, giving the Hoosiers the ball on their own twenty-five yard line.

Hursh combined on a series of short and long passes. Two went to Harris. Two went to Zimmer. An eighteen yard run by Tofil, up the middle of the field, left Indiana with only five yards separating them from scoring again. Indiana's offense was in sync.

Hursh went back into the pocket and found Rucinski in the corner of the end zone. Enich blocked the extra point kick but momentum had clearly shifted to the visitors. Indiana 29, Iowa 20.

All the running since February had increased the endurance of this small band of young men in black and gold. They had run to exhaustion many evenings, only to be told they weren't done, yet. Now, though, it wasn't just the players in the other uniforms they were battling. The oppressive heat and warm wind were also their opponents. The Hawkeyes' conditioning was being tested in the fourth quarter just when tragedy again struck the team. Henry Luebcke buckled over with severe abdominal pain. Lying on the turf, he couldn't straighten the trunk of his body. His face was distorted in agony.

The game stopped again as the trainer and five of his staff labored to carry Luebcke off the field on a stretcher. They headed directly to the locker room. From there he would be transported by ambulance across the practice field, through the parking lot, to the University Hospital's emergency entrance three blocks away.

"Hawkins, you're in at right guard!" bellowed Dr. Eddie. Dr. Eddie felt the pain of losing his humorous big man with the strong Chicago accent.

Luebcke's weight had ballooned to three hundred thirty pounds after the 1938 season. When Anderson started running the team in early February, he told Luebcke to lose sixty pounds or not bother coming out in the fall. Hank Leubcke didn't lose sixty pounds; he lost seventy pounds to prove he belonged on Dr. Eddie's team. The coach had great admiration for Luebcke's efforts at wind sprints, too. He knew the running was particularly difficult for his large guard. Now, Dr. Eddie feared, his big man was gone for the year.

Hawkins grabbed his gold helmet and fastened the single strap under his chin.

His jersey was soaked with perspiration from just standing in the sun, watching the game.

Kinnick looked at Mike Enich. "Mike, are you okay? You're looking pale."

"I think I'm okay. I'm not sure."

"We need you Big Mike. We can't lose you, too." The timeout ended.

Indiana slowly marched down the field. They kept running plays at Max Hawkins, hoping to catch him making a mistake or being caught out of position. But Enich got tougher on the right side of the defensive line in the absence of Luebcke, acting like a big brother to Hawkins, protecting him from the playground bullies.

Hursh handed off to Tofil in the backfield just as Walker and Enich leveled him to the ground. It set up another third down.

Trailing 29 to 20, with less than a quarter to play, the Hawkeyes' Bill Diehl followed Zimmer downfield on a pass pattern. He reached up and snared Hursh's pass, intended for Zimmer, deep in Iowa territory. Diehl ran the interception back to the twenty-seven. Behind by nine points, the Hawkeyes knew they had to act quickly.

Kinnick hollered out a pass play to Prasse. The ball was overthrown and fell to the ground incomplete. On second down he called for another pass, this time to Buzz Dean. Kinnick faded back to avoid the rush, looked away from Dean's direction, then looked back as Dean cut over the middle. Buzz Dean grabbed the ball and fell to the ground for a first down. Next, a running play by Dean took the Hawkeyes to midfield.

Kinnick then called for an 'end around' play. Kinnick faked the handoff to Bill Green running through the middle of the line, and lateraled to Prasse coming from the left side.

Prasse ran across the backfield and then turned up field for a seven yard gain and another first down into Indiana territory. Successive runs, Green behind Tollefson and Walker, and then Kinnick behind Hawkins and Enich, took Iowa to Indiana's nineteen yard line.

The crowd sensed the excitement but didn't know if the upstart Hawkeyes had enough willpower and confidence to create the miracle finish. Nile Kinnick felt the emotions of the people in the stands. Seven minutes were all that remained for the thirty-three players in black and gold to create magic. Kinnick knew it would largely be up to him. His thoughts flashed to his father once saying, "Challenge affords the opportunity to rise above." Calmness was exuding from Kinnick and emanating to his teammates.

Kinnick called for Prasse to do another 'end around.' This time, instead of running around the right end, Prasse cut back up the middle between Diehl and Tollefson. The defense overreacted to the end sweep, leaving a wide open path for Prasse to gain seven yards. He fell just short of the first down.

Kinnick shouted the next play for Buzz Dean to run between Hawkins and Enich. He was tackled hard, but not until he reached the first down markers. The Hoosiers were tiring even though they substituted frequently. Indiana wasn't reacting to the quick shifts. The no-huddle offense was still producing results.

Kinnick thought about calling a running play for himself, but he anticipated the defense focusing on him; so Kinnick used himself as a decoy while Bill Green fell across the goal line for the touchdown. Kinnick missed another extra point. Indiana 29, Iowa 26. Five minutes remained.

The excitement lifted the energy of the crowd, which in turn, added to the team's own energy. The enthusiasm momentarily caused all but one Hawkeye to forget the excruciating temperature. Mike Enich went to the sideline, pale and staggering. He told Coach Harris, "I'm alright, I just can't stand up." He walked towards the bench but collapsed before reaching it.

Couppee, Luebcke, and now Enich were out. Al Couppee was standing in front of the bench with his arm in a sling. Mike Enich was headed to the hospital to join Hank Luebcke.

"Bergstrom, you're in for Enich," Coach Anderson yelled.

"Are you sure, Coach? I've only practiced at left tackle." Wally Bergstrom was feeling the pressure not to make a mistake at a crucial time against the strong Hoosier linemen. He had never played in a football game, high school or college, prior to the win over South Dakota, and that was at the end of the game after the outcome had already been decided.

"Tell Kinnick to use a huddle the next time we're on offense. It'll give you a little more time to process your assignment. And remember, you've got to wait one play before you talk to anyone. But first, go in there and hit that guy across the line with everything you've got. They will most likely keep the ball on the ground to run the clock down. Got it, Bergstrom?"

"Got it, Coach."

The Hawkeye defense did just what they needed. Walker slid off Archie Harris and tackled Zimmer for a loss. Then Bergstrom, maybe because his nerves were in high gear, maybe because he was fresh, pushed Uremovich to the side and hit Hursh for no gain on the play. Bergstrom's football career just began against a lineman headed for the National Football League next year. Bergstrom's time had arrived.

Hursh faded back on third down. He saw Harris across the middle but Bill Green, the fastest player on Iowa, darted in front of Harris. He grabbed the interception and charged down the left side of the field. As he was about to get forced out of bounds at the fifty yard line, he remembered Dr. Eddie saying, "We don't run out of bounds. There are no yards to be gained out of bounds." The Hawkeyes had also been taught not to stop the clock and give the opposing defense extra time to think about the next play; so Green stopped suddenly and stiff-armed the defender who missed the open tackle. Green gained nineteen more yards.

It was Iowa's ball on the Indiana thirty-one yard line. Iowa needed three points. They were a field goal away from a tie or thirty-one yards from a victory.

Kinnick felt it was his time, and he knew he needed to use the huddle to make sure Bergstrom and the others knew what to do. "Bergstrom, I'm headed right, around Evans, but then cutting back between Evans and you. I need one more big play from you, Wally." Then he called his favorite running play off right tackle.

The Hawkeyes shifted into the box formation. Again Kinnick was directly behind the center. Bill Diehl snapped the ball to Kinnick. Evans pushed the defensive linebacker to the outside. Bergstrom made another nice block on Uremovich to the inside. Kinnick scampered for sixteen yards to the Indiana fifteen yard line.

"Bergstrom, that was great!" Kinnick hollered before addressing the huddled team. "We're not done, yet. Let's get the job done before we celebrate."

The players realized huddles weren't so bad when tired. It gave them a slightly longer break before their next collisions. In the huddle, Kinnick called for Buzz Dean to run left. He was stopped for no gain. Another huddle. Kinnick called a pass play but his intentions were strictly to throw the ball out of bounds and stop the clock.

Just under two minutes remained. It was third down on the fifteen yard line. Kinnick called a pass play to Prasse in the corner of the end zone. Diehl hiked the ball. Kinnick stepped back. Kinnick's right foot slipped out from under him as Uremovich knocked him to the ground.

With the loss on the play, it was fourth down on the twenty yard line. The exhilaration of the crowd deflated to a solemn, anxious quiet. The victory was fading. It would come down to

Kinnick's drop kick for a three point field goal, and a tie. The team formed a huddle to receive the instructions.

"Forget the tie!" Kinnick shouted. "We're going all the way! We didn't play all afternoon for a tie! We're going to win!" Nile Kinnick radiated confidence to his fellow Hawkeyes, and it was what they wanted to hear. He was the leader that would only accept victory. Suddenly, their exhaustion abandoned them.

Kinnick refused to look to the sideline because he knew Dr. Eddie would most likely want to go for the tie. Instead, Kinnick called for the 'thirty-four, one' play. Prasse and Kinnick looked at each other. It was up to them. Prasse was to streak ten yards to the ten yard line, then head for the deep corner of the end zone for the pass. Kinnick took the center snap. Indiana knew it wasn't a field goal attempt when Kinnick didn't start deep enough behind the line of scrimmage for his drop kick, so the Hoosiers rushed hard. Kinnick dropped back into the pocket created by his blockers. The clock showed one minute thirty seconds. He darted left to avoid Uremovich who had gotten around Bergstrom, then he moved back to his right to elude another defender. Kinnick released the ball in Prasse's direction. The ball had good height as it arched upward, but Kinnick thought it was overthrown as soon as it left his hand.

Erv Prasse was six feet two inches tall, with great speed. The ball angled to the corner as it descended. With one final exertion, Prasse leaped forward while running at full speed. He reached out as far as his shoulders pads allowed. The ball touched his fingertips. He pulled it into his chest just before running out of the back of the end zone. Touchdown for the Hawkeyes. Iowa 32, Indiana 29.

Kinnick missed the extra point again, leaving an opportunity for Indiana to tie with a field goal; but they would first need a great drive deep into Iowa territory. The crowd didn't seem to mind the missed extra point as jubilation echoed from the stands with Iowa's lead. The Hawkeyes appeared to be real.

The win over South Dakota didn't reveal their potential, but this game did.

Prasse ran up to Kinnick. "That was a terrible pass, Kinnick, it was way too long. I guess I saved you, huh?"

"I thought the pass was perfect," responded Kinnick good naturedly. "Obviously, you're not as fast as I thought. Next time I won't lead you so much." They exchanged bear hugs knowing the game should soon be a victory.

Couppee found two of his Boars' Nest roommates on the sideline, Red Frye and Oops Gilleard. "You guys know the lyrics to 'Indiana, My Indiana?'"

Iowa kicked to Indiana one last time. Hursh ran the ball back to the twenty-seven yard line. The Hawkeyes' defense and the noise of the emotionally charged crowd made it impossible for Indiana to move the ball. Three times Hursh dropped back to pass with no success. On fourth down, they tried one final pass; it fell to the ground incomplete. The fans' cheering intensified.

The Hawkeyes took possession. Kinnick called three running plays, two for Green and one for himself, to run out the clock.

Couppee, Frye, and Gilleard headed across the field looking for Uremovich. He was in no mood for the exhuberant threesome's rendition of Indiana's song but he heard it, anyway, as they ran beside him. Victory was a much sweeter revenge, thought Couppee, but singing this song felt good, too. It had been eighteen years since Iowa had beaten Indiana, but that record didn't matter, anymore.

Kinnick ran for one hundred three yards, threw three touchdown passes to Prasse, gained one hundred seventy-two yards returning kickoffs, and punted ten times while averaging forty-two yards per punt.

In the locker room, Dr. Eddie addressed the team. "For the past three hours, you showed me something. But I'm curious to know – fourth down and three points behind – was that you, Kinnick, that decided to go for it?"

"Yes, sir," replied Kinnick.

"It appears to have been the right call," said Coach Anderson. The room echoed with laughter. "We have plenty of time to talk about the game later but I do want to mention a few things. Again, I was impressed by the effort and character displayed. I think all of you gained a tremendous amount of confidence today. The win last week was nice, but it didn't give us a barometer to gauge ourselves. Today, we beat one of the better teams in the Big Ten. Tomorrow, the newspapers will take note of your accomplishments.

"Kinnick and Prasse, that was special. But all of you fought, and fought hard. All of you won. The linemen were outstanding. Bergstrom, you came of age today. Walker, you took on one of the best all day long and you came out on top. Everyone on this team was spectacular. I mean that.

"I need to get over to the hospital and check on Luebcke and Enich. I think Enich may have been dehydrated, but I don't know what happened to Luebcke. Couppee, get dressed quick and come with me so we can have someone look at that shoulder.

"Gentlemen, celebrate a great performance tonight. But make sure I don't hear about any of it Monday morning."

"Dr. Eddie, can Erv and I go with you to the hospital?" Kinnick asked.

"We'll leave in fifteen minutes," Coach Anderson replied.

Dr. Eddie, Al Couppee, Erv Prasse, and Nile Kinnick walked into the emergency room area. Mike Enich was lying on a bed getting fluids.

"How are you feeling, Mike?" Dr. Eddie asked.

"Good, Coach. They turned the radio on so I could listen to the end of the game. So, I'm feeling really good right now," Enich answered. "I knew Bergstrom could do it."

"I'm going to make sure you stay overnight, Mike," replied Dr. Eddie. "I'll bet you lost ten pounds out there today. We just need to get some water and salt back in your system."

"They weighed me when I came in. I was down thirteen pounds," Enich said. "I haven't seen Luebcke. He was out of the ER before I got here."

"We'll find him," Kinnick said. "Mike, you played a great game today. We wouldn't have won without you out there. And you, too, Coup."

Then Prasse added, "You're wrong, Nile. We did win without either of them out there in the end."

Before Enich or Couppee could respond to the jab, Dr. Eddie interrupted. "Let's go find Hank. I'll have someone here take a look at that shoulder, Al, so you stay here."

Prasse and Kinnick followed Coach Anderson into Hank Luebcke's room. He was still in pain and in an uncomfortable fetal position. Just then, a doctor, making his rounds on the floor, walked into the room. "Mr. Luebcke has a severe hernia. We will want to operate very soon."

Luebcke was almost in tears from the pain. "Dr. Eddie, how long do you think I'll be out? Can I make it back this season?"

"Hank, there are six games left, six weeks left. In all likelihood, I don't believe there is any way you'll recover in time and get your strength back. I'm sorry, son. Football can be cruel sometimes. Your health and recovery are far more important than playing a game. Next year awaits you. Just don't balloon up to three hundred thirty pounds again."

"I was telling the doctor how much weight I had lost, Dr. Eddie. They said if I hadn't lost the seventy pounds in the off season, they might not be able to operate. I don't know why, but that's what they told me. So, thanks Coach, for making me lose the weight."

The Iowa Hawkeyes would no longer be an automatic win on an opponent's schedule. They successfully wiped away years of frustration in one of the most exciting comebacks in school history. Twice they came back after trailing. Twice they displayed the traits of a great team.

A Chicago newspaper wrote:

> *A resurgence occurred in Iowa City yesterday, gloriously conducted by Nile Kinnick and the expeditious Erwin Prasse.*

The Des Moines Register said:

> *A small group of young men put their stamp on the Midwest gridirons. Opposing teams will always have more personnel, but none will ever have more heart than these ironmen.*

CHAPTER FIFTEEN

Saturday night. Downtown Iowa City was overflowing with students, parents, and alumni after the Indiana victory. The Iowa Band was playing loudly in the streets, and marching through the bars, to the delight of the already festive fans. Footballers caused commotion wherever they went. The Academy was packed with people ordering food, playing pool, drinking beer, and anticipating the congregation of their gridiron heroes. Racine's was full, noise and excitement releasing into the street every time the front door opened. The D&L Grill and Joe's Place had long lines of people waiting to get in, though no one really cared if they did. The boisterous party had spilled into the streets.

Ray Murphy and Bill Green were the first players to arrive at Racine's. Several of the band members broke into the "Iowa Corn Song" as they entered. Everyone was congratulating Green for his touchdown run and key interception late in the game. Chuck Tollefson walked in and was immediately offered a beer. The Hawkeyes didn't need their billfolds tonight. Tollefson grew emotional as he looked around, holding back tears, his lower lip quivering. He recalled riding the rails from one farm to another not too long ago. He privately reminisced about the feelings of loneliness and not knowing what tomorrow would bring. He dredged up the pounding he would feel around his temples, trying to sleep in a barn while suffering from dehydration and malnutrition. The farmers were kind, but unable to feed and shelter every hobo that passed by.

How different all this seemed now, he thought. He was a hero for what he had done earlier in the day. Everyone wanted to talk to him as he made his way towards Murphy and Green, two of his thirty-four brothers. Pride was something that escaped him after he had quit college. He grabbed the beer that was handed to him, and made a silent toast to himself for surviving.

Buzz Dean, Russ Busk, and Bill Gallagher walked in proudly with their black leather jackets displaying gold 'I's over their hearts, their off-field uniforms of honor. Some patrons didn't know the players by their faces, but when large, athletic young men walked together, people assumed they were footballers. The thrill of 'winning football' had returned to Iowa City. The sport was a means of escaping the oppression many were still experiencing from the economic downturn. Many in this room were fortunate enough to rise above that financial tragedy, but football was still a key diversion for many across the state. It brought a moment of fun and distraction from tribulations, if only for an afternoon.

Tonight would be a celebratory night. The evening plans originated in the locker room before they disbanded. Some players had dinner commitments with parents before their families headed home. Others went to their dorms or apartments so their aching bodies could rest and recover before the celebration began. But they wanted to be together on this victorious night. Eventually, thirty players were at Racine's, and only five players were missing the hoopla. Mike Enich and Hank Luebcke, two students that had delivered ferocious blocks and tackles earlier in the day, were both in the hospital. Enich's prognosis was good. He would be fine in a day or two. Luebcke's future was bleak. He was gone for the season. It was a huge loss for the right side of the offensive and defensive lines. Al Couppee, the oftentimes party leader, was doubtful for the next game against powerful Michigan following his shoulder injury. Nile Kinnick and Erv Prasse decided to stay with Luebcke until his parents arrived from Chicago. The hospital had called his parents immediately upon his arrival.

Enich, Luebcke, Prasse, Kinnick, and Couppee were the heart and soul of the Iowa Hawkeye football team. Tonight, they would be together, just not partying with the rest of the team.

"You guys should head downtown to celebrate this one," Luebcke said. "You don't need to stay here with me. There really isn't anything you can do."

"I kind of enjoy seeing you in pain, Hank. It reminds me of how lucky I am," responded Erv Prasse.

Kinnick added, while looking at Luebcke's distorted body position, "We can't leave you Hank. It wouldn't feel right being downtown knowing you're here imitating a pretzel. Do you know when your parents will get here?"

"They'll probably be here around ten o'clock tonight. I think the doctors were talking about surgery tomorrow. And, you know, they want a family member here." Luebcke was in pain, but he appreciated his comrades being with him. Other than being sequestered by Dr. Eddie before the game, he had never stayed in a hospital room.

An hour later the silence of the long, sterile hallway was broken. They could hear two familiar voices laughing and talking. The voices grew louder as they neared.

Turning the corner into Luebcke's room were the other two Hawkeyes missing the downtown celebration. Mike Enich was wearing a white hospital gown barely covering his broad girth. He sat in a wheelchair with an IV dangling above his head, strapped to the back of the seat. Couppee, one arm in a sling, was pushing the big tackle's wheelchair.

"We heard the party was down here," Couppee chortled. "And we wanted to check out the nurses. There's a lot of them."

"How are you doing, Hank?" Enich asked.

"Well, besides needing a hernia operation first thing in the morning and being done for the season, I guess I'm alright."

"I'm sorry to hear that, buddy. I'm going to miss having you beside me on the line, and every day in practice. I don't know what to say." Enich's sadness was obvious.

"I'll be alright," said Luebcke. "What about the two of you? What's your prognosis?"

Couppee spoke first. "I just need to keep my shoulder immobile for awhile. I'll probably miss the Michigan game, but maybe not."

Mike Enich followed, "Well, the biggest danger I face is Couppee pushing me back to my room with only one arm. He ran me into the wall twice coming up here." The light-hearted comment broke the serious tone of the conversation. Then Enich added, "You know, it's just like our end sweep. I'm blocking my assignment for Kinnick, but I can always count on Couppee to hit me from behind and knock me into someone, or to the ground."

"Some things never change, Big Mike," Kinnick added. Then Kinnick turned to Prasse. "Prass, you seem a little subdued."

Prasse was staring out the hospital window towards the stadium. "On both those catches in the fourth quarter I saw this young girl sitting in a wheelchair. Enich's wheelchair just reminded me of her. She was eight or nine years old. And right next to her was a boy about the same age also in a wheelchair.

"The first catch I was running right towards them when I ran out of the end zone. They were in the grass behind the end zone, smiling and cheering. They were as much a part of the celebration as everyone else. They both looked so happy. And both were missing a leg, yet there they were on the field, enjoying the moment, enjoying watching us running, something they'll never do."

"I know exactly who you are talking about," Enich said. "I saw them, too."

Kinnick asked, "Did you notice who was with them? Did it look like nurses or hospital workers?" Neither Prasse nor Enich recalled who was accompanying the two children.

Kinnick had an idea. "I'll be right back." Nile Kinnick headed for the pediatric floor. Maybe, he thought, they were staying at the hospital and the staff wheeled them over to the game for some sunshine and a break from their daily routines. He was right.

"Hello. I was wondering if there are two children, a girl and a boy, that may have gone to the football game today. They were in wheelchairs."

"Yes, there are two kids here that you're talking about. They had a great time." The young woman at the nurses' station knew who was standing across the counter, but she asked anyway. "Are you Nile Kinnick?"

"Yes, I am."

"I saw you speak at a Boys and Girls Club in Cedar Rapids last summer. I used to volunteer there on the weekends."

"That's great that you did. What is your name?" Kinnick asked.

"Martha."

"It's nice to meet you. Would it be alright, Martha, if four of the members of the team stopped by to see them? We noticed them in the stands. It would just take a few minutes. We could do it right now, if it would be okay."

Ten minutes later, Kinnick walked into Luebcke's room. "Hank, we need to leave you for a few minutes.

"Follow me, gentlemen, we've got some good will to spread. Those two kids are here. Let's go say hello. Prass, can you take over Couppee's duties on Enich's wheelchair?"

150

Nile led them back to the floor where two young kids were about to be surprised. The nurse had moved Jimmy Scranton into Adel Swanson's room for the meeting, but hadn't told either of them why.

The nurse escorted the four players to the room. "Jimmy and Adel, I've got some visitors that wanted to stop and see you. They are four of the Hawkeye football players you watched today." Nile Kinnick and Al Couppee were the first to walk into the room. Erv Prasse was the last to enter, pushing Enich's wheelchair.

For the next fifteen minutes, two children sat wide-eyed talking to their new heroes. And during those same fifteen minutes, four footballers sat wide-eyed talking to their new heroes. Adel had been in a car accident three weeks ago. Jimmy had been riding with his grandpa on a farm tractor when he fell in front of the rear tire.

When the visit was over, all six left the encounter feeling good about themselves. After Jimmy asked for their autographs, four college students asked the young Hawkeye fans for their autographs. Jimmy and Adel both told the Hawkeyes they couldn't wait until tomorrow to tell their families and friends about their visitors. Jimmy also said his grandpa was a Hawkeye fan.

Kinnick, Couppee, Prasse, and Enich didn't speak as they made their way back to Hank Luebcke's room. Speaking would only ruin the moment, a moment of greatness they had not expected to encounter tonight - two children overcoming physical pain and emotional devastation, with mental toughness. All four were deeply moved by the demonstration, and lesson, of courage and bravery they had witnessed up close.

Iowa 32, Indiana 29 seemed a long time ago, and a little less important.

CHAPTER SIXTEEN

Sunday morning, following the Indiana game, was time for walking. Dr. Eddie Anderson preached that the best therapy for bumps, bruises, stiffness, and soreness was walking. The players would meet at the locker room and take off in groups of six or eight people. The less injured players walked faster to the eastern side of Iowa City, then turned around and headed back to campus. In all, everyone traversed six miles. On this particular Sunday, many local citizens hollered encouragement and support from porches and passing cars. Children joined the players along the route, many circling on bicycles. Only Hank Luebcke and Mike Enich were missing.

The excitement of being undefeated for the season, and victorious in the first Big Ten game of the season, had subsided by the end of Monday night's practice. There were few contact drills because Dr. Eddie wanted everyone to have another day to recover from Saturday's dehydration. Chuck Tollefson was nursing a sore foot. Al Couppee's shoulder caused his status to be uncertain for the upcoming game in Ann Arbor. Michigan was the next opponent. The Wolverines were once again a Big Ten powerhouse featuring Forest Evashevski, Archie Kodros, Ed Frutig, Tom Harmon, and Bob Westfall. All five were

All-Big Ten selections last year, the latter two also being All-Americans.

"Michigan will be tough, especially in their huge stadium," Dr. Eddie said. "Tomorrow night we'll work on our defensive schemes to counter Harmon and Evashevski. Nile, see me after the sprints.

"Okay, gentlemen, let's wrap up practice here with some wind sprints," Dr. Eddie's usual last comment every night.

One hundred yard sprints, goal line to goal line, tested their resolve. After seven sprints, many of the linemen were bent over, their arms braced against their upper legs, waiting for the next whistle. As much as the players disliked the running, everyone believed in Dr. Eddie's regime. Victories made them believe, and look beyond the pain.

Nile Kinnick walked over to Dr. Eddie after the last run. "Coach, you wanted to see me?"

"Yes, Nile. I've been asked to speak at the Iowa City Rotary Club luncheon on Wednesday. If it would fit in your schedule, I wanted to invite you to join me, and also ask you to give a short talk to the businessmen."

"Sure, Coach, I'd be glad to speak. Is there anything in particular you'd like me to address?"

Dr Eddie paused for a moment. He had gained tremendous admiration for this young man leading his squad. "I'll let you decide your topic. Just a short talk, and then I imagine they'd like a question and answer session."

The phone rang at the Phi Psi annex. It was nine o'clock Monday night. Bob Hobbs answered. "Phi Psi House."

"Is Nile Kinnick there?" a young woman asked. Her voice sounded unsure, but also anxious to talk to him.

"Just a minute and I'll see if he's in his room."

Two minutes passed. "This is Nile."

"Hi Nile. This is Era. Is it okay to call so late?"

"Sure it is. How are you, Era?"

"Good. I was hoping I might run into you this weekend after the game. I talked to some of your teammates downtown. Max Hawkins and Wally Bergstrom thought you might show up."

"I would have enjoyed that a lot. Prasse and Couppee, the swing dancers at your party, and I went over to the hospital after the game. Coup needed some medical attention on his shoulder and Prass and I went to see Hank Luebcke and Mike Enich. We ended up being there quite awhile."

"How are they doing?"

"Hank had surgery yesterday for a hernia. He's doing okay, though. And Mike showed up at practice this afternoon, so he's fine."

"And the swing dance star?"

"Couppee's shoulder is okay. He might not play this weekend. We have to wait and see." Nile was happy to be talking to her. "It's nice to hear from you, Era. I'm sorry I haven't called lately. Football and school don't give me much time off."

"That's okay, Nile." Era understood the long hours football consumed. "I wanted to ask you if you'd like to see a movie this week."

"Sounds fun. I can't tomorrow because I need to prepare for a Wednesday luncheon. Dr. Eddie asked me to join him and speak to a local business group. Wednesday night would work, though."

"Wednesday is fine with me," Era Haupert said.

"Is there any movie in particular you'd like to see?" Nile asked.

"I thought you might enjoy *Only Angels Have Wings*. Cary Grant and Jean Arthur are in it. I know you're fascinated with flying. It's a movie that involves pilots delivering mail over a dangerous mountain pass in South America. So we can see some flying and learn a little about South America, not to mention a love story, of course."

"How about the late movie after our football meeting?" Nile inquired.

"Perfect. Nile, what are you going to talk about Wednesday?"

"Probably the team, our hopes, how lucky we are to be here getting an education. What do you think?" Nile was curious if this sounded too conventional. He valued her input.

"It sounds good," Era said. "Besides, they'll enjoy just seeing the person they normally only see from the stands. I know they'll like whatever you have to say."

The two discussed the details of where and when to meet Wednesday, and then said good night.

October 11, 1939. The Michigan game was three days away. Kinnick looked around the room filled with Iowa City businessmen while Dr. Eddie spoke.

Coach Anderson was telling the audience about his coaching philosophies. He elaborated on what he had learned from Knute Rockne in the early 1920s. He said he incorporated his own beliefs and ideas into the system he had learned from his Notre Dame mentor. He spoke about the importance of bringing Frank Carideo, Jim Harris, and Bill Hofer with him to the University, all having played football for Knute Rockne.

> *So I'd like to close by saying how honored I am to be here with you today. This opportunity is a tremendous challenge for the players and coaching staff. And this opportunity is so gratifying when you have the likes of Nile Kinnick and the other thirty-four players showing up every night.*

The crowded room gave Dr. Eddie a rousing applause. This was the first time many of them had heard the new coach speak. Dr. Eddie concluded,

I have asked Nile Kinnick to join me today. I can honestly say, and I mean this, I have never coached a better player in all my years in football. And I can tell you with confidence, you have not yet seen the full talent of this fine young man. Our coaching staff will be focused on getting the ball in his hands as often as possible. Please don't call your friends in Michigan and share that with them. And, of course, it's up to Nile to get his hands on the ball defensively from his safety position.

Laughter floated from the tables.

So, I'd like to introduce Nile Kinnick, the finest football player and the most disciplined athlete I have ever coached.

Applause filled the room as Nile walked to the podium.

Thank you. Thank you very much. It's an honor to be invited to this fine organization today and meet so many of Iowa City's business leaders. I must say that, to me, this is one of the nicest communities I have ever seen. It is such a pleasure to live here and be part of this city while attending the University of Iowa.
When I first visited the campus as an eighteen year old, I instantly felt a warm

and friendly atmosphere that played a significant role in my choosing this school.

It's particularly pleasing to be here when you look at the dire situation in Europe and the tremendous sadness that is enveloping so many lives. We are blessed to be part of the United States. Hopefully, FDR makes the right decisions for our country. And I personally hope that Winston Churchill will soon be the new Prime Minister of England. His words, and his leadership, are needed during this world crisis.

Churchill recently said, "Every day you may make progress. Every step may be fruitful, yet there will stretch out before you an ever-lengthening, ever-ascending, ever-improving path. You know you will never get to the end of the journey but this, so far from discouraging, only adds to the joy and the glory of the climb."

At first the crowd sat in silence listening to a young man who seemed so much older than his years. And then the sound of hands clapping rippled through the room. Everyone was applauding the thoughtfulness of this football player, a young man that carried their hopes on Saturday afternoons. His subject matter was unexpected.

He continued.

Just as Mr. Churchill points to the future and progressing towards a better life, I think all of us have learned a great deal from Coach Anderson. He instills a confidence and a purpose to what we do. What he teaches isn't just football, but a way of living, trying, and succeeding - a lesson I believe that will remain with us long after the 1939 season and our academic years.

Not many predicted a good season for us, but now we are all believing. Not many had confidence in us, especially when we have half the number of players as our competitors. But never once has that caused us to think less of our 'ever-lengthening, ever-ascending, ever-improving path.' In fact, instead of being discouraging, it 'only adds to the joy and glory of our climb.'

Nile paused and looked around the room. Heads were nodding in agreement. People were smiling. He had accomplished what he wanted. He had reached them. He was reminded for just a brief moment of his talks on Sunday evenings at his grandparents' home.

The season is still young. We may find a pothole or two along the way. But this I know: we will be successful.

Every player on our team understands how fortunate we are to be here in Iowa City, going to a great university, and playing football.

Thank you for this opportunity to speak here today.

The crowd again applauded loudly.

A gentleman in the back hollered out, "Nile, are you going to win the Big Ten this year?"

"Dr. Eddie said we will and so, yes, I think we will." Laughter reverberated back to the podium and Kinnick. He grew more comfortable as the group revealed a lightheartedness.

"Is it true your grandfather was the Governor of Iowa?"

"Yes, sir. George Washington Clarke was governor from 1913 to 1917. I have great memories of him. We used to go to his house every Sunday night and the grandchildren read aloud to the parents and grandparents. It gave my grandfather and the other adults great joy. All four of my grandparents would be there along with my parents, and my aunts, uncles and cousins. We read while my grandfathers smoked cigars and my grandmothers served dessert after dinner. It was a great time in my life."

Another question came from the front. "What are your thoughts on the game this weekend?"

"Michigan always has a good team. This year is no different. Tom Harmon and Forest Evashevski are great football players. And, in addition to these players, Michigan has always been a difficult place for visiting teams.

"The loss of Hank Luebcke certainly will have an impact. You don't replace a player with his size and abilities, but we have several other players that will step up to the challenge."

Dr. Eddie listened as this young man spoke. Nile Kinnick was believable, something Dr. Eddie noticed the first time he met his star player. His words reached out and affected the listeners. Dr. Eddie knew his plans rested on the shoulders of this speaker.

Today, the audience was a group of men eager to hear from this young warrior, a person able to give this community and state great joy and hope on weekends, something long overdue after too many dreary gridiron seasons. But those seated in the room were also getting a glimpse of youthful brilliance. They were surprised with the ease and eloquence of his delivery.

They seemed eager to hear more. "What do you contribute the turn around to?"

Kinnick knew the answer but he wanted to be correct in his reply. He had been taught to express goodness because every act has a rippling effect, reaching others in sometimes unexpected ways. Kindness, he knew, is always paramount.

"I would like to, first, preface my response by saying this: Irl Tubbs is one of the finest men I have ever known. He had the utmost respect for every player on the team. He's a gentleman and someone I hope will always be part of my life. But for whatever reason, the fortunes of the program did not meet his expectations. Through it all, though, I always witnessed true character in him.

"My father once told me 'the ultimate measure of character is how one helps others while facing his, or her, own adversities.' Irl Tubbs was always most interested in the well-being of his players, every single one of us, while he faced his own hardship. I recall Coach Tubbs being questioned on why I wasn't getting some medical attention my junior year. Well, Coach Tubbs knew my faith was deeply rooted in the credence of self-healing and he promised my mother, and me, that he would always honor my individual beliefs.

"I learned a great deal about human kindness and decency from him in those locker rooms after our losses. His kindness never wavered even though the seasons weren't going well. He cared most about us, even while being scrutinized by the public. He was truly a man of character."

Applause again rang from the room, this time in honor of Irl Tubbs, but also to acknowledge Nile Kinnick's compassion and ability to interpret the situation. Some in the audience felt a little embarrassed for wanting Coach Tubbs' ouster last year as Kinnick's illustration reminded them about human benevolence. Dr. Eddie was applauding louder than anyone.

"But to answer the question, Dr. Eddie Anderson is the reason for the turnaround. He brought a Notre Dame swagger to our very first meeting. It carried over to our practices. His offense is innovative. His style is hard to explain in words. He and his staff tell you something and expect you to remember it. It instills a confidence in us when we know we will only be told once. You do it correctly and move on." Kinnick looked over at Coach Anderson and saw him smiling proudly. Then he added, "And, he has run us to death."

The group laughed again while Coach Anderson displayed his amusement. He rocked back in his chair, looked up at the ceiling and laughed out loud.

"I have never run as much as I have these past eight months. But as a result, we have taken on a swagger of our own. Though we don't have as many players as our opponents, we feel we have the endurance to get to the fourth quarter with just as much energy.

"I believe we are in better shape than any team we will face. We have heard Coach Anderson say many times that the team in the best shape has a much greater chance to win. Our offense seems to confound the opposition at times. And I must say, I've never had so much fun playing any sport as I do football right now. It's fun to confuse the defense with our no-huddle offense. It's fun to play defense with a bunch of guys that rush to the ball. It's fun to win. It's fun to go into the game, not just hoping for a victory, but expecting it. And this is all due to Coach Anderson's unique abilities, and the coaching staff he assembled."

The monitor stood up next to Kinnick and said they had time for one more question.

"Nile, do you have any plans after college?"

Kinnick paused for a moment. He had pondered that question many times over the past year. Law school was a definite possibility. Maybe applying for a Rhodes Scholarship. But he decided to avoid answering directly. "I have thought about that a great deal. There is a fine line one must walk between living in the present while enjoying this gift of life, and dedicating your time to helping others by providing a service to enhance the well-being of humanity. It seems that many people work hard to get ahead and sometimes miss out on the very essence of life: to live, to love, and to share life. I want to find a balance that allows me the enjoyment of this gift we have, while also helping others toward a better existence. I know that sounds idealistic, but I also believe it's important that we think ideally.

"So, to answer your question, I am open to any suggestions." Nile laughed. "Do you have any openings in your company?" Nile smiled broadly and thanked his audience again for the opportunity to speak to them. The audience clapped robustly one last time, as they were both impressed and entertained by someone they were proud to have representing the University of Iowa.

People were beginning to notice Nile Kinnick.

CHAPTER SEVENTEEN

Couppee was an integral part of Coach Anderson's offense, blocking for Kinnick's sweeps behind Enich to the right or Walker to the left. Occasionally, Couppee was rewarded with the chance to slip into the opponent's backfield to receive a pass from Kinnick. His shoulder had improved enough to make the travel squad, but he was still questionable for Saturday's game. It was Thursday morning, nine o'clock. The Rock Island Rocket was leaving the train station for Chicago.

Chuck Tollefson was sitting next to a window, staring at the autumn colored trees lining the train tracks. It seemed like a painting, he thought. Gold, amber, red, orange. After surviving his earlier hobo days, subtle moments of life's beauty seldom escaped Tollefson. He absorbed what each day offered. His appreciation and happiness for life inspired his teammates. Everyone respected him for entering college a second time and doing it with his own style. Gratitude permeated his appearance. His persona was a living example that quietly shouted to those around him to enjoy the moments they were experiencing. He knew too well what it was like when a path wasn't lined with opportunities, the way these tracks were lined with the different hues and shades of the changing leaves.

Remembering old times, he knew, could be both good and painful at the same time.

Nile Kinnick sat down in the seat beside him. "Tollie, you look deep in thought."

Tollefson turned and smiled. "I was thinking how much nicer it is riding here in a comfortable seat, rather than a boxcar. Although, I must admit, I've slept in some comfortable beds of hay while cruising through the countryside."

"Were you alone a lot?" Kinnick enjoyed talking with Tollefson. It seemed there was always something to learn.

"Not usually. You'd meet some other guys and then stop at the next farm together to see if they needed help bringing in the crops. The farmer might not be able to hire all of us, but usually he'd hire more than one so you formed groups."

Kinnick, curious by nature, wanted to know more. "Where did you travel?"

"I stayed in the Midwest. I'd go down to southern Missouri where the crops were ready for harvest sooner than up north. I'd head for Kansas, and then crisscross back through Nebraska, Iowa, and Illinois. Then I'd end up in Minnesota or Wisconsin. Slowly you worked your way north, following the harvesting season. Obviously, you didn't make much money. We were cheap labor for those farmers. Sometimes you just worked for food. But I eventually saved a little money. I'd hide it in my shoes and then wear my shoes while I slept. You couldn't take the risk of someone stealing your money. There was a strong sense of trust among us, but yet, everyone was trying to survive."

"You know we all look up to you, right?" Nile stated more than asked.

"I appreciate that, Nile."

"How's your foot?" Kinnick asked.

"It's good. I'll be okay. Just tell Couppee to call plays to the right so I can have an easier day of it."

"I always tell him to go that way." Kinnick smiled and slapped him on the shoulder, leaned back against the head cushion, and closed his eyes.

The trip to Chicago was routine for the seniors. The first leg was usually to Chicago and then they would transfer to another train. The next three games were all on the road. Today, the connection was to Ann Arbor. Next week, they would travel to Milwaukee from Chicago, and then take a third train to Madison to face the Wisconsin Badgers. In two weeks the connection would be to West Lafayette and the Purdue Boilermakers.

Ken Pettit's voice boomed from the back of the train car. "Who's in for some poker? Come on, Tollefson. We need another."

Tollefson looked over at Kinnick. "I can't pass up a chance to take Pettit's money, right?" He got up and joined Pettit, Red Frye, Bruno Andruska, and Ham Snider. The game would last all the way to the Chicago depot. The coaches didn't mind the gambling as long as the stakes didn't get high. But even small wagers were a lot to these young men from meager backgrounds, so the coaches occasionally walked by to make sure the pots didn't get too large.

Kinnick looked around behind to see who was joining the card game. His glance stopped when he saw Mike Enich intensely absorbed in a book. Enich intuitively felt Kinnick's stare and looked up. Enich propped up his hulky body and sauntered down the aisle towards Tollefson's vacated seat.

"Are you reading any interesting novels, Nile?" Enich asked the question, knowing the answer. Mike Enich and Nile Kinnick were both voracious readers.

"Not a novel. I'm reading *A Further Range* by Robert Frost. It won a Pulitzer not too long ago." Kinnick responded. "It's interesting. How about you?"

Mike Enich flashed his book so Kinnick could see. "Surprisingly, some poetry, also. *The Prophet* by Kahlil Gibran."

"I'm not sure but I think he said something like, 'My every thought, my every word, my every action is my religion.'" Kinnick surprised Enich with his familiarity of the author. "Wasn't he Lebanese?"

"Yes, he was," Enich said. No one ever asked Mike Enich about his ancestry, but he had an eastern-Mediterranean appearance with his olive skin and dark eyes. "Gibran had an interesting and insightful outlook. I guess I always enjoy learning about someone else's viewpoint. For instance, Nile, I'm very curious about your religious beliefs, and what you were going though emotionally while you were injured last year."

"I have to admit," said Kinnick, "I was second-guessing some of the things I grew up believing. Christian Scientists believe in a strong mind/body/soul link. Injury might be due to something out of balance or something we need to change. It's one thing to grow up believing something, it's another thing to find yourself being tested. There were times last year when I thought maybe my approach was wrong. I found myself thinking strongly about getting medical attention."

Enich responded, "I think most of us are all, in a sense, victims of our environments, especially when it comes to religious views. From the time we are infants, we are taught by our parents, and they teach us what they know. I'm sure it would be a rarity for a young child to belong to a religion other than his or her parents.' I know I grew up believing the same things my parents believed."

"Me, too, Mike." Kinnick enjoyed philosophical topics. "You bring up an interesting thought. I admire a person that can look at their life and their principles objectively, not believing what they do just because it's what they had been told since childhood, but rather, actually being able to step back and analyze why they believe what they believe. It's too easy to never question our rituals and routines."

"I know what you mean," said Enich. "When you're faced with a tragedy, you seem to find God a little easier. You pray. Sometimes the prayers go unanswered, but then, no answer is an answer, isn't it?" Kinnick looked over at Enich and smiled, then Enich continued. "I was once faced with a serious catastrophe, or what seemed like one. I was praying harder than I've ever prayed in my life. And nothing changed. I started questioning divine intervention.

"Then one day, I was sitting on a park bench. I looked around at the trees bending with the wind and the beautiful manicured lawn. And I started thinking about the science of it all. It dawned on me that there are only so many elements in the world. And we are made up of the same elements as a leaf on a tree or a blade of grass, hydrogen, oxygen, carbon, iron; but I decided I was more important than a leaf or a piece of grass."

Nile continued the thought. "We don't have to understand to believe, right? In fact, I don't think we are ever privy to information as to exactly what to believe. That's why it's called faith. We believe because we want to, or maybe it seems like a safe bet."

"And sometimes, Nile, something happens that is too coincidental. It puts a smile on your face. There's something comforting to know that, maybe, there is more than we comprehend."

"What religion are you, Mike?" Kinnick asked.

Enich paused, then remembered Kinnick quoting Kahlil Gibran earlier. "My every thought, my every word, my every action is my religion."

"Well, then, I hope your religion on Saturday is to create big holes for me to run through."

The two football stars had great admiration for each other. They sat in silence for the next hour, Enich reading and Kinnick pondering his future with his eyes closed, until their stillness was interrupted by Coach Anderson, standing in the aisle at the middle of the train car.

"Gentlemen, I'd like everyone to take a seat, put away the cards and books, and just relax for the rest of the ride. We've got a short layover in Chicago before the next train. We'll all meet at the restaurant in the depot for a late lunch." Dr. Eddie was aware of the importance of rest on a road trip. He knew young players can act in robust, youthful ways and not get the rest they need. Coach Anderson thought it was important for them to enjoy themselves, not thinking too much about the game, but he also valued introspection. "So, please take a seat, and think about what we've been working on these past few days, and what we want to accomplish Saturday."

Nile Kinnick reflected on the past week. He also thought about the past two years, one victory in 1937 and one victory in 1938. Already they had matched the number of wins in those two years. Kinnick remembered the long rides home after some of those losses. He wondered how this season would end. Can this season be a miracle season? Or, did they just finally have some luck this year and Michigan would bring them back to reality, proving that the Hawkeyes are not yet a top caliber team? He knew the task ahead was daunting. He couldn't help but think about those All-Big Ten Wolverines and how hard they would be tackling him. Michigan had speed in the backfield and linemen with size and quickness. If only the ride home could be a good one, he thought. If only they could ride home with three victories.

CHAPTER EIGHTEEN

October 14, 1939. Leaves were falling in Ann Arbor with the slight breeze from the south, bringing unusual autumn warmth to the northern state. It was a perfect day for football. The Wolverines had beaten their in-state rival, Michigan State, 26 to 13 the previous week. With no injuries in that game, all seventy-two players were dressed for Iowa. The Michigan roster was deep and talented. Tom Harmon, Forest Evashevski, Bob Westfall, Archie Kodros, and Ed Frutig were All-Big Ten players; Harmon and Westfall were also All-Americans.

Coach Fritz Crisler addressed his Wolverine team in the locker room. "I want to share some statistics with you from last week: one hundred three yards rushing, one hundred eight yards passing, three touchdown passes, two hundred one yards returning punts, one hundred seventy-one yards returning kick offs, four punts for a total of one hundred seventy-two yards, an interception with a return for twenty yards, and two extra points. If you total all these yards, it equals six hundred three yards advancing the ball and another one hundred seventy-two yards punting the ball down the field. All together, that totals seven hundred seventy-five yards. Then add in an interception and twenty points scored. And this, men, was done by one individual, in just one game against a good Indiana team. Nile Kinnick is the best we'll face all year.

"And that is why we have practiced all week to stop him. He is not only the best we'll face all year, he is quite possibly the best football player in America. Evashevski and Kodros, you've got your work cut out at linebacker determining whether he's running or passing. He'll disguise it. His play action fakes will make your decisions to attack the line or fall back in pass coverage crucial. And Harmon, as you know, your assignment all day on defense is to shadow Prasse. He caught all three of Kinnick's touchdown passes last week.

"Fortunately, we have some fine players sitting in this room right now. And I'm sure Iowa is concerned about Harmon the same way we are concerned about Kinnick. These Hawkeyes haven't had a lot to cheer about in recent years. That makes them all the more dangerous. They are a different team now. Emotions play a big part in sport and these Hawkeyes are excited. They don't have the personnel and depth that we have, so we'll be substituting freely and, hopefully, wearing them down in the second half. But make no mistake, even though they don't have the depth, they are well coached, and playing with a lot of passion.

"They beat Indiana last week and they are capable of beating us today. Let's make sure they don't. I want the headlines tomorrow to read how we crushed an up-and-coming team in the Big Ten."

The visiting team's locker room was bursting with animation. "A high-spirited vivacity can sometimes be a team's greatest asset on game day," said Dr. Eddie Anderson, "and at other times be a team's greatest adversary. It can bring out the best, a focus and quickness not normally displayed; or it can bring on nervousness and disaster. Coaches Carideo, Harris, and I know there is a fine line between flawless execution and catastrophe. Young men," continued Dr. Eddie, "can get too animated, which in turn, can cause poor decisions. The enthusiasm must be complemented with execution, leadership, and vision. We must be at an emotional level that will allow the performance we expect."

Ham Snider was starting his first game in place of Hank Luebcke. He would be facing one of the best defensive lines in the country. Dr. Eddie walked over to Snider. "Ham, you don't have to be great today. You just need to be good. If someone blows by you on offense, or knocks you to the ground on defense, don't get frustrated. It's going to happen. Just stay focused and get ready for the next play. Okay?"

"I'm ready, Coach."

Dr. Eddie next walked to Al Couppee who was putting on his shoulder harness. "Couppee, if you think you can do it, I'll let you start."

"I want to try, Coach. If it hurts, or if I don't think I can go, I'll come out. I don't want to hurt the team."

Couppee was primarily a blocker from his quarterback position. Whether or not his shoulder could take the hits, even Couppee didn't yet know. Dr. Eddie felt each individual possessed his own pain threshold. He was willing to let Couppee make his own decision about today. "I want you to let me know if you feel any pain at all," commented Dr. Eddie. "Even though this is a big game, I don't want any further injury, and then lose you for the season. We've got two weeks until our next game and that should be plenty of time to heal, provided the injury doesn't worsen. Okay?"

"Okay, Coach."

Dr. Eddie motioned Nile Kinnick to follow him to the other side of the locker room where they could speak privately. "Nile, today can be your greatest hour. Beating Michigan in their own stadium would be an achievement you'll be telling your grandkids someday. But be prepared for an all-out attack on you every snap of the ball. They are well aware of your achievements. And they know if they stop you, their chances of winning take a quantum leap. This game is going to be at a pace you've never experienced before. You will have to play with reckless abandon. But I've got faith in you, Nile. If anyone can do it, it's you."

Kinnick's lips pressed tightly together. His jaw protruded out. He looked Dr. Eddie directly in the eyes. "I'll do my best, Coach. Our journey is just beginning."

"You've got a target on your back, Nile. The Wolverines will be looking for you on every play."

NBC Radio was broadcasting the game to the entire nation. It was a feel-good story about a team on the rise against a perennial football power. It was a story of the downtrodden hoping for that seamless moment of over-achievement.

Captains Forest Evashevski and Erv Prasse met with the referees at mid-field for the coin toss. The Hawkeyes won and elected to receive the ball.

Tom Harmon - Michigan's triple threat at passing, running, and kicking - watched the kickoff fall into Kinnick's hands. Like Kinnick, Harmon also handled the punt returns as well as the kick returns. The only difference between the two footballers was that Kinnick was the only place-kicker in the country still using the drop kick style for field goals and extra point attempts.

Kinnick returned the kickoff to the Hawkeye twenty-seven yard line. Bill Green ran the first play behind the middle of the Hawkeye offensive line for no gain. Kinnick ran two plays off Enich's right tackle position for six yards. Fourth down and Kinnick punted to Harmon.

While Michigan was in their offensive huddle, Couppee shouted to his ten defensive teammates. "Prasse and Norgaard, watch for Harmon and Westfall on end runs. Dean, be ready for Frutig going out for a pass from the backfield if Harmon fades back to pass. Especially watch him on the down and out patterns." Jens Norgaard and Buzz Dean were starting their first games at end and in the backfield, respectively. Couppee wanted to make sure they were both focused on their respective assignments.

After two lackluster runs and an incomplete pass to Frutig, the Wolverines punted to Kinnick who called for a fair catch at Iowa's twenty-two yard line.

Couppee called a trick play on first down, a reverse run by Bill Green. Michigan was not surprised by the reverse and stopped Green after a gain of three yards. Thinking that the Wolverines were waiting for Kinnick on an end-around play, Couppee called for the shift from the T formation into the Notre Dame box to the left. Buzz Dean ran between Jim Walker and Chuck Tollefson on the left side for four more yards. The Hawkeyes were faced with third down, needing three yards in order to retain possession.

Couppee looked over to the sideline and saw Coach Anderson pointing to the end zone. With the line of scrimmage on Iowa's twenty-nine, the end zone was seventy-one yards away. Couppee knew what the coach wanted, a big play. Couppee smiled and looked at Kinnick.

"Four, seven, three, twenty-three, seventy-five, thirty-six!" The third single digit was less than five; the ball would be hiked on the count of four. The first digit of 'twenty- three,' because it was an even number, told the team to shift right into the Notre Dame box. Kinnick was directly behind Diehl at center. The second digit of 'twenty-three' and the first digit of 'seventy-five' meant the play was 'thirty-seven.'

When the Hawkeyes knew the play was 'thirty-seven' they reached deeper for that inner strength, anxious to unleash their energy on a Wolverine on the other side of the line of scrimmage. Couppee continued, "Hike," the shift started, "one, two, three, four." The ball was snapped to Kinnick.

Nile started to his right with the option to run behind Couppee and Enich, or to look for Prasse angling across the middle of the field. Kudros and Evashevski were closing in on Kinnick. Prasse was tightly covered by Harmon. At the last second, before Kudros slammed Kinnick to the ground, Nile launched the ball to his secondary receiver, Bill Green, on the forty yard line. Green's tremendous quickness silenced thousands of stunned Wolverine fans as he raced sixty yards to the goal line after the catch. Kinnick's drop kick for the extra point was good. The Hawkeyes' belief in themselves took a huge step forward with the 7-0 lead.

Jens Norgaard's ensuing kickoff went into the end zone. Michigan had the ball on their twenty yard line following the touchback.

"They're not going to try anything fancy from their twenty and down seven points. Watch for the run," Kinnick yelled to his teammates. Westfall was hit hard by Diehl and Walker on the first play. Snider and Enich stuffed Westfall at the line of scrimmage on the second play. Surprisingly, Trosko quick-kicked a punt on third down and the ball rolled to a stop on the Iowa thirty-six yard line.

Both teams struggled to sustain offensive drives. Punts were exchanged back and forth. Finally, a short punt by Michigan gave the Hawkeyes good field position. But Kinnick did something that was unexpected, something he had never done before; he fumbled the punt. A Wolverine pounced on the loose ball at the Iowa forty yard line. The home crowd came alive as the Wolverines again prepared to play offense.

After an incomplete pass and a short run by Harmon, Frutig grabbed a pass from Harmon at the ten yard line and was forced out of bounds by Kinnick at the two. Westfall tried a run up the middle but was again stopped by Diehl. Next, Harmon took the snap and crossed the goal line untouched. Just like Kinnick, Harmon kicked the extra point and the game was tied, 7-7.

Buzz Dean grabbed Tom Harmon's kickoff and ran it back to the thirty yard line. Couppee thought the Wolverines were over-playing both sides of the field so he called for Buzz Dean to run up the middle behind Snider's and Enich's blocking.

Ham Snider took out the defensive guard. Mike Enich leveled the tackle. Couppee led Dean through the hole created by the linemen and hit the middle linebacker. His sore shoulder made a slight popping sound. Dean raced to the forty-four yard line but Couppee was laying back on the turf, his face contorted from the sharp pain shooting from his collar bone.

Kinnick motioned to the sideline for help. "Just stay still. The doctor is coming."

"My shoulder. I can't move it." After Couppee got up slowly, he was helped off the field by the team doctor and an assistant. He was done for the day.

Coach Anderson walked down to Bill Gallagher. "Gallagher, you're in. But remember, you can't talk to anyone until one play has been run."

Kinnick immediately realized what needed to be done. "Let's huddle up. I'll call the plays. You've got to listen up, though. I don't have Coup's volume and I'm going to be further back from the line. If you can't hear me, we'll need to huddle every time."

Kinnick called a play that shifted him from his left halfback position. It was a formation they often used, leaving Kinnick in the backfield with half the team to either side of him. The ball was hiked to Kinnick and he ran straight ahead for a two yard gain. On the next play Kinnick handed off to Bill Green who gained one yard.

On third down Kinnick called a pass play. Bill Green slipped out of the backfield where a linebacker picked him up. Kinnick delivered the ball right to Green's hands and Green took it to the Wolverine twenty-nine yard line before Harmon and Kodros sandwiched him to the ground. The play was good for a first down. Kinnick then called a running play for himself around the right end but the Wolverines were ready and brought him to the ground. The next play was an incomplete pass to Dean after Kinnick first looked for his favorite target, Erv Prasse. Green followed with a run to the twenty yard line on third down. The first quarter ended and the teams exchanged ends of the field.

The Hawkeyes were faced with fourth down, needing one yard for the first down. Kinnick called for a huddle. "We came here to win, right? Green, you got us down here, so I'm calling your number for this one yard. Shift right and then I'll hand off so you can follow Enich. Ready, Mike?"

"Follow me, Greenie." Enich loved knowing it was up to him. Kinnick gave the ball to Green and Enich created a large path through the defensive line. It was first down for the Hawkeyes at the seventeen.

Kinnick stayed with Green on the next two plays and the Hawkeyes moved to the twelve yard line. On third down, Kinnick attempted a pass to Prasse. Harmon slapped the ball to the ground. Fourth down. Kinnick wanted the touchdown, not a field goal. He called the 'thirty-seven' play. Kinnick slid to the right and watched for Prasse across the middle. Harmon shadowed Prasse along the goal line and this time slipped in front of Prasse just as Kinnick released the ball. Harmon reached out as he fell to the turf where 'MICHIGAN' was painted across the end zone, holding onto the ball with his fingertips for the interception and touchback. Having thwarted the Iowa drive, Michigan took possession at their own twenty.

On first down, Harmon gained seven yards before Kinnick tackled him from his safety position with the help of Prasse. Second down gained nothing as Enich snuffed the play. On third down, to everyone's surprise except big Jim Walker, Michigan tried a reverse with Trosko. Walker held his position instead of over-running the play and waited patiently for Trosko to come right at him. It was a five yard loss for Michigan, forcing the Wolverines to punt.

Neither team could move the ball with consistency. After Iowa ran a few plays, Michigan recovered a fumble. Iowa, in turn, intercepted a Harmon pass intended for Frutig, but the Hawkeyes were again unable to move the ball, and Kinnick punted again.

Trosko received the punt and raced down the middle of the field behind a wedge of blockers. Just as Dean attempted a tackle, Trosko changed directions and scampered down the sideline for fifteen more yards before Kinnick forced him out of bounds at the Iowa twenty-six.

The Iowa players stood at the line of scrimmage waiting for Michigan's next play. Kinnick hollered out, "They're going to Harmon! This is his territory down here. Watch for the run!"

He was right. Harmon took the snap from center and ran off tackle behind Evashevski and Kudros. Harmon slipped through the grasps of the Iowa players for an eleven yard gain. First down on the fifteen yard line.

On the next play, Evashevski pretended to be setting up as a blocker, then suddenly left his blocking assignment and glided past the defensive line, looking back to Harmon for a pass. Harmon fired the ball to Evashevski who then dragged a much lighter Bill Green to the four yard line.

Westfall ran next and made it to the two. He tried again and Diehl stopped him at the line of scrimmage. Third down and Kinnick knew again what would happen. "It's Harmon's time. Track him!"

Harmon took a handoff from Evashevski as he started to his left. After three long strides, he changed directions and cut back against the grain of the blockers. He made one final lunge to the goal line and the Michigan fans let their approval be known. Touchdown. The extra point by Harmon sailed right of the goalpost but the Wolverines still led 13 to 7.

The teams lined up for the kickoff. Harmon kicked to Kinnick standing at his five yard line and Kinnick sprinted along the sideline to the twenty-seven.

Kinnick continued to call the plays. The Michigan defense continued to be stubborn, causing failed runs by Kinnick and Green, and an incomplete pass to Norgaard. The Hawkeyes were forced to punt again.

All of a sudden the Hawkeyes' fortunes took a turn for the worse. As Diehl hiked the ball to Kinnick, Savilla, a second string Michigan linebacker, wedged his way through the middle of the line and did something that hadn't ever been done against Kinnick. Savilla blocked the punt. The ball sailed awkwardly, seemingly in slow motion, past the line of scrimmage, landing in front of Prasse who jumped on it at the thirty-six yard line. The Wolverines took possession; their fans sensed an opportunity to score again.

Harmon followed Evashevski around left end, racing to the eight yard line as Evashevski left a stunned Norgaard lying on his back.

Harmon tried the same play again, only this time to the right. Evashevski blocked two Hawkeyes at the same time, leaving a clear path to the end zone for Michigan's star runner. Harmon crossed the goal line again. His extra point landed in the bleachers as the Wolverines took a commanding 20 to 7 lead.

On the sideline, Coach Anderson found Kinnick. It was time to regroup. "Let's just finish the half conservatively. Take the kickoff up the middle and then call some running plays to let the clock expire."

Kinnick did what the coach requested. Both teams headed for their locker rooms.

Inside the locker room, Coach Anderson spoke to his players. "Gentlemen, the game is as physical as I have ever witnessed. Football, when played by two evenly matched teams, comes down to five or six plays that are the difference between winning and losing. The ball bounced their way a few times in the first half. We just need to keep playing as we are, and waiting for the bounce to come our way."

He looked around the room knowing he needed to make some changes. "Diehl and Walker, I don't know when I've been prouder of two young men. Both of you were hurt and neither one of you stopped for a second. You really showed me something out there. But I can't let either of you continue with your leg bruises. You're not at full speed and I don't want to gamble on worsening your injuries. Take the rest of the day off. Andruska, you're in at center for Diehl. Bergstrom, you're in at left tackle."

Bruno Andruska was a good football player. The Hawkeyes lost little man power with him replacing Diehl. Now, with Hank Luebcke out for the season, and Couppee, Diehl, and Walker injured, the Hawkeyes were down to thirty-one athletes.

Coach Anderson continued, "Nile, we'll go to a huddled offense to start the second half until the new players get a feel for the game. Andruska, you've got Tollefson and Snider on either side of you. Talk to them if you aren't sure what to do. Bergstrom, the same goes for you. Ask Tollefson or Prasse if you're unsure.

"We are just two plays from making this game even. Go out there and give me those two plays! If you keep hitting the way you have so far, our opportunities will come."

Tom Harmon kicked off to Kinnick to start the second half. From his own six yard line, he headed straight up the middle of the field where Frutig jarred him at the twenty-seven yard line. Bill Gallagher was dazed on the play, got up slowly, and walked to the sideline. With Couppee and Gallagher out, Dr. Eddie walked down to a nervous third string quarterback, Jerry Ankeny. "This is your moment, son. Just go do what you do in practice. Kinnick will continue to call the plays."

Ankeny ran out to the huddle. Kinnick knew he had to call some plays not relying heavily on the new quarterback. The first play was a double reverse, Kinnick handing off to Buzz Dean, who in turn handed off to Prasse. Kinnick was ahead of Prasse as he made the turn up the right side of the field. Kinnick took Westfall to the ground, but Harmon came up and forced Prasse out of bounds. The play gained two yards.

Another Hawkeye was motionless on the ground. Buzz Dean took a hard hit from Evashevski. He, too, retired to the sideline. That meant Ed McLain was in to play right halfback. The Hawkeyes were playing with a second string guard replacing Luebcke, a second string center after Diehl's injury, a second string tackle in for Walker, a third string quarterback after Couppee's and Gallagher's departures, and now a second string right halfback to replace Buzz Dean. The absence of Couppee and Dean hurt the most because now the Wolverines knew the ball would be in Kinnick's hands all the time. Michigan's focus could narrow to stopping just one player.

Nile Kinnick had great confidence in McLain's quickness. Kinnick knew Michigan wouldn't be concerned about a player just entering the game, so Kinnick decided to counter conventional wisdom. "Ed, we're going to you."

The Hawkeyes shifted into the Notre Dame box. Kinnick took the center's snap and dropped back to pass. He saw McLain just beyond the line of scrimmage and fired a quick pass. McLain was stopped by Archie Kudros after the reception just shy of the first down. After an unsuccessful third down run, the Hawkeyes punted.

It was first down for Michigan on their twenty-nine yard line. Enich tackled Harmon after a gain of seven yards. On the next play, Westfall stretched as he was hit by Tollefson, barely getting the first down at the thirty-nine.

Iowa's new players displayed hesitation on offense, needing to think through each play, but defense allowed them to react instinctively and so the Hawkeyes' defense more than met the challenge of the potent Michigan offense. Bergstrom stopped Harmon at the line of scrimmage. Next was a Michigan penalty and the referee marched off the fifteen yards against the Wolverines. On the following play, Bill Green dashed through the Michigan offensive line and stopped Westfall for a five yard loss. Michigan was assessed with another penalty, and then another loss of yardage as Enich knocked Evashevski to the ground before grabbing Harmon. The ball was on the Michigan two yard line. The Wolverines' punter stood in his own end zone, barely getting off the punt under a heavy rush. The ball traveled a pitiful sixteen yards before going out of bounds at the Michigan eighteen, giving Iowa great field position.

On first down, Kinnick dropped back to pass. He dodged the first wave of tacklers and stepped forward to release a pass to Jerry Ankeny in the end zone. Harmon left Prasse and moved over in front of Ankeny at the ten yard line, intercepting the pass. No Hawkeye was near him as he quickly high-stepped away from Ankeny. The crowd noise became deafening as he raced down the right sideline. The euphoric bystanders were delighted knowing nothing would prevent Harmon's fourth touchdown of the day. The Hawkeyes' short-lived momentum was crushed. It simply wasn't their day. With the 27 to 7 lead, Coach Fritz Crisler substituted his key players for the remainder of the quarter. The battered Iowa players were now faced with eleven fresh faces while Michigan's regular players enjoyed the luxury of resting for a few minutes.

The third quarter ended. Iowa had only fifteen minutes remaining to overcome a twenty point deficit, a daunting task against a talented team.

Michigan's first string players returned for the start of the fourth quarter. Harmon faded back to pass and saw Evashevski near the left sideline. He launched the ball across the field from the right hash mark, only this time Kinnick grabbed the interception in front of Evashevski. Nile's momentum carried him out of bounds at midfield. With twelve minutes left, a false sense of hope returned to Iowa. But Iowa's offense struggled the remainder of the game and the fourth quarter soon came to an end.

Prasse, Enich, and Kinnick walked off the stadium field together. Prasse had virtually been stopped by the Wolverine defense. Enich had played brilliantly. Kinnick had good moments as well as bad. Prasse spoke first. "I hope the Indiana game wasn't a fluke." Kinnick and Enich knew what he meant. They didn't want a repeat of the last two seasons.

"I don't think so, Prass. I think we're good." Kinnick knew the Hawkeyes were formidable. "Today, we just got beat by a really good team having an exceptional day. We'll be alright."

The locker room was quiet. Everyone kept to themselves as they took off their equipment and showered. As the Hawkeye players were packing their gym bags, Coach Anderson entered. "Today we played a great ball game. The score doesn't indicate the closeness of this battle. In fact, we outplayed Michigan in several ways. We had over a hundred more passing yards than they had, and about the same difference in total yards. First downs were fairly even. But there were some timely plays that went their way. That's football. I think we learned a lot today about our team, and our weaknesses.

"I want us to leave this game in Ann Arbor. Let's not take it out of the locker room and onto the bus with us. The game is over. We have two weeks to prepare for Wisconsin. I want everyone thinking about the next game. We've got a lot of football ahead of us." Coach Anderson looked around the room. "Wow! That was a splendid game. But you know what, it's over. Let's get on the bus."

An hour later the bus stopped at the train station. The players immediately found seats on the train for the long ride back to Iowa City. They had been told not to dwell on the

Michigan game, but heads hung low and shoulders slumped from the emotional drain and physical exhaustion.

The train slowly started as these combatants stared out the windows at the city where dreams were so immense just a few hours ago. In one afternoon their hopes, that had been building in recent weeks, were dashed by an unkind scoreboard.

The coaches were talking with uncharacteristic smiles on their faces after the loss. They were practicing what they preached, thought Kinnick, and moving on from the game. After all, it was part of sport. No one goes undefeated forever. There will eventually be a loss. He remembered a letter he wrote to his father after one of the devastating losses last year. Nile Kinnick Sr. wrote back: "All victories are not won on the playing field, son. It takes a better man to be outstanding in defeat than in victory. I want you to also know I take great pride in your mental alertness, your eagerness for knowledge of the type that will later make you useful as a citizen, your inherent sympathy for others, and your capacity for friendliness. So even in these swirling, tumultuous times of defeat, don't lose your balance in any degree. The hidden reward is often worth the risk."

Coach Anderson moved away from where the coaches were sitting in the front two seats. He turned to his team. "Our train was supposed to arrive in Iowa City late tonight. But Coach Carideo, Coach Harris, and I have changed plans. Before we boarded, I placed a phone call to a friend of mine in Chicago. We are going to stay at the Morrison Hotel tonight and go to the Chicago Bears game tomorrow at Wrigley Field. They're playing the Green Bay Packers."

For a single moment, the Hawkeyes completely forgot the Michigan loss. The young footballers were suddenly excited about the immediate future. The Bears and Packers were two of the best teams in the National Football League. Prasse was the only player that had ever attended a professional football game.

"I can't believe I'm going to Wrigley Field to see Sid Luckman," Al Couppee exclaimed, "and spend a night in downtown Chicago."

"Couppee, just make sure you make it back to your room tonight." Team captain Erv Prasse enjoyed a friendly taunt of the famous socializer from Council Bluffs. "You've got to be a little careful downtown."

"How bad can it be?" replied Couppee. "I'll just stay with Tollefson and Andruska. They can protect me."

Coach Anderson overheard the discussion. "Couppee, make sure my decision to stay in Chicago wasn't a bad one." Then Coach Anderson addressed everyone. "A few rules, though, gentlemen. I'll make a deal with you. There will be no room checks tonight, no curfew." Cheers and smiles came from the bruised athletes. Coach Eddie continued, "However, in return, I expect all of you to act with decorum. You are representing your team and your university. I have two rules. The first is no hard liquor. The second, no women. Tonight is not a night for either of those.

"In the morning, we will be giving everyone a wake up call for breakfast, and then church for anyone that wants. We'll have a list of different denominational churches at dinner tonight. And we'll provide the transportation.

"So to repeat, what's rule number one?"

In unison the team shouted back, "NO HARD LIQUOR!"

"And rule number two?"

"NO WOMEN!"

"And then there is no curfew." Coach Anderson looked around and smiled at the players. He sat down with the other two coaches. He knew it was almost an impossible task to constrain young men in a big city. So, rather than control them, he gave them freedom with responsibility.

"Coach Anderson," Frank Carideo said, "I think we have successfully left the Michigan game in the past for all these guys."

"I think you're right, Frank," Coach Eddie responded. "We'll know in two weeks in Madison if it worked. It might be one of our greatest coaching decisions."

The Hawkeyes were again spending a night at the "World's Tallest Building." The Morrison Hotel majestically graced the corner of Madison and Clark Streets. Last year, after the only victory of the season against the University of Chicago, the Hawkeyes came here for one night. The upperclassmen all remembered Tommy Dorsey playing in the Terrace Garden Restaurant and Ballroom that night. Tonight, Benny Goodman was the headliner.

Just like last year, the team dinner was in the Grill Restaurant. The restaurant's staff remembered the Hawkeyes. They hadn't experienced so many orders for the porterhouse steak since their last visit. Finally, after dessert was finished, Dr. Eddie stood up. "Before you leave tonight, I want to introduce a special guest I have come to know and respect very much over the last fifteen years." Dr Eddie looked at the black man sitting next to him at the head table. "This is Judge Fred Slater. He's better known in the football world as 'Duke' Slater. He was an All-American end at the University of Iowa in 1921. And for those of you who remember my speech when I took the job at Iowa, I was captain on an undefeated Notre Dame team that year, at least until we played the University of Iowa. Duke's team won that game. It was the only game we lost that year. So, I can tell you, I learned how much Knute Rockne pushed his players after a loss with extra running drills, and I can thank Judge Slater for that lesson.

"I didn't know Duke then, but we certainly ran into each other, literally, a few times that afternoon. And then later, when I was coaching at DePaul while playing and coaching for the Cardinals, I got to know Judge Slater quite well. He's now a municipal judge here in Chicago. I have asked him to join us and talk to us tonight."

Applause spread through the dining room. Even though he played when most of the Hawkeyes were infants, many knew of him. All-Americans didn't come along that often at the University of Iowa. Pictures of Duke Slater hung on various walls throughout Iowa's athletic offices.

Judge Fred 'Duke' Slater stood up and smiled at the Hawkeyes. The large black man gazed across the room at the team to which he once belonged. "Thank you, Coach Anderson. I am honored to be invited here tonight.

"I hope all of you embrace every single day you have in college. It certainly was an integral part of my life. I played football at Iowa at a time when many universities didn't allow blacks to even attend school. I was lucky to have found a home at Iowa.

"As Coach Anderson said, Notre Dame wasn't supposed to lose that day to Iowa, but they did. And the next week Coach Anderson's Notre Dame team bounced back and didn't lose another game the rest of the season. I tell you this because I believe you may have a similar fate. You lost today to a team that you could have beaten. You have a lot of football left to play. I believe you will bounce back, and when the season is over, you'll look back and see that the Michigan game just might have been the turning point in your season. It might be the defining moment where you truly became a great team, even though you lost. We'll wait and see. I'll certainly be watching. And, in fact, if Coach Anderson can get a ticket for me, I'd really like to see that Notre Dame game in four weeks."

Coach Anderson interrupted, "Consider it in the mail, Judge." The players joined the laughter of these two men.

As Judge Slater continued his talk, Kinnick reflected on the camaraderie he witnessed between these two adversaries from long ago. He wondered if any of his opponents on the gridiron this year would be his friends fifteen or twenty years from now. It was nice, he thought, to see the respect these two former footballers shared.

The banquet ended and it was time for the young men to discover Chicago. Many of the underclassmen weren't traveling with the team last year and many were from families unable to afford family vacations. Being in such a big city was a new experience for them, causing uncertainty as well as excitement.

The ballroom's cover charge was four dollars, so the players mingled in the Morrison's hallways to listen to the band they couldn't afford to see, and to absorb the sights of the well-to-do Chicagoans enjoying a Saturday night.

"Tollefson, Frye, let's go down to State Street and walk around." Al Couppee wanted to see the city lights and feel its vitality. "We can check out some bars and hit the Sherman Hotel."

Red Frye felt a little intimidated by the big city. "Do you know where you're going, Coup?"

"Not really. But I'm sure we can find the Sherman. That's where they do the 'College Inn' radio show every Saturday. What do you say?"

Erv Prasse walked by and overheard them. "I think you need Enich and me to join you. I know the way."

"I'm in," replied Chuck Tollefson.

"Me, too," chimed Mike Enich.

"Let's do it." Suddenly Red Frye felt confident.

"You got room for one more in your posse?" asked Jim Walker. Walker, from South Bend, Indiana, was one of two blacks on the team, the other Fred Smith from Cedar Rapids, Iowa. On this football team, color didn't matter; Walker and Smith were as much a part of this group as Kinnick, Prasse, and Enich.

"The more the merrier, Walker." Enich slapped his arm around Walker. "Let's follow Prasse and see if he can keep from getting us lost in his hometown."

The six strode down the bustling streets. Though they looked lost, they had a peculiar physical presence with Frye, Walker, Enich, and Tollefson walking together. Couppee and Prasse followed closely behind their linemen. The streets were busy. Parking spots lining both sides of the streets were filled. People walked briskly along the sidewalks, seeming to be in a hurry and knowing exactly where they were headed. Others stood at the curbsides waiting for the next taxi.

State Street was two blocks from the Morrison Hotel, but then they needed to walk several blocks north on State Street to reach the nightclubs.

As they walked along Madison Street they came upon three women and a man standing under a street light. The man was dressed in a dark suit. The three women wore provocative dresses with plunging necklines, their overcoats opened. Couppee noticed the heavy make-up and pungent perfume.

"You boys from out of town?" the man asked. It was obvious with three of the Hawkeyes wearing their letter jackets.

"Yes, we are," replied Mike Enich hesitantly.

"Are you looking for something to do?"

Prasse quickly responded, "We've got some plans."

The group slowed but kept walking.

"These ladies can show you a good time. You don't need to go spend your money at a bar looking for a good time. It's right here in front of you."

Erv Prasse again spoke up for the group. "Sorry. But you people have a good evening." The man was used to hearing refusals. He turned to look down the sidewalk at his next approaching prospect.

Red Frye chuckled. "I think Dr. Eddie would come down on us less if we just found the hard liquor. You know, he left it open that beer was okay."

"I agree," replied Tollefson. "I thought his rule clearly meant beer was okay. And I'm guessing Prasse is leading us that way."

Couppee looked at Prasse. "You know, I think one of those women might have been interested in me." The group let out a collective laugh.

Finally, after walking about ten blocks Prasse said, "Let's stop. I think we can get a beer here."

It wasn't an elegant State Street nightclub, but it looked like a place that wouldn't question serving beer to college-aged young men. A neon sign with a man's name in lights hung straight out from above the front door, reaching halfway across the sidewalk. Music drifted out into the street from the small, neglected bar. "Johnny's" was a place where people went to party and dance to the big band sounds created by local musicians in the rear portion of the building. The patrons' attire matched the drab walls with cracked paint. The lighting was dim in contrast to the bright lights along the street. No one here had an expensive car parked outside.

The six college footballers from Iowa walked through the crowded bar, looking at the different patrons. A tall, overweight man in his late fifties approached them. "Boys, I'm gonna have to ask you to leave." As he said this, several men along the bar and others sitting at the tables along the wall turned to look.

"It's alright. We're all old enough," replied Mike Enich.

"That's not it." His eyes glanced at Jim Walker.

"We just came for a couple of beers," said Chuck Tollefson. Three men slowly walked over behind the owner, immediately creating a standoff. Emotions took over as the other four white Hawkeyes, not to be bullied, stepped forward next to Tollefson.

"No, you guys, this isn't worth it," said Jim Walker. He was protected by a line of teammates. "Come on. Let's go."

After a brief stare down between the two sides, the Hawkeyes turned and walked out. Jim Walker looked at his comrades when they were on the sidewalk. "Guys, I appreciate you taking a stance for me. But maybe I should just head back to the hotel."

"No way, Walker," said Mike Enich. "At least, not without us going back with you. We're a team, right?"

The six jostled with each other, appreciating how they had reacted together against the unexpected bigotry.

"You know, Walker," said Prasse, "after the Michigan line earlier today, those guys back there looked a whole lot easier. Oh well, I guess one dog fight in a day is enough. So, Jim, how does it feel having Couppee blocking for you?"

"I never realized," answered Walker, "how scary it must be for Kinnick, sometimes." It was good-natured kidding only best friends can share with each other after having fought side by side in games and practices, reaching out a hand numerous times to help each other off the turf.

The walk back to the hotel was a walk they might remember for a lifetime, engulfed by the city, surrounded by strangers. Six Hawkeyes were having fun taking it all in, feeling more comfortable than when they had left earlier in the night. It was a big city, and tonight they caught a glimpse of the depth of their friendship.

Nile Kinnick Sr. with sons, George, Nile, and Ben

Frances Kinnick with sons, Nile, George, and Ben

Nile Kinnick's grandfather, Governor George Clarke, Governor of Iowa, 1913-1917

Kinnick originally played on the University of Iowa's basketball and baseball teams

*Nile Kinnick practicing punting the summer of
1939 at Benson High School in Omaha, NE*

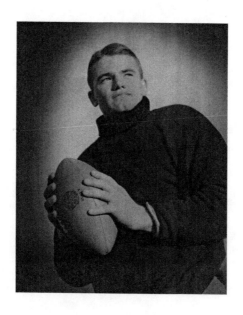

*Kinnick practicing punting with
Coach Frank Carideo, 1939*

Dr. Eddie Anderson, 1939

Notre Dame football game at Iowa Stadium, 1939

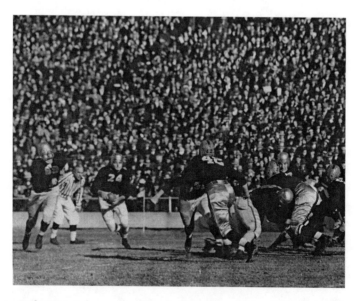

Nile Kinnick carrying the ball against Notre Dame, 1939

Kinnick intercepting a Notre Dame pass. (Nile is on the far right behind the receiver. The ball is crossing the 40 yard line.), 1939

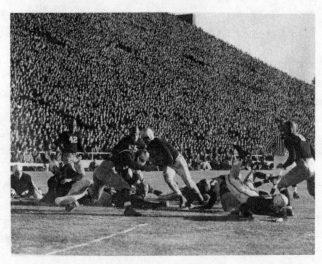

Kinnick scoring the only touchdown, and winning touchdown, against Notre Dame, 1939

Kinnick's late game punt against Notre Dame that sealed the victory, 1939

Dr. Eddie Anderson speaking at a pep rally. Nile waiting to speak. President Gilmore is seated.

Kinnick preparing to speak at the Old Capitol, 1939

Kinnick with Barbara Miller

*Nile Kinnick with Dr. Eddie Anderson
before the Northwestern game, 1939*

*A team photo prior to the last game of the
season against Northwestern, 1939*

Nile Kinnick accepting the Heisman
Trophy in New York, 1939

Nile holding the Heisman Trophy, 1939

*Kinnick with Dr. Eddie Anderson and
Virginia Eskridge at the Kit Kat Club*

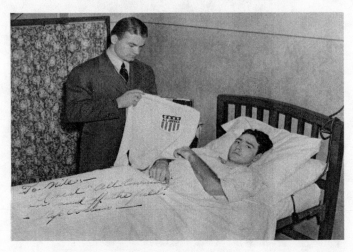

*Nile at the hospital with the injured high
school football player, Rip Collins, 1939*

Kinnick in Navy whites

*Nile standing in front of an open cockpit
plane while learning to fly for the Navy*

*Nile Kinnick Sr. attending the ceremony re-naming
Iowa Stadium to Kinnick Stadium, 1972*

CHAPTER NINETEEN

"Hello."

"Hello. Is Era Haupert there?" Nile Kinnick held the phone with his left hand. His right hand was still stiff from a late-game tackle in Ann Arbor five days ago.

"I'll see if she's in her room. Is this Henry?"

"No. This is Nile Kinnick."

"Oh. Okay." There was a surprised tone in her voice. Nile wasn't sure if she was surprised to be talking to him, after all, he was well-known on campus. Or, was she surprised the caller wasn't the person usually calling Era?

Two minutes later. "This is Era."

"Hello, Era. How are you?"

"Hi, Nile. Good. Just studying for a test."

"So am I. I've been studying Money and Banking all night.

"Era, I called to ask if you would you like to go out for dinner tomorrow night? I would enjoy seeing you, that is if you're done with your tests, and would like to get together." As confident as Nile Kinnick was on the football field or in front of an audience, he felt awkward asking her on a date. Not wanting to be exposed to possible rejection, he knew, was probably a trait he shared with many his age. Football he understood. Speaking he did regularly. But, dating, that was a relatively new experience he felt uncomfortable doing. But he also felt there was an exciting mystery to it, especially with someone like Era. He continued, "Judging by the person that answered the phone, and asking if I was Henry, maybe you're unavailable." He tried to laugh at the situation. He still was unsure what to think about the reaction of the person that answered the phone.

Era Haupert joined his uncomfortable laughter. "Oh, Nile. Yes, I have been seeing someone, Henry Wolfe. I think you know him. He's a Sigma Nu."

"Yes, I have met him. He seems like a nice guy." Neither knew what to say next.

Quickly, Nile broke the silence. "Is your relationship with him an exclusive relationship, I mean, not dating others?"

"Right now, I think it is. We haven't been dating that long, but we have seen each other frequently."

"Your voice sounds happy, Era. I'm happy for you. Right now, I wish I had spent more time - "

Era quickly interrupted, "You couldn't, Nile. I understand that. And I am happy. I really enjoy my time with him. It all happened very suddenly."

"He's a lucky person."

Nile was about to say goodnight when Era spoke. "Nile, I'm sorry about the Michigan game. Several of us listened to the game here at the sorority."

Nile's thoughts quickly shifted to the night they talked while Prasse and Couppee danced in the sorority's living room. "Well, thanks. It hurt to lose that one, even though I'm still quite well conditioned at losing." Both laughed. "You don't forget that feeling fast enough. Walking off the field and then feeling down all night, and all weekend, was something we've experienced too often in the past. Coach Anderson had changed our outlooks so much that I truly felt we might go the entire season without losing."

"You're still doing great," Era said.

"You're right. I was hoping the feeling of losing was in the past. Then, one game, and you start wondering how it will all play out. You question yourself. You start thinking 'can we get back to winning?' I think we can, but we have Notre Dame and Minnesota coming up soon. So, time will tell how the season goes.

"But I don't want to bore you with football. Era, I want to say that I hope everything works out well between Henry and you but a part of me, selfishly, hopes it doesn't."

"Thank you, Nile, for wishing me well, and hoping it won't be at the same time." She laughed again. "It's actually quite flattering."

"Good night, Era. And good luck."

"You, too, Nile. You know, there's something very special about you. It's as if greatness awaits you. I'll be watching."

"My turn to be flattered." Nile put the receiver back on the wall-mounted phone in the hallway, feeling an emptiness as he walked back to his room. A pang of loneliness overcame him, knowing he had missed an opportunity. He hadn't seen Era that often, but still, she was important to him, someone he always looked forward to seeing. *Destiny keeps you wondering, and hoping,* he thought. A Money and Banking textbook sat on his bed. But first, he decided to write a letter to his parents:

> *Dear Mother & Father,*
> *First, thank you Mother for your prayers that I stay healthy. You are doing fine work. I came out of the Michigan game relatively unscathed, except for my pride taking a beating. My ankle feels very good and I know I have your prayers to thank.*
> *Father, thank you for your encouraging words. I want you to know I am in complete agreement with you that "nothing is more*

ephemeral than public hero-worship." And
I also agree with you that *"he who seeks it,
and personal aggrandizement, is doomed to
disappointment."* I shall always keep that
in mind. And I shall always strive to make
Mother and you proud by trying to do what
is right.

Concerning football, we have one more week
before Wisconsin. I'm afraid Jim Walker is
out for the season, although he might return
later. He was injured at Michigan and he
has since aggravated the injury. So, with
Henry Luebcke and now Walker gone, we
have lost two key linemen. Coach Anderson
has changed our practice routines due to
injuries. He has been working the second
string players very hard every day to see
which ones might rise to the task. The first
string had light contact most of the week to
avoid any needless injuries.

But the coaching staff, as always, still runs
us more than I can describe - forward,
backwards, sideways, innumerable laps
around the practice field. And it may be
that our superior conditioning will prove
even more beneficial if injuries continue.

Coach Anderson believes winning at Camp
Randall, in Madison, will be our turning
point. And he has additional incentive.
Harry Stuhldreher, Wisconsin's coach, was
one of the 'Four Horsemen' at Notre Dame.
In fact, Stuhldreher was a freshman when

Coach Anderson was the All-American captain of Rockne's 1921 team.
I need to study a little more before going to bed. Good night.
And Mother, please keep Henry and Jim in your prayers.
Love,
Nile

October 27, 1939, Friday. The Hawkeyes were very familiar with the 9:15 a.m. boarding onto the Rock Island Rocket. Dr. Eddie had arranged for a brief workout at the University of Chicago's Stagg Field before boarding the second train to Milwaukee, where the Hawkeyes would spend the night, then one more train to Madison Saturday morning.

After checking in at the Schrader Hotel, and having the team dinner, Coach Anderson asked for everyone's attention. "Gentlemen, that was a good practice we had today. I think it was just what we needed to break up the ride to Milwaukee.

"I picked up a copy of the Chicago Daily News. There was an article by James Kearns in the sports section. In that article he mentions that Kinnick leads the nation with an average of 7.89 yards per carry, and leads the nation in punting yardage per kick and passing yards per game. He also quotes Minnesota's coach, Bernie Bierman, predicting Iowa will beat Wisconsin because of Nile Kinnick." He looked over at Kinnick. "Frankly, I hope no one in Madison, Wisconsin, saw this article but I imagine they will. And if I was the coach of Wisconsin, some guy named Stuhldreher –" Dr. Eddie paused for the room's laughter. The Hawkeyes all knew Harry Stuhldreher was an underclassman to Coach Anderson at Notre Dame. "Then I would make sure all of my Badgers read the article. So Kinnick has a bullseye on his back, and most likely will the rest of the year. And it's up to our offensive linemen to keep the Badgers from hitting their target."

Coach Eddie looked at everyone. "It's been a long two weeks. With the injuries we sustained at Michigan, the coaches were provided an opportunity this week to evaluate the second string. And I'm proud of the way you men stayed focused on the task: learning, improving every day, and not allowing one set back at Ann Arbor to stop our momentum. With all obstacles you face in life, or goals you want to achieve, it's consistent effort that overcomes. Intelligence alone won't do it. Strength alone won't do it. Continuous effort toward your goals is the secret to getting there."

Kinnick was sitting at a table with Prasse, Enich, Couppee, Tollefson, Bergstrom, and Pettit. Kinnick continued listening to Dr. Eddie, a person who knew how to reach goals, Kinnick thought. Dr. Eddie gave the impression of being successful at everything he did. Even now, in Iowa City, Kinnick often saw Dr. Eddie walking from the University Hospitals to the football locker room before practice in his white hospital jacket.

Coach Anderson continued. "Coaches don't usually talk about games too far in the future. We normally focus on the next game. But I've got to tell you, the next three weeks are what it's all about. Next week we play Purdue, a team many think can win the Big Ten this year. In two weeks, we play Notre Dame, considered to be the national champions last year by some polls. But more importantly, they are currently ranked second in the nation. Three weeks from now we play Minnesota, the national champions three of the last five years. They are currently ranked sixth in the nation.

"Gentlemen, the next three weeks is a window in time you will never forget. So I want all of you to close your eyes for just a moment." He looked around the room. "I'm serious. I want everyone to close their eyes.

"Now, I want you to picture yourselves twenty years from now. You are forty years old, give or take a couple of years. It's 1959. You are attending your twentieth Hawkeye reunion of the '39 season. You are there with your old teammates, the people sitting in this room right now. Your wives are with you. Some of you brought your children. It's homecoming weekend on a glorious, beautiful Saturday afternoon in Iowa City. Can you see it? Can you feel it? What will you say to each other? Will you be talking about the 'what ifs?' Or, will you be talking about 1939 and how that year changed your life? Will you be talking about that moment in time when you learned anything is possible with dedication and effort? Will you bask in your achievements on the gridiron, remembering those wonderful days when your waistlines were smaller and your hair a bit fuller?

"Every action has a reaction. Life is about cause and effect. The choices you make, the things you do, all have consequences. So let's promise each other to make this moment in time a historical, significant moment in each of our lives. The achievements of the rest of our lives start now.

"What will you say at that homecoming reunion? What will you remember about 1939? The real laurels, the glory, will be emblazoned in your hearts and minds forever based on your achievements in this small window of time.

"I speak from experience. That moment for me was 1921. You know the story. We were undefeated and on our way to being national champions for Knute Rockne. It was my senior year. It was a terrific year I'll never forget, but coincidentally, Iowa ended up as national champions after beating us. It was the only loss Notre Dame had in my three years of playing. Our record those three years was 28 and 1. Our achievements were great, but still, I know personally what it means to look back and say, 'if only.'

"I don't want that to happen to you. That's why I want this team to always strive for perfection, while accepting mere excellence.

"Your lives will be shaped by these next few weeks. What do you want to accomplish? What do you want to be talking about twenty years from now at that reunion?"

There was silence in the banquet room. Twenty-six players, three coaches, a team doctor, and two student managers sat with their eyes closed. The footballers were 'here and now' people, youthful spirits of immortality. The future had always been exactly that - the future, something in the far off distance. But now Enich, Prasse, Couppee, Kinnick, Tollefson, Pettit, Diehl, Andruska, Frye, Hawkins, Snider, Smith, Evans, Norgaard, Gallagher, Ankeny, Murphy, Green, Vollenweider, Dean, McLain, Busk, Gilleard, Endling, Moore, and Otto realized they were connected for the rest of their lives. It was a new concept for these young men. Their futures were beginning.

Coach Eddie was finished. Slowly they opened their eyes and looked around at each other. Mike Enich and Nile Kinnick started clapping slowly and everyone joined in as the crescendo grew. They had three hours before the team curfew. The players decided to have their own team meeting and they all agreed this was not the time to leave the Schrader Hotel for Milwaukee's night life. Instead, everyone headed to their rooms for an early bedtime.

Saturday. The Hawkeyes were finishing their pre-game rituals in the locker room before taking the field. Kickoff was fast approaching. It had already been a long day. The morning train to Madison had left the Milwaukee depot at 8:30.

"Nile, you are the team captain today for the coin toss because I'm not starting Prasse." Then Coach Eddie turned to his usual starting ends. "Evans and Prasse, I want you on the sideline to start the game. Our scouting reports show the Badgers always run wide to start the games. Norgaard and Smith, the two of you are starting at the end positions. I want Norgaard and Smith to give every ounce of energy they have on the initial Badger drives. Prasse and Evans, it's a gamble I'm willing to take because I want both of you with fresh legs later in the game. I want our team to have the strongest passing attack possible in the second half. Smith and Norgaard can wear them down during the first half."

The players were stunned at the news. Prasse and Evans were two of the best ends in the conference. But no one questioned Coach Anderson's philosophies. He had already reinvented these believing Hawkeyes.

Many in the stands wore winter coats in anticipation of the temperature dropping through the afternoon. A northerly wind brought a chill through Camp Randall Stadium on the late October afternoon as the Hawkeyes kicked off against their rivals dressed in bright red jerseys and white pants. Wisconsin returned the ball to their twenty-three yard line.

George Paskvan was a bruising fullback usually requiring more than one tackler to bring him to the turf. The first three plays from scrimmage were carries by Paskvan around the right end. The last run gave Wisconsin a first and ten at their own forty yard line. On the next two plays, Mike Enich reminded the Badgers why he was considered one of the best tackles in the nation. He knocked his Wisconsin counterpart to the side and hit Paskvan for a one yard loss. Next, Wisconsin's halfback, York, started to his right but cut back against the blocking, only to have his face smashed against the ground with Enich blanketing him. Another run by York netted four yards before Diehl grabbed his right ankle. Diehl's tackle caused fourth down and a punting situation for Wisconsin.

Fred Gage's high hanging punt gave Kinnick little time to set up behind blockers. Eckl tackled Kinnick immediately at the Iowa twenty yard line.

On Iowa's first play from scrimmage, Kinnick tried a run around the right end following Enich and Couppee. He was stopped after a one yard gain. The Hawkeyes positioned themselves at the line of scrimmage, waiting for Couppee to call out the next play. He shouted out a play for Ray Murphy to take a handoff straight ahead behind center Bill Diehl and right guard Max Hawkins. Paskvan slammed Murphy to the ground before Murphy reached the line of scrimmage.

The home crowd got excited with the defensive efforts of the Wisconsin Badgers. The roar was deafening. Kinnick hollered at Couppee, "We need a huddle so everyone can hear the next play!"

The Hawkeyes broke from the huddle, turning to face the wound up Badger defense. When Kinnick was stopped on third down the noise became even more deafening.

"Prasse, get in there for Smith." Coach Anderson couldn't keep his best blocking receiver off the field any longer. "I need more blocking up front!"

Fourth down. Kinnick needed a good punt to keep Wisconsin from getting field position. The punt sailed high and to the right side of the field. Gradisnik caught the ball, started up field, and was hit by Jens Norgaard head-on, causing a cracking sound heard by everyone nearby. Both men groggily returned to their feet and continued, but Norgaard was obviously feeling severe pain. Mike Enich, playing next to Norgaard at right end, saw the dazed look in his eyes. "Jens, are you okay? We can call a timeout."

"No, I'll be alright. Really, I will."

The Badgers failed to move the ball as the Hawkeyes' defense similarly toughened. The Badgers punted.

Iowa again failed to move the ball and Kinnick punted again. It was almost a replay of the last Hawkeye punt. The ball moved diagonally down the field to the right. Gardisnik again fielded the punt and headed up the left side of the field. Norgaard again slipped through the wall of blockers and, again, hit Gardisnik at full speed. This time Norgaard was motionless, his back against Camp Randall's turf.

Prasse was close by. "Jens, can you hear me? Where is it hurting?"

"My neck!"

Prasse hollered at the nearest referee, "Timeout! We need a doctor!"

The crowd's volume, even though they were all standing, went from ear piercing loudness to utter silence. Coach Anderson was the first person to arrive from the sideline. Kinnick and Enich stood behind him.

Coach Anderson knew it was serious. "Son, just lie still. The stretcher is coming. I don't want you to lift your head up. Understand?"

A trembling, fearful voice answered back, "Yes, Coach.

"Coach?" inquired Norgaard, staring up at the blue sky.

"Yes, Jens."

"Tell the team to win this one for me, like 'for the Gipper.'" Norgaard showed a feeble smile, referring to Knute Rockne's famous halftime speech during a game against Army.

Fifteen minutes later the battle resumed. Dick Evans took over his role at right end. Norgaard's injury was causing Dr. Eddie much angst as he looked solemnly towards the ground. Thoughts of 'why did I do it?' tormented him, even though he knew no one could have predicted the injury. In an odd way, he thought, the calculated strategy of starting Norgaard and Smith at ends, in order to save Prasse and Evans, may have worked, but not in the way he had intended.

After two first downs and advancing the ball twenty-five yards, Gradisnik faded back to pass. Kinnick, from his safety position, saw Fred Gage coming across the field from the opposite side. Gage had Murphy, the Hawkeyes' defensive cornerback, beaten by two steps. Kinnick moved forward when he saw Gradisnik's arm release the pass. Kinnick darted in front of Gage, intercepting the pass at Iowa's twenty-two yard line.

After Iowa failed to move the ball, Kinnick was again in punting position. Gradisnik fielded the kick at Wisconsin's twenty-six and returned it to the thirty-seven yard line.

Gradisnik then carried the ball twice for ten yard gains each time. Next, Gradisnik passed to Lorenz who was brought down by Buzz Dean at Iowa's fourteen yard line. Paskvan ran around right end and was tackled by Prasse and Bergstrom.

Momentum clearly shifted to Wisconsin as Gradisnik pedaled backwards again while looking for a receiver. He drilled a pass to Fred Gage in the end zone as the crowd stood, ending the defensive struggle. Gage's extra point made the score Wisconsin 7, Iowa 0.

The Hawkeyes ran back to their sideline prior to the kickoff. Kinnick realized, counting the Michigan game two weeks ago, that they had given up thirty-four unanswered points. He called the players together. "The second half of the season starts right now! Right? We regroup right now and start putting some points on the board. Losing is no longer acceptable! Injuries cannot, and will not, be an excuse!" Eleven Hawkeyes sprinted back onto the field to receive the kickoff.

Fred Gage kicked off to Nile Kinnick standing at the ten yard line. He sprinted straight ahead, advancing past the Badgers angling towards him from the outside positions. Schmitz grabbed Kinnick's left thigh at the thirty yard line, but Kinnick fooled him. Just as the defender was making the tackle, Kinnick relaxed his body, fooling Schmitz into thinking he was going to the ground and ending the play. But instinctively, Kinnick released a burst of energy as the defender was also falling and loosening his grip on Kinnick's leg. Nile broke free of the Badger grasp. He darted left, stopped suddenly, then veered to his right. Kinnick was brought down at the Wisconsin thirty-five yard line, a fifty-five yard return.

Misfortune struck the Hawkeyes again. This time Bill Diehl, the starting center, picked himself off the ground and hobbled to the sideline. Bruno Andruska grabbed his helmet and entered the game to replace Diehl.

Coach Eddie decided to relieve Ray Murphy at fullback and Ed McLain at right halfback with Bill Green and Russ

Busk. On the first play, Bill Green lateraled to Russ Busk who was immediately hit in the backfield by Paskvan for a loss. Next, Kinnick took the center snap from Bruno Andruska, hitting Bill Green with a pass as the first quarter ended.

The Hawkeyes were faced with third down and seven yards remaining for a first down. Kinnick tried running around the right end for the first down, hoping Wisconsin would be playing Iowa to throw in the obvious passing situation. It didn't work. He was stopped two yards short of the first down.

Iowa was too far from the goalpost to try a three point field goal on fourth down. Kinnick wanted more than a punt that could possibly pin Wisconsin deep in a precarious position. "Let's go for it, Coup!" Kinnick hollered to Couppee. "Have the ends cross over the middle, and you slip out to the right sideline. I'll be looking for you. Just make sure you're past the first down marker."

Couppee called the pass play. Prasse and Evans crossed over the middle drawing both defensive halfbacks into the middle of the field. Couppee pretended to block for Kinnick, hoping the defensive backs would ignore him, then raced toward the sideline's first down marker. Wisconsin was deceived by the disguised play. Couppee ran alone at the twenty-five yard line. Kinnick lead Couppee down the sideline with a throw ahead of him. Couppee caught it, and spun around as a defender approached, before being tackled by two Badgers at the fifteen yard line. First down.

Green ran up the middle behind Andruska's and Hawkins' blocking for three yards. A handoff to Prasse on a reverse play lost two yards. Green then ran around Mike Enich and gained the two yards back.

The Hawkeyes were faced with another fourth down. This time, though, they were within field goal range. Kinnick again ran over to Couppee. "We're only down seven. I know what I want to do. What do you think?"

Couppee was unprepared for Kinnick's question. This was the first time the senior had asked the underclassman for his opinion. "What's our mantra in these situations?" Couppee asked as he volleyed a question back to Kinnick. "Go for it?"

"Go for it!" replied Kinnick. "We didn't come here to lose."

Couppee called a pass play. Kinnick dropped back into the pocket and found Al Couppee in the end zone for the touchdown. The visitors' bench exploded. The Hawkeyes suddenly realized they could do this, even though Jim Walker at left tackle, Bill Diehl at center, Henry Luebcke at right guard, and Jens Norgaard at right end were missing from the front line.

The Hawkeyes celebrated in the end zone, but before running back to the sideline bench, Kinnick missed the extra point attempt. Wisconsin 7, Iowa 6.

"We can do it again! Let's play some defense and get the ball back!" exclaimed an excited Couppee to anyone within hearing distance. "It's our game!"

Cone caught Prasse's kickoff and returned it to the thirty-five yard line before being forced out of bounds by Russ Busk. The Badgers ran five plays, three running plays and two passes, bringing them to a third down and eight for the first down.

Kinnick hollered at Busk, Green, and Murphy - the other defensive backs playing behind the linebackers. "Watch for Gage and Schmitz out of the backfield!"

Kinnick saw the play developing in front of him. Cone, who had replaced Gradisnik, fired a pass near Kinnick's safety position. Gage cut to the ball. Kinnick had an angle on Gage and leaped in front of the Badger, gathering in his second interception of the game.

With little time remaining in the first half, Kinnick threw twice to Prasse for gains of twelve and six yards, respectively. A seldom used quarterback sneak behind Andruska, who was still in for Diehl at center, lost four yards as Paskvan crushed Couppee to the ground.

It was third down and eight for the first down. Just over a minute remained in the second quarter.

"Let's fake the punt," Enich said softly enough so only Couppee could hear him. "If we go into quick-kick formation on third down, they'll think we just want to punt the ball out of this end of the field with the clock running down."

"Nile on a fake punt," Couppee, in turn, said to himself under his breath. It was up to him to call the right play, he thought, so everyone knew what to do. Instead of blocking to protect the punter, everyone would have a different assignment. The Hawkeyes had practiced it yesterday at Stagg Field in Chicago.

"Twenty-nine, ninety-nine, thirty-six!" yelled Couppee. "Hike!"

Bruno Andruska hiked to Kinnick standing eight yards behind Andruska. Instead of leaning back into punt blocking position, Andruska shot straight ahead looking for Wisconsin's safety. Tollefson and Hawkins, the guards on both sides of Andruska, purposely let the defensive linemen streak by them on the outside. The play was designed to trick them into coming across the line of scrimmage untouched by any Hawkeye linemen. Both defenders headed straight at Kinnick. Al Couppee and Buzz Dean, standing in the backfield to protect the punter, cross blocked the two rushing Badgers. Neither defender saw it coming as Couppee and Dean blind-sided the two helpless linemen from opposite directions. Enich and Bergstrom shot forward, looking for linebackers downfield to take out of the play.

While all this was transpiring in a mere three seconds, Kinnick skipped forward and swung his right leg high as if he had punted, but instead, he quickly tucked the ball under his arm and raced straight ahead into the wide open lane created by his teammates. Kinnick ran past Couppee and Dean, both sprawled on the ground after their blocks. He followed Andruska, with Enich and Bergstrom on his right and left. Kinnick reached midfield and still had not been touched by a defender. Finally, two Badgers converged on him after he had gained fifty-four yards to the Wisconsin twenty-five yard line. But the play was not over, yet. As Kinnick fell to the ground, Prasse ran beside him. Kinnick pitched a lateral to Prasse who impulsively headed for the end zone. Touchdown on a fake punt. The home crowd fell silent, but only for a moment. The referee, standing at the twenty-five yard line, thought it was a forward lateral and threw a yellow penalty flag on the field. "An illegal forward pass nullifies the play. There will be a ten yard penalty from the previous line of scrimmage!" he bellowed while making the corresponding arm gestures to inform the officials in the booth. The Wisconsin sideline and the fans cheered the call. The Hawkeye bench and the players on the field were dismayed, yet they were experiencing contradicting emotions. It was excruciating to have run the play perfectly, only for it to be called back, but it was also exhilarating to know they had acted out their roles to perfection. They were once again sensing the ability to win.

Prasse called out to Couppee as they jogged back to the original line of scrimmage, "Let's just run Murphy up the middle twice and let the clock run out."

In the locker room, Kinnick spoke first. "That lateral was my fault. We would have had the ball on their twenty-five yard line if I hadn't made that mistake."

As Anderson walked into the room hearing Kinnick's apology, Prasse responded, "That's okay, Nile. It still felt good to cross that goal line with the ball in my hand. We're moving the ball. We'll be okay."

Dr. Eddie added, "Frankly, I'm feeling confident after what I just witnessed. Wisconsin is focused on stopping our run. I think the pass will work the second half. And somewhere in the second half, we will run the other fake punt we practiced. So, Buzz Dean and Nile Kinnick, be ready for that play call.

"I also want to try our reverse, Dean to Kinnick, on our first offensive possession.

And one more thing, I think Norgaard is done for the season. He was taken to the hospital for x-rays. He asked me, with a smile on his face, to tell the team to win this game for him - like the Gipper. So, gentlemen, you have your orders. Win this one for Norgaard. Now, let's bow our heads for a moment in silence, and in your own thoughts, ask or hope that Jens will be okay."

The team obliged. An eerie silence fell over the locker room. The team was growing fewer in numbers, but stronger in mind and spirit. Luebcke, Walker, and now Norgaard, were gone.

Iowa started the second half kicking off to the Badgers. Enich stopped Paskvan trying to run outside. Couppee hit Schmitz from his linebacker position after a two yard gain. On third down, Kinnick knocked down a pass, forcing Wisconsin to punt.

Kinnick caught the punt on his own thirty-five yard line, started straight ahead, and after getting past the first two Badgers, cut left. Dean and Prasse led Kinnick down the left sideline, each taking a Wisconsin player to the turf as they cleared a path for Kinnick. Gage then brought Kinnick down at Wisconsin's forty yard line.

Kinnick was hit hard by Gage on the next play. Nile got up slowly, looking down, his chin resting against his chest. He walked slowly back to his position, staggering once while he tried to get his equilibrium back.

"Nile, you okay?" asked Couppee. "If you leave the game, we're without you until the fourth quarter."

"Just call Green on a play around right end so I can just rest a minute. I'll be okay, but I need a minute." Kinnick felt the same worry Couppee expressed. The substitution rule would drastically hurt Iowa if Kinnick had to sit out the rest of the third quarter.

Bill Green ran behind Evans and Enich on the right side for a short gain. Kinnick trailed the play slowly.

Coach Anderson wanted the reverse called during the first series. The Hawkeyes were faced with third down. Couppee was concerned Kinnick wasn't ready.

"Coup, call the reverse. I can do it. I just got stunned for a moment. I'm ready."

Couppee smiled with relief as he belted out the next play. "Six, five, two, thirty-six, fifty-three, twenty-seven, hike, one, two, three, four!" The backs shifted left. Couppee moved behind Bergstrom at left tackle. Buzz Dean shifted directly behind Diehl at center who had recovered enough from his first-half injury to play again. Bill Green moved from fullback to left halfback while Kinnick positioned himself at the left wingback.

Wisconsin thought it was a run to the left, especially with Kinnick positioned far to the left. Diehl hiked to Dean. The Hawkeye linemen and backs all started moving left, looking for an opponent to block. But suddenly, Kinnick stopped and spun back to his right. Dean ran with the flow of the linemen, then slipped the ball to Kinnick running in the opposite direction of the blockers. Kinnick had no one in front of him for protection. Two Badgers moved towards Kinnick. Prasse and Evans ran the crossing routes fifteen yards down field, trying to create space between the Wisconsin defenders and themselves.

Kinnick, with the option to pass, spotted Dick Evans at the fifteen yard line and unleashed a high arching pass. Evans caught it at the ten yard line in full stride, running across the field at an angle and crossed the goal line. Kinnick missed the extra point again, but the Hawkeyes took the lead, 12 to 7.

Buzz Dean kicked off to Gradisnik. He ran back to the twenty-three yard line before Prasse brought him down. On the first play from scrimmage Gradisnik gained eight yards before Tollefson leveled him. Gradisnik was unable to get up, and after the trainers attended to him for five minutes, a stretcher was brought out to the field. Bill Schmitz replaced him.

The proud Badgers were determined not to let the visiting Hawkeyes leave with a victory on this beautiful late autumn day. Losing to the Hawkeyes was unacceptable; after all, these were the Hawkeyes that had been the worst team in the Big Ten for the past decade. George Paskvan and Bill Schmitz took over. The two combined for a ferocious ground game the Hawkeyes were unable to stop. Together, the two Badgers took turns running the ball, eventually reaching the Iowa nine yard line. Then Schmitz surprised the Hawkeyes by going to the air. He found Al Lorenz in the back of the end zone for a touchdown to regain the lead. On the extra point play, Dick Evans and Mike Enich did a cross block, Enich surprising the Badger assigned to block Evans. Evans slipped around Enich's backside with a clear path to the kicker. Evans leaped at the last moment, his fingertips grazing the ball just enough to knock it off line; but the Badgers had seized the lead, 13 to 12.

Again, just as in the Indiana game, the Hawkeyes trailed in the fourth quarter.

Coach Anderson summoned Kinnick. "Nile, you are the leader. It's up to you if we are to have a chance." Then he smiled at Kinnick. "I think the Minnesota coach was right. Remember, he said Iowa will win this game because Iowa has Kinnick. Let's prove Coach Bierman knows what he's talking about."

"I think we'll have a lot more success passing than running, Coach," Kinnick responded.

"Tell Couppee to keep going to the Notre Dame box with the passing options," Dr. Eddie said. "And remind him we've still got the other fake punt in our arsenal."

"Okay, Coach."

Gage's kickoff sailed to Couppee at the eighteen yard line. He started left, then ran back to his right, traversing the entire width of the field. Paskvan tackled him at the thirty-four yard line.

A run by Bill Green was stopped at the line of scrimmage. A pass to Prasse fell incomplete as Kinnick unloaded the pass just to escape a heavy rush. The incomplete pass, though, kept the ball at the original line of scrimmage. Another short gain on a run by Dean brought fourth down.

"Coup, time for the other fake punt." Kinnick gave Couppee the play to call and looked at Buzz Dean. "Ready, Buzz?"

"I've been waiting for this play for two weeks," said Dean.

Couppee called for the punt formation. Wisconsin sent their two safeties back to receive the punt. Nile lined up only eight yards behind Diehl. The ball was snapped and Kinnick stepped forward with his left foot to begin his rhythmic kicking motion. Bergstrom, Tollefson, Diehl, Hawkins, and Enich formed a wall, not only to block the oncoming rushers, but also to block their vision. Kinnick swung his right foot high, but as he did, he reached back with his right hand and handed the ball to Buzz Dean streaking behind him. The Badgers saw his right leg swing upward, thinking the ball was sailing through the air. Several in the stands - with their unblocked view - hollered 'fumble,' realizing the ball hadn't left Kinnick's foot. By the time the Badgers had figured out it was a fake punt, Dean was five yards down the sideline and headed for the first down, and more. One of the Wisconsin safeties grabbed

Dean's ankles but not until he had gained twenty yards to the Wisconsin forty-six yard line.

The Hawkeyes were sensing a confidence good footballers experience when out-playing and out-smarting their opponent. The Hawkeyes were still behind but it didn't seem to matter. They felt they would reach the end zone again. The coaching staff had them prepared, and they had Kinnick doing magic in the backfield. In that moment, the game became fun for the Hawkeyes. Their glances at each other were with bold, self-assured eyes.

Kinnick faded back, looked downfield, and found Prasse for a ten yard pass near the left side line. Iowa had first down at the Wisconsin thirty-six. Next, Couppee ran past a rushing linebacker and gathered in a seven yard pass at the twenty-nine yard line.

The Missouri River flows gently between Omaha, Nebraska, and Council Bluffs, Iowa. In a very nice two-story house in Omaha, two parents sat in the parlor, both leaning forward with anticipation, listening to WHO Radio broadcasting the Iowa-Wisconsin game. In a small, cold house in the lower west side of Council Bluffs, a mother was listening to the same broadcast, but not with her husband. The furnace hadn't been ignited yet in order to save money on the heating bill. Her husband was busy delivering feed and seed for a local grain elevator to farmers in his old, rusted Ford pick up. It was one of three jobs he worked whenever he was needed. The truck didn't have a radio.

Nile Sr. and Frances listened as their son moved the Hawkeyes down the field for what would possibly be the winning score. They were nervous, but this temporary uneasiness was over-shadowed by their unending pride. They were proud more for the person than the athlete. They had raised a son with unparalleled empathy for others.

While their son kept them informed on his football experience, he spoke more on topics other than sports. His interests centered on social issues, the disadvantaged, dreaming of one day working in government to positively affect those in need. He regularly wrote letters to his grandparents and brothers, expressing gratitude to the former and teaching the latter with his own experiences and concerns. Nile's two younger brothers had idolized him for years.

Mary Couppee held her hands together, almost as if in prayer. A blanket draped over her shoulders. She could only imagine what it was like in Madison. She had never seen a large stadium. Her son had scored Iowa's first touchdown. And he just caught another pass to get Iowa closer to the winning score. She loved hearing his name spoken on the radio. She loved even more that Al Couppee was going to college, something few from the neighborhood ever accomplished.

As Al Couppee walked back to his quarterback position to call the next play, he approached Bill Green and Nile Kinnick. "Boys, it's time. You'll like this next play call, Greenie." Couppee then started calling the signals.

Even though they were only twenty-nine yards from scoring, he called for a short punt formation, but that was only to put Kinnick in a great position for a pass play. Couppee then called for the pass routes. Green moved closer to the line of scrimmage.

As Kinnick shuffled back into the protective pocket created by his linemen, he saw Green fake a defender to his right, before turning left at full speed. Kinnick saw space between Green and the Badger widen and knew it was a touchdown if he could just get the pass to Green. As the protective pocket moved backwards in unison, pushing the Wisconsin linemen out wide from the center of the field, Kinnick stepped forward and released the ball. The pass was perfect. Green caught the ball in his chest for Iowa's third touchdown pass of the game.

Kinnick dropped kicked the extra point to give Iowa a 19-13 lead.

Nile Sr. and Frances held hands, relaxing into the back cushion of the couch. Mary Couppee smiled, a tear streaming down her cheek. She missed her son's smile and laughter. She didn't know her son instructed the other Hawkeyes on what to do before every play. But she knew he was having the time of his life, and she was proud.

The team's backslapping was interrupted by the sight of Bill Diehl struggling to stand up. His knee was re-injured on the touchdown play to Green, but he wanted to center the snap to Kinnick for the extra point. Now, this warrior's day was over. In fact, it was obvious to his teammates, and to Diehl, that his season just ended. Diehl's left leg dangled loosely, tilted to the side. Enich and Tollefson instantly put their shoulders under Diehl's to carry him off. Bruno Andruska would take over the center's duties again.

After Wisconsin received the kickoff, and ran two unsuccessful plays, they had one last opportunity to reclaim the lead with time running out. On third down, Mike Enich and Max Hawkins breezed through the left side of Wisconsin's offensive line. Schmitz threw a desperation pass that landed in Buzz Dean's arms. Dean's interception at midfield all but assured the victory.

The men in black and gold were exuberant. The Iowa sideline was ecstatic. All that was left was what every footballer loves to experience: quietly celebrating in the huddle, running a few innocuous plays, while watching the game clock come to a halt. Bill Green took the first handoff. Jerry Ankeny suddenly left Coach Anderson's side and ran onto the field.

"Coup, you're out," Ankeny said.

"What? Why now?" asked Couppee. Enich, Hawkins, Tollefson, Bergstrom, Kinnick, and Couppee had played all fifty-nine minutes of the game. Only one minute remained. Couppee wanted to go the distance with the other ironmen.

Couppee ran towards Dr. Eddie. Obvious disgust showed in his furrowed brow and clenched jaw. Why only him, he thought?

Coach Anderson smiled at the disgruntled quarterback. "Al, I just had to make sure the play caller knew to sit on the ball. I'm proud of you, young man. You played one helluva ball game." Coach Anderson smiled as he slapped his assertive quarterback on the shoulder pads. "You just quarterbacked your best game against the former quarterback of the Four Horsemen. That should mean something to you. Beating Stuhldreher means a lot to me. Take the rest of the day off, Al."

Couppee walked to the water cooler. This was a life changing moment for him, he thought. His coach, whom he had tried to please for the past eight months, had finally praised him. This game, too, was a major hurdle. If the Hawkeyes had lost, their season record would have been two wins and two losses. But now, this team was making a mark for itself, not only in the Big Ten, but throughout the nation. His thoughts quickly erased the disappointment of being taken out of the game. No one had predicted that the 1939 Iowa Hawkeyes would have much success. Now, their record would stand at three victories against one defeat. They had come from behind in both Big Ten wins. Couppee also remembered this was Iowa's first win at Madison in ten years. The drink of water was the sweetest he had ever tasted.

The Hawkeye bench and the eleven on the field swarmed together after the final quarter ended. They hollered, hugged, and slapped hands, congratulating each other for their shared accomplishment. They slowly moved toward the tunnel and the glorious experience of a winning locker room. No journalists, no photographers, just the soldiers who stood side by side during the battle could enter their private clubhouse and enjoy the celebration. The soreness, the bruises, the aches from collisions with opponents and the hard turf were temporarily healed, except for the injuries of Norgaard and Diehl. Both were lost for the season. Diehl sat in a wheelchair in front of his locker with a radio next to him, waiting for his team, and smiling. Norgaard was at the University of Wisconsin Hospital.

The 'Ironmen,' a term Coach Anderson used prior to the game to describe the few players on the traveling squad, made several newspaper headlines Sunday morning. "They'll need to be ironmen," Dr. Eddie was quoted saying.

Sunday morning Bert McGrane's headline in The Des Moines Register read,

The Ironmen Showed Their Mettle!

James Smith of the Chicago Times wrote,

A sellout crowd in Madison witnessed Nile Kinnick displaying the game of football with a style that will never be seen again at Camp Randall. He did it all.

Another Chicago newspaper quoted Wisconsin's coach, Harry Stuhldreher, in the post-game interview.

You find a player like him once in a generation. Usually when you find a great football player, he is great because he has one exceptional talent. Kinnick is exceptional

at everything. In addition, he is a great morale man. He is another coach on the field.

He beat us and that's where the credit should go. I think he is the greatest player I've ever seen, and I've seen quite a few.

What he did today was amazing. He had a fourth quarter touchdown pass to take back the lead. In all, he threw three touchdown passes to Couppee, Evans, and Green. He had timely runs for first downs, several punts over forty yards, a kickoff return for more than fifty yards, a beautiful fake punt and run with a lateral for a touchdown that - fortunately for us - was called back, two interceptions, tackles from his safety position, another fake punt and handoff for a first down, and something not in the statistics - leadership.

A star was shining in the Midwest.

CHAPTER TWENTY

October 29, 1939. It was nine o'clock in the evening and Nile Kinnick, Senior Class President, was finishing his duties presiding over the monthly class meeting. "Unless there is any further new business to discuss, I move to end this meeting. Is there a second?"

"I second the motion," said someone in the second row.

"Anyone opposed?" Kinnick asked. No one responded. "The meeting is hereby over. We will meet again next month at the same time. Thank you for attending."

Nile Kinnick had campaigned for Senior Class President in May at the end of his junior year. He won by a landslide against three classmates. He felt somewhat guilty using his celebrity to run for the position. He was well-known on campus, and he knew many voted for him for only that reason. But, he thought, that is the nature of politics, using your unique advantages to garner attention. Kinnick was proud of his position. But he quickly learned being class president was not very glamorous. Topics discussed, although important on campus, held little significance in the overall scheme of things, he thought. Still, it was interesting and a learning experience.

As Nile walked from the auditorium into the hallway, he heard a familiar voice. "Mr. President. Mr. President."

"I like the sound of that," Kinnick responded as he walked towards Erv Prasse sitting in the window sill. Two women, holding books in their arms, were standing next to Prasse. Nile recognized one of them from the meeting that just concluded.

"Nile, this is my friend, Mary Stellman. And this is Mary's roommate, Barbara Miller."

"It's nice to meet you, Mary, Barbara."

"Mary and I were on our way to The Academy when we saw Barbara walking out of your meeting. Can you join the three of us?" Prasse asked.

"Sure, I'd be glad to but I can't stay long." Kinnick wondered if this was a purposeful arrangement by his star receiver, or just a coincidence, but it didn't matter. The four left Schaeffer Hall, walking towards downtown.

"Did you enjoy the meeting tonight, Barbara?" Kinnick asked.

She looked at Nile. "It was the first one I've attended. I thought it was interesting, but I was surprised by the formality."

Kinnick noticed the softness of her voice as she walked with a stylish elegance. "Some meetings are more interesting than others. We usually have the good fortune to either agree on issues or quickly form a committee to address the topic in more detail at the next meeting. I'm not sure we accomplish a lot, but I've met some interesting people."

The two continued talking as they walked along the sidewalk, almost forgetting Erv Prasse and Mary Stellman were right behind. Nile discovered Barbara Miller was from Sioux City. She was a senior, majoring in English, with plans to teach next year.

"Nile, I must confess, I know a considerable amount about you. You're in the headlines and the radio broadcasts all the time. My dad will be impressed that I met you, but he might be disappointed if I don't talk about football." She paused for a moment. "I won't be able to give him any inside story."

Nile laughed. "Tell your father that Dr. Eddie has us ready to upset some teams we aren't expected to beat."

The four sat in a booth for nearly two hours. Several Hawkeye teammates wandered by the booth and exchanged friendly banter with the two senior footballers.

"Well, I should get going. I have to do some early morning studying. Will you be alright getting back to your room, or will you join Mary?"

"Mary and I will be fine. Thank you for asking, though. Good night, Nile."

Kinnick looked over his shoulder at Barbara as he slid to the outside of the booth to stand up. "I hope we can get together again sometime."

"I hope so, too," she responded.

Erv Prasse stood up from the other side of the booth. "I'll walk with you, Nile. Maybe the four of us should go out sometime, maybe a movie or dancing. I think you'd be impressed if you saw Kinnick and me on the dance floor."

"Let's talk sometime," responded Mary Stellman. "Good night, Erv."

Prasse and Kinnick walked towards one of the bridges that crossed the Iowa River. "Was that a setup, Prass?"

"You mean the three of us being at Schaeffer Hall when your meeting ended?" Prasse smiled. "If it was, I may have promised not to tell."

Kinnick laughed. "I hope you're as evasive against the Purdue defensive backs, but whether or not it was a setup, thanks.

"Prass, four more weeks and college football is over. I'll miss it."

"You know we could always use you again on the basketball court," Prasse said. "Or we could use you behind home plate in the spring if you start missing the applause." Prasse would start practice with the basketball team as soon as the football season ended, and then baseball in the spring. "Nile, you and I both know you could probably play major league baseball if you wanted."

"No, I think I'll be done with sports," Nile said. "It's time for me to move on to other endeavors. I don't think my purpose is to continue hearing applause in a sports venue. Anyway, our decisions will come soon enough, right?"

Prasse looked at Kinnick. Kinnick was surprised by his friend's solemn eyes because Prasse was never serious. "When you're not around, Nile, sometimes we talk and wonder what's in your future. Most of us see you someday as a governor or senator. We all agree we've never known someone quite like you. I think someday I'll be telling my grandkids I knew Nile Kinnick."

Kinnick looked squarely at Erv Prasse after the compliment. "I've never known anyone that enjoys life more than you, Prass. I've always been a little envious of that."

They reached Riverside Drive. Prasse turned to walk up the hill towards the Phi Gamma Delta fraternity. Kinnick continued north on Riverside to the Phi Psi annex.

"And when you're talking to your grandkids," Kinnick continued, "make sure they know you might have been faster than me, but I did a better jitterbug."

As Kinnick walked alone the final few blocks, he reminisced, thinking about how fleeting his college years had been. He pondered what the future held. Law school? Some type of public service? Frances Kinnick's strong religious beliefs taught her son to give to others in whatever he did. "Happiness can only be attained through giving, not receiving," he remembered his mother saying. Maybe Prasse was right. Maybe he should think about professional baseball. After all, he thought, one of his best friends growing up was Bob Feller, from Van Meter, Iowa. They were a great pitcher/catcher duo on the American Legion baseball team during their high school years. And now, Feller had already won fifty-five games for the Cleveland Indians since 1936, twenty-four games this past year alone. Maybe baseball for awhile would be alright; he could save some money and then attend law school. It would certainly be less taxing on his body than football, if he ever had to choose between the two sports. But somehow, these thoughts didn't feel right. Maybe it was his mother's influence.

His mind drifted to Europe. War seemed imminent, but when? Tyranny, he thought, had no place in the world. Oppression by one against another was wrong. But right now, he was in Iowa City and this weekend the Hawkeyes would be facing Purdue in Ross-Ade Stadium. He knew their third game in a row away from Iowa City would be a daunting task. Purdue had three great running backs, Lou Brock, Mike Byelene, and Jack Brown. The end was anchored by an All-American, Dave Rankin. The Boilermakers finished second in the conference last year, and some predicted Purdue winning the Big Ten conference this year. Somehow, Nile reasoned, a group of college students playing a game on a football field seemed so unimportant compared to the bigger, more complex world stage.

Then his thoughts drifted to Barbara Miller. Prasse had made it an interesting evening.

Friday came quickly after preparing for the Boilermakers all week. Without Norgaard and Diehl traveling, the Hawkeyes were down to thirty-one players. The Rock Island Rocket was leaving Friday morning at 9:15. The footballers were to meet, as usual, thirty minutes before departure. Slowly they gathered at the depot, but this morning was different.

Nile Kinnick turned to walk down Benton Street and was shocked by what he saw. The parking spots along the streets were filled with cars belonging to Iowa City residents. In front of him were at least seven or eight hundred students standing in the midst of the local citizens. Next to the depot, under the wooden overhang, the Iowa Marching Band stood together playing songs, pumping up the crowd's enthusiasm. The mayor was there. So was the University's President Gilmore. The players were surprised by this outpouring of support.

Mike Enich walked to the front just as Kinnick and Couppee also arrived. Enich had to yell to be heard over the band. "This is amazing. This isn't even a victory party; it's just a farewell."

"I guess they like us," Couppee added.

"I think Hawkeye fans have been denied winning for too long," added Enich.

"We have an obligation to keep it going," Nile said, "and not just for ourselves."

After President Gilmore spoke, the crowd started chanting, "Kinnick! Kinnick!"

The President turned to Dr. Eddie first to make sure it was okay with him. Dr. Eddie nodded his approval. Then President Gilmore looked at Nile Kinnick. "Nile, can you give us a few words?"

The players humorously joined in, "Kinnick! Kinnick! Kinnick!"

Nile walked towards the makeshift podium. A microphone was attached to a stand between two speakers. He stopped and gazed out at the people cheering his name. He smiled, turning his head slowly from left to right as if to recognize each person individually. He absorbed their passion.

"Thank you. Your expression of kindness, being here this morning, is overwhelming to all of us. If your purpose was to send us off feeling a tremendous exuberance, then I must tell you, you have been successful. You have given us something to carry with us, on the ride to West Lafayette, and into the stadium Saturday. Your passion reinforces our determination. You give us even more purpose. Bringing back a victory is something we want to share with everyone here, as well as the

University and the state of Iowa. Thank you for coming this morning."

Applause broke out. An appreciative smile appeared on Dr. Eddie's face, approving again of his leader. He noticed, too, that journalists from the Cedar Rapids Gazette, Iowa City Press Citizen, and Des Moines Register were on hand. Dr. Eddie leaned over to speak into President Gilmore's ear, trying to be heard over the band's final song. "That night in The Academy when I accepted the coaching position, I knew if I had one player like him, things would be alright."

"Doctor, if things progress as they have, and you beat Purdue, I anticipate large crowds at our Notre Dame and Minnesota games. If we sell out both of those games, we can finally pay off the debt from 1929 when we built Iowa Stadium. The timing of the stadium's construction, followed by the depression, has been a burden on the University. That can all change with fifty-three thousand in the stands for both games." President Gilmore beamed a smile as he shared his thoughts with Coach Anderson. "Frankly, though, first and foremost, I'm a sports fan and what you are accomplishing with this team is wonderful. This turnaround has been simply magnificent."

"Thank you, Mr. Gilmore."

After the team changed trains in Chicago on their way to West Lafayette, Indiana, the second train passed through the south side of Chicago. All along the ride, the players stared out the windows at the poverty surrounding them. The train traveled through an industrial park adjacent to a deprived neighborhood, then another neighborhood, and another. Grayness filled the air from the coal burning in the plants' furnaces, bestowing an austere presence to the endless landscape. The rear sides of the three and four story apartment buildings faced the train tracks. The cramped back porches, adorned with laundry strung across the railings, conveyed a sharp contrast to the spaciousness of Iowa. Dilapidated furniture also decorated the porches of many of these premises. People walked along the alleys and sidewalks lined with tall weeds that no one cared to mow. Children played kick ball in the grassless backyards. No one looked at the train passing by. It was an ordinary sight occurring frequently throughout the day. Sadness permeated these stark neighborhoods. Nile Kinnick was affected by the plight of these Americans as he also contemplated their destinies. Why does our nation consent to people living this meager existence, he asked himself. The bleak scene, perpetuating mile after mile, then caused him to be reminded of Germany invading Poland last month. Why do we allow these things to happen? It struck a chord with what his mother had told him. There is a "duty to help mankind." Surely, though different from the cruelty facing some Europeans, these people in Chicago were suffering their own oppression.

Chuck Tollefson sat across from Kinnick. He wasn't playing tomorrow due to an injured foot from Wednesday's practice. Nonetheless, Dr. Eddie wanted him to travel with the team because Tollefson, in his own quiet way, was an inspiration to his teammates. Everyone knew his story of riding the rails. Tollefson noticed Kinnick's serious expression as he watched the neighborhoods pass by the train window. "There's a lot of grief in the world. I know. I've been there. It just becomes so magnified when it's all condensed into one area like this. It's hard to look past it," Tollefson said.

Kinnick, knowing Tollefson was referring to his days as a hobo, asked, "What did the hopelessness feel like, not knowing what would happen next?"

"It sits in your stomach. You're always uneasy." Tollefson also looked out the window while speaking. "Sometimes you can't distinguish between the feeling of anxiety and the pain of an empty stomach. They feel the same. But you start to get used to both feelings after awhile because it becomes part of your existence. It's what you know."

"How did you break away from it?" Kinnick asked.

"I was lucky, I guess. I was able to step outside myself and look at my life objectively. I decided this wasn't acceptable. One night while I was lying in a barn alone, I started asking myself all the 'what if' questions. And the one that struck me was, 'what if I had stayed in school?' I had lost a lot of weight, and strength, but I decided to approach Irl Tubbs. He welcomed me back with open arms. I cried the night Coach Tubbs said he would give me another chance. I cried a long time. And then Hi Jennings called me the next day, lined up a place for me to stay, and a job.

"Those people you're looking at right now, they don't have that opportunity waiting for them. What they have is what you see. But as sad as it looks from this seat on the train, I know there can be a lot of love and a lot of togetherness within those families. Poor people possess those attributes, too. Poverty and love can coexist."

Kinnick's eyes were moist listening to his friend. "I'm glad you're on this train now, Tollie."

The locker room grew quiet when Dr. Eddie entered. All thirty-one players were dressed in their black and gold uniforms and gold helmets. "I used the term 'Ironmen' last week saying, 'the Hawkeyes will need to be ironmen,' referring to our few players against Wisconsin's full squad. Last spring we had eighty players. But I didn't want any players that weren't truly committed to being their best. Through attrition, or should I say running drills," a nervous laughter swept through the room, "a strong bond and commitment to each other grew. Frank Carideo, Jim Harris, and I witnessed it.

"But now we have lost Hank Luebcke, Jim Walker, Jens Norgaard, and Bill Diehl. And even though Tollefson is dressed, we won't play him today. A week off should have him ready for Notre Dame next week." Dr. Eddie paused. "You truly do need to be 'Ironmen.' With Bergstrom at left tackle and Pettit at left guard, we'll need to run more often to the right. Bruno Andruska will do a fine job at center and I'll be substituting Max Hawkins and Ham Snider for each other at right guard because I want a fresh guard alongside Enich at his tackle position. Snider, you'll start. Hawkins, I want you to substitute halfway through each quarter. Ray Murphy starts at fullback today and Ed McLain at right halfback." Coach Anderson didn't need to say who was starting at left halfback. And everyone also knew Couppee was at quarterback.

"Purdue knows we will be going to our strength, the right side, since we have relatively new and untested players on the left side of our line. So I expect a slugfest. When we are on defense, I anticipate they will be playing to our inexperienced left side.

"Several of you will play the entire game. Today, you'll earn the 'Ironmen' moniker. And that doesn't concern me in the least because your conditioning is far superior to the men across the line. Today will be fun!"

A brisk wind from the north swept through the stadium. Purdue elected to kick off with the wind to their back.

Eleven players gathered around Coach Anderson along the sideline.

"We're going into a strong wind, so let's just start conservatively," Anderson yelled. "Couppee, just keep the ball on the ground for now. Nothing fancy. Let's just play good, fundamental football. We'll open up the offense in the second quarter when the wind is with us, or if we get good field position this quarter. Got it?"

"Got it," replied Couppee.

August Morningstar kicked off for Purdue. Maybe it was the excitement of the moment, maybe a gust of wind moved the ball slightly just as his foot made impact, but the ball traveled only fifteen yards where Ken Pettit fell on it. The battle had begun.

Anticipating Purdue's defense zeroing in on Kinnick, Couppee called a running play for Ray Murphy. The play was directed to the right side behind Ham Snider and Mike Enich. The Hawkeyes crept into Purdue territory.

The players moved back to their positions awaiting Couppee's no-huddle signal calling. He called the same play again which netted six more yards.

Purdue shuffled back quickly into their defensive stances. Their assistant coaches had scouted Iowa's last two games in Ann Arbor and Madison. They were ready for Iowa's quick offense without the use of a huddle.

Kinnick ran around the right end as Enich took out the Purdue tackle and middle linebacker. Dick Evans dropped the left linebacker to the ground while Kinnick raced along the sideline. The nine yard pick up left the Hawkeyes facing second down and needing one yard for another first down. This time Murphy was to run straight ahead behind Couppee and Bruno Andruska. After hiking the ball, Andruska pushed the guard to his left and Couppee moved the linebacker to the right. Murphy gained eleven yards to Purdue's eighteen yard line, and another first down.

"Pettit! Bergstrom!" hollered Couppee after the play. "This next one is coming behind you. Let's show Anderson we don't have to run to the right all day."

Kinnick smiled hearing Couppee guide the team. Couppee always acted a little tougher and walked with a little extra swagger during a good drive. The team fed off his confidence.

From the T-formation, the backfield shifted to the left. Kinnick moved to the left wingback behind Prasse. Ray Murphy and Al Couppee both slid left, Couppee behind Pettit's left guard position. That put Ed McLain at tailback to receive Andruska's snap. Ken Pettit and Wally Bergstrom were ready for the challenge. They pushed the Purdue linemen backwards as McLain raced forward for seven yards.

The Hawkeyes were moving. It almost seemed too easy. It was second down and three yards to go on the Purdue eleven yard line. It was time to unleash Kinnick's arm, Couppee thought; after all, Coach Anderson said it was okay to pass once they had good field position. The next play called for Kinnick to find Prasse in a slant pattern to the corner of the end zone. Bergstom, Pettit, Andruska, Hawkins, and Enich stepped back into pass blocking stances. The protection was good. Purdue couldn't reach Kinnick as he pedaled backwards to avoid the mayhem. Meanwhile, Prasse faked towards the middle and then cut back to the outside. Kinnick delivered the ball for what looked like a touchdown. But the wind fought against the trajectory. The ball seemed almost motionless fighting against the strong breeze. Purdue's Jack Brown cut in front of Prasse, grabbed the interception, and ran back to the forty-three yard line.

The Hawkeye defenders took their positions. Lou Brock ran behind his tackles on two consecutive plays. First, he was stopped by Enich and Murphy. Then he tried the other side of the line only to discover Prasse and Bergstrom withstanding the challenge. Needing four yards for a first down, Byelene charged through the middle of the line. Andruska hit him at the ankles as Pettit reached for the ball. It came loose from the Purdue runner's grasp and Couppee lunged to the ball. The Hawkeyes recovered the fumble and it was time to try the ground game again into the strong wind.

The remainder of the first quarter saw an exchange of punts as the two teams fought for field position. Most of the game was played between the thirty yard lines as both teams struggled trying to advance the ball. The hitting was tenacious. Neither the Boilermakers nor the Hawkeyes would give in. The struggle stopped momentarily while they exchanged positions on the field at the end of the quarter. Bill Green and Buzz Dean replaced Ray Murphy and Ed McLain.

Both teams continually stopped the other's attacks for the first ten minutes of the second quarter. With five minutes left in the first half, Iowa began a charge. A reverse had Dean handing off to Kinnick. The line of scrimmage was advanced eight yards. Next, Bill Green charged straight ahead behind Andruska and Pettit for twelve yards. Prasse ran an end-around play successfully for fifteen yards. Kinnick passed to Buzz Dean for seven more yards. And then Kinnick ran to Purdue's eight yard line. Finally, the Hawkeyes had a chance to break the deadlock.

"Huddle! Let's huddle!" hollered Kinnick. "Coup, let's go on a five count."

The Hawkeyes formed a rare huddle. Dr. Eddie, watching from the sideline, wasn't sure why. Couppee took over. "We're going on a five count. Hold your positions for that extra count. I'll make it sound as if we are hiking on 'four.' If we can get them offside, then Andruska hikes it, and it's our ball half the distance to the goal line."

The Hawkeyes took their T-formation positions. Couppee called for a shift to the left. The count went to 'five' without drawing Purdue across the line of scrimmage. Buzz Dean was in motion from his right wingback position. Kinnick took the center snap from Andruska and handed the ball to Dean crossing in front of him. Couppee and Prasse escorted Dean as he raced towards the left side of the goal. Dean crossed the goal line for the touchdown just before running out of bounds; but a referee had thrown a yellow flag. An offside penalty was called on the Hawkeyes because Pettit had jumped before the fifth count from his offensive line position. The score remained Purdue 0, Iowa 0 as the teams jogged to their locker rooms for halftime.

The wrestling mats were rolled up and stored against a wall in the Hawkeyes' locker room. Several of the players were either sitting on the floor relaxing in front of the mats, or sitting on top of them with their backs leaning against the wall. The wrestling mats were a small luxury to a group that had been falling on the hard turf for the past two quarters. Couppee and Kinnick sat side by side. Enich was on the other side of Kinnick.

Dr. Eddie walked in with Frank Carideo and Jim Harris. "Pettit, you've got to be ready when there's a five count. You've got thirty minutes of football to make up for that mistake.

"Where's Couppee?" bellowed Coach Anderson with an unusual display of anger in his voice. "Good. You're sitting with Kinnick.

"Couppee, even though we crossed the goal line on our last possession, when we get inside the ten yard line, I want Kinnick carrying the ball. Mr. Couppee, allow me to introduce you to Nile Kinnick? He's one of the top offensive players in the country! I want you to shake his hand. Nile, this is your quarterback. Meet Mr. Couppee. I want him to know who you are the next time we get inside the ten yard line! Go ahead, shake hands." Dr. Eddie stood over them until they reached out and shook hands while the rest of the team looked on with bewilderment. "Now, for the rest of you, that was one tough half. I'm extremely proud of the relentless defense we displayed. Enich, that was one of the best performances I've ever seen from a lineman. They quit trying to go your way. So instead, Purdue tried out our new left side of the line. Bergstrom and Pettit, you two also did a marvelous job.

"Now when we get the ball again, Couppee, let's keep it on the ground. Brown has two interceptions for them. That wind is too strong. I think one score just might win this game. Let's get it right away and then continue with what you've shown me on defense.

"One more thing, I was just told coming in here that Illinois is beating Michigan and Northwestern is ahead of Minnesota. If those games continue like that, and we get that elusive score in the second half, we could end up tied for first place in the league."

The possibility of being in first place with only two Big Ten games left on the schedule stunned the upstart Hawkeyes. They had hoped this moment would arrive if they kept playing well, but the realization that it might happen today was overpowering.

Kinnick gazed at the ceiling. This season, he thought, was shaping into the season he had hoped it would be. Feeling triumphant, even if for only one magical season, would make it all worthwhile. The struggles of the past two years could fade away. His indecision about his future seemed unimportant right now. This moment was all that mattered.

Dr. Eddie continued. "But I shouldn't even mention the other games because all I want you thinking about right now is the next play. Always think about the next play. Everything else will take care of itself."

The battle-weary legion of black and gold clad Iowa Hawkeyes felt glory thrust upon them by merely thinking of first place. No one throughout the nation would have ever thought that the worst team in the Big Ten the past two years would suddenly be vying for a championship. They stood up and gathered in the middle of the room. No one seemed tired. They were ready to battle for a title.

The normally quiet Mike Enich spoke up. "This is it! This is our moment! We've been waiting for this a long time! Are we going to let it slip out of our grasp?!"

In unison, and with everyone yelling at the top of their lungs, the answer was a resounding, "NOOOOO!!"

"Then let's go play the best half of our lives!" Enich added.

Collectively, "YEAHHHH!" echoed through the room, and continued echoing as they walked out the door.

The third quarter saw more of the same, eleven young men unleashing all their strength against eleven others they knew only by name. The defensive struggle continued. Purdue had worked all week on stopping Kinnick. They were prepared for his option pass or run that had been so effective in the South Dakota, Indiana, and Wisconsin games. Purdue shifted their defensive linemen and linebackers slightly to their left to combat Iowa's stronger right side.

Punts were exchanged three times by each team through the third period. Kinnick was intercepted again by Jack Brown. On defense, Enich halted any attempts by Purdue to run plays behind the Boilermakers' left side. Evans, too, shored up that side of the Iowa line along with Ham Snider or Max Hawkins. Snider and Hawkins continued sharing the right guard position. Prasse, Bergstrom, Pettit, Andruska, Enich, and Evans had played every down on the line of scrimmage. Couppee at quarterback and linebacker on defense, and Kinnick at left halfback and safety on defense, had also been on the field for every play. The 'Ironmen,' Kinnick thought, was a name that would be remembered if they kept winning. And if they lost the rest of the season, with Notre Dame and Minnesota coming to Iowa City, the 'Ironmen' would eventually be forgotten. They had to win, he thought. Enich was right. This was their moment.

Kinnick returned the favor of intercepting a pass late in the third quarter, but again Iowa was forced to punt. Both teams became more determined, fighting with every ounce of energy they could muster. Neither side backed down. They couldn't. The Boilermakers and the Hawkeyes had invested too much to let the opponent have an opportunity now.

The fourth quarter began without either set of warriors having scored. The stakes kept increasing as the time on the clock continued decreasing.

On fourth down, Kinnick punted again. With the line of scrimmage on Iowa's own forty-eight yard line, Kinnick moved back to his forty to receive the snap from Andruska. The Hawkeyes again performed the play to perfection, giving Kinnick enough time to recoil his right leg and unleash the ball. The punt sailed fifty yards in the air before hitting the Ross-Ade turf with a thud at the ten yard line, bouncing almost straight left, and going out of bounds on the Purdue five yard line. Suddenly, a crack appeared in Purdue's armor. The Boilermakers were ninety-five yards from scoring. Coach Carideo's daily punting exchanges with Kinnick, before practice every afternoon, were paying dividends.

"This is it! No first downs for Purdue! Let's not let them out of here!" Kinnick took charge this time for all the seniors on the team who had weathered the past two years. "Don't worry about Rankin going out for a pass. I don't think they'll do that this close to their own end zone. It will be Byelene or Brown on a run."

Kinnick was right. Byelene advanced the line of scrimmage to the nine yard line before Kinnick, coming up from his safety position, dropped him to the ground. Then Brown ran for no gain. On third down, Evans stopped Brock for a one yard loss.

Ten minutes remained in the scoreless game. Purdue was faced with fourth down. Kinnick retreated back to return the punt. But he never received it.

Mike Enich lunged across at his opponent as the ball was snapped. With one sudden forward movement, he thrust forward knocking two Boilermakers to each side of him. He was relentless in his pursuit of the punter. He reached out with both hands and tipped the ball as it left Brown's foot. The ball bobbled forward to the fifteen yard line where Prasse picked it up and advanced the ball to the two yard line before a swarm of Boilermakers stopped him. The Hawkeyes were delirious.

Couppee, knowing Dr. Eddie wanted Kinnick to have the ball in these situations, was equally concerned that Purdue was focused on Kinnick going for the touchdown. He called a play for Buzz Dean who dove forward for a half yard gain. Then Kinnick leaped over Enich but was stopped on the one yard line. Kinnick took the next snap from Andruska but a Purdue linebacker was in the Iowa backfield almost as quickly as the ball. Kinnick was sacked for a two yard loss. It was fourth and goal on the three yard line.

Couppee looked at Kinnick. "Do we take the three points, or go for it?"

"The wind is a factor so let's take our chances and keep it on the ground. Let's go for the touchdown!" Kinnick answered.

"Then I'm calling your number. I don't want Anderson making me shake your hand again."

From the T-formation, Couppee called the 'thirty-one' play, Kinnick around Enich and Evans on the right side. A foot race ensued. Kinnick tried to outrace two Boilermakers to the corner of the end zone, but Purdue had anticipated the play. They rode Kinnick out of bounds at the goal line. Bedlam broke out. The Iowa players congregated where Kinnick was tackled, all holding their arms extended above their heads, signaling the touchdown. The Purdue footballers were all pointing down the field, imitating a referee's signal for a Purdue first down, hoping to persuade the referees. A referee signaled that it was Purdue's ball; the Hawkeyes failed to score. It was a superb goal line stand by Purdue but now Purdue was ninety-nine yards from the other goal line. The home crowd, having cheered endlessly for every defensive play of the series, immediately increased their volume.

"It's okay that we didn't score!" shouted Couppee to everyone that could hear him on defense. "We can stop them again!"

Purdue tried to catch Iowa off-guard. Rather than risking the possibility of getting caught in the end zone for a safety, Brown moved to the very back of the end zone to try a quick kick on first down. Kinnick and Green raced backwards to receive the punt. Jack Brown, standing just inside the out of bounds chalk line, crouched down into position to receive the center's snap. Then it happened; Brown mishandled the hike. The ball fell to the ground in the end zone, wobbling in front of the kicker. Brown picked it up, but Prasse was charging hard from his left end position. Prasse slammed Brown to the turf. The referee signaled a safety. Iowa scored the first two points of the game, a score indicative of the defensive performance by both teams.

Ten Hawkeyes swarmed their captain. Kinnick had both arms around his good friend and fellow senior. "Prass, those two points might be the most important points of the season! Nice attack of the prolate spheroid!"

Couppee added, while hugging Prasse and Kinnick, "Convex prolate spheroid!"

And coming up from behind all three, "Pebble grained, leather convex prolate spheroid!" bellowed Enich with his deep voice as he reached his massive arms around all three. Iowa 2, Purdue 0.

Mary Couppee leaned over to her husband. "I've got to see Al play at least one game while he's at Iowa. Let's go to the Notre Dame game next week."

"Oh, Mary, I wish we could afford it. But we can't. Besides, the weekend is just too busy for me hauling the feed," he said. Then seeing her melancholy eyes, he added, "But maybe we could afford one train ticket for you. I'll look into the cost, okay?"

She nodded with a sad smile.

Seven and a half minutes remained in West Lafayette's brutal battle for field position. Coming into the game, Iowa had been concerned about Purdue's backfield trio and their rugged running style. Purdue's ability to run the ball was the main reason many considered the Boilermakers to be contenders for the championship. But on this day - led by Enich and two newcomers on the other side of the defensive line, Bergstrom and Pettit - the Hawkeyes had held Brock, Byelene, and Brown to sixty total yards rushing. Mike Enich, considered to be the best tackle in the Big Ten, was showing that he might be the best tackle in the country.

The Hawkeyes huddled on the sideline next to Coach Anderson. "Will they try an on-side kick?" asked Couppee.

Dr. Eddie answered, "They're kicking from their twenty yard line, so they're too close to their end zone to try an on-side kick. If they don't recover the on-side kick, the game is over. They've got plenty of time. They'll kick away and try to stop us.

"Gentlemen, you've been stellar all afternoon. Give me a few more minutes of your very best, whatever you've got left in your tanks! I want smart football! No mistakes and we'll walk off this field possibly tied for first place. These are the times you discover who you are and what you're made of!

"I want Green and Kinnick on our thirty-five yard line for the kick. Prasse, I want you deeper just in case they elect to kick instead of punt. They have the option to do either."

Kinnick noticed Jack Brown, Purdue's punter, standing in the middle of the field at the twenty yard line. "Prass, they're punting but stay back there as a safety valve," Kinnick yelled from Iowa's thirty-five.

The punt spiraled high into the air. Kinnick moved forward and caught it at the forty. He started forward as a wedge formed in front of him by Couppee, Green, and Evans. At the fifty yard line, he darted right to avoid the midfield congestion. A Boilermaker tackled him in Purdue territory at the forty-five.

Kinnick ran over to Couppee before the Hawkeyes went into the T-formation. "Let's just get a first down and keep the clock running!" he said. "They're going to be keying on me so give it to Green."

Bill Green ran straight up the middle between Andruska and Hawkins. He was stopped after a one yard gain. Again a play went to Green on an off tackle play so Enich could lead the way, but this time he was stopped by a Purdue linebacker shooting in at an angle from the other side of the field. The line of scrimmage remained the same. On third down, Couppee thought he had to call a play for Kinnick. He hollered out the play. It was the 'thirty-one' play for Kinnick to run to the gap on Enich's right side, and then cut back to the middle. Purdue again showed their gutsy determination and stopped Kinnick again.

Fourth down and Kinnick was ready to punt. Nile was well known for the consistency of his long punts, but this one needed to be a short, high punt. If he could just keep it short of the goal line, he thought, Purdue wouldn't get the touchback and first down at the twenty yard line.

Andruska centered the ball perfectly to Kinnick. Nile stepped forward with his right leg, then one step with his left. He let loose of his grip on the ball so it could fall to meet his right foot. The ball floated high, reached its apex, and descended rapidly to the ground. It landed at the fifteen yard line as the Purdue player stepped away from the ball to avoid it bouncing into him. Iowa didn't need to down the football before it reached the goal line. Instead, Kinnick did what he did so well. The ball bounced sideways and out of bounds at the ten yard line.

Five minutes remained before the Hawkeyes could celebrate. Purdue needed to advance the ball at least sixty yards for a legitimate opportunity at a three point field goal.

But the Iowa Hawkeye Ironmen weren't about to give up any of those yards without a fight. They did what Dr. Eddie had asked them to do. They found something extra.

Ken Pettit, Bruno Andruska, Wally Bergstrom, Mike Enich, Erv Prasse, Dick Evans, Al Couppee, and Nile Kinnick had played all fifty-five minutes of the game. Only three starters ever left the field to substitution. Max Hawkins had relieved Ham Snider at right guard. Bill Green and Ray Murphy shared time at fullback. And Buzz Dean had exchanged playing time with Ed McLain. The 'Ironmen' were again earning their new nickname.

Byelene tried a conservative play around left end. He wanted to get out of bounds to stop the clock but Couppee alertly kept him in bounds. Second down. Byelene faded back to pass, looking for their star end, Dave Rankin, who had been kept silent all afternoon by the pressing Hawkeye defense. Kinnick batted down the pass intended for the All-American. Third down. Byelene again went to pass. Iowa rushed the quarterback harder than they had all day, forcing Byelene to pass quickly to avoid being sacked. He had no alternative but to throw it long over everyone's heads to avoid an interception. Fourth down.

Less than four minutes remained for these courageous players on both sides of the line of scrimmage. Again Jack Brown went back to punt, this time standing on his goal line. Kinnick and Prasse retreated to midfield to receive one final punt.

This time, Brown didn't mishandle the hike. He caught it cleanly and stepped forward. But from his left, Mike Enich came barreling towards him after sliding off a Purdue blocker. At the last moment, Enich dove towards the kicker, reaching as far as he could from his prone position. His left hand slapped the ball hard as it left Brown's foot. It careened to Brown's right side and behind him. Wally Bergstrom, a step behind Enich, lunged towards the ball as it went into the end zone. Brown fell on the ball with Bergstrom landing on top of him. The Hawkeyes scored a second safety. The players were ecstatic. The points didn't matter as much as the fact that it would be Iowa's ball after Purdue was again forced to kick off.

Dr. Eddie stood next to Frank Carideo with the Hawkeyes surrounding him for last minute instructions. He shook his head looking up at the scoreboard. "Four to nothing! That is possibly the oddest score I've ever seen! We've got a little over three minutes to make sure their score remains at zero. No passes. No end runs. Just three plays up the middle and we'll punt for the umpteenth time if we need. Three minutes! Three minutes!"

The Iowa Hawkeyes ran back onto the field for one last series. They weren't thinking about how tired they were. Right now, the bruises and soreness inflicted by this Big Ten foe weren't even considerations.

Iowa fielded the punt and, after a Purdue penalty, had the ball at midfield.

"One huddle, guys!" Kinnick shouted. "Smart football and we've got a fun ride home. No mistakes!"

A rousing response followed.

A Chicago Tribune reporter stopped Nile Kinnick as the team walked off the field after the final seconds had ticked off the game clock. "Can I get a quote, Nile?"

Kinnick kept walking with his companions but acknowledged the journalist. "What would you like to know?"

"Your eighty yards rushing was more than Purdue's big three combined," the reporter said. "How do you feel about that?"

"The yardage isn't about me. Those yards are because of what the other ten players are doing. Today was one of our best performances. And most of the success can be attributed to Mike Enich." Kinnick kept walking. He was walking beside Enich.

"Mike, what inspired the second blocked punt? Were you trying to run up the score?" Kinnick grinned.

"I just wanted to make sure the score was decisive," Enich answered with a laugh.

"That's the quote I'm looking for," said the reporter.

The sendoff at the Iowa City depot the morning before had caught the Hawkeyes by surprise. But they were completely unprepared for what was occurring now. As the train slowly pulled to a stop in Iowa City, a noise outside the train grew louder and louder. The players and coaches looked out their windows. Over two thousand people had gathered for the welcoming. They stepped off the train to the accompaniment of the band. There were no speeches this time. It was an impromptu gathering that was organized after some band members looked into the Rock Island Rocket's arrival time. News of the event spread quickly.

Al Couppee became teary-eyed when he turned away from the window and saw his suitcase. Not too long ago he packed everything he owned into that suitcase and headed to Iowa City, not knowing what the future held. He thought about his parents struggling in Council Bluffs. He hoped they had listened to the game on the radio.

Ten convertibles lined the street next to the depot. The players hopped in. An unorganized parade ensued through the streets of downtown Iowa City. The parade had no official beginning, or end. It just was. It was an unmitigated display of support for the Ironmen heroes.

Illinois had beaten the powerful Michigan Wolverines. Northwestern had upset the Minnesota Gophers. The Hawkeyes, with a record of four wins and one loss for the season and three wins and one loss in the conference, were tied for the Big Ten lead.

CHAPTER TWENTY-ONE

"I can be there, Dr. Eddie. I'll see you at your office tomorrow at nine o'clock. Good night, Coach." Nile Kinnick hung up the phone and walked back to his bedroom. This weekend's game meant everything to him but it meant even more, he thought, to the coach. Dr. Eddie wanted to meet with Prasse, Enich, Couppee, and Kinnick tomorrow morning.

Nile paused and reflected on the personalities of his teammates. They were natural leaders. Mike Enich was revered by the entire team as a silent leader. Enich, though a person of few words, was one of the most scholarly people Nile had ever met. Everyone on the team implicitly trusted his judgment.

Erv Prasse was the team captain. He was an out-going person, always happy, and intuitively grateful for his good fortune. His attitude was contagious. Everyone enjoyed being around Prass. Erv Prasse enjoyed life more than any person Kinnick had ever known. Maybe it was his upbringing in a hard neighborhood in Chicago before experiencing the ease and openness of life in Iowa City. Equally likely though, Kinnick thought, Prasse knew professional sports awaited him and he was enthralled with the idea. For whatever reason, Prasse was a joyful person celebrating life.

Then Nile's thoughts turned to Couppee. Al Couppee grew up surrounded by poverty. Sports, Kinnick assumed, had been his identity. Athletics offered Couppee recognition as a young teenager that he otherwise would not have experienced growing up in the flat lands on the poorer side of Council Bluffs. Kinnick had a great deal of respect for Couppee. His brashness was endearing to those who knew him well. A night out in Iowa City with Al Couppee was always a memorable event. He knew how to play, both on and off the field. It seemed as if Couppee never studied but Kinnick also knew Couppee had one of the highest scores ever recorded on an aptitude test for incoming freshmen. He had refused a full academic scholarship because, had he accepted it, he wouldn't have been allowed to play football. Couppee, instead, wanted to do what the other footballers did: work a job that the University arranged, spend summers with the guys, and enjoy autumns in Big Ten stadiums. Al Couppee, though an underclassman, was a leader. His humble background kept him grounded while his self-confidence continually grew. Nile Kinnick respected the self-assured style of the Hawkeyes' quarterback. Nile knew he wouldn't want his play caller any other way.

"Good morning, gentlemen. I'm glad you could make it this morning." Dr. Eddie entered his office after his secretary had seated the four players. He walked over behind his over-sized oak desk and sat down, leaning forward, placing his forearms on stacks of reports. Some piles were all football related. Others displayed the University of Iowa Hospital's letterhead. Coach Anderson was still wearing the white hospital jacket from his seven o'clock rounds with the third year residents. "It's a beautiful day. It's a great week for all of us." A broad smile formed on his face. "Eighteen years ago I came to this campus as the captain of Notre Dame. I know you already know the story but I want to tell you how much that one day changed my life.

"Everyone had us picked to win the national championship. We were ranked number one in the country. Every newspaper across the country, every radio station, predicted Knute Rockne leading his team to another title. The 'Four Horsemen' were on that team, though they were underclassmen and not playing yet. There were always two stories circulating. One was Notre Dame being on the verge of another championship year. The other was Knute Rockne. Rockne was larger than life.

"Well, you know how the game turned out. Iowa won. Our lofty goals were shattered in one single afternoon at the old Iowa Field. But that's where the story I want to share with you begins. Right after the game, Coach Rockne took me aside and said, 'let's go for a walk.' So we walked out of the locker room, just the two of us, and walked out into the middle of the football field. Iowa Field, where Iowa played their home games at that time, was on the other side of the river right next to the student union. Everyone had left the football field except for the volunteers cleaning up the litter underneath the bleachers. You could hear the journalists typing in the press box, trying to get their stories finished. And it was a big story, a big upset." Dr Eddie paused for a moment as he searched for the best way to convey the reasons for today's meeting. "I was feeling very frustrated. Coach Rockne looked at me and said, 'I know how you feel Eddie. It's not fun. But sometimes you need to remind yourself that it's only a game.' Then he smiled. I was surprised at how he seemed to have already moved on from the loss.

"Anyway, Coach Rockne said, 'Eddie, you're like a son to me. Football is a great game. It has given me a wonderful life. But I was like you when I was younger. I, too, wanted to be a doctor. The glory and applause eventually fade. Now, in my case as a coach, I do still hear the applause because my profession is still on the sideline. But I will always regret that I didn't pursue medicine. I will always wonder how I could have affected others if I had pursued my dream. I don't want you to have regrets, son. Do what's in your heart. I am always here to help you.'

"Then we walked a little further and Coach Rockne said, 'Today's game is over. Tomorrow we start preparing for next week's game. And you start preparing for your future. Remember, this is only a game.'

"That loss, that talk, is probably what convinced me to pursue medicine. And maybe it made me realize I enjoy the applause, too. And so I couldn't give up football. I thought about that the other day. I thought about Coach Rockne wondering how he would have affected others as a doctor, when in reality, he had such a huge impact on so many of us." Dr. Eddie paused again. "And I want you to know I am always here to help you in any way I can. I feel that way about the entire team. I've never known a group of footballers as determined as this team. I've been pushing all of you hard. I thought it was time to let you know I'm here, outside of football.

"Rockne eventually had his Four Horsemen. And now I've got my Ironmen." Coach Eddie paused as he looked at his players.

Kinnick spoke first. "Thank you, Coach. I think I can speak for the four of us, and for the entire team, in saying that we all appreciate what you have given us. Right now, we are experiencing things we have only dreamt about in our pasts. Before this year, those dreams were slipping away. And now, not only are the dreams back, but they have materialized into something none of us has ever known."

"My aspirations are unfolding as well," Dr. Eddie said. "Now, gentlemen, I want to discuss the other reason I called you here today. The four of you are in charge of practice tomorrow. There won't be any coaches." Four bewildered looks stared back at Coach Anderson. "Prasse, you're in charge of conditioning with the backs, and by conditioning I mean running. Enich, you do the same for the line. Then, Couppee, you're in charge of running some offensive plays after the conditioning to keep everyone in sync with the play calling. And finally, Kinnick, you finish the practice with more running, the backs and line together. Forty-five minutes of conditioning, forty-five minutes of play calling, and then another forty-five minutes of running. I want them running harder at the end of practice than at the beginning. The coaches will be back on Tuesday."

After promising to do their best, the four Ironmen walked out of the building together. Erv Prasse said, "That is either one of the best coaching motivations I've ever seen, or there's something up that we haven't been told. We've got Notre Dame this weekend, and they're putting us in charge of practice?"

"I think it's a way to get us to work harder than we've ever worked," responded Mike Enich. "He's changing the routine. If we continue to do things the same way, we continue to get the same results. This is different. And besides, Mondays are fairly routine, anyway. He just added a new dimension to an otherwise predictable workout."

"He left it up to us," Nile said. "I agree with you, Mike, that he will get a great Monday practice from us. And while we are motivating each other, he can spend the entire practice time strategizing with Coaches Carideo and Harris. This game is big for all three of those Notre Dame alumni."

Couppee added, "Then let's make it the greatest Monday practice we've ever had."

"Did I just hear Coup say we need to make this our best practice? Is this the guy who is always the last to practice and the first to leave?" asked Prasse. "Couppee is proof that Coach Anderson's plan is working."

Besides these four footballers, there were only ten other Hawkeyes that had played regularly. Every other Big Ten team was using at least twice as many players. The Ironmen had been born, and these four were the heart and soul of the Iowa Hawkeye Ironmen. The four stalwarts headed for campus and their classes.

Tuesday afternoon. "Okay, gentlemen, let's work on the defense for awhile." Dr. Eddie didn't need to blow his whistle a second time. Everyone gathered immediately. "Not coincidentally, Notre Dame happens to run out of the Notre Dame box just like us."

Laughter wafted through the team. "And so," Dr. Eddie continued, "we know what they run. We know the key players on their roster, and their tendencies. You are all familiar with Harry Stevenson and Benny Sheridan. Together, they give Notre Dame the equal of one Nile Kinnick at left halfback."

Laughter again broke out as Kinnick shook his head, smiling with his teammates. The Ironmen jeered at the mention of anyone, even if it was two players, equaling Kinnick's ability.

Dr Eddie interrupted the players' lighthearted banter. "When Stevenson is in, they are more likely to pass. Sheridan will most likely mean it's a running play. Bernie Crimmins is an All-American guard and I'm sure some of you will find yourselves looking up at him after a play with the blue sky silhouetting his gold helmet. He delights in putting people on their backs. Bud Kerr is an All-American end and Johnny Kelley anchors the other end of the line. Steve Sitko will come up with some big plays at quarterback. And Milt Piepul will be the hardest running fullback we'll face all year. It'll take two players to bring him down.

"They are good. They're ranked number two in the country. They've been rotating about thirty players every game. But frankly, I think we will match up well. Our size matches up well. Our athleticism is equal to theirs. But they'll keep bringing in fresh bodies. And, I believe, the Ironmen's endurance will prove again that conditioning will overcome numbers." At the mention of 'Ironmen' everyone let out a loud holler. They had seen the nickname in the newspapers and they were proud to have earned it. And Dr. Eddie was equally proud to refer to his 'Ironmen.'

"Coach, look over there." Mike Enich was looking over everyone's heads and past Dr. Eddie. Coach Anderson turned to look in the direction of the locker room. The other coaches and players likewise turned in unison.

Slowly strolling across the cleat-torn grass from all the practices and running drills, an injured Hawkeye was returning. It was the player the Ironmen missed most.

The limping Hawkeye wore his sweat pants, football shoes, and jersey. It had been three weeks since the hernia operation following the Indiana game. He was pale. Because of his mammoth size, the recovery had required a longer than expected stay in the hospital.

Everyone initially waited in silence for their feeble friend's arrival. But then a rousing chant of "Lueb-cke, Lueb-cke, Lueb-cke" grew louder and louder as he approached. The coaches joined in. The players started clapping in unison with their vocal outburst, slowly at first, then more rapidly.

A smile crept over big Hank Luebcke's face, camouflaging the tears welling up in his eyes as he approached his former teammates. Everyone knew he wouldn't be able to play again which made the moment all the more special.

He didn't need to walk the last forty yards because the Ironmen ran to greet him, led by Dr. Eddie.

"Mr. Luebcke, you look like you are dressed for practice," Dr. Eddie said as he shook his player's hand vigorously.

"No, Coach. I just came for the running drills," he answered and paused while the players chuckled. "You don't know how much I wish I could do those running drills. The team is peaking and I just wish I was part of it." His voice broke slightly toward the end of his response.

Dr. Eddie handed him a whistle. "You are part of it. Today, you'll be in charge of the drills. It's good to have you back.

"Now before Mr. Luebcke blows his whistle, we need to work on the defense. These will be no-contact drills. In fact, we're going all week without contact to avoid injuries. So, let's set up with the starting eleven on defense, second string on offense."

The practice became more animated. Luebcke's presence inspired the already high-spirited Ironmen. The nearness of playing the number two team in the country inched closer; anxiety grew stronger. The whole nation would be paying attention to the Hawkeyes and Fighting Irish.

Thirty minutes later Dr. Eddie motioned for the team to gather. "I have just one more thing tonight, men. Everyone take a knee.

"I have a personal motivation for this game, just like our Wisconsin game. This is another coach from the famed 'Four Horsemen.' As you know, Wisconsin's coach was the quarterback for that Notre Dame team. Notre Dame's coach, Elmer Layden, was the fullback. Nothing would be sweeter to me than to not only beat Notre Dame, but to beat another member of the 'Four Horsemen.' Elmer Layden will have his team ready. He always does. But I am confident we will be just as ready, if not more so. It will be a war.

"Okay, Mr. Luebcke, they are all yours."

Luebcke blew his whistle twice. "Okay, men," Luebcke hollered with all his energy, "everyone on the goal line. To the fifty and back on the whistle. Linemen first."

"I have to admit, Al, I'm a little nervous about coming alone, but it will be so wonderful to see you play." Mary Couppee informed her son she was planning on attending the Notre Dame game in three days without her husband. "Everyone is talking about Iowa and Notre Dame. I just read an article in the newspaper at the library about it. Your name was mentioned three times. I'm so proud of you, Al."

For Al Couppee, this was the greatest phone call he had ever received at the Boars' Nest dorm. He missed his family two hundred forty miles away on the other side of the state.

"Since the train doesn't arrive until noon, Mom, I won't be able to see you before the game. The game starts at two. But I'll meet you afterwards outside our locker room. Just ask someone and they can tell you where it is, okay?"

"I'll find it, Al," she said. "I won't be able to stay very long after the game, but it will be so nice to see what I listen to on the radio every Saturday and, especially, to see you."

Al knew a hotel room was too costly for his parents, but he was pleased she would finally see him play. "It will be great to see you, too, Mom. Tell everybody hello. I'll see you after the game. And remember, just give them your name at the 'will call' window on the west side of the stadium. The train stops right by the west side. I'll have a ticket waiting for you. I love you."

Al Couppee walked back to the Boars' Nest thinking about the upcoming weekend. It was the most important game of his life. He would be on the playing field taking on a team ranked second in the nation. Every newspaper's sports section was talking about the Iowa Hawkeyes resurgence, and Nile Kinnick as a possible Heisman Trophy candidate along with Tom Harmon of Michigan. Kinnick was ranked fourth in the nation in running, Harmon sixth. His thoughts shifted to Coach Anderson. Dr. Eddie had turned the program around in one year and was now facing his alma mater. But the biggest story was the Ironmen. The name had stuck.

Couppee had heard yesterday that several journalists were unable to secure seats in the press box, so their only alternative was to spend two dollars for a ticket. And he had also heard scalpers might be asking as much as ten dollars for a ticket. Luckily, he had gotten his mother a ticket through the athletic office. Fifty-three thousand people would fill the stadium on Saturday, the first sellout since it was built ten years ago, but only one fan mattered to Al Couppee.

Nile Kinnick was talking to Red Frye and Chuck Tollefson when Al Couppee entered his room. It seemed odd to see

Kinnick at the Boars' Nest, Couppee thought. Here was the grandson of a former Iowa governor sitting in the makeshift dorm room. "My mom's coming to the game Saturday. She never even saw me play a high school game!" Couppee still couldn't quite believe she was coming.

"That's hard to believe," said Tollefson. "But if this is the first one, she sure picked the right one to see. This game is already making me toss and turn all night. I used to sleep better in boxcars."

"Just don't injure your foot again with that tossing and turning," Kinnick joked. "We finally got you back and ready to play." Kinnick then turned to Couppee. "Al, how are your parents doing?"

"They're still struggling," Couppee said. "Dad is working any job that pops up: ice cream parlor, delivering feed and seed to farmers. It just doesn't seem to get any better for them."

Kinnick sensed his pain. "Something will change, Al. It might not happen as quickly as you want, but something will change." Couppee nodded in hopeful agreement.

"I'm going to The Academy for a snack before I head home," Kinnick said. "Any of you want to join me?"

Red Frye, Chuck Tollefson, Al Couppee, and Nile Kinnick strode down the hill to the Iowa River, and across the bridge. They passed the Old Capitol on their way to the adjacent downtown. Already university custodians were preparing a stage for the Friday night pep rally at the top of the outdoor stairway leading to the Old Capitol. The enormity of the event was creeping into their psyches.

It was a long walk for a snack, but it wasn't about food. It was four guys spending time together, laughing, joking, and kidding each other. Four of the thirty-one Ironmen were releasing anxious energy before the weekend battle, a fight they knew would be the toughest and most scrutinized of their lives. These were the moments important to a team, moments when they were out of the public's view, far away from the football field. Camaraderie was an unseen virtue important to this team's chemistry. Dr. Eddie had charged Kinnick, Prasse, Couppee, and Enich with being the glue of this solidarity. The bond was strong. This cohesive unit drew strength from each other. Several other Hawkeyes would probably be at The Academy tonight for one reason only, to be together. It didn't matter that they only numbered thirty-one, or that only half that number would play in the game. The Ironmen were proud of their small alliance. Victory against Notre Dame was a long shot, but the remote possibility existed. Every game they had played, so far, further reinforced a belief in their physical superiority. They knew it was Dr. Eddie's conditioning drills.

Kinnick entered The Academy behind the other three. He quickly spotted Barbara Miller and Mary Stellman. They were seated together at a booth along the outside wall. Barbara and Nile smiled, acknowledging each other's presence. He walked towards them.

"Hi, Barbara. Hi, Mary. Prasse told me you might be here tonight. May I join you for a little bit?"

"Please," said Barbara, sliding her french fries and root beer towards the wall, and then herself, giving Nile room to sit next to her.

Erv Prasse soon joined them, walking out from the billiards room. The four spoke briefly before Kinnick and Prasse excused themselves, saying they needed to join the guys in the back. But before they left Barbara and Mary, the four made plans to get together Saturday night after the game.

As the two walked back to the billiards tables, Prasse put his arm across Kinnick's back, resting his hand on Kinnick's far shoulder. "Nile, I've got a feeling about this game."

"What's that, Prass?"

"I think we've got a good shot. And if we do, it might be the greatest moment we ever experience."

Kinnick smiled. "Dr. Eddie had November 11th circled on his calendar last February. I would venture to guess all the conditioning we've done has been aimed, in no small way, towards this one game."

"How do you feel about the game?" Prasse asked.

"I feel like I've been waiting my entire life for this moment. It's as if every other game I've ever played was just an opening act leading up to Notre Dame. The stadium will be packed. The entire country will be focused on this David and Goliath story. It's remarkable.

"I remember looking at this year's schedule a year ago and wondering what it would be like to play Notre Dame. And honestly, my thoughts weren't real pleasant. But now, I think we've got a chance. Those fifty-three thousand voices will get our adrenalin flowing."

The two walked into the back room of The Academy. Several footballers stood around the billiards table, finding comfort in spending these hours together. The apprehension was much more tolerable here than in their dorm rooms, fraternity rooms, or apartments. Prasse stood at the end of the pool table. "Okay guys, I do have one item to discuss tonight. I've been informed that the student council has asked that we show up for the pep rally Friday night.

"I asked Dr. Eddie about it and he reminded me that we would all be 'sequestered' in the same wing at the hospital Friday night. He doesn't want us walking around campus Friday night and tiring our legs. But he did say I should represent the team as captain and take one other player."

Immediately everyone boisterously shouted together, "Kinnick!"

"And since you have all voiced your opinions so eloquently, Nile, you have been chosen to speak at the rally."

Then a rousing "Kin-nick, Kin-nick" floated through the air.

Nile smiled and nodded in acceptance. In fact, he looked forward to it. His childhood lessons from his parents and grandparents left an indelible mark: speak whenever someone asks.

The group disbanded. It was ten o'clock. With the most important game of their lives fast approaching, sleep was paramount. Dr. Eddie had again mentioned to them that sleeping would be difficult on Friday night, so it was important to sleep well during the week. This weekend, they would be the center of the sports world, thrust into the limelight against the Notre Dame Fighting Irish.

The fraternity brothers were talking and speculating about the upcoming game when Nile got back to the house. He joined his friends for an hour before retiring to his room. He hadn't written his youngest brother, George, for a long time. Now would be a good time. Writing brought a sense of calm, organizing his thoughts and deliberately choosing the words to express a point of view; his mind slowed.

> *Dear George,*
> *This year is so different from any I have ever experienced.*
> *The enthusiasm of the season could cause one to get caught up in the hype, if not careful. But Mother and Father have taught us well. With all the excitement, my mind keeps projecting forward and wondering what it all means or where it all leads. The accolades are nice, but they are fleeting.*
> *It's far more important to strive for self-improvement, rather than self-importance. Tell Mother and Father I shall keep my eyes on what is truly important: to be the best person I can possibly be, hopefully affecting*

others positively through my words and actions. Rightful thinking will persist.

Speaking of words, I hope you are making good use of the Sunday night speeches. I now look back on those moments and realize their impact. They were preparing us to be leaders and good citizens, able to express our thoughts and feelings. I'm sure you are learning the virtues of speaking and writing, even now in eighth grade. So keep writing and speaking, my young brother. I shall try to set the bar high for Ben and you, so you can both someday raise it.

I must close now. I need to spend some time planning what I shall say to a pep rally Friday night.

George, I'm very proud of the accomplishments Mother and Father have told me about you.

They are extremely proud of you.

I am proud to call you my brother.

Please write soon.

Love,

Nile

Friday night. Erv Prasse and Nile Kinnick left the training table to join the pep rally at the Old Capitol.

"I can't believe the weekend is already here," exclaimed Prasse. "The days roll by when the tension is high." He paused. "Look at that!"

Nile stared in disbelief as his teammate spoke. The sight was unbelievable. They continued walking, but neither spoke. They were stunned by the spectacle.

As they drew nearer to the rally on the other side of the Iowa River, people were chanting, yelling, and cheering as loudly as any football game crowd. Stretching from Madison Street all the way up the lawn to the final steps of the Old Capitol, students, fans, and faculty were standing alongside each other. Some held signs above their heads proclaiming "Kinnick for President." Other signs hailed the Ironmen, or declared the Hawkeyes toppling the Irish. Over ten thousand rabid Hawkeye followers were showing their support for their Iowa Hawkeyes.

Prasse and Kinnick stopped and watched in astonishment. At the top of the massive lawn, they could hear the band playing as the cheerleaders led the raucous crowd. A podium stood on the top step in front of the Old Capitol, the symbol of the University.

Prasse and Kinnick were spotted in their letter jackets as they started to walk through the rear of the crowd. An approving roar rippled from the participants, out fifty yards to either side of the footballers and forward one hundred yards to the podium. The crowd parted as the two walked side by side. Everyone turned to watch. Nothing had prepared Kinnick or Prasse for this unbridled adulation. For a brief moment, Kinnick sensed the feeling of being a politician - seeing these people assembled, waiting for a speaker to deliver motivational words.

Off to the side, away from the frenzied participants, two parents stood holding hands. They had traveled from Omaha a day early to make sure car problems or flat tires didn't prevent them from seeing the greatest game they would ever watch. Their two other sons, Ben and George Kinnick, stood by them in amazement. They had seen stadium crowds cheering for their older brother, but they had never witnessed him walking through a swarm of admirers like this. Nile Sr. and Frances were spellbound, too, watching their eldest son walk through the bystanders.

T. Lidd

After many handshakes, waves, and smiles, Prasse and Kinnick made their way to the steps leading to the podium. The crowd was overjoyed. President Gilmore knew what the euphoric crowd wanted. He motioned to Prasse and Kinnick that the microphone was theirs. Prasse looked at Kinnick. Nile politely swept his arm toward the podium, gesturing that Prasse could speak first.

> *Thank you. Thank you very much. This is truly overwhelming. Coach Anderson would only allow two of us to join the pep rally tonight.*

Good-hearted boos interrupted Erv Prasse from continuing. They were hoping for the whole team.

> *But if Coach Anderson knew how difficult it would be to walk through the crowd, he would certainly have sent some linemen to block for us and create a bigger lane.*

Again he was interrupted, but this time by laughter and cheers. He turned and looked at Nile who was laughing and nodding in agreement.

> *I just hope Notre Dame's defense is easier to run through than all of you.*

Erv Prasse told the crowd that Nile and he would be joining the rest of the team shortly, and would definitely share with them the enthusiasm and passion they had encountered tonight. He closed by again thanking the fans for all their support.

Applause broke out, then slowly changed to a chant. "Kin-nick, Kin-nick, Kin-nick!" Nile stepped to the microphone. About forty feet from the front row he noticed Barbara Miller and waved to her. "Kin-nick, Kin-nick, Kin-nick!" continued. Slowly the noise faded.

> *It is so incredible to see so many here tonight. The entire team has been amazed by the support you have given us this season. And I can assure you, your participation on Saturday afternoons brings out that extra effort in us that is crucial to victory. So thank you, the entire team thanks you, for being that twelfth Ironman on the field.*

The crowd was overjoyed at being considered part of the Ironmen. Nile waited for the noise to subside before continuing.

> *As we walk around campus, along the city streets, in the stores, or movie theaters, many people have approached us and asked if we can beat Notre Dame.*

The crowd again cheered, anticipating what Kinnick would say next.

> *And the answer is, 'Yes!'*

To Kinnick, the flailing arms above thousands of heads resembled a field of corn waving in the wind just before harvest, only the sounds of this field were much louder than the gentle noise of wind rustling across a sea of corn stalks.

Coach Anderson always has a game plan for the next opponent. We always feel we are better prepared than our competition. We know our competition's strengths and weaknesses when we step on the gridiron and that gives us an edge in the many, various game situations that occur. But more than anything else, Coach Anderson has consciously instilled a positive anticipation in all of us. We expect to win.

Again he was interrupted by the group's response echoing off the Old Capitol, serving as a backdrop with floodlights illuminating the stately limestone structure.

He has taught us that extraordinary dreams can turn into extraordinary results. This Saturday, you will see two teams battle for sixty minutes. And I guarantee, you will witness the greatest effort the Ironmen can give until the final second of the final quarter.

Nile again paused for the applause to quiet, remembering their last reaction when he mentioned the 'twelfth' Ironman.

I hope all of you are there Saturday afternoon as the twelfth Ironman. Thank you.

Erv Prasse and Nile Kinnick stood side by side as the Iowa Marching Band played. As Nile looked out over the crowd, he leaned towards Prasse. "I wish the whole team could share this moment."

Prasse replied, "They aren't going to believe it."

After President Gilmore's concluding remarks, the President turned to the two footballers. "If you follow me, I'll give you a ride back to the hospital. I don't think you want to try walking back through the crowd."

Minutes later, the band could still be heard from President Gilmore's car as they drove down Burlington Street to avoid the congestion. Nile watched the rally from a distance as they drove across the river. He remembered his decision to attend Iowa was for an opportunity to play a role in a program's rise to prominence. His father had talked to him about the value of this sort of personal gratification, as opposed to being a member of a well oiled machine like the Minnesota Gophers.

He had made the right decision.

CHAPTER TWENTY-TWO

"One final comment before we head to the stadium." Dr. Eddie was finishing his pre-game talk. It was twelve o'clock, noon; kickoff was in two hours. He knew his players didn't need to be reminded of the magnitude of the situation. The moment was here. "I can't express how excited I am about this day. It's simply unbelievable. To not only have the opportunity to play Notre Dame, but to have had the season that we have experienced leading to this game, goes beyond description. This is a moment waiting to be seized." He paced as he spoke. "Five hours from now we will know the outcome. And I know in my heart that you will not lose! You won't let that happen. The celebration at the end of the game will be on our side of the field. The headlines tomorrow will read, 'Notre Dame loses to the Ironmen.' Now go out there and play this game the way you know - with precision!" Dr. Eddie was very convincing to his Hawkeyes, but personally, he had his doubts. It was, after all, Notre Dame in the visitors' locker room.

Notre Dame's uniforms resembled the Hawkeyes' attire. The gold helmets were similar. The Fighting Irish's navy blue jerseys were only a shade different from the Hawkeyes' black jerseys. The primary distinction was Notre Dame's gold pants compared to Iowa's white.

The teams completed their warm-up drills. They were finally - after all the preparations by the players and coaches, and countless newspaper articles written from coast to coast - awaiting the kickoff.

The clock started as Prasse caught the ball at the five yard line. The sellout crowd boisterously cheered, some for the visiting team. They were primed to enhance the efforts on the field with their own display of energy. For one brief moment, nothing else mattered at this remote location in middle America on a cool November afternoon. Many wore gloves, which made a deep base echo when hands were clapped together, a noise that accompanied the higher pitched sounds of constant voices yelling in unison. Everyone's attention was on the twenty-two soldiers doing battle before them.

Neither offense could generate a drive. The Hawkeyes, like the Irish, ran the famed Notre Dame box alignment that Dr. Eddie had brought with him to Iowa. Each team was stellar on defense, knowing the other's offense by heart.

An exchange of punts floated from end to end. Harry Stevenson was Notre Dame's version of Nile Kinnick. He played left halfback for the Fighting Irish, and he shifted behind the center when it was his turn to punt. High arching punts continually rose above the field before floating downward. Neither team had experienced a punting exhibition like this one, between Kinnick and Stevenson. Good field position eluded both squads.

Notre Dame focused on Kinnick. He was swarmed by the Irish each time he touched the ball. An occasional pass to Prasse - or a short run by Kinnick, Murphy, or McLain - garnered little yardage.

The teams had several players going head to head on every play no matter which team had the ball. Bud Kerr was an All-American end battling Erv Prasse on every down. All-

American Bernie Crimmins fought against Wally Bergstrom and Chuck Tollefson. Milt Piepul, Notre Dame's All-American fullback, often felt the brute force of Mike Enich. Neither the Hawkeyes nor the Irish gave ground.

Iowa made its first substitution ten minutes into the second quarter. Buzz Dean entered the game in place of Ed McLain. Dr. Eddie wanted to send in a play, even if Dean had to wait one play before passing the information to Couppee.

Al Couppee called for a shift right into the Notre Dame box. The ball was centered directly to Kinnick. He ran to his right and then cut back behind the blocking scheme. Milt Piepul and Johnny Kelley, the Irish captain, flung Kinnick to the ground.

"Let's huddle," yelled Al Couppee, looking at Buzz Dean. "Buzz, what's the call?"

"Coach wants a quick punt," Dean said.

Couppee took over. From the T-formation, he called for the shift. Only this time, the numerals hollered by the quarterback signaled everyone to block for two seconds and then break downfield to cover the punt. As they shifted right, Kinnick was again behind the center, but instead of his usual four yards off the line of scrimmage, he was eight yards back. The Irish weren't anticipating the Hawkeyes' second play. Kinnick's foot struck the ball as it descended from his hands. The ball sailed high over all eleven Notre Dame players. Fifty-two yards later, Erv Prasse downed the ball at the Notre Dame eighteen yard line. Finally, the Hawkeyes had an advantage.

On first down, Milt Piepul ran straight up the middle, only to again be shoved to the ground by Mike Enich who pursued the runner from his tackle position.

Second down. Prasse yelled to the defensive backs and safety. "Stevenson is at left halfback! Watch for the pass!"

It was a good observation by Prasse. Stevenson shifted into position, took the snap and started pedaling backwards. Tollefson, Andruska, and Enich swarmed in. Just in time to avoid being sacked, Stevenson fired a pass in the direction of Bud Kerr. Kinnick was waiting. Nile darted in front of the receiver, intercepted the pass, and raced towards the Notre Dame end zone with the ball tucked tightly under his right arm. He avoided two tacklers before Sitko grabbed his lower legs.

The crowd became ecstatic after the play that seemingly broke the defensive stalemate. It was Iowa's ball on the Irish thirty-five yard line. Everyone was standing. For the first time, one of the teams had penetrated into scoring territory.

Elmer Layden was furious on the Notre Dame sideline. He immediately sent seven fresh players into the game to join Steve Sitko and his three All-Americans.

Couppee belted out the signals. Kinnick stepped back to pass. Erv Prasse was at full speed, slanting from his left end position towards the right corner of the end zone. This time, Steve Sitko executed the perfect defensive play. Running stride for stride with Prasse, Sitko turned at the last second to look over his shoulder just in time to react. He reached out and intercepted the pass at the goal line. Harry Stevenson had been exchanging punts with Kinnick the entire first half; now Sitko was trading interceptions with him, too. Sitko changed direction and started running out of the end zone. Bruno Andruska hit Sitko with all his might at the six yard line. Then, another break befell the Ironmen. Sitko, while trying to escape Andruska's grip, made one of the biggest mistakes of his football career. He tried to lateral the ball to a teammate, but there was no navy blue jersey behind him. Andruska rolled towards the bouncing ball. Dick Evans and Mike Enich were also chasing after the loose ball. It was unclear which of the three Hawkeyes landed on the ball, but it didn't matter. The referee pointed in the direction Iowa was headed, signaling a first down for Iowa on Notre Dame's four yard line. None of the Hawkeye fans were sitting. None were quiet.

Al Couppee tried to restore order to the Ironmen. The excitement camouflaged their fatigued bodies as a surge of adrenalin swept through all eleven. Then, Couppee flashed back to the Purdue game. He again remembered the handshake he was forced to give Kinnick at halftime. Dr. Eddie's point was well made that day, and not forgotten. There was only one person to carry the ball to the goal line.

From the T-formation Couppee called Iowa's best play, thirty-one right. Kinnick took the snap and started right. He was behind Enich when he cut back behind the blockers in front of him. Notre Dame wasn't fooled as they matched the strength of the Ironmen. Kinnick fell under the weight of two Irish linemen. The line of scrimmage remained the same.

Second down and four yards remained for the score. Again the Hawkeyes ran thirty-one right, counting on sheer football performance to create that one seam, that one narrow path for Kinnick to follow. Again, Notre Dame responded. Only one yard was gained. The Hawkeyes were faced with the three most difficult yards of the season.

Sitting in the thirty-eighth row at the forty-five yard line of the west bleachers, a petite, gray-haired woman watched her first football game. She didn't understand exactly what was taking place, but it was an electric environment she had never felt listening on the radio. A gentleman two seats to her right hollered loudly, "Call the same play again, Couppee!"

She asked the woman sitting next to her, "What is Al Couppee's number?" The woman barely heard her frail voice over the surrounding noise.

"I don't know. I'll ask my husband," she said, and then leaned towards him. "Dear, what is Al Couppee's number?"

"Number thirty," he hollered with a smile, turning to look at the inquiring woman.

His wife then asked, "Are you here alone?"

"Yes," shouted the petite, gray-haired lady so she could be heard over the thunderous noise. "I came to watch my son, number thirty."

"Huddle!" shouted Couppee. "They're stuffing us on thirty-one right! Dean, you switch places with Kinnick at left half. Nile, you're at right half. We're running thirty-one left!"

"I don't know, Coup. Let's not do something we haven't practiced. I can run the play from the right," said Buzz Dean.

"No! We're running it as I call it! Kinnick is carrying it and we've got to go left!" Couppee didn't have time to reconsider his play call. Also, he didn't want to be yelled at again by the coach at halftime. "The huddle is not a place for conversation! Got it? Kinnick at right half. Thirty-one left! When we break the huddle, everyone run to their spot. We're hiking on the first count."

The Hawkeyes turned and ran to the line of scrimmage. There was no shift since they were going on 'hike.' Andruska centered the ball perfectly to Kinnick. Prasse took two steps forward and shoved the linebacker towards the left sideline. Wally Bergstrom pushed the right tackle back. Ken Pettit made the greatest block of his life turning the All-American guard, Bernie Crimmins, to the inside. Nile Kinnick did the rest.

Milt Piepul, the best of Notre Dame's All-Americans, playing middle linebacker when on defense, slid over and collided with Kinnick at the two yard line. Kinnick lowered his right shoulder, hitting Piepul with the most force he had ever hit anyone in his life. Too much mattered on this one single play. Piepul rocked back onto his heels as Kinnick pressed forward, dragging the beaten All-American those two precious yards. Still embracing the ball in his left arm, Kinnick fell to the ground in the end zone. The fans cheered louder than they ever had in Iowa Stadium; their exalted Ironmen had finally reached the end zone. The game clock stopped. For a moment, time also stood still in this new mecca of college football. The live radio broadcasts informed the country of what just happened in Iowa City.

The extra point was crucial in this low scoring game. Kinnick took his position behind Bruno Andruska. Andruska snapped the ball to Kinnick. The hike was high and to Kinnick's right. Kinnick slid to his right and grabbed the ball above his shoulder. Carefully, and quickly, Kinnick dropped the ball to the ground in front of him as he took one step forward with his left foot. He swung his right leg forward, timing the movement perfectly so his foot made contact just as the ball touched the ground. The football soared into the air and past the goalpost. Radio announcers, unfamiliar with Iowa, were astonished to see a drop kick. Iowa 7, Notre Dame 0.

Duke Slater had driven from Chicago for the game. It had been ten years since the Chicago municipal judge had been back to Iowa City. After speaking to the Hawkeyes earlier in the season, he wanted to see this showdown in person. After all, he was Iowa's first black All-American who had played in the famous 1921 game between these two teams. Judge Slater's Hawkeyes beat Knute Rockne's team that day, a Notre Dame team led by captain Eddie Anderson. A tear rolled down Duke Slater's cheek while remembering that afternoon eighteen years ago.

Dutch Reagan, a former Hawkeye broadcaster on WHO radio in Des Moines, was standing next to Judge Slater in the stands, a result of complimentary tickets both had received from Dr. Eddie. Dutch had flown in from Los Angeles. Just like Slater, but for different reasons, Dutch Reagan didn't want to miss this epic battle.

In row thirty-eight, number thirty's mom was meeting jubilant strangers.

"Mrs. Couppee, my name is Fred. This is my wife, Alice. Hey, everybody, this is Al Couppee's mother."

From behind Mary Couppee, another Hawkeye fan introduced himself. Then another person, and another, and another.

Two plays after the Hawkeyes' kickoff, the first half ended. Both teams jogged off the field to their respective locker rooms. The deafening crowd roared their approval for the toughness of these Ironmen. The dream season's plot was becoming more dramatic.

"We can beat this team!" shouted Mike Enich to the players in the locker room. "We've just got to do it again for another thirty minutes!"

"Then let's do it! This is our stadium! That's our crowd out there! Come on, Ironmen!" exclaimed Chuck Tollefson. Kinnick looked at Tollefson and felt a warmth overcome him. Kinnick couldn't help but reflect on the contrast of this moment with Tollie's former life.

Pettit shouted, "Way to punt, Kinnick! We can play defense if that's what this game is all about, and just let Kinnick keep punting deep!"

Kinnick and Couppee sat next to each other. Kinnick sipped on a Seven-Up while Couppee poured sugar into his coffee. The group quieted as Dr. Eddie walked in with coaches Carideo and Harris.

"Who called the shift of Nile to right half?" Coach Anderson's voice made it clear he wanted to know the answer immediately.

The eleven players in the huddle before the touchdown were silent, except one. "I called the switch, Coach," said Al Couppee, not knowing what to expect, but proud that his decision gave the Hawkeyes the lead.

Dr. Eddie walked over and stood in front of Couppee. "That was the smartest thing I've ever had a player do." Couppee gave a sigh of relief.

Dr. Eddie stepped to the middle of the room so everyone could hear. "Every team in the country would like to be seven points ahead of Notre Dame at halftime. It doesn't happen often.

"This game is within your grasp. How badly do you want it? Are you satisfied with just being a part of this game, or leading at halftime? Right now, gentlemen, right here! This game goes beyond today."

Only fifteen Ironmen played the first half, the same fourteen that played at Purdue, plus Tollefson. Eight players never came out of the game during the first half and most likely would remain on the field for the rest of the game. Ken Pettit, Bruno Andruska, Wally Bergstrom, Mike Enich, Erv Prasse, Dick Evans, Al Couppee, and Nile Kinnick, along with Chuck Tollefson, continued earning their nickname.

When the teams came out of the locker rooms for the second half, Notre Dame had made an alteration everyone noticed immediately. A buzz was heard throughout the stadium as fans voiced their opinions, many laughing amongst themselves. Maybe it was to change the contrast of their uniforms, which had resembled the Hawkeyes' black and gold. Maybe it was a psychological ploy used by Notre Dame's coach to rally his troops and make them feel new and refreshed, taking on a new direction for the next two quarters. Maybe it was to call on the luck of the Irish. Whatever the reason, Elmer Layden had the entire team change jerseys. No longer were they wearing navy blue. They now wore shamrock green jerseys that projected an entirely new visual of a different team coming to battle the second half.

The game continued with the same ferocity as before. Mike Enich continued his relentless pursuit of the ball carriers.

He was in the Notre Dame backfield creating havoc play after play. Sometimes it seemed there were no Irish linemen blocking him. Prasse and Kinnick both made touchdown saving tackles to protect the slim lead.

Notre Dame's defense was equal to the challenge. The Irish and the Hawkeyes constantly thwarted any advances by their adversary. Both defenses played with an unparalleled passion neither club had exhibited in prior games.

The battle continued. Elmer Layden and Eddie Anderson kept the offenses very plain, waiting for that one mistake by the opponent. Sitko's fumble that lead to Iowa's touchdown was the only mistake by either team thus far. The punting duel continued while Notre Dame kept sending in fresh substitutions.

Late in the third quarter, Notre Dame fielded another Kinnick punt on the twelve yard line and returned it to their twenty-five. Bernie Sheridan and Milt Piepul took turns on two consecutive running plays. Piepul ran for twelve yards; Sheridan took the next play another nine. A pass from Sitko to Johnny Kelley covered twenty-three yards. Notre Dame had moved the ball to Iowa's thirty-one yard line on three plays.

Piepul ran again for five yards and a second time for seven more. It was first down and ten at Iowa's nineteen.

"Timeout, ref," shouted Kinnick. He felt his teammates needed a moment to gather themselves. After fighting so valiantly all afternoon, the Ironmen suddenly resembled a losing boxer taking an eight count in the final round. The trainers brought a bucket of water and some cups out to the huddle. But the temporary effect of the quick refreshment paled in comparison to the rested legs of their challengers. Notre Dame's confidence was growing as the Hawkeyes' weakened.

"Just keep doing what we are doing, guys," said Kinnick. "They just had a few nice plays. Battle back! We need one good play to stop this drive! I think they'll keep running the ball."

Kinnick was right. They kept the ball on the ground. But three plays later it was first and goal from the six yard line. Again Notre Dame shifted. It looked like Sheridan was headed for the lane between their right tackle and end. But he handed off to Piepul who ran straight up the middle of the field. Touchdown. A collective sigh deflated the crowd's hopes as the lucky green jerseys thrust their arms upward, finally able to celebrate. Iowa 7, Notre Dame 6. Notre Dame needed the extra point.

Couppee heard Dr. Eddie yelling for a timeout. Couppee ran to the closest black and white striped shirt. "Timeout, ref!"

The Hawkeyes huddled again while Prasse ran to the sideline to get Dr. Eddie's play call.

Prasse quickly sprinted back to the place no defense wants to huddle, their own end zone. "Dr. Eddie thinks they'll probably go for the extra point kick, but he wants us to watch for the two point conversion. They've lined up in kicking formation twice this year and, instead of kicking, the holder takes the snap and goes up the middle. So, Tollefson, Enich, and linebackers, watch for the run. That means Evans and I are rushing hard from the outside."

The referee placed the ball on the three yard line. The players took their respective positions on the line of scrimmage. Sheridan dropped to his left knee seven yards behind the center and pointed to the spot on the ground where he would place the ball for Lou Zontini, Notre Dame's placekicker. Zontoni stood three yards behind Sheridan, looking at the goalpost, lining up his kick. The Hawkeyes were ready. If it was a run, they wouldn't be fooled by Notre Dame's acting.

Coach Elmer Layden was concerned that if they tried for the two point conversion and failed, the already frenzied crowd would give Iowa the momentum. He chose, instead, to go for the easier one point kick and the 7-7 tie. Sheridan took the snap, placed the ball on the turf, and Zontoni started forward for the kick.

Erv Prasse, from the left side of the line, and Dick Evans, from the right side, headed for Sheridan. The kick barely missed Prasse's hands and sailed towards the goalpost's left upright. The crowd was silent awaiting the referee's signal. Arms outstretched above the referee's head meant a tie ball game. Arms waving back and forth meant the Ironmen were still ahead.

The fans behind the goalpost didn't need to wait for the referee's signal. Their view allowed them to watch the angle of the kick as the ball drifted wide. The end zone fans started the celebration that immediately rippled and swelled to the grandstands on both sides of the field. The Ironmen maintained their one point lead over the Fighting Irish, 7-6.

After the Notre Dame kickoff, the clock again reached zero, ending the third quarter. Players rushed to their respective sidelines for Elmer Layden's and Eddie Anderson's final strategies.

One quarter remained for the Hawkeyes, Dr. Eddie, Mary Couppee, Nile Sr. and Frances Kinnick, Duke Slater, Dutch Reagan, and all the Ironmen fans. The possibility of a magical moment grew closer. The wind would be at the Hawkeyes' backs, and, more importantly, behind Kinnick's punts if the game continued as a defensive struggle.

"Nothing fancy, Couppee. We are leading. Simple plays. Simple handoffs. No mistakes." Dr. Eddie knew one mental mistake could cost everyone their dreams. Only fifteen minutes remained in the game. "Clock management, and then pray Kinnick keeps booting it deep."

"Got it," was all Couppee needed to reply.

His coach nodded. "Nile, we'll call some plays to give you the option to run or pass, but unless a receiver is wide open,

I want you to run it. Couppee, don't call the option until we get to mid-field."

The fourth quarter emotions triggered an unforeseen vitality in the eleven Hawkeyes. Adrenalin took over. A new strength emerged. Minds became more focused on the tasks at hand. The Ironmen had a chance to upset the Fighting Irish.

Both coaches played their cards close to the vest, taking no chances while waiting for that one single mistake by the opponent. Kinnick punted after three offensive tries. Then it was Stevenson's turn to punt after the Ironmen's defensive spirit again matched the freshness of the Notre Dame players.

The clock continued. With each passing minute, the crowd grew more anxious with Iowa's narrow lead. Kinnick punted again.

On Notre Dame's first play from scrimmage, Milton Piepul ran into Tollefson after a one yard gain. Then Stevenson faded back on second down, looking for Johnny Kelley on a deep pass pattern. Kinnick saw the play unfold and raced step for step with Kelley before knocking down the pass.

Third down. Stevenson attempted a pass to Zontoni coming out of the backfield. Again, Kinnick anticipated it perfectly and slapped the ball to the turf. The crowd's roar was deafening as the teams regrouped.

Quickly, it became fourth down and nine yards to go with six minutes remaining. The line of scrimmage was at the Notre Dame thirty-three yard line. The Irish were forced to punt once more or risk giving the ball back to Iowa if they came up short of the needed yardage. Stevenson again kicked a high spiraling punt fielded by Kinnick at Iowa's twenty. Nile eluded one tackler before being brought down on the twenty-four yard line.

The Hawkeyes exploited their rarely used huddle. Mike Enich had been animated all afternoon, playing the game of his life with reckless abandon. "Come on guys! We just need two first downs to run out the clock! This is it!"

Kinnick interjected, "Enich's right! Smart football! Key blocks! We don't need great plays right now, just good ones! Just do what we practice day after day!"

"I'm not calling your number, Nile," said Couppee. "They will be keying on you like never before. I'm going with Murphy up the middle and then Dean wide. No passes now! We've got to keep it on the ground and eat up the clock!"

Murphy gained two yards to the twenty-six. Next, Couppee belted out the thirty-one left for Buzz Dean, the same play Kinnick had scored on from Dean's right halfback position. Dean was smothered by the two All-Americans, Bernie Crimmins and Budd Kerr, for no gain.

Iowa was faced with a third down and eight from their own twenty-six yard line. "Huddle," hollered Couppee. "Same play. And if we don't get it, Nile's punting."

Again Buzz Dean followed the blocking of Bergstrom and Pettit. He gallantly fought his way to the thirty-one yard line, three yards short of the first down.

Notre Dame used one of their two remaining timeouts.

In that brief span while the players collected their thoughts, the decibel level intensified. Nile looked around at the standing crowd. This game, he thought, meant as much to the people in the stands as it did to those on this coliseum stage. He sensed the fans trying to will the Hawkeyes to the unexpected finish. Less than three minutes remained.

The teams took their positions for what would be Kinnick's sixteenth punt of the game. Andruska hiked the ball. Kinnick, standing on his own twenty-three yard line, caught the ball and began his forward movement. The linemen held their blocks for a count of three. Kinnick released the ball softly from his hands before launching it one last time with all his might. The other ten Hawkeyes started racing down the field toward the Notre Dame punt returner, but this time, they didn't need to converge on the ball carrier.

This kick was unlike Kinnick's previous fifteen punts. This one sailed higher and farther. As it crossed the fifty yard line, it had not yet reached its apex. It kept floating. The ball started its descent but continued traveling downfield.

Steve Sitko, standing on his own twenty-five, turned and started sprinting back as the ball soared over his head. It landed on the ten yard line. Sitko tore his helmet off in disgust and flung it to the ground. He knew Kinnick had all but ended the game with this last, majestic punt. It would take a miracle, clock management, and a great play if the mighty Notre Dame Fighting Irish were to have a chance to score again.

The ball bounced left and hopped three times before crossing the sideline markers at Notre Dame's six yard line. A sixty-three yard punt. No one, not even Nile Kinnick or Coach Carideo, would have ever guessed a punt would seal Notre Dame's fate. Triumph began to unfold on the field, in the stands, on the Iowa sideline, in the press box, in front of radios in thousands of living rooms throughout the nation, in a living room in Council Bluffs, Iowa, and in the thirty-eighth row on the forty-five yard line of the west grandstand. Mary Couppee cried joyously as she watched her son display unadulterated emotion she had never before seen from him. But she also cried for all the moments she had missed in her son's life for so many years. Nile Kinnick Sr. hugged Frances Kinnick.

"Nile, where did that one come from?" exclaimed Prasse, joking about the distance of the punt. "Have you been saving that one?"

Kinnick smiled. "I've had a lot of practice at it this afternoon. I was due to unload one sooner or later. I am officially done kicking that prolate spheroid today!"

"One more time guys!" shouted Couppee. "One more defensive stand and this game is ours!"

Eleven Ironmen were ready to finish the epic battle.

"They've got to pass! Watch for the pass!" Couppee yelled. "Come on linemen, don't give the quarterback any time! Backs, don't let anyone get behind you! Play soft. Keep everything in front of you! Four plays! Four plays!"

On first down from their six yard line, Notre Dame's Stevenson faded back into his end zone, looking downfield for Johnny Kelley. Buzz Dean and Ray Murphy guarded Kelley tightly, forcing Stevenson to throw the pass out of bounds.

Second down. Stevenson rolled to his right and delivered a pass to Bud Kerr cutting across the middle. Couppee's helmet crashed into Kerr's side, jarring the ball from his grasp. The crowd started chanting, "Coup-pee, Coup-pee," as both players groggily struggled to their feet.

"Are you okay, Coup?" Tollefson said as he leaned over Couppee.

"I'm okay. I'm okay. I'm not leaving now."

Third down. The Hawkeyes' defensive backs were playing deep. Notre Dame tried a delayed hand off to Piepul for a run up the middle. Pettit and Bergstrom formed a wall Piepul couldn't penetrate.

Fourth down. One minute and thirty-five seconds stood between the Ironmen and history. Stevenson took the hike and again dropped back to pass. Notre Dame needed to reach the sixteen for a first down. The Irish's Joe Thesing ran straight down field to the twenty yard line and cut sharply to his right. Stevenson delivered the ball perfectly just before Thesing stepped out of bounds, stopping the clock. Notre Dame was still alive with the first down.

Once more, Stevenson tried to pass. Kinnick ran alongside Bud Kerr. With perfect timing, Kinnick leaped forward and again batted the ball to the ground. The noise was deafening. Fifty-seven seconds remained. Stevenson's only option was to pass. Every play had to be either a first down, a catch at the sideline that could be run out of bounds, or an incomplete pass. Any of these three options stopped the clock. Notre Dame didn't need a touchdown; they needed to get inside Iowa's thirty yard line for their placekicker to have a realistic chance at a winning field goal.

Second down. Stevenson took the hike and moved to his right, trying to avoid Enich's rush. This time, Johnny Kelley was open at the thirty, but only for a brief second. Kinnick anticipated the pass to Kelley, noticing Stevenson staring at his receiver a moment too long. This time Kinnick ferociously slapped the ball with both hands. The crowd grew louder. The air vibrated.

Third down. The line of scrimmage remained at the Notre Dame twenty yard line. Stevenson went back and made the mistake of moving towards Mike Enich. Enich chased him sideways and backwards. At the six yard line Enich made his final play of the day. He lunged forward, grabbing the shoulder pads of Notre Dame's highly regarded halfback. Stevenson landed hard under Enich's weight.

Notre Dame was facing fourth down and needing twenty-four yards for the first down. The Irish desperately called their final time out. They had one last chance to change their misfortunes.

Coach Anderson spotted Bernie Sheridan, Notre Dame's fleetest runner, standing on the sideline next to Coach Elmer Layden. Kinnick and Couppee joined Dr. Eddie on the opposite sideline. "Sheridan's taking off his pads for quickness," said Coach Anderson. "They did the same thing last week on a punt return against Army. He ran it back for the win! So, the ball is definitely going to Sheridan!"

Kinnick and Couppee ran back to the huddle. "Sheridan will be carrying the ball. Buzz, you and I will play forty yards off the line," Kinnick said. "Coup, you and the linebackers play twenty-five yards off the line. Everybody play wide and make him come to the middle of the field where we've got help from each other!"

Sheridan ran to the Notre Dame huddle without shoulder pads, knee pads, thigh pads, or hip pads. The gold helmet was his only piece of protective equipment. The final play began. Sheridan took the snap and started to his left. Mike Enich headed straight at him. Sheridan veered right to elude Enich and then had to change direction again to evade Prasse and Bergstrom, holding their positions on the left side of the Hawkeye line.

Max Hawkins, who had battled Notre Dame's All-American guard Bernie Crimmins all afternoon, charged towards Sheridan. No one heard their helmets collide because the Hawkeye fans were cheering so loudly. The Irish luck had ended, and Hawkins was mobbed by his delirious teammates. The crowd's emotions brought them down to the field, swarming their heroes. This day would never be forgotten. The Hawkeye Ironmen 7, Notre Dame 6.

Fifteen Ironmen withstood the onslaught of substitutions Coach Elmer Layden had made in hopes of wearing down Iowa's overachievers. Ends Erv Prasse and Dick Evans, tackles Wally Bergstrom and Mike Enich, guard Ken Pettit, center Bruno Andruska, quarterback Al Couppee, and left halfback Nile Kinnick played the entire sixty minutes. Max Hawkins, Ham Snider, and the recovered Chuck Tollefson had shared the other guard position. Buzz Dean and Ed McLain had substituted for each other at right halfback. And Bill Green and Ray Murphy had taken turns at fullback.

The journalists had the fairy tale ending to the story they came to see, but they didn't expect to see such a classic defensive struggle. The Hawkeyes capitalized on one mistake, the missed lateral by Steve Sitko after he had intercepted Kinnick. And except for one drive by Notre Dame, the Hawkeyes played consummate football against thirty-two great Notre Dame players. Mike Enich recorded fifteen solo tackles. Nile Kinnick batted down six Irish passes from his safety position. But the most amazing statistics involved Kinnick's punting.

Hugs and handshakes were abundant in the boisterous locker room.

"Gentlemen, great things are accomplished by people everyday. Today, it was your turn to exceed expectations. That was a game I shall always remember." Dr. Eddie displayed a satisfied smile as he walked among his squad. "Everyone contributed in a huge way to this victory. Even those that didn't play today contributed because you were worthy adversaries in our practices every night. It was a team win. And, personally, I can't begin to describe how much it means to me.

"Your effort today was something to behold. That was a great team you faced today. They tried to wear you down, but you held your ground, every one of you. So go enjoy your win tonight. Enjoy your families for those who have family in town today. And tomorrow as usual, in order to get the stiffness out, we'll meet right here and walk to the east side of town and back.

"I can't tell you how proud I am of your performance. That was the greatest victory I have ever been associated with! Your determination will be the headlines across the country tomorrow. Everyone will know about the Ironmen.

"Nile, the statistician told me you punted sixteen times for seven hundred thirty-one yards. Incredible! And of course there was the seventeenth kick, the extra point."

Dr. Eddie turned to introduce two people standing just inside the locker room doorway. "We invited two men to join our celebration. I'm sure you remember Judge 'Duke' Slater, from Chicago, who has now witnessed his beloved Hawkeyes triumphing over Notre Dame twice." Cheers greeted his introduction as Judge Slater nodded approvingly while returning the applause to his former team. Coach Anderson continued, "And I want to add that I am now, finally, on the winning side of one of those clashes."

A player yelled from the other end of the room, "You're a Hawkeye now, Dr. Eddie."

"Yes, I am. And I'm proud to be a Hawkeye.

"And the other gentleman I want to introduce to you was previously a broadcaster for Iowa football games, and Chicago Cubs games, before finding success in Hollywood. I'm sure I don't need to introduce him since you probably recognize him from the big screen. This is Dutch Reagan, or do we call you Ronald Reagan now?"

Applause echoed again through the room as the battered, happy footballers greeted the familiar Hollywood star.

"My agent says I should go by Ronald from now on," said Reagan. "But here in Iowa City, you can call me 'Dutch.'"

In the locker room that afternoon, no one was in a hurry to shower or rush out the door and into the night. They stayed together for as long as they could because only they understood what they were experiencing in that instant, and they didn't want it to end.

Dutch Reagan walked over to Nile Kinnick. "That was a fine performance you gave today, Nile. I've never seen two teams play with that much intensity."

"Thank you, Mr. Reagan. It's nice of you to say and it's an honor to meet you. I used to listen to your broadcasts. And it's inspiring that you came back here for this game."

"Well, Nile, it seemed like a perfect opportunity to come back. I really wanted to see this game. But I also came back because I'm doing a movie next year based on football."

"What's the movie about?" Nile asked.

"It's a movie about Knute Rockne. I'm playing the role of George Gipp, the 'Gipper.' And since Coach Anderson and Coach Layden knew those individuals, I came for the opportunity to talk to both coaches," Reagan responded. "Most of all I wanted to see this game and get a feel for the Notre Dame mystique. But you boys certainly changed the script today."

"How did you get into acting, Mr. Reagan?" Nile asked with curiosity.

"I think I've always wanted to be in front of a crowd. In fact, I was your age when I first recognized it. I was attending Eureka College in central Illinois, class of 1932. The college was planning on cutting some faculty positions. Well, I ended up leading a campus strike and for the first time in my life I felt my words reach out and grab an audience."

Nile smiled at Ronald Reagan. "I have experienced similar feelings. I think, next to playing in a game like today, it's the most satisfying feeling I've ever encountered."

"I have heard of your speaking prowess. And I understand you're the Senior Class president. That tells me a lot about you."

Nile asked another question. "Did you accomplish your goals with the strike?"

Reagan laughed loudly. "Yes, we did. The college didn't lay off anyone. And I remember thinking, at the time, I wanted to go into politics. Maybe I will someday if I ever grow tired of acting.

"It's nice to meet you, Nile." Ronald Reagan thrust his hand forward to shake Nile's. "Would it be alright if I called you sometime this winter, after the football season, to ask questions about playing major college football? It would help me get a feel for the upcoming role."

"That would be great, Mr. Reagan. I look forward to it. What's the name of the movie?"

"*Knute Rockne, All-American*. Pat O'Brian is playing Rockne."

Nile smiled again. "I'll make sure I see it."

"Hey, Couppee, where are you going?" Prasse saw Couppee walking towards the door.

Couppee's hair was still damp from his shower. "My mom's waiting outside. I'll catch up with you later at The Academy."

Al Couppee walked up the stairs leading to the outside of the bricked Iowa Stadium. The anticipation of seeing his mom suddenly engulfed him. Six months had passed since he last saw her. Couppee thought it was wonderful that she ventured away from Council Bluffs, by herself, to see him play for the first time.

Standing outside the locker room door, Mary Couppee was saying goodbye and thank you to her new friends, Fred and Alice, who had helped her find the locker room. She was standing in the front of a large group of fans and well-wishers, all hoping to greet the Hawkeyes when they exited the locker room.

"Tell your son he played one great game today," Fred said as they turned to walk away. "You can be mighty proud of him."

The locker room door was pushed open. Al Couppee was the first to appear. The fans burst into cheers.

"Way to go, Couppee!"

"Go Hawkeyes!"

"Ironman Couppee!"

Shouts were coming from every direction. Al finally spotted his mother. His first thought was how proud and happy she looked, smiling as the crowd applauded.

Then Al did everything he could to keep from crying. It wasn't tears of joy. The elation in the locker room over the Ironmen's new triumph quickly drained from his face. He tried with all his might to hide his feelings from his mom and the many standing close enough to observe. "Hi, Mom! Wow, it's great to see you again!" He put his arms around her frail shoulders.

"Oh, Al. I'm so proud. I had no idea these games were so dramatic. I wish I had attended them sooner."

Al sensed an apology coming so he interrupted, "And seeing you here is what really makes this one special. Mom, there's a little restaurant not far from here. I borrowed a friend's car so let's go get something to eat. I'm starved."

Once they got in the car, Al asked his mother about her health. "Why have you lost so much weight?"

She was reluctant to talk at first. But then she told Al that finances were very tight, and she had been working more hours. Then Mary said, "Your dad wanted me to tell you how proud he is. And that thirteen year old brother of yours is at the park every night playing football and bragging about his big brother."

They talked for two hours during dinner and then Al drove her back to the train depot. After a farewell hug, Al got into the car. He sat there for several minutes before turning the ignition key. What should he do, he thought? His family needed him in Council Bluffs. Emotions burst out as he broke down crying.

He headed downtown to The Academy, but instead of joining his teammates, he drove aimlessly through the streets. He watched the students and other Hawkeye fans walking in and out of the bars. Everyone, except one, was in a celebratory mood after the win over Notre Dame. What a great night it should be to celebrate, he thought. He had played sixty minutes in the biggest game of his life. But he wasn't feeling the excitement. Suddenly, football just seemed like a game. He was torn between joining his friends, or just driving back to the Boars' Nest and going to bed. He chose the latter.

Sunday morning, November twelfth. The Boars' Nest bunch was headed for Dr. Eddie's day-after walking ritual. Chuck Tollefson, Red Frye, and Oops Gilleard were walking with Al Couppee. They were soon joined by Prasse, Kinnick, and Enich. Most hadn't slept much, having tried unsuccessfully at keeping the prior evening from ending. The morning conversations covered many topics: the next game against

Minnesota, reliving the big plays from yesterday's game, hilarious activities at The Academy last night, and girlfriends.

Nile Kinnick noticed Couppee wasn't his usual self. "Al, you seem distracted. Is everything okay?"

"Not really. I'm thinking of quitting," Couppee responded.

"What?" said Prasse. "You're kidding, right?"

"No. I'm not. I think I need to go home and be with my family."

"What happened, Al?" said Kinnick.

Couppee's swollen red eyes looked at Kinnick. "My family isn't doing very well financially. When I saw my mom yesterday, she couldn't have weighed a hundred pounds. I think she's been eating less so my brother and sister would have more."

The Boars' Nest group lived together because the university made it affordable for them. Chuck Tollefson had ridden the rails. Red Frye had been raised by his single mother. Oops Gilleard was an orphan who had lived with several different families. All were silent while listening to their roommate retell his story.

"We'll get you through this, Coup," said Tollefson, not a stranger to hopelessness.

"I was wondering why we didn't see you last night," Enich said. "There must be something we can do."

Kinnick spoke next. "You're right, Iron Mike. There is something we can do. We'll talk to Dr. Eddie after the walk."

Couppee was still down, but he found a degree of solace knowing these footballers were also his best friends.

"Hello, gentlemen. How was your walk this morning?" Dr. Eddie had driven to his office after picking up Coach Carideo. Al Couppee had called Coach Anderson two hours earlier, after they finished the walk. He asked if he could meet with the two coaches. Couppee said it was urgent. He asked Kinnick to join him.

"It was good, Coach. We had a lot to talk about this morning." Then Nile added, "And that's why we're here now."

"I'm here to listen, gentlemen," said Dr. Eddie.

"Coach, I saw my mom after the game yesterday. My family isn't doing well. There's little income and barely enough food. My mom has lost a lot of weight and seems weak. I told the guys that I'm thinking about quitting school and going home to help out. Nile suggested I talk to you."

Dr. Eddie's face saddened. A look of concern spread across the face of Coach Carideo, as well.

"What's their situation right now?" asked Frank Carideo.

Al Couppee described what his mother had told him. They were cutting back on all expenses, even food. And of course, winter was looming and that meant the additional cost of heating the house.

"How's your dad's health?" asked Dr. Eddie.

"It's good. He can do physical work, if that's what you mean," replied Couppee.

Dr. Eddie then inquired, "Do you think they would be willing to move from Council Bluffs if a good job came along?"

"Right now, Coach, I think they would consider any possibilities."

Coach Anderson let out a deep sigh before speaking. "Al, you can't quit school. And I'm not just saying that because I want you on the team. If you quit, it's very likely you'll never resume your education. Your parents might appreciate your kind gesture in the short term, but eventually, they might regret that your impulsive decision caused you to miss out on college. They might feel terrible if they felt it was their fault. And you, too, might grow to regret a life-changing decision you make right now.

"You've got to believe that things will work out. Right now, I want you to go have some fun. Go out and enjoy the day with your friends and celebrate what you did yesterday. I mean it. I want you to trust that Frank and I will address the problem. I want you to quit worrying about it. Okay?"

"Okay, Coach. I'll try."

Nile and Al got up to leave.

"Thank you, Coach," Al said, his eyes tearing up.

Nile looked back through Coach Anderson's glass door after exiting his office. He saw Dr. Eddie saying something to Coach Carideo while reaching for the phone.

CHAPTER TWENTY-THREE

Monday, November thirteenth. "I've got Enich and Tollefson calling the linemen. Dean and I are contacting all the backs. Everyone's to meet at the Old Capitol at noon." Erv Prasse's voice was animated, informing Kinnick of the plan. "Tell everyone you see, and tell them to tell everyone they see!"

Nile Kinnick hung up the phone. He agreed it was worth doing. But he needed to make one phone call, first.

"Hello. This is Barbara Miller."

"Hi, Barbara. This is Nile."

"Hello. It's nice to hear from you. It's a coincidence you called just now," said Barbara Miller.

"What's the coincidence?" Kinnick was surprised, and curious.

"I was just reading Bert McGrane's article in yesterday's Des Moines Register. His words are so expressive describing Saturday's game. Did you see his story?"

"No, I didn't," replied Kinnick. Nile found it comforting to be relieved from the nervousness of calling for a date. Discussing a newspaper article would be a nice distraction, helping ease into the reason for his call.

"Would you like me to read it?" asked Barbara, also nervous about speaking to Saturday's hero.

"That would be nice." Kinnick silently shook his head at the thought that calling one person can be almost as nerve-racking as fifty thousand people watching him play football on a Saturday afternoon.

"Okay. Here goes," responded Barbara.

> *An amber autumn landscape in Iowa Saturday received the remains of the Notre Dame's 1939 championship hopes.*
>
> *Eddie Anderson's wonder team – Nile Kinnick and his Iron mates – took over the opportunists' role held through the years by the Fighting Irish, forced the great Notre Dame array to make a single, glaring mistake, slammed across an Iowa touchdown and won a titanic triumph, 7 to 6.*
>
> *With a solid human embankment of fifty-three thousand viewing every move of the crackling, reverberating battle, Iowa's 'heroic handful' withstood every savage thrust through sixty chill-choked minutes to do what teams from many a section couldn't do with something like twice the number of able bodies.*

Kinnick thought Barbara was done reading, "McGrane always makes things vivid in his own unique way."

"There's more, Nile." She continued.

> *It was a mad, relentless defense that won this game for Iowa. A defense that beat down every Notre Dame threat save one – ripped the thunder off a chilling, rocking running attack and put a wall of fiends between Irish passers and their eligible receivers.*

Barbara paused, "I think he's talking about you. You must have knocked down four or five passes, not counting interceptions."

"I got lucky on some of those plays. I could easily have been the goat if I had anticipated wrong, and the receiver turned for the goal line."

"But you didn't." Barbara smiled with her response. "Shall I continue reading? Maybe I shouldn't because the rest of the story might give you a big head."

"Then you better not. Those helmets are tight enough," Nile said with a laugh. "Barbara, would you like to do something fun this afternoon?"

"Sure, but I've got a class at three o'clock. What is it?"

"I'd like to invite you to go for a walk at 11:30. Can I stop by then?" Kinnick hoped the answer would come quickly. And it did.

"Sure, I'll see you then. Where are we walking?"

"We'll go to the Old Capitol, and then walk to East Fairchild. It's Dr. Eddie's fortieth birthday. We're walking to his house to sing happy birthday. Tell everyone you see to come and join us. I'll see you at 11:30."

The word spread fast. The athletes told others in their respective fraternities and dormitories. Several phone calls informed the sororities and women's dormitories. Kinnick walked by the Old Capitol at 11:15 on the way to Barbara's sorority house. Already several hundred people had congregated. Some were carrying makeshift signs with messages to boycott classes the rest of the day in order to celebrate the Notre Dame win. The victory still permeated the air in this small university town.

It was a relatively warm day for mid-November. Nile wore his black letter jacket. Briefly he reflected on how different this season was from the previous two. Winning made this year fun, but his mood could not be entirely celebratory. He thought about his friend and teammate, Al Couppee, and how he must be feeling. He put his faith in Dr. Eddie's involvement, but still, he knew the Couppee family was facing significant obstacles.

"Hi Nile." Barbara Miller's smile changed Nile's focus. Her engaging personality was irresistible to Nile, who smiled too as he greeted her.

"Good morning. I'm glad you could join me." Nile leaned forward to kiss her right cheek. He realized how fortunate he was, standing on the sorority porch with this very kind and charming person. "It looks like our plan to serenade Dr. Eddie is turning into a rally to postpone classes for the rest of the day. Maybe your three o'clock class won't happen."

As they walked down the stairs, Nile reached for her hand. She looked at him with another smile as she squeezed his hand gently.

"Somewhere along the grapevine of spreading the word, the idea of getting out of classes seems to have been attached to our original idea, and it appears to have taken on a life of its own," said Nile.

"I know. I saw students with banners headed that way. I guess you can never underestimate the unity of students when the subject matter involves getting out of school, especially after all the partying Saturday night," Barbara added.

Barbara noticed Nile was somewhat withdrawn as they walked quietly after their initial exchange. "Nile, something seems to be on your mind. Is everything okay?" she asked.

Nile paused. "Sometimes, Barbara, football seems so trivial in contrast to hardships all around us." He looked over and sensed her genuine interest to his reply. "On the walk over, I was thinking about Couppee. His family is going through a difficult time. You may have noticed he wasn't around Saturday night. The past ten years have been hard on many people, but his family is still suffering from the economy. I wish our government could help people in distress."

Barbara turned from looking at Nile to see the group forming ahead. "In a Contemporary Affairs class last week we were discussing Europe. It's all so hard to comprehend."

Nile continued on her thought. "There, too, our government is taking a stand of neutrality, and I don't believe we can continue thinking that way." He shook his head as he spoke. "The German Nazis invaded Czechoslovakia earlier this year and I can understand the United States not getting involved immediately. But now, they've gone into Poland, too."

"And now the Soviet Union has overtaken Poland on its eastern border," Barbara added.

"And Germany and the Soviet Union are now discussing how to divide Poland as if it's theirs to divvy up," Nile said. "At least Britain, France, Australia, and New Zealand declared war on Germany two months ago. And more recently Canada joined the cause. I don't think we can wait much longer to get involved. I just don't understand how we can stand by while this sort of tyranny seems to be expanding rather than retreating."

"It all seems so senseless," said Barbara. "We should have learned a lesson from the world war twenty years ago."

Nile let out a large exhale. "For now, singing Happy Birthday to a great person is our goal. In a way, though, it seems rather inconsequential, don't you think?" He smiled at his friend.

"Yes. But we need to enjoy our slivers of happiness when we can, Nile."

"You are right, my friend. You are so right," he said.

"Hey, Nile! Over here." Mike Enich's baritone voice echoed from across the street. He was standing with Erv Prasse and Al Couppee. "I'm not sure what we started here, but it will be one memorable birthday party."

"I guess there's no reason why everyone can't join us to Dr. Eddie's," said Erv Prasse.

"We took a vote and decided we needed you to talk to the crowd. At least a thousand people are already at the Old Capitol."

"You took a vote?" laughed Kinnick. "What, the three of you voted? Okay, I'll speak. Let's go do it."

Most of the football team were on the top step of the Old Captiol when Enich, Prasse, Couppee, Kinnick, and Barbara Miller joined them. Various roars came from different corners of the crowd. Some shouts invoked the Hawkeyes' new nickname, "Ironmen." Other hollers were about Dr. Eddie, and Iowa being "Number One." But the dominant cheer was "Cancel classes! Cancel classes!"

There was no podium or microphone for the impromptu gathering on the east side of the imposing building, so Kinnick stood ready to yell as loud as possible once the crowd noise faded. The throng swelled enough to cause traffic problems at the intersection of Clinton Street and Iowa Avenue.

"Thank you all for coming. This started off as a rally to walk to Coach Anderson's house because it's his fortieth birthday today. But somehow, this assembly has transformed into a rally to cancel classes." Cheers rose from those assembled. While Kinnick turned to laugh with his teammates standing behind him, he noticed President Gilmore standing at the doorway of Schaeffer Hall. Schaeffer Hall stood stoically in the southeast section of the Pentacrest, one of four grand buildings surrounding Old Capitol. The lawn's majestic oaks stood barren without their leaves, providing Nile a clear view to Schaeffer Hall and President Gilmore.

"In fact, I see that we have even earned the attention of President Gilmore." Kinnick pointed towards Schaeffer. "President Gilmore. The people have spoken!"

"Cancel classes! Cancel classes! Cancel classes!" started up from the students again.

President Gilmore raised his hands above his head and moved them several times in downward motions, asking for the crowd's silence. Then he spoke as loudly as he could. "In the spirit of Saturday's win, classes are canceled for the rest of the day!"

The jubilant crowd was overjoyed at hearing his words. President Gilmore again waved his arms so he could be heard. "And we will have a campus party to celebrate Saturday's win, beginning in two hours at the Student Union."

President Gilmore turned and looked at Nile Kinnick. The two smiled at each other and then waved. Nile reflected back to Ronald "Dutch" Reagan's story of realizing for the first time, at a Eureka College strike, that his words impacted others.

The Hawkeye Ironmen led the way north four blocks on Clinton Street and then right at East Fairchild.

Erv Prasse walked to the front door of Eddie and Mary Anderson's home, flanked by his teammates, with a good portion of the Old Capitol crowd standing in the yard and spilling into the street. Inside, Mary Anderson was on the phone contacting her husband. She had heard the mob as it marched through the normally quiet neighborhood. "Eddie, you need to come home right away. And come down the alley and in through the back door."

"What is it?" questioned Dr. Eddie.

"It's a surprise. And you've got to see it to believe it. Come quickly!"

"I'm on my way."

Mary answered the door. "Hello, everyone. I'm going to assume this has something to do with my husband's birthday?"

"Yes, Mrs. Anderson," replied Erv Prasse. "We came to sing Happy Birthday. A few more than what we had expected showed up."

"I just called him at the hospital. He should be here soon."

The news that he wasn't home, but was on his way, spread through the three hundred people that made the march. Fifteen minutes later Dr. Eddie appeared in the doorway next to Mary. Immediately, the crowd broke into the popular song.

Happy birthday to you. Happy birthday to you.
Happy birthday, Dr. Eddie. Happy birthday to you.

Dr. Eddie's eyes blinked rapidly as he looked out over his front yard. He and his wife stood arm in arm.

"Everyone inside for cake and ice cream!" he shouted after the birthday song, looking at his wife with laughter. "Seriously, thank you so much. You have again demonstrated to Mary and me how wonderful this university is. We couldn't ask for a greater community, student body, or faculty. And these gentlemen in the front are the ones who have made this so special for Mary and me. We are experiencing some success and it's because of their commitments. So I say thank you to all of you, but especially these Hawkeye Ironmen."

After one more rendition of 'Happy Birthday' the crowd slowly dispersed, most heading straight to the Student Union.

"Al and Nile, do you have a minute?" Dr. Eddie asked.

"Sure, Coach," responded Couppee.

Nile Kinnick stepped closer with Barbara Miller by his side. "Happy birthday, Coach. This is Barbara Miller."

"Hello, Barbara. It's nice to meet you." Then Dr. Eddie turned to Al Couppee. "How are you doing?"

"Okay, Coach. Still have a lot on my mind, but I'm okay."

"Good. Good. Keep your head up young man. Something will work out. Nile, keep an eye on this guy."

"I will, Coach. We all will," said Kinnick.

"Good. Then I want all of you to head down to the Union for the celebration. I heard you convinced President Gilmore to forego classes this afternoon. But practice is still on. Make sure everyone knows."

CHAPTER TWENTY-FOUR

Tuesday night, November 14, 1939. "Thank you, Mother, for all your prayers. You have helped me make it through the season unscathed. I know I owe much to you for my health and the healing I've experienced." Nile was talking to Frances Kinnick by phone. "I'll write again soon. I just didn't have enough time this week because we've put in extra hours preparing for Minnesota."

"We understand, Nile," Frances said. "I'll put your father on now. We are so proud of you. Stay rightful. I love you. Good night."

"Hello, Son. How are you feeling?" Nile Sr. asked.

"Good." Nile hadn't felt this healthy since he came to the University three years ago. "My right hand is a little stiff, but it won't pose any problems."

"Nile, your team is playing great football. The battle with Notre Dame was phenomenal. I can't remember a team showing more heart than the Ironmen did Saturday. I like the name 'Ironmen.' It fits your team."

"Thanks, Dad. The team earned it. Somehow, Dr. Eddie knew back in the spring that he would need a lot of playing time from certain individuals so he was merciless with the constant running, but looking back, I wouldn't have wanted it any other way. We are all experiencing something extraordinary."

"It goes well beyond Iowa City; in fact, it goes beyond Iowa," said Nile Sr. "You have caught the attention of the nation. You are showing what the little man can do against the odds. And I'm not talking about the physical sizes of the Hawkeyes, or the number of players on the team. I'm not even talking about football. I'm talking about the down-trodden realizing that they, too, can pick themselves up and get on with life, no matter what the circumstances. It's a message people need to hear because many are still suffering financially. A lot of people are discovering joy by merely watching your story unfold. They are attaching themselves, emotionally, to the storyline.

"And I want to reiterate what your mother said. We are extremely proud of you. We are proud of the gridiron accomplishments, but we are prouder of the person you've become along your journey."

"Thank you, Dad. Mother and you, especially Mother, have reinforced the idea of rightful thinking into me as far back as I can remember. In a sense, when you look at me, I hope it is you that you see."

There was silence on both ends of the phone. 'Senior' and 'Junior,' as they were known by family and friends, knew their bond was strong. Nile Jr., in that instant, recognized that neither a father nor a child can experience a greater relationship than one involving mutual respect.

Nile Sr. changed the subject. "I've read about Minnesota's size. The Register said the linemen outweigh the Hawkeye linemen by twenty-five to thirty pounds at each position."

"There's some truth to that, although maybe a little exaggerated. Their linemen are clearly bigger than ours. Minnesota's Coach Bierman likes to pound the ball down the field. I think this game will be more difficult than Notre Dame. And when I remember the scores of the last two years, beating us 35 to 10 and 28 to 0, I'm not sure what to expect. We are much better now, but Minnesota is still ranked high and has a shot at another Big Ten title."

"And with a Hawkeye win, I think you are practically guaranteed the title!" exclaimed Nile Sr. "I'm glad you didn't go to Minnesota. Now just go get that Floyd of Rosedale trophy back in Iowa City. Minnesota has had that border-state trophy for too long. Good night, Son."

"Good night, Dad." Nile walked down the hallway to his room. He leaned down and put his hands on the floor for his customary one hundred push-ups before bed. It was a ritual he started his junior year in high school. It was a reflective moment every night. His thoughts frequently drifted to what was on the forefront of his mind. Tonight, it was Al Couppee. He knew Couppee's family was as close as his own, but faced different circumstances. He wondered how his teammate was feeling right now.

Nile walked back down the hallway to the floor's only phone and called his father again collect. "Dad, I know you are aware of Al Couppee's family having a difficult time of it. And since they just live across the river from you in Council Bluffs, I was wondering –"

Nile Sr. interrupted his son. "I'm aware of the situation. I can't tell you why I'm aware of what is happening but trust me, Son, sometimes things are better left unsaid, and this is one of those times."

"Okay. I'm not sure what you mean, but I'll respect your decision to not discuss it. Good night, Dad."

Nile placed the phone back on the wall unit's prongs. He stared at the phone in astonishment not understanding why his father cut him off. It was late. Nile went back to his room and went to bed.

Wednesday morning, November 15, 1939. A loud knock on the door stirred the Boars' Nest residents from their sleep.

Chuck Tollefson, Red Frye, Bill Gallagher, Oops Gilleard, Bob Otto, and Al Couppee were sleeping in late. Last night's poker game ended at two o'clock in the morning. No one answered the door so the knock repeated, but louder.

"Al Couppee. Mr. Couppee. There is a telephone call downstairs for you. Mr. Couppee?" The voice on the other side of the door sounded anxious.

Tollefson spoke. "Coup, get up. It's for you."

Couppee stood up next to his bed. He grabbed the pants lying on the floor next to him, slipped them on, and walked to the door. "Yes?"

"There is a long distance telephone call for you."

"Okay. Let me get some shoes on."

Couppee hurriedly walked downstairs to the athletic office. He was nervous, not knowing who would call long distance and wait for his arrival. His parents didn't have a phone in their home. He picked up the phone from the cluttered desk. "This is Al Couppee."

"Al, this is your father." There was a sudden awkwardness felt by both. The two had never spoken to each other in a long distance phone call. "I'm in Mr. Dodd's office here in Council Bluffs. I just got offered a nice job in Davenport. They even lined up an apartment for me until Mary and the kids can join me."

"That's great, Dad. What will you be doing?"

"Well, you know all the liquor stores in Iowa are owned by the state. I will be managing the Davenport store." Mr. Couppee's voice trembled slightly from both the excitement and the nervousness of the moment. He told Al the job he was just offered paid three times more than he had ever made. Mr. Dodd, the Council Bluffs liquor store manager, placed the call so Al could know right away.

Al was speechless. The good news surprised him. Dr. Eddie, he thought, evidently made some contacts with alumni and state officials. And then he realized something else, but his father's voice interrupted his thought.

"I'm not sure why this is all happening, Al. A grocer brought a car full of food. And then someone dropped off a truckload of coal."

Al then finished his previous thought; he had been told not to worry. Dr. Eddie had been true to his word. But, clearly, Coach Anderson had bent the rules to help his family. Al still didn't know what to say; he was ecstatic that his family was about to experience better times, but he wasn't sure what he would say to Dr. Eddie. "I guess we don't need to know why it's happening, Dad. I'm just happy that it is."

"Son, go take care of business this weekend with Minnesota. We'll all be listening. I've got to run, but wanted you to know right away."

"Thanks for the great news, Dad. Goodbye."

Nile Kinnick sat in the trainer's room getting his ankles wrapped before practice. He had noticed Al Couppee displaying a sense of calm earlier in the locker room. Chuck Tollefson sat next to Kinnick.

"Chuck, Coup seems very relaxed today and in a good mood. Do you know why?" Nile asked.

"Coup got a phone call from his old man this morning," said Tollefson. "His dad got a good job. But he hasn't talked about it much."

The trainer finished Kinnick's ankle wraps. Nile walked over to Couppee and sat down on the bench next to him.

Couppee spoke first. "Dr. Eddie came through. He took care of my family. It's incredible what he did. I don't know whether to thank him or just wait for him to mention something to me."

"What do you mean?" asked Kinnick. "What happened?"

"My dad got a job working for the state. He's got to move to Davenport right away, and then my mom, sister, and brother will join him as soon as they can."

"That's great, Coup. What's the job?"

"Working in a state liquor store. And that's not all. A grocer stopped by the home in Council Bluffs and dropped off some food. And another truck dropped off a load of coal."

Nile looked at his quarterback and knew Coup was perplexed. "That's amazing, Coup. I'm happy for you. It's great, right?"

"Yeah, it's great. I suppose Dr. Eddie contacted some alums or boosters in the state government, and in Council Bluffs. I'm really happy, too, but I'm not sure it's something you go to your coach and say 'thank you' for."

Kinnick smiled to himself, remembering his recent conversation with Nile Sr; "sometimes things are better left unsaid." Now he knew what his father meant. Dr. Eddie may have stepped over the line, breaking some rules, Nile thought, but to rescue a family and improve their lives seemed a justifiable means to an end. Who could question Coach Anderson's compassion? How could facilitating a family's basic needs for food and warmth be considered disrespectful to college rules? Obviously, Dr. Eddie thought more about assisting people experiencing hardship than about staying within some guidelines. For the first time, Nile realized what is truly right sometimes goes beyond what is lawfully right. Because of Dr. Eddie's benevolence, a family's luck was changing. "I understand your feelings. You don't want to draw unnecessary attention to it. Coup, why not just wait and let Dr. Eddie bring up the subject? He'll let you know if it's appropriate. In the meantime, just know your family is doing fine."

Couppee nodded. "It's a nice feeling."

Saturday, November 18, 1939. Inside the locker room, the Hawkeyes could hear the high-spirited crowd growing more rambunctious by the minute as the kickoff slowly approached. Again the stadium was sold out. Once more the nation would tune into the NBC Radio broadcast to follow the Hawkeyes and their leader, Nile Kinnick.

Last week, the Ironmen put their footprint on college football. Today, the Hawkeyes could place themselves in position to win the Big Ten championship. Only one game would remain in their remarkable season after today's clash with powerful Minnesota.

Minnesota had won the national championship in 1936. Under Coach Bernie Bierman, the Gophers had won four Big Ten championships and three national titles in the past seven years. Like Notre Dame, they traveled to Iowa City with hopes of another national crown. Coach Bierman's success rested on his proven style. He was able to recruit size and speed from all across the country. The best athletes naturally wanted to play for Elmer Layden at Notre Dame or Bernie Bierman at Minnesota. Bierman had shown little interest in Nile Kinnick three years ago coming out of Benson High School in Omaha. At five foot eight inches tall and weighing only one hundred sixty pounds, Kinnick had neither the size nor the speed Coach Bierman preferred.

Minnesota brought sixty able-bodied footballers on two busses from Minneapolis. The Hawkeyes countered with thirty-two giant hearts, twenty-eight that could play and four that were suited up purely for emotion. Big Hank Luebcke, Jens Norgaard, and Bill Diehl - all out for the season - were still just as much a part of the team as anyone else in the locker room. So was Jim Walker who also wasn't healed enough to play. But even though these four would never set foot on the turf today, not even for warm up drills, they all wanted to dress for this game. Dr. Eddie thought it would be a morale boost just to have these four young men putting on the black and gold in the locker room. This crew of Ironmen, thusfar, had withstood the rigors of a Big Ten season. They had withstood the pain and agony of Dr. Eddie's drills. As the practices continued, the numbers had slowly diminished but that was offset by greater solidarity and increased strength.

The Iowa Hawkeyes were 'the' story in sports across the nation. Joe Louis, Joe DiMaggio, and horse racing were also making news, but it was the fifteenth ranked Iowa Hawkeyes making the front pages and being talked about at breakfast tables and in diners from New York to California. It was Iowa's first national ranking since 1921. Everyone outside the state of Minnesota was cheering for this madcap collection of under-sized, out-numbered over-achievers.

"Gentlemen," began Dr. Eddie for the last home game of the season, "I don't think I need to tell you what looms ahead. I believe today's game will be tougher, harder hitting, and more grueling than any game you have ever played. Notre Dame was a hard fought victory. But Minnesota has much greater size, and probably better speed, than Notre Dame." He paused for a moment, thinking of what next to say. "Last week was one of those highlights of a lifetime. But I want you to know, the luster of that victory will soon fade if we don't pick up today where we left off last Saturday. A loss today would stop the tremendous momentum we're building.

"I don't want that to happen. I want this team to keep climbing upward to the next hurdle. One game at a time! One play at a time!

"The Gophers will keep substituting and bringing in fresh bodies. They'll try to wear us down just as Notre Dame tried. But I don't think they know what they're up against!"

Everyone jumped to their feet and simultaneously started yelling. The Ironmen's pride brought an undeniable confidence to the thirty-two. Dr Eddie looked around and observed his courageous players. "I don't think they know how well conditioned we are. They can bring in wave after wave of new players to beat us down, but they won't succeed! You are the Iowa Hawkeyes! You are the Ironmen, a name you've earned!"

Again the coach was interrupted by the players' cheers. They drowned out the crowd noise coming through the ceiling of the locker room from the people above them in the stands. Coach Anderson continued. "This season has been astounding. President Gilmore told me recently of an accomplishment that you have achieved this year.

"Iowa Stadium, as you know, was built in 1929. The Depression hit right then, people couldn't afford to come to football games, and consequently the University has struggled to pay off the loan that built this magnificent brick arena. But the financial picture has changed. This year changed it. With the attendance you've caused, especially last week and the sellout again today, Iowa can finally pay off the debt after today's game." He paused again, shaking his head as he smiled. "I think someday they should name the stadium after you.

"As I call out your names, I want you to step forward. Dean. McLain. Kinnick. Evans. Prasse. Smith. Busk. Moore." One by one the eight seniors stood and walked over to Coach Anderson, standing in a line facing their underclassmen.

"Gentlemen, this is your final home game. You seniors have done a wonderful job in leading this team. All eight of you experienced one-victory seasons your sophomore and junior years. And then you endured the rigors I put you through physically this year. I can only hope you can look back now and say it was worth it. I know I can. I'm proud of this entire team, but this is the last time I get to talk to you eight seniors before a home game.

"Today is your final day in front of our fans. When you run onto the field, I want the eight of you holding hands, forming a line for the rest to follow. But before we run out through the tunnel, I want to make sure you have been paying attention these past nine months since spring football began." Coach Anderson felt a bit of levity often took the edge off nervous intensity. He remembered the first chalk talk after the first practice. "Dean, what's the shape of the field this fine game is played on?"

Buzz Dean, along with his thirty-one teammates, let out a laugh, and then he answered, "The field is a rectangle, Coach."

Coach Anderson moved to the next unsuspecting student. "McLain, what are the dimensions of that rectangle?"

"Three hundred sixty feet in length, counting the end zones, and one hundred sixty feet in width."

"Very good, McLain. Evans, what do you call the lines at the back of the end zone?" Anderson was trying not to smile. It was hard to do with everyone else laughing.

Dick Evans said, "Those are termed end lines, sir." He shouted his answer, doing his best imitation of a rookie Marine responding to his drill sergeant.

"Smith, you didn't think I was going to leave you out, did you?"

"No, Coach," Fred Smith replied.

"Okay, Smith, the out of bounds lines on the sides of the field are called what?" asked Dr. Eddie.

"Sidelines, sir," Smith barked back, as Evans did, to the drill sergeant.

"Busk, front and center." Coach Anderson accepted his new role as the Marine sergeant. "The ball is made of what?"

Russ Busk yelled back, "Pebble grained leather, sir, without corrugation of any kind, enclosing a rubber bladder, sir." The locker room went into hysterics. If anyone outside the locker room doors, or in the stands above, could hear them, they had to wonder what was going on. Unrestrained merriment was not a common sound heard emanating from a locker room before a big game.

"Joe Moore, even though you didn't get to catch that ball too often this year, how much pressure should it have?"

Joe Moore surprised everyone with his correct answer. "It should be inflated with a pressure of not less than twelve and a half pounds and no more than thirteen and a half pounds."

"Moore, if I had known you were paying that much attention, I would have gotten you in the games more often. Be ready to play today." Coach Anderson slapped him on the top of his shoulder pads. Dr. Eddie had great admiration for the players who practiced but rarely played on Saturdays.

Coach Anderson looked at the two remaining seniors. Erwin Prasse and Nile Kinnick. Both were destined for All-Big Ten honors and, most likely, All-American status as well.

"Prasse, what is the shape of the ball?"

Coach Anderson didn't know the entire team, when he was not around, referred to the ball by its nickname after that first chalk talk. Prasse couldn't hold back his laughter. "It has the shape of a prolate spheroid!"

Everyone burst into laughter again. Anderson sensed an on-going joke was on him. "And Kinnick, what do you do with that prolate spheroid?"

"Never, and I mean never, run out of bounds!" Kinnick answered, trying his best to impersonate Coach Anderson.

Coach Anderson looked around the room. He could only shake his head as he watched this team fuse together just a little bit more.

The moment had come for the game to begin. The anticipation of entering the stadium before a game, Kinnick thought, was almost as satisfying as the feeling of victory afterwards. It was now time to take the field for his last home game. The approval and applause, as the eight seniors led the way, already had the same feeling as the Notre Dame game. The voices echoed from the stands, accompanied by the bass-sounding thunder resonating from gloved hands. The crowd cheered constantly as the Ironmen went through their warm up drills; the vapor mists from the spectators' breaths floated above their overcoats and hats. It was a short-lived fog that kept repeating, and then disappearing, with the fans' exhalations and inhalations.

The Hawkeye faithful never sat during the first half. Nile Sr. and Frances stood with the parents of the other seven seniors. Sixteen seats were reserved for them in the tenth row behind the Hawkeye bench. Twenty-five rows above them, Harry Bremer stood with a group of Iowa City businessmen. The seating on both sides of the field rose seventy-nine rows and extended from end line to end line, and above the seventy-ninth row on the west side, the press box was packed with journalists from major wire services and large city newspapers. The journalists had placed their typewriters in front of wooden chairs. It was a means of reserving their seats. The desk top counter, holding the typewriters, stretched from the twenty yard line to the other twenty. The athletic department provided one program and one notepad in front of each chair.

The students sat in the northwest corner of the stadium. Barbara Miller and Mary Stellman watched intently as number twenty-four, Nile Kinnick, and number thirty-seven, Erv Prasse, practiced an assortment of passing routes. Al Couppee's parents were listening to the radio broadcast, one in Council Bluffs with Al's sister and brother, the other in a sparsely furnished apartment in Davenport. It was the first time they listened to a game free of the worry and anxiety that had been etched so deeply into their psyches.

Mike Enich walked by Kinnick and Prasse. "Have you looked at the Minnesota players? The scouting report said they were maybe fifteen pounds bigger per man than us, but I think the rumors were more correct. It's more like twenty-five to thirty pounds, at least for the linemen."

"It'll give you something to do today, Enich," Prasse said. "I know I'm going to be running a little bit faster today to keep my distance. How about you, Nile?"

Nile's answer took on a serious quality. "I think if we duplicate what we did last week, we end up winning the Big Ten championship and, possibly, the national championship. I noticed Dr. Eddie, with his humor in the locker room today, never mentioned these possibilities to us. Today could be a very special day." Enich and Prasse were aware a Big Ten title was within their grasps, but neither had thought about the possibility of a national championship.

"Let's do it, guys," Enich said. "Let's just do it! One more time!" Three Ironmen did a three way hug, each with their hands on the other's shoulder pads. The three knew, most likely, they would never come out of the game.

"Coup, are you able to go one hundred percent with your left shoulder taped?" Kinnick asked as Couppee walked by.

"This collar I'm wearing doesn't seem too bad. I think I'll be okay as long as I don't get a direct hit on it." Couppee had re-injured his shoulder the last day of practice when Pettit rolled across him. Couppee was determined not to let anyone know the amount of pain he was experiencing. This game was too important. He knew he would regret it the rest of his life if he told Dr. Eddie how much it hurt. He couldn't watch from the sideline, especially after Coach Anderson's generosity toward his family. He had to play today.

Six thousand Gopher fans had driven from different towns across Minnesota to cheer on their team. They drove to Iowa City hoping to cap the season with yet another Big Ten championship. But the visiting Gopher devotees were no competition for the volume and intensity of the Hawkeye admirers who were feasting on victories after having gone hungry for too long.

Minnesota won the coin toss and elected to receive the ball. The Ironmen's good fortune quickly changed on the opening kickoff.

Prasse's kick went to Mernick on the ten yard line. After eluding two Hawkeyes, he darted for the sideline at the twenty-seven yard line. Al Couppee had a good angle on Mernick and delivered a brutal tackle. The Hawkeye crowd cheered loudly to praise Couppee's hard hit but Couppee was motionless on the turf.

Kinnick ran to Couppee. "Coup, is it your shoulder?"

Couppee's face showed lines of acute pain. "Yes, but it's not the left shoulder. Just help me up."

Prasse was ready to holler to the bench for a replacement. But Couppee couldn't let him do that. The pain didn't matter, Couppee thought. Hopefully, the initial sting would subside and he could continue. "Prasse, I'm okay! I'm okay! If I go out now, I'm out until the second quarter. Just let me see how it goes for a few plays."

"Okay," Prasse said. "But I'm watching you. If you can't play, I've got to ask for a substitute. Okay? You've got to let me know."

"Right." Couppee knew Prasse was right. But it was Minnesota on the other side of the line of scrimmage. His team, he thought, needed his play calling if nothing else.

Harold Van Every played Minnesota's left halfback. He was much like Nile Kinnick, taking the center snap directly from his halfback position rather than having the quarterback take the snap, and then handing off. Van Every was also a deft passer. He gave Minnesota the lethal option that made Kinnick so difficult for teams to stop. He could start a play as a run, and pass instead if the situation warranted it. Likewise, he could fake a pass and then turn up field if the linebackers and defensive backs were too cautious dropping deep to defend against a pass.

As the two teams lined up for Minnesota's first offensive play from the line of scrimmage, it was clear the Gophers were bigger at each position. Even Enich looked like an underclassman standing across from Gordon Paschka and

Urban Odson. Bill Kuusisto and Win Pederson towered over Iowa's Chuck Tollefson and Wally Bergstrom on the other side of the line.

The Minnesota running attack began from their twenty-seven yard line. Coach Bierman had so much depth at the halfback positions, he substituted running backs on the opening drive. Harold Van Every, Bruce Smith, Sonny Franck, and Bob Sweiger took turns running through the holes created by the Minnesota linemen. It was an impressive display of players working in unison to advance the ball. Next, Van Every ran to his right and launched a deep pass in the direction of John Mariucci. Mariucci ran parallel to Buzz Dean, lunging forward to haul in the long bomb before falling to the ground at the Iowa thirty-two yard line. On the ensuing play Smith ran behind Paschka and Odson, but Enich slipped through both blockers and dropped Smith for a loss. Two more running plays advanced the ball to the Iowa twenty-six yard line before Van Every threw an incomplete pass to Joe Mernick. Coach Bierman elected to punt, rather than go for the field goal, hoping to pin the Hawkeyes deep near their goal line - but Van Every's punt sailed beyond the goal line. Iowa had a first down on the twenty yard line following the touchback.

"Let's get out of here on our first play," Couppee hollered over the constant roar of the crowd. "Kinnick, quick kick."

Couppee called the play after everyone took their positions. "Six, eight, two, forty-nine, thirty-six, forty-five." The 'two' gave the variation of the play. The 'forty' meant shift right. The 'nine' told the team that the shift was to the quick kick formation.

The crowd, and the Gophers, saw what seemed like a normal Iowa shift, but Kinnick slipped seven yards behind Andruska at center. The Gophers never thought Iowa might punt on first down from their own twenty, but Dr. Eddie liked to deliver surprises so he had ordered Couppee to call the play. Kinnick punted deep before Minnesota was ready. The ball sailed high, dropping to the Minnesota twenty-five yard line and bouncing to the left out of bounds. Though it was once again Minnesota's possession, Kinnick improved Iowa's field position by fifty-five yards.

"Toughen up, linemen," Prasse shouted. "Come on Enich, Hawkins, Tollefson, Bergstrom! You do your jobs and our linebackers can clean up!" The Hawkeyes responded. They held their ground as Enich, Prasse, and Kinnick all made tackles on consecutive plays.

Kinnick fielded Sonny Franck's punt at Iowa's forty yard line but could gain no ground against the swarming Gopher tacklers.

"Prass, can you beat that guy long?" Kinnick asked, referring to Sonny Franck. Prasse nodded yes. Kinnick then hollered towards Couppee, "Let's try it. Coup, let's do our favorite play." Prasse loved knowing the pass was coming in his direction.

Couppee stood behind Andruska. "Four, eight, four, forty-three, seventy-six, eighteen." Again the shift to the Notre Dame box. Kinnick took the snap and drifted to his right. Prasse streaked across the field from his left end position. Kinnick saw Prasse one step ahead of Franck and let the ball fly. Sonny Franck's tremendous speed caught Prasse and even took a slight lead as Franck wedged his way between Prasse and the pass. The ball nestled into the Gopher's arms at the goal line. Prasse made a desperate attempt to upend Franck, reaching forward for his ankles. But Franck took off, heading back up field with the interception, where Andruska stopped him at the twenty-one yard line.

The first quarter ended in a scoreless tie.

The second quarter involved more hard hitting tackles, tremendous defense by both teams, and a flurry of punts. The fans cheered every play. Slowly, though, the Gopher size and strength started showing its superiority. From midfield, behind the strong running of Van Every and Franck, they inched their way slowly to Iowa's ten yard line.

The Hawkeyes grew steadfast in defending their end zone against Coach Bierman's substitutions. Ham Snider, now relieving Max Hawkins at Iowa's right guard position, made two incredible tackles – one at the line of scrimmage, and the other seven yards deep in Minnesota's backfield.

Minnesota tried running again into the right side of the Hawkeye line. This time, Mike Enich rose to the occasion, shedding his blocker and grabbing Franck by his shoulder pads. There was a loud thud as Franck hit the ground for a three yard loss with Enich's weight on top squeezing the air out of Franck's lungs.

Fourth down. The Gophers had the ball on the twenty yard line, ten yards further from the goal line than they were three plays earlier.

Joe Mernick stood on the thirty yard line, ready to take his two steps forward to kick a field goal from the twenty-seven yard line. The Minnesota place-kick holder grabbed the hiked ball, quickly set it on the ground, and held it still for the kicker. The kick went between the uprights. Minnesota 3, Iowa 0.

The Gopher fans grew louder. But even though the size and strength differences were becoming more apparent, the Hawkeyes had prevailed with their own small victory. As Iowa ran back to the sideline, the Hawkeye faithful returned to their feet and quickly began to drown out the Minnesota cheering. The Iowa players had risen to the occasion. The defense had stiffened, preventing the touchdown, after Minnesota knocked on the door from the ten yard line.

Dr. Eddie walked briskly to Al Couppee on the sideline before the kickoff. "Couppee, just run to the right, or up the middle. Call an occasional pass to keep the defense honest. No trick plays. If we're faced with a fourth down, Kinnick can kick us out of our end of the field."

"Got it, Coach." Couppee leaned slightly to his right. His arm hung motionless as he turned to run onto the field.

"Couppee, are you okay?" asked Coach Anderson.

Couppee looked back at his coach. "I'll be alright. The trainer can look at my arm at halftime."

"Can you block?"

"I'm calling Kinnick to the right three plays. My left shoulder's okay."

Gordon Paschka put the kickoff five yards deep in the end zone. Kinnick backpedaled to retrieve it. A wall formed with Prasse and Couppee a few steps ahead of Kinnick as he ran at full speed straight up the middle of the field. Bill Kuusisto's two hundred thirty pound body leveled Kinnick's one hundred seventy pound frame to the ground at the twenty-five yard line.

For just a brief moment, Kinnick stayed on his stomach, his face against the grass. Silence instantly swept through the stadium. "Get up, Nile, get up," Nile Sr. whispered to himself, almost as if saying a prayer. Frances Kinnick stood helplessly.

The ten Hawkeyes on the field moved closer to help their fallen star. Nile slowly rose to his elbows, then to his hands and knees. Slowly the air released from a crowd holding its collective breath. A sigh emanated from the stadium all the way to the seventy-ninth row and press box.

Kinnick's legs were wobbly. Prasse ran to the nearest referee and signaled for a timeout.

The Ironmen stood together ten yards behind the line of scrimmage, collecting their thoughts and sipping water from cups handed to them by the trainers. Kinnick, too, reflected for a moment. He saw the concern of his teammates.

Mike Enich looked worried. "Nile, do you want a sub?"

"No, just give me a minute," Kinnick said. "You know that this is where I want to be right now, with you guys. We've got these Gophers right where we want them, right?" Kinnick paused. "Besides, it's much better than being on the battlefields of Europe, isn't it?"

"Only you would be thinking about political issues at the most important moment of the season." Enich shook his head as he spoke. Eleven Ironmen smiled.

Three running plays gained little yardage. The speedy Sonny Franck then returned Kinnick's punt to the Minnesota forty. On first down, Mike Enich buried Bruce Smith, limiting the Gopher's right halfback to a three yard gain. Second down. Harold Van Every dropped back for a deep pass to Bob Sweiger. Kinnick ran alongside Sweiger, swatting the pass to the ground. Third down. Van Every tried rolling out around Minnesota's right end. Bruno Andruska hit Van Every hard, jolting the ball loose. The fumbled ball bounced once and came to rest in Prasse's arms. Iowa took possession at the Minnesota forty-two yard line with three minutes left in the first half.

In a small Davenport apartment, Couppee's father jumped out of his chair and thrust his right fist above his head. His wife was also standing in their Council Bluffs living room on the other side of the state.

Bill Green and Buzz Dean replaced Ray Murphy and Ed McLain. On first down, Couppee called Kinnick on a run around Enich and Evans on the right side of the Iowa line. With second down and seven yards remaining for a first down, Kinnick faded back, scanning his receivers as two of them ran a crossing pattern just beyond the line of scrimmage. Prasse was guarded tightly by Mernick. But suddenly, Kinnick spotted Dick Evans slowly creating some separation from the Gopher defender. Kinnick threw a perfect spiral to Evans, leading him enough so Evans never had to change speed. Evans pulled the pass into his arms at the thirty yard line as the crowd cheered wildly; then he raced nine more yards before being tackled by Harold Van Every and Bruce Smith. Suddenly, the Hawkeyes' aching, tired bodies found new life. A calm confidence returned to their eyes.

The crowd was deafening. Couppee called for another huddle to combat the noise. "Let's huddle every time now! I've got to make sure you can hear me!"

On the next play Bruno Andruska fell to the ground from a hard hit. His left hand went limp. Fortunately, it wasn't the arm he used when centering the snaps, but pain was etched deeply into his tensed face.

"Bruno, can you hike the ball?" Couppee, with his own bad shoulder, asked.

"I think so. Let me try."

Couppee didn't believe him but with Bill Diehl out of action, an underclassman, Red Frye, was the only backup center. Couppee called for a reverse play with Buzz Dean trying to follow Erv Prasse and Wally Bergstrom down the left side of the field. Dean gained one yard.

"Ready, Nile, to throw the pass of your life?" Couppee hollered but still could only be heard by Kinnick walking next to him.

"Call the play, Coup," Kinnick responded.

Again, the Hawkeye backfield started in the T-formation before shifting to the right. Andruska hiked the ball to Kinnick. Kinnick faded back while running to his right, then darted to his left to avoid the onslaught. He saw Prasse making a final cut to the inside before changing direction one last time toward the end zone.

Kinnick's pass sailed toward Prasse. But Harold Van Every hauled in the interception at the two yard line. Van Every fell to the ground but got up quickly and pumped the football above his head in celebration, ending the Hawkeye hopes for a first half touchdown. The noise level quickly changed from a deafening roar from all corners of the arena, to cheers from the small Minnesota contingent in the southeast corner of the stadium. It was Minnesota's ball. The Gophers ran two plays before the second quarter ended.

The final play of the first half ended near the north goal line. The Hawkeyes' locker room was at the opposite end of the field. As the Ironmen ran the entire length of the field to the locker room, the fans stood and cheered their gold-helmeted soldiers as they paraded past. They were only down three points against the most physical team in the country. They had stood their ground.

The scoreboard showed Minnesota 3, Iowa 0. Thirty minutes of football remained.

Continuing their halftime custom, Couppee and Kinnick sat next to each other in the locker room. Couppee looked sadly at the floor as he spoke. "I can't go any longer, Coach. I can't move my arm. Nile will have to call the plays in the second half." He couldn't look Coach Anderson in the eye. He didn't want Dr. Eddie to see the tears, afraid his tears of disappointment might be misconstrued as tears of pain. This game meant too much. He couldn't imagine not being on the field. He had always been a key contributor ever since he first put on the pads in junior high school.

"Okay. Go have the trainer take a look at it." Dr. Eddie felt the loss as much as Couppee. This was not the time to lose your starting quarterback. "Nile, you're taking over the play calling.

"Where's Andruska? Bruno, how's the hand?" Dr. Eddie looked at Andruska's bruised and swollen wrist, knowing he might be without his center for the second half.

"It's not bad enough to keep me out of the game, Coach. I can play."

"It looks awful. Get some tape on it." Dr. Eddie knew it was more serious than Andruska thought. "And let me know if you can't go."

The players rested while Dr. Eddie spoke. He praised their efforts and applauded their mental and physical toughness. He again reminded them how proud he was to be part of this team. Then he gave them one final challenge. "Gentlemen, outside those doors is an opportunity that goes beyond description. Last week against Notre Dame, I thought, was possibly my greatest moment in sports. And now, another high profile game knocks on our doorstep. We're not expected to win this game. But we weren't supposed to beat Notre Dame, either. I believe in you. The few bodies we have doesn't matter. The size of the Gophers doesn't matter. All that matters is execution.

"Couppee is out for the rest of this game." Dr. Eddie's bad news shocked the team. "So Bill Gallagher will be at quarterback. Nile will be calling the plays. And we'll run the T-formation, dropping into the 'box' on most all plays. If it gets too loud, we'll go to a huddle.

"Jerry Ankeny, be ready to sub for Gallagher. And Red Frye, be ready to sub for Andruska." Dr. Eddie scanned the room. His gaze stopped on Nile Kinnick. The two looked at each other. Dr. Eddie knew he didn't need to tell Kinnick how much weight rested on his shoulders. "Alright Ironmen, are you ready?!" shouted Dr. Eddie. "Are you ready to take this game?!"

In unison, the Ironmen jumped to their feet shouting their agreement, surrounding their head coach with a powerful, crushing energy.

"Gentlemen, we are on one of those rides of a lifetime! Let's not get off, yet! We have two quarters to change a three point deficit into our victory. A three point deficit is the same as a tie game, so it's all about who plays better for the next thirty minutes. And I'm betting my money on you!" Dr. Eddie turned towards the door. Twenty-seven players rushed past him.

The struggle for field position continued. Minnesota and Iowa exchanged punts. With seven minutes left in the third quarter, on consecutive plays, Gallagher sprained a shoulder and Dean injured his right leg. Both were gone for the rest of the game. Tollefson began limping.

Kinnick noticed Andruska's blue fingers due to his swelling wrist pushing tighter against the wrapped bandage. "Bruno, this game is important but Red Frye can get the job done if you want to stop."

"What about just staying in the T-formation so I just hike to the quarterback right behind me?" Andruska knew Kinnick would be against his idea. They rarely operated out of the T-formation. This game was not the time to try seldom used plays from the playbook. And with Couppee and Gallagher both out, Ankeny was the only remaining quarterback. It would be better to just use the new quarterback for blocking assignments rather than for handling the snaps.

"Bruno, you've got to be able to hike it back or Frye must come in!" Kinnick was emphatic. There would be no argument from Andruska. He stayed in the game.

It was Minnesota's ball on the forty-nine yard line. Fourth down. Harold Van Every was displaying kicking skills that rivaled Kinnick's. Once again Van Every took aim. The punt sailed towards Kinnick, but Nile didn't try to catch it. Kinnick hoped it would bounce into the end zone for a touchback, giving Iowa possession of the ball on their twenty yard line. But the ball bounced at the seven and was downed by a Gopher at the four yard line.

The crowd noise lowered with Iowa pinned back near the goal line, so Kinnick didn't need to use a huddle. All ten could easily hear him bellow the play over the soft din of the crowd. And he did what the Hawkeyes expected, hoping to catch the Gophers off guard. "Four, seven, two, forty-nine, twenty-five, sixteen!" Kinnick shifted behind Andruska, eight yards off the line of scrimmage, hoping Minnesota wouldn't notice the punt formation, but Van Every did.

Kinnick kicked the ball high and deep. Van Every raced back to midfield and caught it after one hop. He turned and ran his best route of the day, eluding three tacklers before Prasse tackled him at Iowa's twenty-eight yard line. The quick punt formation accomplished little.

The skirmish for field position was slowly turning in Minnesota's favor. Coach Bierman did not want to miss this opportunity. He sent in seven new linemen and Sonny Franck, who had been resting since the second quarter.

Franck ran for five yards on first down on a cutback behind his left guard. Van Every gained six more running behind Gordon Paschka and Urban Odson. The Gophers had a first down on the seventeen yard line.

Sonny Franck bulldozed his way to the twelve yard line and then Bob Sweiger gained five more yards on the next play. With a new first down, Sweiger made the mistake of running straight at Mike Enich for no gain. Franck ran to his right on the next play, but cut back, also into the arms of Enich. Somehow, Enich was trying to will Minnesota away from the score by himself.

The fan noise was back. An anxious crowd knew a Minnesota touchdown might be too much for the Hawkeyes to overcome with the end of the third quarter fast approaching. Holding Minnesota to a field goal would mean Kinnick and his teammates would only be a touchdown behind. The crowd's clamor suddenly rose to a level that didn't allow Minnesota to hear Joe Mernick's play calling. Minnesota called timeout.

"Coach, put me in for this goal line stand. I've got to be out there!" Couppee stood next to Dr. Eddie.

Dr. Eddie looked at Couppee's eyes and knew the fire was burning strong. He liked seeing that look on a player's face. "Okay. Go in for Murphy. But this series only! Just this series!" Dr. Eddie questioned if putting Couppee back in was the right decision, but the season was winding down, and this might be the moment where it ends, or where it escalates higher than everyone's expectations.

Third down. Minnesota had two chances to cover seven yards. This time it was Van Every's turn, but Max Hawkins stopped Van Every after a one yard gain.

Fourth down from the six. Coach Bierman wanted the touchdown. Once again Sonny Franck took his turn carrying the ball. Van Every led the charge around the left side. Kinnick and Couppee both ran at an angle to the spot where the goal line meets the sideline, hoping to cut off Franck. A loud collision occurred at the goal line.

It appeared that Kinnick and Couppee had tackled Franck, knocking him out of bounds short of the goal line. The Hawkeyes and their fans cheered the defensive stop of the mighty Minnesota Gophers. Then, to the astonishment of thousands, the referee raised both hands above his head as he ran to the scene. Suddenly, it was the maroon and gold uniforms celebrating. The black and gold insisted to both referees standing nearby that Franck hadn't reached the goal line. The play stayed as called, a touchdown for Minnesota.

After order was restored, Joe Mernick lined up for the extra point kick. Prasse cut in front of a Gopher and sprinted toward the Minnesota player holding the ball for Mernick's kick. He reached out, deflecting the ball just enough with his fingertips to push it left of the goalpost. Iowa trailed by nine points.

Two hours later, Bert McGrane sat in the press box finishing his story for Sunday's Des Moines Register. Next to him was James Kearns from the Chicago Daily News. A St. Paul sports editor and another young journalist from Cedar Rapids, Tait Cummins, were also still soaking in what they had just witnessed.

These four gentlemen, as did over fifty thousand others, came to Iowa Stadium hoping to see a spectacular game between a national powerhouse and an upstart football program. They witnessed what they came to see, yet, it was a game that left them speechless, smoking cigarettes and cigars, not wanting to rush out into the common, conventional world. They could still feel what they had just observed on this Saturday afternoon. The magic still mysteriously blanketed the stadium like an early morning fog. They didn't want to leave. Not yet, anyway.

For three quarters the most successful team in the nation the past three years slowly built a lead on the undersized and undermanned Iowa Hawkeyes, who had only one-third the number of players of most Big Ten teams. And to further worsen Iowa's chances of victory, Tollefson, Couppee, Dean, and Gallagher had left the game with injuries. Minnesota, ahead 9 to 0 at the end of the third quarter, had what seemed an insurmountable lead. Then the fourth quarter began.

Bert McGrane and James Kearns knew each other well. Many times they shared seats next to each other in the press box. Often, no matter what Big Ten campus they visited through the years, they would find the biggest steak and the coldest beer after sending their stories off to their respective newspapers. Many times they read each other's accounts and stole a phrase or two.

After the game it was learned in the press conference that Nile Kinnick's right hand, his passing hand, was swollen from a hit in the first half. And to add to this tribulation, he was calling the plays in the second half and purposely called running plays when his hand throbbed too much to pass. But the big story regarding Iowa's injuries was Bruno Andruska. After suffering an injury to his wrist in the first half, he asked that it be taped because he didn't want to leave the game. He played through the pain. In fact, he played the remainder of the first half - and the entire second half - with a broken wrist, further augmenting the Ironmen legend.

All four journalists were in the Hawkeye locker room earlier when Dr. Eddie shared these pieces of information. It was, now, a little after six o'clock. Their stories for tomorrow's papers were finished.

"I've never seen anything like it in all my days of reporting," said Bert McGrane.

"It's a storybook, Bert. It's the biggest story we've had in years." James Kearns shook his head while he took a drag on his customary post-game cigar. "I just wonder where it ends."

"It just keeps building," McGrane added. "Few players, injuries, a new coach and coaching staff, and a losing program turned around in one season. And then there's Kinnick. Jim, neither you nor I have ever seen someone like him!" The two sat in silence looking out over Iowa Stadium. They still couldn't believe what this November afternoon had delivered. McGrane turned to his old companion. "You hungry?"

"Hungry and thirsty, my friend. How about that restaurant in Tiffin?" James Kearns knew what McGrane's answer would be. It was their usual destination after an Iowa City game. As they stood and started walking toward the door Tait Cummins, the rookie journalist for the Cedar Rapids Gazette, approached them. "Would you mind if I read your columns?"

"I'll make you a deal, Cummins. You can look at them right now, if you'll then run these over to the telegraph company and send them to the Chicago Daily News and the Des Moines Register. After that, you can catch us for a beer in Tiffin."

"I'd be glad to, Mr. McGrane." It was an opportunity a rookie journalist didn't pass up, not only the opportunity to read their stories, but also to have a beer with two well-known writers. It was his first invitation to join the select club.

"Make sure you don't send my story to the Daily News," McGrane chuckled. "I don't want Kearns getting credit for my efforts."

James Kearns only smiled. "If you hurry, Cummins, you might even get Bert to buy you a steak. I'm almost certain it's his turn."

Tait Cummins sat down and pulled Bert McGrane's report out of its yellow folder.

> *IOWA CITY November 18, 1939*
> *A grizzled observer wiped a tear of admiration off his leathery cheek. Writers hardened to emotion in many a year in the pressbox fumbled for words. Mad, milling thousands hauled an All-American halfback off the field on their shoulders. Pandemonium everywhere.*
> *Iowa, probably the most astounding football team ever to cross the tawny turf of a gridiron, had just written another glorious chapter in its book of hair-raising, breathtaking finishes.*
> *The Iron Hawks, underdogs as usual, had blasted Minnesota off the gridiron with another of their torrid, story book onslaughts that brought them an unbelievable 13 to 9 triumph over a team that had all but smashed them into submission through three bruising periods.*
> *Here was another amazing victory against colossal odds. Outweighed, overpowered at times, outmanned as usual, the invincible Hawks went into the fourth quarter trailing, 9 to 0, moved the length of the field twice on passes and whirled on in the national*

spotlight with a thundering climax that 50,000 spectators still can't believe.

With the echo of the timekeeper's gun still in the air and thousands swarming onto the field in wild acclaim, fans hoisted Nile Kinnick onto their shoulders and hauled him away to the dressing room. Kinnick, the lad who had kept the Hawks together when it seemed fate was against them at the start, had just put the clinching touch on his all-American reputation.

It was Kinnick who fired the two touchdown passes that beat Minnesota. First to Erwin Prasse, later to Bill Green, the Comet of the Cornbelt shot home the winning throws. But it wasn't entirely Kinnick's triumph. His role was to dish up the dynamite that left a stunned, unbelieving Minnesota team the victim at the finish. *

Tait Cummins read on, recounting how the fourth quarter unfolded. Two minutes into the fourth quarter, Kinnick passed twice to Buzz Dean. After sending three receivers to the right as decoys, Kinnick found Prasse on the eight yard line. Catching the ball while sprinting down the left sideline, Prasse easily raced into the end zone.

Minnesota 9, Iowa 7, after Kinnick's extra point drop kick.

Iowa kicked off. On the second play from scrimmage, Andruska hit the Minnesota halfback hard, jarring the ball loose from his grasp. Enich jumped on the fumble at Minnesota's thirty-six yard line.

Iowa couldn't move the ball and Minnesota took over on downs. Then Iowa's defense again found the strength to fight the fresh Gopher faces that had just entered the game. They kept Minnesota from gaining the needed ten yards, so Van Every punted.

Kinnick fielded the ball on Iowa's twelve yard line and ran back to the twenty-one before being tackled.

Two plays later, Joe Mernik intercepted a Kinnick pass but the interception was nullified because he was called for interference on Prasse. It was Iowa's ball on the Minnesota forty-five yard line.

Bill Green ran for seven yards. Kinnick ran for ten more. Next, Prasse and Evans ran patterns deep in the Minnesota backfield on a pass play. And while Minnesota focused on the Iowa ends, Kinnick found his fullback, Bill Green, coming out of the backfield. Green caught the ball in the back of the end zone. Kinnick's extra point kick was blocked. Iowa 13, Minnesota 9.

With one minute left, Minnesota's Harold Van Every tried a long pass to midfield. Kinnick intercepted. Iowa ran the clock out with two running plays.

Cummins put McGrane's story back in the folder and grabbed James Kearns' article that would be in the Chicago Daily News tomorrow morning.

IOWA CITY   November 18, 1939
There's a golden helmet riding on a human sea across Iowa's football field in the twilight here.
Now the helmet rises as wave upon wave of humanity pours onto the field. There's a boy under the helmet which is shining like a crown on his head. A golden No. 24 gleams on his slumping, tired shoulders.
The boy is Nile Clarke Kinnick Jr. who has, just now, risen above all the defenses

that could be raised against him. He has gone out of Iowa's domestic football scene with an explosive, dramatic, incredible farewell party of his own making. He has just thrown the great power and size and strength of Minnesota into a 13 to 9 defeat before an overflow crowd of fifty thousand. Here was courage incarnate, poise personified in the calm deliberation of a twenty one year old boy. Here was Kinnick at the peak of his great career, leading a frenzied little band of Iowa football players to a victory which was impossible. They couldn't win, but they did.

Cummins looked up from the typed paper, out onto the football field. His emotions were stirring. He knew, at that moment, he wanted to do this work for the rest of his life. It was time to get to the telegraph office. He didn't read the rest of Kearns' article. He wanted to meet up with his mentors.

CHAPTER TWENTY-FIVE

"I'll see if Barbara can join me," Mary Stellman told Erv Prasse during their telephone conversation. "I'll see you at Racine's."

"Okay. Around eight o'clock. Tell Barbara that Kinnick won't be there right away. He's speaking at a high school tonight." Erv Prasse was making several phone calls, as was Al Couppee. The two decided the Hawkeyes needed a night of celebration. "But I know he'll be there later. Bye."

Prasse, Couppee, Enich, and Kinnick had walked out of the earlier chalk talk together following the team meeting. It would be the fifth night in a row that students packed downtown Iowa City to celebrate the unexpected successes of the football squad. The culmination of the season, winning back-to-back games against two of the greatest powerhouses in the nation, and come-from-behind wins against Indiana and Wisconsin, had the students rejuvenated. It felt good. It touched everyone. It was a story bringing acclaim to a few football players, several of whom were now injured. It started on a Saturday afternoon in late September. Slowly their following grew week after week. Now, the entire nation was embracing the story. And the leading actor on the stage was an unassuming young man more concerned with social issues than football. Nile Kinnick didn't understand why poverty was rampant. He didn't understand the tyranny taking place in Europe. He had grown up hearing about the legacy of his grandfather governing Iowa, and how his grandfather successfully dealt with the issues of that time. Nile often wondered if he, too, could someday make a difference.

Harold Avery, the principal of Iowa City High School, stood at the podium. "Given the events of the last two weeks, we thought it would be a wonderful opportunity for our seniors to hear from a person making headlines across the country. Then, after our guest speaker had accepted our invitation to join us tonight, and with his approval, we decided we should invite our entire student body to tonight's event. So it is with great pleasure I introduce to you, Nile Kinnick."

The applause echoed from the metal rafters supporting the ceiling above the basketball court. The students filled the temporary chairs on the floor and the bleachers on the south side of the gym. Curious parents and Hawkeye fans packed the north bleachers. Others, unable to find a place to sit, stood along the concrete block walls at the two ends of the basketball court. They had come to listen to a young man now being mentioned by many journalists as a contender for the Heisman Trophy, an award presented to the outstanding college football player in the nation.

Nile Kinnick stood stoically in front of the podium, smiling as he scanned the crowd. The turnout overwhelmed him. Originally, he had agreed to speak to the seniors. Now, as he looked out, he was awed by the Ironmen's obvious impact on others.

> *Thank you. Thank you all for your gracious welcome. I am moved. And thank you, Mr. Avery, for your invitation.*

My very first thought as I stand here is 'what a difference a year makes.' I doubt there would have been a turnout like this a year ago.

Laughter rang through the gymnasium.

So much has changed. And maybe that's the greatest thing I can hope to impart upon you tonight. And that is, how quickly life can change, for the better, with proper effort and preparation. My speech was prepared thinking I was just speaking to the seniors, but my words I hope will have meaning to everyone.
The world is alive, alert, and dynamic. And every person here is a part of it. Whether you make an ultimate effort to reach your goals, or merely accept what life delivers to your doorstep, each day is up to you. With goals and direction, you create a path to follow rather than wandering aimlessly through life like a ship without a rudder. It's your decision. And that decision shouldn't come at some moment in the distant future. That decision can be right here, right now.
I was blessed with great parents. They instilled in me a desire to learn and to always endeavor to make the right decisions, and to never be deterred from what I felt was right. 'Rightful living' was a term I heard endlessly growing up, and I will be eternally grateful for those lessons. I owe much to my

parents. Without them I wouldn't have had the opportunity to attend the University of Iowa, or be here speaking to you tonight.

I hope many of you have the opportunity to attend college. It is a wonderful environment to learn and develop. You are given a chance to study what is important to you. But no matter what courses you choose, what is truly important is the opportunity to 'learn how to think,' to think for yourselves, and to develop an inquiring mind. College presents this wonderful possibility. But it is up to the individual to educate him or her self. Many of you might not have college in your plans, but I still challenge everyone to commit to educating yourself every day. Just imagine how great the world could be if everyone pledged to learn something new and worthwhile every day. How great the world could be with greater knowledge of our planet and greater knowledge of each other, and what is truly important in life. Maybe, someday, we could eliminate the prejudices, bigotries, and injustices sweeping through our country, and the rest of the world.

It is so important that you maintain a dynamic interest in reading, math, science, economics, sociology, and history right now. Literature and language improve your ability to clearly express ideas and convictions. Reading newspapers and periodicals is important for gaining knowledge about current events, our social values, and each other. This knowledge is essential for your future and the future of everyone. With the study of history, we have an opportunity to learn from our past so we can duplicate the good deeds and eliminate the mistakes of our ancestors.

Governmental positions will continually experience turnover until one day our generation will be making the decisions that affect the world. There will come a time, and not in the too distant future, when the responsibility to positively influence the world will rest on our shoulders. Will we be ready?

We all have a tendency to dream about the future. We often think that someday good fortune will be granted to us and our lives will be enriched beyond our expectations. We think everything will fall into place and, eventually, be alright. But the reality is that our destiny is caused by an unseen energy, an energy that is initiated by our decisions and enhanced by our actions. And as these actions build upon each other, they create momentum, and our life's direction - what some call destiny. But we choose it. Every day we choose.

Once we see our personal goals unfolding, we automatically focus more time and effort toward those specific goals, and as a result, an exponential movement begins to take us more rapidly toward our goals. Our dreams, visions, decisions, and ultimately our actions keep the momentum building.

Winston Churchill, a man I greatly admire, once said, "Continuous effort, not strength or intellect, is the key to unlocking potential." I firmly believe this. So I challenge you to begin now. Right now. Begin your future and find your potential.

But I also warn you not to dwell on dreams and forget to live. There is a balance between dreaming, visualizing, and planning your future, and the actions you need to take today to accomplish that which you seek. Dreams are good, they give you direction, but they must be followed by action. Dr. Eddie Anderson told us back in spring practice, I should really call it winter practice because it was February, that 'each day without practice is one more day before you are good.' I must tell you, it was somewhat odd practicing football in the west end of the Fieldhouse while the basketball team was practicing in the east end. And I can also tell you, we are all glad Dr. Eddie got in those extra practices so we could be where we are now.

So take action, and create your momentum, right now. It is not enough to stare up the steps. One must also step up the stairs.

I believe in self-fulfilling prophecies, meaning how you perceive yourself will speak volumes about your life's success. So I ask you, 'how do you see yourself?'

I hope each of you leaves here tonight knowing you are capable of extraordinary dreams and extraordinary results. And you can start right now by being extraordinary today.

My father once told me: "Your thoughts become your words. Your words become your actions. Your actions become your habits. Your habits become your destiny."

For another thirty minutes, Nile Kinnick reached out to the spellbound listeners. He wanted to inspire them, especially the seniors, to boldly proceed forward with the rest of their lives.

I'll quote my father once more. It's something I'll never forget. He said: "You are given three names in your lifetime: the name of your family, the name your parents bestow upon you, and the name you earn for yourself."

I'll leave you with one final thought: As you dream and plan your futures, remember also to enjoy where you are. There is no greater place to be than right here, right now, and I hope you will always be able to feel that way no matter where your journeys take you.

Thank you for this opportunity to be here, now.

NILE

Good night, and good luck.

As he folded the papers with his handwritten notes and placed them inside his sport jacket, applause again echoed in the gymnasium's rafters. Everyone stood. Then the applause increased. He was more than a football player, or hero. He was a leader, a young man with purpose. The parents and teachers in the gymnasium sensed it even more than the students.

Kinnick smiled broadly as he looked around, absorbing the continuing applause. He was enjoying the moment. As he looked to his right, his thoughts quickly shifted. Standing against the wall by the exit door was Barbara Miller. Kinnick then noticed Mary Stellman standing next to her. And beside her, Erv Prasse, then Mike Enich, Al Couppee and ten other Hawkeyes with their golden 'I's proudly displayed on their black letter jackets. They had collectively decided Racine's could wait.

Iowa City High School was thirteen blocks from Racine's. Fourteen Hawkeyes and two women enjoyed each other's company walking along the sidewalks. Distances didn't bother college youth, especially when the camaraderie of friends warmed their spirits on a cold November night. Lighthearted teasing and laughter accompanied this merry group.

Nile and Barbara walked behind the others. "What are your plans after second semester?" Kinnick asked.

"I'm hoping my student teaching in the spring might lead to a job somewhere either around here, I do like Iowa City, or maybe in Des Moines. I don't know where I'll be doing the student teaching, though. What about you, Nile?"

"Most likely I'll be attending law school, and probably here at Iowa. I have considered applying for a Rhodes Scholarship, but if I was lucky enough to get one, it would ultimately delay law school by two years."

"It sounds like you are taking action toward your goals."
Barbara Miller laughed, referring to this evening's speech.

Nile laughed, too. "I can talk a good story. Frankly, I'm a little undecided."

"Would you ever consider pro football?"

"At my size, I don't like the thought of large linemen getting paid money to collide with running backs." Kinnick laughed again as he turned to look at Barbara. He noticed a kindness radiating from her warm eyes and pleasant smile. And then he answered her question again, this time more seriously. "I know law school is an important stepping stone for me. I've entertained the idea of pro football because it could give me the opportunity to attend law school later without having to work at the same time. But then I think about how quickly time passes. If I did play pro football, let's say for three years, that's three years my law degree is delayed. I think I know where I want my journey to take me, and I see pro football as a detour slowing my plan."

"What are your goals, Nile?"

He sighed before answering. "You mean besides enjoying a nice walk with you?" Their eyes met again while the others continued ahead. "I want to have a positive effect on humanity and the environment, whatever that might be. I know that sounds idealistic and generalized, but that's what I want to do."

Barbara perceived what he was alluding to. "I detect an interest in politics. And after hearing and seeing you tonight, I think you would be great. People genuinely like to listen to you. They want to know what you have to say. Just look at the turnout at the auditorium tonight."

Chuck Tollefson and Al Couppee were leading the cluster's hike towards downtown. Red Frye, Max Hawkins, Mike Enich, and Hank Vollenweider trailed the two fastest walkers by thirty yards. Wally Bergstrom, Jens Norgaard, Ham Snider, Buzz Dean, Jim Walker, and Ed McLain formed a snug pack behind the previous four. Erv Prasse walked with Mary Stellman just in front of Nile and Barbara.

Prasse turned to Kinnick and spoke loudly enough for everyone to hear. "Hey Nile, this must be how you feel going down the field. I can't see ahead with all these wide bodies leading the way."

Kinnick jumped on Prasse's verbal hand-off and spoke with equal volume. "Fortunately, tonight, none of them are lying on the ground requiring us to step over them. It can get so tiring having to high step just to keep from injuring them."

Bergstrom defended the linemen. "Kinnick, we just may have to let one of those All-American guards go unblocked this weekend so you'll appreciate us more."

Red Frye spoke up with a nervous high pitch to his voice. "There are two All-American guards at Northwestern?" His teammates laughed. Red Frye would be starting his first college game against Northwestern in place of Bruno Andruska.

"Red, you are about to experience an entire season in one game," responded Jens Norgaard.

"Especially once they hear the scouting report that you're starting your first game, Red." Mike Enich's words didn't console the underclassman Frye, especially when Frye considered the weight of hiking the ball to a Heisman candidate and then blocking for him while trying to win the Big Ten championship. Bill Diehl, the original starting center, wouldn't be back from his season-ending injury at Wisconsin. Andruska couldn't play the injured hero any longer. One game with a broken wrist was more effort and dedication than an Ironman needed to give. It was Red Frye's turn.

The crowd slowly bunched together as they neared Racine's. Couppee and Tollefson were standing next to a new Chevrolet talking to two young women as the others caught up to them.

"Are you two new around here?" Couppee asked.

"I've been here about a year. My sister is just visiting for the weekend." Her tone showed no interest in Al Couppee or his friend.

"This is Chuck Tollefson, a guard on the football team, and I'm Al Couppee, the quarterback."

"Well, I'll have to tell my husband I met the two of you. I'm sure you know him. He's an assistant football coach, Frank Carideo."

Couppee's jaw dropped as his face turned red. Instead of showing his teammates his bold style, he was embarrassed. It didn't help him that he could hear fourteen people behind him laughing hysterically, some bent over at the waist.

"Uh, well, tell Coach 'hello.' Anyway, hope the two of you have a nice dinner, or whatever you're going to do."

The two women, clearly amused by Couppee, walked by the others. The rest of the group couldn't talk because they were still laughing too hard.

Racine's was two doors down, packed with the other Hawkeye footballers and friends. It was a night for the Hawkeyes to bond. One game remained in their remarkable season. One more win and the Ironmen would be Big Ten football champions.

CHAPTER TWENTY-SIX

Tuesday, November 28, 1939. Nile sat alone at his desk. It had been three days since the final game against Northwestern. It was almost midnight. He needed to write one letter before going to bed.

> *Dear Mother and Father,*
> *I don't know where to begin this letter. I just received a most astonishing phone call. But before I share the content of that call, I'd like to tell you my thoughts on last Saturday's game.*
> *Saturday morning I received a telegram from Ed Frutig, Michigan's outstanding receiver. I read it to the team before the Northwestern game. It said, 'You take care of Northwestern, and we'll take care of Ohio State.' It was very motivational for us. If Michigan could win at Ohio State, and if we were victorious against Northwestern,*

then Iowa would tie Ohio State for the Big Ten championship. As you know, Michigan held up their end of the bargain. They didn't want their arch rival winning the conference outright.

I have never seen a more determined group of people than the Iowa Hawkeyes Saturday. We were decimated with injuries. After Andruska played the second half of the Minnesota game with a broken wrist, we turned to a third string center as his replacement. It was Red Frye's first action. He played with remarkable poise, especially when considering the conference championship was at stake. He was a true Ironman. After Bergstrom was injured, Jim Walker returned for the first time since his knee injury in the Michigan game. And Al Couppee played the entire game wearing a harness to protect his collar bone.

Sophomore Hank Vollenweider played for the first time since running a kickoff back for a touchdown against South Dakota in the opening game. Max Hawkins and Chuck Tollefson also left the game with injuries. I have shared with you my admiration for Tollie. He fought his way back to Iowa after riding the rails and helping farmers with their harvests. I've learned a great deal from Tollie. He is a very commendable person who leads by example.

Mother, I want you, especially, to know about my injury. I separated my shoulder on a tackle in the early part of the third quarter. I tried to accept it and continue playing, but it continued to worsen. Finally, I couldn't move my right shoulder to pass. I'm not sure why I sustained this injury. I have tried my very best to live rightfully. Again, please help my healing. I just wish I could have made it two more quarters for my teammates.

Buzz Dean did a great job replacing me. Dean, Prasse, and Mike Enich brought the Hawkeyes back into the game. Iron Mike had more jarring tackles than I have ever witnessed by one individual. And his final tackle, when Northwestern had a fourth and goal at our one yard line, saved the tie, and our season. He is a tremendous athlete, and even more, a tremendous person.

I was so proud to be a Hawkeye Saturday. Sitting on the bench was difficult after having played six complete games. I experienced such a dichotomy of emotions watching the Ironmen from the sideline. Enich, Prasse, Frye, Pettit, Snyder, and Evans played the entire sixty minutes. It was exciting to watch. Yet, at the same time, I felt disheartened realizing I would never set foot on the gridiron again wearing the black and gold. But I know my journey doesn't end here at the University. It begins.

Our 7-7 tie with Northwestern means we finished second in the conference. More important, possibly, we ended up ninth in the Associated Press' final national poll. For once, the long awaited glorious season no longer eluded me.

Dr. Eddie again took the entire team to Wrigley Field to watch the Bears play the Cardinals. We quickly forgot our disappointing tie with Northwestern and, instead, were immersed in realizing what a wonderful and magical year we experienced. And as you probably heard already, Dr. Eddie was voted the National Coach of the Year.

Now, before I retire for the night, I must tell you about the phone call I received this morning. I thought about calling you earlier to inform you about it, but my emotions would have gotten the best of me. I thought it would be easier in a letter.

The call was from a Mr. Willard Prince. The Downtown Athletic Club in New York voted me the recipient of this year's Heisman Trophy.

With love,
Nile

Willard Prince told Nile the results of the voting would not be released for two days. The Club wanted a small window of time to prepare for the media onslaught. Mr. Prince also said he wanted to inform Nile ahead of the media release so Nile could have an opportunity to "absorb the accomplishment, enjoy it, and reflect on his success before being besieged by reporters."

Nile stopped and thought about all that had happened. The 1939 Iowa Hawkeyes were the most written about, and talked about, team in the nation. Dr. Eddie had made it all possible. Then his thoughts shifted to himself. He was Senior Class President, Phi Beta Kappa, and now this phone call from New York's Downtown Athletic Club. He was awestruck by the magnitude of one phone call and how it might change his life forever. It felt 'right,' he thought.

He folded his parents' letter before slipping it into the envelope. He hoped it would arrive at his parents' house before the press was informed. He turned off the light and went to bed. He realized he would never have this moment again, a private moment when no one else knew. A smile widened as he closed his eyes and exhaled.

CHAPTER TWENTY-SEVEN

Tuesday, December 5, 1939. The train station's boarding area was wet from snowflakes gently falling, instantly melting on the surface of the wooden planks. Dr. Eddie Anderson and Nile Kinnick waited inside the depot for the Rock Island Rocket's boarding call. The nine o'clock departure would take them to Chicago, where they would subsequently get on the Twentieth Century train this afternoon for New York.

"Look over there, Nile. We have company," said Dr. Eddie.

Nile peered to his left. Erv Prasse, Al Couppee, and Mike Enich walked briskly toward the depot. They hurried through the door to avoid the cold.

"Gentlemen." Dr. Eddie greeted them as they walked towards the two travelers.

Al Couppee spoke first. "Hi, Coach. We thought we'd come down and send you off in style."

"Congratulations again, Coach, for being the Coach of the Year. You deserve it." Mike Enich stretched his large right hand toward Coach Anderson. Enich reveled in knowing he would get Dr. Eddie's well-known, unyielding handshake. He was ready to grip Dr. Eddie's hand just as firmly. "We would not have had this season without you."

"Thank you, Mike."

"Yeah, congratulations, Coach. No one deserves the award more than you. I wouldn't want to even consider what the season would have been like without you and Nile." Erv Prasse also shook the coach's hand. Then he turned to Kinnick. "Nile, I've played with some great players, but none like you. You're not the biggest. You're not the fastest. But you are definitely the greatest I've ever seen. I'm glad you beat out Harmon. And besides, he's a junior and will have a shot at it next year." Michigan's Tom Harmon received the second most votes for the Heisman.

"Thanks, Prass. That means a great deal coming from you. We've been through a lot together." Nile Kinnick looked at Couppee and Enich who were nodding in agreement with Prasse's assessment. "I'm sorry I wasn't around to see you guys this weekend. My family wanted to have a late Thanksgiving celebration at my grandmother's." The conductor hollered a last call for everyone to board. Kinnick continued, "It doesn't seem right that you guys aren't coming along."

Couppee added, "Well, just mention our names in your speech. We've got to keep our names in front of those NFL owners." Couppee laughed. "I assume they'll be listening to the radio broadcast, just like us."

"I'll make sure I include all of you," Kinnick said. "Seriously, though, this is a team award. I'm not sure one individual should be singled out."

"Time to go, Nile." Dr. Eddie leaned down to his side, reaching for the suitcase next to him. "Thank you, gentlemen, for stopping by, especially you, Couppee. You probably were out all night and just got out of bed to make it down here on time."

"Not really, Coach. Just had to miss a class I don't like to attend, anyway."

"When are you guys coming back? We need to have a celebration," said Enich.

"We fly back December 10th. It'll be fun to get up in the air," Nile said. "I may be riding the Rocket for my last time today."

Dr. Eddie and Nile found their seats. Nile's was next to the window facing the depot. His three teammates still stood inside looking out at the train. "You know, Coach, we couldn't have done it without any one of those guys." Nile continued looking at his teammates.

"You're right, Nile. You are absolutely right. But I can reiterate what Prasse said. You are the best I've ever seen. And I've seen many players in my day, college and professional. But your abilities go far beyond football, Nile. And I know you know that, too." The train slowly started forward. "I went into medicine and coaching because I liked both, but also because I wanted to help others. I couldn't give up one for the other. I help sick people and I help young men become better young men. And I think you feel somewhat the same obligation, an obligation to use your skills to help others. You have a gift. People want to hear what you have to say."

Nile said, "I've thought about it a lot, Coach, what I want to do after this school year. I'm sure pro football is a good possibility, but I think I most want to start law school right away. You know, when I think back to my Sunday evenings growing up, it's almost as if my parents and grandparents were preparing me for politics."

The Rocket was at full speed. Dr. Eddie and Nile would be transferring to another train within four hours. The reality of the moment, and what they were about to do in New York, became more real with each passing hour. The Heisman Trophy would make Nile Kinnick a household name, even to those who didn't follow college football. He wondered what the future held with that kind of fame.

One hour into the journey, Coach Anderson interrupted Kinnick's thoughts. "Nile, have you thought about what you will say when you accept the trophy?"

"Yes, and no. I want to use the moment to thank everyone, but I don't want to have a written speech, or notes. I want it to come from the heart. But I'll be thinking about it on this ride."

"I'm sure you will do fine, Nile."

"I'm going to miss this ride to Chicago, and then wherever we went from there." Nile spoke while gazing out at the Mississippi River flowing under the bridge. "Especially, those rides home after a victory. Those will be some of the best memories of my life."

"Well, I'll be taking this ride many times with different players in the future," said Dr. Eddie. "It's odd in a way. You never leave behind one team and start coaching another. The team doesn't change all at once. It continues. There is always a gradual change of faces. You lose some seniors. Some new players take their place, so the majority of players are always men that were on the team the previous year. There is a continuance. It feels like it's the same team, even though it slowly transforms.

"This team was special. I hope I win some Big Ten championships, but this team will never be duplicated. Even though we were one score away from beating Northwestern and winning the Big Ten, the belief and the conviction were there. The character was there, and we did it with very few players. I'd be a very fortunate coach to have a similar experience again." Dr. Eddie leaned backwards, resting his head against the cushion. He closed his eyes, taking a moment to relax before the transfer in Chicago.

Kinnick reached into his book bag and pulled out the Des Moines Register. The front page news included a column about the Soviet Union's November 30th attack of Finland. After reading the first five paragraphs, he put the newspaper down in his lap. He had thought about Europe many times this past autumn. Germany had invaded Poland. France and Britain had declared war on Germany. Canada had entered the war. The Soviets invaded Poland from the east. And all this, he thought, had happened the same month as the first football game against South Dakota. And now, people in Finland were faced with an enormous catastrophe affecting still more human lives.

Dr. Eddie heard the shuffle of the newspaper. His eyes opened.

"Dr. Eddie, I don't understand it. You think of Europe as being a civilized area. And yet there is so much destruction and death because one country wants to expand."

"War never seems to make much sense, Nile. Most of those people don't want to be involved in their conflict. They are forced into it to protect what they have. The 'Blitzkriegs,' as they have come to be known, are about greed and domination."

Nile shook his head. "I do feel a calling, Coach, to help people. Europe seems so far away, but it's real. And so are the problems facing this country. I look around here as we ride through Chicago and wonder at the plight of the black man. And I wonder how we, as a society, can enjoy all that is good in life when people next to us suffer so much. There is a sickening oppression that needs to be addressed. Is it too simple to dream about a time when men are truly equal, with equal rights and equal jobs? Abraham Lincoln addressed this a long time ago. He didn't want war, but there came a moment when war seemed to be the only answer. And still this racial problem exists, and probably will for a long time until people change their minds and hearts."

Dr. Eddie didn't want to interrupt his thoughtful, articulate football player. He continued listening while watching two elderly people maneuver their way down the aisle, both seeming to brace each other from falling.

"And in a very real way, the problems inflicting Europe are also about a malignant idea of supremacy that needs to be obliterated. September 5th, just three months ago, we declared our neutrality in the European war. But I don't think we can sit idly by much longer. We are not a people apart. Freedom for everyone is at stake. The idea of oppression, in Europe and right here in our own country, must be eradicated."

Wednesday, December 6, 1939. After sleeping poorly on the train the night before, Nile Kinnick was resting in his hotel room at the Downtown Athletic Club in New York. A knock on the door awakened him. A middle-aged man, dressed in a black suit, stood in the hallway.

"Yes?" Nile asked when he opened the door.

"Good afternoon, Mr. Kinnick. My name is Samuel Andrews. I am the concierge. The hotel wanted to make sure you have everything you need."

"Yes. Thank you."

"And we wanted to remind you that the ceremony begins at nine o'clock tonight and hope that you can be at the third floor conference room around eight thirty."

"I'll make sure I'm on time." Nile smiled at the concierge, letting him know not to worry about his attendance. "I don't think I want to miss this."

"Very good, sir. I will also inform Dr. Anderson of the same. Good evening."

"Could you tell Dr. Anderson I'll meet him in the restaurant at seven thirty?"

The concierge nodded yes.

Nile looked at his watch. He had an hour and a half to get ready.

After shaving and showering, he put on the new suit his parents had purchased for him last weekend. He paused and looked in the mirror at the double-breasted, dark gray, pinstriped suit. The white shirt was heavily starched. The tie was perfectly knotted. He looked into his own eyes. A sense of pride overcame him. He had been told his entire life about the virtues of humility, but just for a moment without anyone else around, he smiled approvingly at the image looking back in the mirror.

Kinnick's room was on the twenty-fourth floor. The elevator ride to the lobby was interrupted by two stops for others also going down. Nile was feeling excitement and anxiety at the same time. He wanted to walk around the streets for awhile to relax.

He walked across West Street and looked back at the Downtown Athletic Club. It was a magnificent hotel that had opened just nine years ago. The art deco structure stood thirty-five stories high. The reddish-brown brick building was lined with windows forming vertical stripes. Painted glass spandrels were spaced perfectly between the lower archways. He stood across from 19 West Street in New York, visually taking in his surroundings. It was a sharp contrast to Iowa City's quaint downtown. Also, here, no one recognized him.

The street was lined with high rise buildings in each direction. Hundreds of people walked briskly along the sidewalks, seemingly in a hurry for their own important evening event. A woman walked hastily past Kinnick but not before he noticed her elegant beauty and confident posture. The two strangers exchanged smiles. She wasn't used to seeing a man her age dressed as dapper as Kinnick. She also noticed his chiseled chin below the friendly smile. As she passed Nile, she caught one of her high heels in the sidewalk's iron grate, a delivery door to the skyscraper's basement storage. She stumbled slightly, falling to one knee. Kinnick lunged quickly to her aid, grabbed her arms, and helped her up.

"Are you alright?" he asked, picking up the loosened shoe and handing it to her.

"Yes, I meant to do that." She smiled again. "Thank you. I guess I was in too much of a hurry to watch where I was walking." Her hand reached for his forearm as she leaned to put the shoe back on. "You don't seem like you're in a rush like everyone else."

Kinnick laughed. "I have a little time before a meeting. I wanted to spend a few minutes just walking, observing the city."

"Oh. Where are you from?"

"Iowa."

"That's interesting. Isn't that where that good football player is from?" she asked.

"Yes, he's from Iowa." He looked at her eyes, feeling a slight selfishness for indulging himself with a little personal humor.

"In fact, I'm meeting my parents right now for dinner before we attend a trophy presentation for him. My dad is a member of the club that presents an award every year."

"That's nice. I hope you have a good time." Kinnick realized he might have an opportunity to talk to her later.

"Well, thank you again for helping me," she said. "I should get going so I don't keep my parents waiting. I'm already late, as you might have noticed."

"Yes, I noticed. And be careful. I won't be there next time to help you up." Kinnick looked at her as if she were the only person that mattered in that moment, everything else fading from his peripheral view. Silence followed.

She knew it was just another chance meeting in the big city. It happened frequently. But, this time, she didn't want to just walk away and allow their interchange to slip into the past. "My name is Virginia Eskridge."

"It's nice to meet you, Virginia. I'm Nile Kinnick."

They stood facing each other shaking hands, neither letting go of the innocent embrace.

"I'm sure you don't do this with strangers," Nile said, "but I feel I must ask you something, otherwise, this might be a missed opportunity for me. Could I have your phone number so I could possibly call you before I go home?"

"Yes. That would be nice." She pulled a paper and pen from her purse and wrote the number down. "Good night, Nile." She walked away slowly, backwards at first, both exchanging a final glance.

"Good night, Virginia."

Virginia Eskridge walked into Donnelly's Restaurant one block past the Downtown Athletic Club. Her parents were already seated. Mr. and Mrs. Eskridge were conversing as Virginia approached. "Hi, Mom. Hi, Dad." Virginia took her seat at the table.

"Hello, Virginia. I was just telling your Mom about this evening's plans. This year's Heisman Trophy winner is a young man of real substance. He's Phi Beta Kappa, headed for law school, and I understand his grandfather was once Governor of Iowa."

"I just met a person from Iowa," Virginia said, as she took off her coat and put her napkin in her lap. "I should have asked him if he's here for the ceremony. What's the Heisman Trophy winner's name?"

"Nile Kinnick," her father said.

"Nile Kinnick?" she responded. "Nile Kinnick?"

Dr. Eddie and Nile had finished their dinner in the hotel restaurant. The elevator ride to the third floor only took seconds. "When I was told I won the Heisman, time seemed to stand still for an instant. I was taken aback. I had never dreamt of receiving such an award. I don't think the immensity of the Heisman has fully sunk in. It's still difficult to imagine when you consider all the great players across the nation."

"Nile, I have no doubt that you are the most deserving person to win this award. It rightfully should go to you. Be confident in accepting it." Dr. Eddie knew Nile needed to hear this in his final moment before taking the stage.

"Then let's go do it, Coach." Kinnick opened the twelve foot tall oak door leading into the Downtown Athletic Club's ceremony room. Dr. Eddie led the way to the front tables.

The start of the ceremony was thirty minutes away. Both had been given a program to familiarize themselves with the event's timeline. It would start at nine o'clock, but the trophy presentation would not be until ten fifteen. Twelve chairs were on the stage for the ten speakers, Dr. Eddie Anderson, and Nile Kinnick. The speakers would take their turns at the podium before Kinnick would be presented with the trophy. Three hundred people were already seated.

"Tonight's the night, Nile. Just make sure you have fun, and enjoy all of it." It was Dr Eddie's final inspirational quote for his star player.

"I will, Coach. And tomorrow night, just before your award presentation, I promise to give you the same advice."

Nine men - including two previous Heisman winners - took their turns at the podium, each speaking briefly. Finally, Walter Holcombe, the President of the Downtown Athletic Club, walked to the dais. He had many accomplishments to read about the night's recipient.

> *Good evening, ladies and gentlemen. We are here to honor the greatest college football player in the country, and more impressively, an intelligent young man who makes us all proud of college athletics.*
> *Nile Kinnick averaged over twenty yards per pass this season. One third of his passes went for touchdowns. He was involved in one hundred seven of his team's one hundred*

*thirty points by running, passing, or kicking.
After taking a seat on the bench at the end
of the first game of the season, because
the Hawkeyes were well ahead of their
opponent, he played four hundred two of the
remaining four hundred twenty minutes.
A separated shoulder in the final game was
the only reason he missed the last eighteen
minutes of the season. Running, passing,
and punting made him a triple threat on
offense from his left halfback position and
caused the opponents to strategize every week
on stopping one player. Defensively, he set a
school record with eight interceptions from
his safety position. He also holds the Iowa
record of eighteen interceptions in his career.
He returned kicks and punts. In fact, he
returned nine punts against Indiana for
two hundred one yards, both records.*

*In a defensive struggle against Notre Dame,
he held the Fighting Irish at bay with sixteen
punts for a total of seven hundred thirty-one
yards. Again, both records.*

*The following week, he played a key role in
beating another national power, Minnesota,
with two touchdown passes in the fourth
quarter.*

*And, in addition, he did the place kicking.
Pro football may be involved in his future.
But most impressively, you realize our
country is in good hands as long as we keep*

*producing Nile Kinnicks. Once you talk to
him, the football part seems incidental.*

*He is an honor student, Phi Beta Kappa,
and probably headed for law school at his
grandfather's alma mater. And I might add,
his grandfather was a two-term Governor
of Iowa. Also, Nile is President of his senior
class at the University of Iowa.*

*Ladies and gentlemen, it is with great pride
that the Downtown Athletic Club has
chosen Nile Kinnick as this year's recipient
of the Heisman Trophy.*

Enthusiastic applause burst from the conference room. Kinnick shook Walter Holcombe's hand and was then handed the trophy signifying the best college football player in the country. Willard Prince, the chairman of the award committee, walked to Nile's side to also congratulate him. Nile Kinnick looked out at the standing crowd, smiling the broadest smile of his life while holding the Heisman with both hands. The applause continued as flashbulbs popped countless times from all around the front of the stage.

Virginia Eskridge, sitting near the back with her parents, thought maybe she understood why the smartly dressed young man was outside during their coincidental passing on the sidewalk. He probably needed a contemplative moment, knowing he would be center stage all night.

Nile Kinnick looked over to his right and saw Dr. Eddie Anderson nodding approvingly while clapping with the crowd. He recognized a few journalists from the Big Ten area. He waved to Bert McGrane, from the Des Moines Register.

Kinnick set the trophy on the table next to the podium. It was obvious he was without notes as he looked out at the audience and began speaking.

Thank you very, very kindly, Mr. Holcombe. It seems to me that everyone is letting their superlatives run away with them this evening, but nonetheless I want you to know that I am mighty, mighty happy to accept this trophy this evening.

Every football player in these United States dreams about winning that trophy and of this fine trip to New York. Every player considers that trophy the acme in recognition of this kind, and the fact that I am actually receiving this trophy tonight almost overwhelms me, and I know that all those boys who have gone before me must have felt somewhat the same way.

From my own personal viewpoint, I consider my winning this award as indirectly a great tribute to the new coaching staff at the University of Iowa headed by Dr. Eddie Anderson…

Applause interrupted as Dr. Eddie accepted the acknowledgement.

…and to my teammates sitting back in Iowa City.

Applause again stopped Nile as he shared his achievement with his teammates.

A finer man and a better coach never hit these United States, and a finer bunch of boys, and a more courageous bunch of boys,

*never graced the gridiron of the Midwest
than that Iowa team of 1939. I wish that
they might all be with me tonight to receive
this trophy. They certainly deserve it.*

In Iowa City, all the Ironmen sat together at the Student Union to listen to the nationally broadcast event. The radio's volume was turned as high as it could go.

"Mention our names, Nile, our names," Couppee shouted to the amusement of the Hawkeyes.

In Omaha, Nebraska, Frances and Nile Sr. sat on the living room couch in front of the fireplace. Tears streamed down Frances' cheeks. Nile Sr.'s jaw was clenched with pride. A lump grew large in his throat. Nile's brothers, Ben and George, listened intently.

*I want to take this grand opportunity to
thank collectively all the sportswriters and
all the sportscasters and all those who have
seen fit, have seen their way clear, to cast
a ballot in my favor for this trophy. And
I also want to take this opportunity to
thank Mr. Prince and his committee, the
Heisman Award Committee, and all those
connected with the Downtown Athletic
Club for this trophy and for the fine time
that they're showing me, and not only for
that, but for making this fine and worthy
trophy available to football players of this
country.
Finally, if you'll permit me, I'd like to make
a comment which in my mind is indicative
perhaps of the greater significance of*

football and sports emphasis in general in this country, and that is, I thank God I was warring on the gridirons of the Midwest and not on the battlefields of Europe.

Three hundred people were unprepared for the social commentary, then responded strongly. They broke into a spontaneous ovation lasting over a minute. The fear of the United States becoming involved in the European war seemed real to the entire nation.

I can speak confidently and positively that the players of this country would much more, much rather, struggle and fight to win the Heisman Award than the Croix de Guerre. Thank you.

Nile Kinnick had captured his audience. Everyone stood again and applauded one more time for this young man who humbly accepted this great award and, at the same time, reminded them how fortunate they were to be Americans. He was aware of world affairs. He felt it important to mention the tyranny on the other side of the ocean. The nation realized Nile Kinnick's character and charm transcended mere sport.

The praise continued with clapping and cheering, a sound very familiar to the young man from Iowa. He couldn't hear the applause at the Student Union in Iowa City. He couldn't see the happiness and pride sitting in his parents' living room. But his thoughts shifted to both locations, knowing his family and teammates were listening.

The next morning Nile awoke and called room service for breakfast and a newspaper. Last night was an amazing night, he thought, but this morning he just wanted a little private time away from journalists, photographers, and anyone wanting a handshake or conversation.

He couldn't help but scan the front page for the most recent developments in Europe. The Soviet Union was being expelled from the League of Nations after the Finland invasion. Next to the European article was a story about a high school football player in New Jersey, Edwin 'Rip' Collins. He was at the Newark hospital following a football injury in October. His leg had not responded well to treatment and had to be amputated.

Kinnick set the paper down. He couldn't stop thinking about the misfortunes of this young footballer, and how he was laying in a hospital bed right now while Kinnick was enjoying the accolades from the New York Athletic Club. He quickly read the sports section about his magnificent evening, then took the elevator to the lobby, went outside, and stood at the curb. He motioned for a taxi.

Nile hopped into the back seat, carrying a brown paper sack, and asked the taxi driver, "How far away is Newark, and how long would it take to get there?"

"About fifteen miles," was the response. "I could get you there in thirty minutes. But I'd have trouble getting a return fare from Newark, so I'm not that interested in going there."

"How much would it cost to get there?" Nile asked.

"Three dollars."

"I'll pay you ten dollars to take me to the Newark Hospital, wait about thirty minutes, and then bring me back here."

The New York cab driver could tell it was important and he knew he wouldn't feel too good about himself if he didn't honor a request to a hospital. "Close the door, young man. We're headed to Newark."

"Hello. I'd like to know what room Edwin Collins is in." Nile stood at the hospital's information counter looking down at the smiling receptionist.

"He's in room six eighteen. But I need to call to see if he is seeing visitors. Are you family?" she asked in a heavy Jersey accent.

"No, I'm not. And I'm not a friend of the family, either," said Nile. "I'm a football player who would like to stop and say hello. I understand he was injured badly in a football game."

"Your name?"

"Nile Kinnick."

Nile spotted a water fountain and walked twenty feet down the hallway while she placed a call. He turned and looked at the woman to see if she was off the phone yet. The woman was smiling as she hung up the phone. "So, you said you are a football player?" she asked.

"Yes, ma'am."

"The elevator is down the hall on your right side. Room six eighteen is on the sixth floor. I believe the nurses' station is anxiously awaiting, Mr. Kinnick. Oh, and also, my husband was real excited that you won the Heisman. He's been talking about you ever since November. Congratulations."

"Thank you, ma'am." Kinnick gave her a big smile as he headed for the elevators.

As Nile approached the nurses' station a young nurse, not much older than Nile, approached him while three other nurses beamed with excitement to see the new celebrity.

"Hello. I'm Nile Kinnick and I was hoping I might be able to see Edwin Collins."

"Hello, Nile. I'm Marjorie Bluhm, Edwin's nurse today. He is going to be very pleased to see you. Follow me."

Nile followed the nurse to the injured footballer's room.

"Edwin, we have a visitor who would like to see you," Marjorie said.

Nile stepped into the room, still carrying the brown sack under his arm. The morning sun was shining brightly on the young patient's bed. His father was sitting in the corner reading the newspaper. Edwin Collins' mother sat in a chair next to the bed. All three turned simultaneously toward the door, curious who was stopping by at such an early hour.

Nile Kinnick didn't need to introduce himself to the high schooler.

"Nile Kinnick! Wow! What are you doing here?" Edwin exclaimed.

"I was doing just what your father is doing right now, reading the paper, and I came across your story. It was very inspirational. I wanted to meet you and tell you how much I admire your courage." Kinnick instantly caught the attention of Edwin's parents when they saw how excited and happy their son was for the first time in a long time. "And since my flight back to Iowa doesn't leave until tomorrow, I wanted to stop by."

For the next thirty minutes, Nile, Edwin's parents, and the nurse all stood next to the bed talking about Edwin's injury, the difficult decisions that had confronted his parents, and Big Ten football.

"Edwin, I want to stay in touch and follow your journey and recovery. I'll give you my address so you can write and let me know how you are progressing." Nile scribbled his parents' address on a piece of paper. "My address will be changing, but if you send it to my parents, they will get it to me.

"And one more thing." Kinnick reached into his paper bag. "This is a sweater I was given for making the All-America team. I want you to have it."

Nile handed Edwin the sweater with the All-America logo sewn on the front. His mother started crying. His father reached out and shook Nile's hand, but he couldn't speak, either.

"Not every All-American is found on the gridiron," Nile said. "Some have a tremendous impact on others by who they are and how they live. You are my All-American, Edwin. I want that sweater to remind you of that." Nile started walking toward the door. "And don't forget to write."

CHAPTER TWENTY-EIGHT

Saturday, December 24, 1939. The broken shafts of the harvested corn stalks pierced through an otherwise white blanket of snow shrouding the rolling hills of his childhood. Nile Kinnick felt the peaceful serenity of this farmland. It presented a sharp contrast to his recent visit to New York, and Saturday afternoons in Big Ten stadiums. He stopped the car, rolled down the window, and breathed the air one last time before continuing the journey home for Christmas. He drove past his grandparents' home in Adel, Iowa   He missed his grandfather. The wisdom of the former governor and the way he carried himself, always wearing a vest and tie, were memories he would never forget. His grandmother was already in Omaha with Nile's parents and brothers, and he would see her again in just a few hours. Next, he drove past his childhood home. The memories were so vivid he could visualize the grass-stained pants his mother would wash after he had played football with his brother, Ben, and other neighborhood friends. He stared at the back yard where he pretended to throw game-winning touchdown passes to Ben. He remembered how the grass never grew where dirt patches marked first base, second base, third base and home plate. The old metal swing set was still cemented into the ground behind the garage. He laughed to himself, thinking he almost spent more time in the yard than inside the house. It seemed so long ago, he thought, even though they moved from Adel only five years ago.

The short drive through Adel to reminisce added only twenty minutes to the journey across the state. He was halfway done with the two hundred sixty mile trip along Highway 6. Al Couppee sat silently in the passenger seat. He respected Nile's stillness, evoking childhood memories. Neither said a word. Their plan was to do the same in Council Bluffs before Nile dropped Coup at his mother's. It had been over a year since Al had been back to his hometown. His dad wouldn't be with the family this Christmas. His new job at the Davenport liquor store didn't allow him any time off during the busy holiday season. But it didn't bother Al that his father wouldn't be there for this holiday. His family would soon be together in their new home, only an hour from Iowa City. Maybe in the next two years, he hoped, they could all attend some Hawkeye football games.

Nile reached for the radio knob and tuned in WHO Radio broadcasting from Des Moines.

> *And that was Tommy Dorsey's latest hit song, 'I'll Never Smile Again,' featuring his new vocalist, Frank Sinatra.*
>
> *We have a new story just in from the Associated Press. Another award will be presented to Iowa's own Nile Kinnick. As you know, Mr. Kinnick won the prestigious Heisman Trophy earlier this month and followed that by also winning the Walter Camp Award and the Maxwell Award, all recognizing the nation's top college footballer. Well, today, the Associated Press has voted*

*him the Male Athlete of the Year, finishing
higher in the voting than Joe Louis, Joe
DiMaggio, and Byron Nelson.*

Al Couppee looked over at Kinnick. "They just keep rolling in for you, my friend."

"Joe Louis and Joe DiMaggio?" said a bewildered Kinnick. "That's hard to believe. Wow! I'm speechless."

"That's a first," Couppee quickly replied. "But I agree. Wow! Those names are as big as it gets. Pro football is waiting for you."

Nile was silent for a moment, absorbing the news and contemplating its importance. "I've come to the realization that politics is my passion, Coup. I'd like to someday be a voice for the underprivileged. Law school will be a great stepping stone for me. I need to move on from football. Besides," Kinnick smiled at Couppee, "pro players are too big and too fast."

"What about Barbara Miller?" asked Couppee.

"We've talked several times about our futures and our goals. One of the things I really like about Barbara is that she and I both understand we are young, and need to establish our own paths, first. We're great friends, but neither of us wants to make a decision right now based on the other's proximity."

"You mean you're not that serious about her," Couppee quickly interjected.

Kinnick shook his head and smiled at Couppee's directness.

Couppee continued, "Well, let me be the first to congratulate you on the Athlete of the Year. I'm assuming I'm the first person to congratulate you, since you just learned of this, here, in the middle of nowhere. You earned it, Nile. I'll miss you the next two years. The entire state will miss you."

The snow quit falling as they approached Council Bluffs. Couppee told Kinnick where to turn as they maneuvered through the streets. Couppee sat erect, passing by youthful memories scattered throughout his old neighborhood.

Nile knew Al had grown up in an impoverished section of town. But he was unprepared for the widespread deprivation. Cracked windows had tape restraining the cold air from entering homes. Personal belongings were stored on front porches. Many cars in the street were old with rusted wheel wells and lower panels. The city's snow removal plans seemed to have forgotten the area, though the nice neighborhood ten blocks prior had snow-cleared streets. No more than fifteen feet separated one house from the next in Al Couppee's old neighborhood.

"That's it, the white house with the brown shutters. Come on in and say 'hello' before you head to Omaha."

"I'd be glad to, Coup."

As they stood on the front porch, Couppee looked inside. He could see his mother cooking in the kitchen. "She looks better, Nile. She looks healthier. Dr. Eddie cures from a distance."

"Yes. He's got a huge heart, Coup." Kinnick put his hand on the quarterback's shoulder. And then he tried to lighten the mood before their entrance. "Besides, he couldn't let you leave the team to come home. Who would have been around to try hustling his assistant coach's wife?"

"Let's forget that one." Couppee turned the door knob and started to walk in. "It was an honest mistake. Who would have known he had such a young looking wife?"

Mary Couppee walked hurriedly to the door. The hug lasted much longer than the hug in the front yard, the day he hitchhiked to his new university. And it was much firmer than the frail hug outside the stadium after the Notre Dame game.

"Mom, I want you to meet Nile Kinnick."

Kinnick extended his right hand. "It's a pleasure to meet you, Mrs. Couppee. I've heard a lot of great things about you. I'm sorry I didn't get a chance to meet you after the Notre Dame game."

"And I have heard much more about you, Nile. Al and I barely had time for a quick dinner before rushing back to the train depot. The day went too fast, but it was so wonderful. Please come in."

Kinnick stayed long enough to ruin his appetite with two pieces of apple pie even though a big family dinner would be waiting for him in Omaha. But he knew desserts were probably not routine in the Couppee household just a short time ago, so eating the second piece of pie was a celebration, he thought, of abundance for Al's family.

Saturday, January 20, 1940. The footballers gathered at The Academy for the usual burgers, fries, and a few games of billiards. Big Hank Luebcke was sitting next to Nile Kinnick in the corner booth by the coin operated phonograph, or 'jukebox,' as it was rapidly getting to be known across college campuses. Erv Prasse was selecting some Benny Goodman and Tommy Dorsey songs. Mary Stellman and Barbara Miller stood next to him, pointing to their favorite dance songs.

"Hank, I'm really glad you were drafted by the Packers even though your season was cut short," Kinnick said. "But how is a Chicago boy able to rationalize playing for Green Bay?"

"I think they drafted me because they needed some speed on the line," chuckled the oversized lineman. "As for being a Packer, my dad will eventually forgive me, but it might take two or three seasons, or a couple of blocks of cheese sent home.

"One of the oddest experiences I'll have will be that first game against the Detroit Lions and Prasse being in the Lions' blue and gray on the other side of the line of scrimmage. I'll try to go easy on him." Luebcke's Chicago accent made him sound so much more menacing than the easy-going giant everyone loved.

"I'm sure he'll appreciate that, Hank. But Prasse told me he might just opt for professional basketball or baseball."

"What about you, Nile? I've heard you're not going to accept an offer from the Brooklyn Dodgers. I guess that's the cost of going high in the draft, you end up on a team that isn't that good, but they'll probably offer you a big contract."

"The money would be nice, Hank, but I've decided to hang up my cleats."

"For good?" asked Luebcke. "You've got to play in the All-Star game in August. It's tradition that the all-star seniors take on the NFL champs, and you received more votes than anyone in the country. And besides, wouldn't you like to see what you could do against the Green Bay Packers?"

"I'll play in the All-Star game. But it will be my last. I'm sure of that now." Nile almost sounded relieved to admit his final decision.

Prasse, as usual, was the first Hawkeye on the dance floor. "Are you ready, Mary? Come on, Nile, let's show these people some steps."

Kinnick walked over to Barbara Miller. "May I?" he asked, reaching out his hand for hers.

"Yes, of course," Barbara replied.

The next two hours passed quickly dancing, eating, and reminiscing. It was a grand time, shared by young men that had grown together under the tutelage of Dr. Eddie. They were grateful for these moments and were realizing their time together, especially for the seniors, was fleeting.

Suddenly, Max Hawkins whispered loudly to Jens Norgaard and Mike Enich who were both standing next to him, "I think that's Sonja Henie that just walked in the door!"

Eyes turned towards the front door. Mike Enich looked up from the pool table where he was aiming his next shot. "That is Sonja Henie! Why would a Hollywood star be standing here at The Academy?"

"And three time Olympic skating champion!" proclaimed Barbara Miller.

"I know why," said Al Couppee. "She's here to see Nile. Or, I should say, she's here with her husband who is here to see Nile."

Nile Kinnick got up from the booth and walked by Chuck Tollefson and Buzz Dean, toward Sonja Henie and her husband.

"Hello, Mr. Topping."

"Hello, Nile. Let me introduce my wife. Nile, this is Sonja Henie. Sonja, this is the young man we came to see."

"It's nice to meet you, Ms. Henie. It's quite a surprise to see you. I had no idea Mr. Topping was bringing you."

"It's a pleasure to meet you, Nile. I wasn't planning on coming, but it just worked out that I could join him. Dan has said that you are a great athlete." Sonja Henie wore a long black wool overcoat over her ankle length red dress.

"I am nowhere near being an Olympic gold medalist," Kinnick said.

"May we sit down somewhere, Nile?" Dan Topping looked somewhat out of place in his dark suit and hat, surrounded by letter jackets, flannel shirts, and khaki pants. But he also seemed very comfortable being the center of attention.

"Would you mind if I introduced you, since everyone is curious?" Nile asked.

"Not at all. Go ahead," replied Dan Topping.

"Everyone, can I have your attention for just a moment. We have two special guests with us tonight. This is Dan Topping, the owner of the football Brooklyn Dodgers. And accompanying him is his wife, whom I think everyone recognizes, Sonja Henie.

"Mr. Topping was in Chicago today, and called me earlier to ask if we could get together sometime. I had mentioned we were having a team party tonight, and he was generous enough to offer to come here.

"Mr. Topping and Miss Henie, these are the Iowa Hawkeye Ironmen, and friends. A finer group of people will never be assembled, at least until we have our first reunion."

Laughter followed his comment. Dan Topping took note of Kinnick's ease at speaking extemporaneously while commanding everyone's attention. Topping witnessed what he had heard of Nile Kinnick. He was a natural leader, the kind of person Dan Topping wanted on his team.

Kinnick continued his introduction. "This group, Mr. Topping and Miss Henie, has become a family. It might even be said at times that we were a dysfunctional family, but a family nevertheless. That's the reason for our success this year."

"It's nice to meet all of you Ironmen," said Dan Topping. "I've followed your season in the New York papers every week. And, since you are allowing me to barge into your party, I'd like to do something in return. Food and drinks are on me tonight."

A roar went up from the footballers. The eyes of linemen Luebcke, Enich, Tollefson, Bergstom, Hawkins, Walker, Snider, Andruska, Pettit, Frye, Evans, and Diehl grew large just thinking about how much they could eat.

"Mr. Topping, you may regret making that offer," hollered Chuck Tollefson as he walked to the closest bar stool.

"By the looks of some of you, I already do." Dan Topping knew how to win over a roomful of people, even college students in Iowa City.

Nile Kinnick, Sonja Henie, and Dan Topping sat down in a nearby booth.

"Miss Henie," Nile began.

"Please, call me Sonja."

"Sonja, I've seen three of your movies this past year. *Happy Landing* with Don Ameche. Then *Second Fiddle*, although playing a skating instructor from Minnesota is, of course, very adversarial to the Hawkeye State. Minnesota is our biggest rival. But my favorite was *Everything Happens at Night* with Ray Milland and Robert Cummings. I believe it was your first time outside the romantic comedy role."

"You know your movies, Nile. And thank you for mentioning them. I've been very lucky."

"I'm the lucky one," said Dan Topping, looking at his wife. There was a pause before he addressed his reason for coming. "Nile, the Dodgers drafted you high even though we had heard law school might be your next move. It was a gamble we were willing to take. A name like yours can help fill Ebbets Field.

"And, of course, we did some background checks. Your credentials are impeccable. But one of the things that really stood out to me, besides your football prowess, is that you were a very good baseball player for the Hawkeyes, too. In fact, I heard you used to catch for Bob Feller on an American Legion Team."

"And I still have swollen knuckles on my left hand to show for it." Kinnick noticed Barbara Miller watching from a distance with Prasse and Mary Stellman. "Why the interest in baseball, Mr. Topping?"

"Two colleagues and I are thinking about the possibility of buying the New York Yankees. Jake Ruppert, the previous owner, died about a year ago and the Yankees are currently owned by his estate. Jake is the man who famously bought Babe Ruth from the Boston Red Sox in 1919. Anyway, the purchase of the Yankees, if we are successful, would take some time. If things went according to plan, and you played football for me, it would be a huge story in New York that a Heisman winner, and current football player in Brooklyn, would try to make the Yankee roster. If you turned out to be a good baseball player, too, great! And if you just played sparingly for the

Yankees, that would be fine, too. New York likes personalities and stories. You would be bringing both."

Silence filled the next several seconds as Kinnick considered the possibilities.

"I'm willing to pay you $1,000 a game for the Dodgers. That's a guaranteed $11,000 for the season, and an additional $1,000 for each playoff game. I can't make any promises about baseball because that hasn't happened yet, but obviously, there could be additional money if the Yankee purchase goes through. So, right now, I can only talk about football, but I want you to know there are other plans down the road."

"I'll think about it, Mr. Topping. It's a very generous offer. I believe my heart is set on what I want to do, but I will give this some consideration. Thank you. And Mr. Topping, regardless what my decision will be, your coming here tonight does not go unnoticed. I realize you made a special effort to be here."

"It was our pleasure, Nile," replied Dan Topping. "And even if your decision is still law school, it was worth meeting you. We've heard too much about you."

"Would the two of you mind meeting some friends?" Nile asked.

"Not at all. We'd be glad to," said Miss Henie.

"Yes, who knows, there could be another future Dodger in this room right now," added Mr. Topping.

The two shook hands and Nile motioned for Erv Prasse, Barbara Miller, and Mary Stellman to come over and meet the celebrities. Soon after, Sonja Henie and Dan Topping walked around the room and met everyone before leaving.

That evening, Nile leaned back on his bed to enjoy those precious, hypnotic moments before sleep. His eyes lost focus, his mind quieted, no longer thinking with words and sentences, but instead, absorbing thought without being analytical. It was a moment that allowed him to be his own omniscient author, writing his own future. He would tell Mr. Topping in the morning of his decision. Unfortunately for Dan Topping, Nile had already weighed the possibilities, and had decided on his life's course.

May 20, 1940. "Did you finish preparing your speech last night in time to get a good night's sleep?" Frances Kinnick displayed her motherly concern.

"Yes, Mom. It went relatively well. The thoughts came easily for some unknown reason. The typing took some time, though. With Germany invading Holland and Belgium, and now the Nazi's campaign in France, I felt it was necessary to address these current events.

"Hi, Dad. I'm glad both of you could come to the commencement."

"Nothing could prevent your mother or me from being here on your last day of college, Son. I wish Ben and George could have made it, but their lives are getting busier, too." His father found it difficult to keep from showing the emotion he felt. After all, his son was Phi Beta Kappa, graduating cum laude, the Heisman winner, and headed for law school.

"I'll see you afterwards," Nile said. "I need to meet with the other speakers so we know exactly what we're supposed to do."

"That's fine, Son. We'll see you later."

Nile took his seat on the stage, facing the graduating class, their families, and friends. Everyone was seated. The Class of '40 filled the Fieldhouse floor where he once had played basketball for the University. Twenty chairs on each side of the center aisle stretched the entire length of the basketball court. Quitting basketball and baseball to concentrate on football and studying were difficult decisions, he thought, but in the end, he had no regrets.

The families and friends of the graduates, including all the underclassmen footballers, occupied the bleachers on both sides of the basketball court. As President Gilmore began the ceremony, Nile looked around the crowd. Barbara Miller was sitting halfway back in the seniors' alphabetical seating. Then Nile spotted the other six Hawkeye football players graduating with him. Russ Busk and Buzz Dean were near the front. Dick Evans was in the row after Dean. Ed McLain was just one seat away from Barbara Miller. He discovered Erv Prasse smiling right back at him. Fred Smith sat just behind Prasse.

Nile looked over at the bleachers. He instantly spotted Al Couppee and Mike Enich sitting together. Then he looked at Chuck Tollefson and remembered the story he shared on the train ride to the Michigan game, talking about the life and dignity of riding the rails and helping with the Midwestern harvests. Kinnick couldn't take his eyes off Tollie. In one year, he thought, Tollie would be sitting on this same floor with his graduating classmates. Tollefson had tried college life, failed, and then came back again. No one in the audience sat taller than the former hobo.

Nile's thoughts were wandering, thinking about his four years while President Gilmore spoke. Then suddenly, he was quickly awakened from his daydream when he heard President Gilmore say, "And now, your senior class president, Nile Kinnick."

Kinnick stood up, walked over to the podium, and shook President Gilmore's hand. While the audience applauded, President Gilmore spoke softly to conceal a private comment. "How about one more performance for the University, Nile?"

"I'll do my best."

Nile pulled out the type-written pages from his inner lapel pocket, the same suit he wore to the Heisman banquet. He looked out at the crowd, spotting his parents to his left in the fifth row of the bleachers. He looked at Al Couppee, Mike

Enich, and Erv Prasse one more time. He looked at Barbara
Miller and smiled as the polite applause faded to silence.

> *The remarks I have to make tonight are*
> *very brief, but nonetheless, with your*
> *permission I am going to read them rather*
> *than attempt to render them without the*
> *benefit of a text. I prepared this short talk*
> *several weeks ago but since then so many*
> *events of terrible and ominous significance*
> *have taken place in the world that I almost*
> *revised it. The bloody holocaust raging in*
> *Europe with its possible repercussions in this*
> *country tends to exert depressive influence*
> *on all of us, and as a result, many of you*
> *will scoff at many of my remarks as foolish*
> *hopes and mere fictions. However, whether*
> *we know it or not, or like it or not, we in*
> *this country live by idealistic hopes and by*
> *fictions. And it may be that in the last*
> *analysis these seeming fictions and idealisms*
> *will prove to be the only realities. With this*
> *thought in mind I shall read this speech*
> *with absolutely no apologies for the hopes*
> *and aspirations expressed.*
> *Tonight, we seniors are gathered here as*
> *college graduates. Four short but dynamic*
> *years have gone fleeing by. It seems only*
> *yesterday we entered this University as the*
> *very greenest of freshmen. Each one of us*
> *has treated and experienced these four years*

in different ways. To some it has been one grand holiday at father's expense marred only by the necessity of a certain amount of study and classroom attendance; to others it has been a grand opportunity to fulfill the hopes and aspirations of posterity-minded parents; and to still others it has been a stern and intense experience - an opportunity, yes – but realized only by treading the rough and rocky road of unmitigated hard work. I speak of you courageous men and women unfavored by financial assistance from home, who have earned your way by outside work on this campus; who have struggled desperately to meet your physical needs and at the same time maintain a decent classroom average – no social pleasures or frivolous pleasures have been yours – but you have asked for no quarter nor given any. You have been willing to pay the price for that which so many of us take as a matter of course; you hold your heads high tonight – and rightly so – for you have fought and won.

But regardless of what this college experience has meant to different students, this evening we stand as one body, and in a few days we shall stand together once more to receive that which is emblematic of four years of academic study well done – our diploma. Some of us will treasure this scrap of paper, some will be indifferent, and some will be cynical and unappreciative. But to all of us it will serve as a sort of "union card;" hence forward, we are members of that great group who have "been to college." Unfortunately, it can't honestly be said that we are now educated – but certainly, at least, this diploma indicates that we have been satisfactorily exposed to the process.

And what now – where do we go from here? Certainly, it isn't a very pretty picture – unemployment and uncertainty here at home and international anarchy abroad. What part are we to play in this dynamic ever changing world? We are told on the one hand by the pedagogues of this University that the salvation of this nation is on our shoulders, and on the other hand depicted in the honorable Ding Darling's cartoons as naïve, intellectually doped youngsters without any ideas of practicality. But be that as it may, I know we are all full of ambition, courage, and a desire to do well for ourselves and for the society of which we are a part. We shall struggle to be sufficient unto the need – if it means better government, we shall be active there; if it means a more enlightened business leadership, we shall strive for that; and if it means a broader, more responsible international outlook, count on us to be alert and ready.

Are we capable of successfully meeting the problems that face us? Have we been adequately equipped to fulfill our manifest duties and obligations? Only time can honestly answer. But we may be sure that if this great University is succeeding in her aims then we shall be successful in ours. Fundamentally, all true education is composed of mental discipline and inspiration – and one is of no avail without the other. All successful teaching must hinge on these two necessary fundamentals. Nobly have our professors endeavored to embody these principles in their lectures and personal associations with us. Hopefully, now they will watch our progress to see if we make use of the tools with which they have tried to provide us.

However, the successful use of what we have learned here will be contingent entirely upon the addition of another element which we alone can provide. For whether we realize it or not, we have lived a rather sheltered life here at the University; here our ideals are lauded, appreciated, and protected – the development and expression of a social consciousness has been easy. But you know and I know this period of easy idealism is now at an end. And it is here that this other element of which I speak, and which can be provided by the individual and the individual alone, enters into the picture.

I refer, fellow graduates, to a real, positive, mental courage. We all seem to have the courage to face the physical forces of life - sickness, poverty, unemployment — even war itself — but how about courage of conviction, of morality, of idealism, courage of faith in a principle tangible proof of which is slow in appearing. Herein lies that phase of these problems which we must meet by ourselves, unaided by any university-given tools. Here is that angle of the greater difficulty which most often has proven the weak point in graduates of the past. True, we must learn to face adversity with equanimity, and even philosophically; but at the same time never for a moment losing sight of the ultimate goal, never failing in our ambition, or our ideals. By now we should have learned that success and happiness and attainment come only periodically, not permanently — that they really are only passing moments in our experience — and that therein lies the explanation of the law of progress, and human dynamics. By now we should realize that the "battle is life itself" and that our joy and happiness should lie as much in the struggle to overcome as in the fruition of a later day. So let us confidently take courage in what we deem to be right, and no matter what our line of endeavor may be, cling to its concomitants of persistence, desire, imagination, hope and faith. Our competitive urge must not only be objective but subjective, not only physical but spiritual. Injustice, oppression, and war will ultimately bring on their own destruction; suffering and misery eventually awaken the human race. But that is the long, sad, unenlightened road we have taken in the centuries past. Now is the time for these problems to be solved by enlightened thought and understanding. We can accomplish much if we implement mental discipline and inspiration with real mental courage. The task is not easy. Wishful thinking will not do the job. We shall have to battle until we seemingly have reached the end of the line, then "tie a knot" and "hang on." This is not just a figure of speech, but an imperative necessity.

Nile Kinnick stopped and looked out, scanning the people from his left to his right. In that moment, he knew his college experience had ended. The audience was standing and applauding. The ovation continued in waves. The seniors had looked forward to hearing from their most famous classmate, the Heisman Trophy winner. The audience collectively realized this young man's commencement speech was exactly that, a beginning. Nile Kinnick was the epitome of what he articulated: mental courage and its impact on others.

Nile looked at his proud parents. Frances waved with her left hand while wiping a tear with her right. Nile Kinnick Sr. beamed an enthusiastic smile as he clapped his hands vigorously.

CHAPTER TWENTY-NINE

Thursday, July 4, 1940. Mike Enich gazed at the library adjacent to the city square in downtown Charles City, Iowa. They had just walked away from the farm trailer that had served as a makeshift stage on the south side of the city park. "It's amazing how you can go to any small town and find a Carnegie Library. I've enjoyed these trips, Nile. Too bad Prasse can't join us anymore."

"It's his fault for leading the Hawkeye baseball team to the Big Ten championship. If he hadn't, maybe the Cardinals wouldn't have drafted him. I hope he makes the St. Louis squad. He might get tired of playing on their Asheville farm club." Kinnick looked around as the crowd dispersed. More than a thousand people had been in attendance, larger than the last five speaking engagements in June.

Mike Enich changed the subject. "Wow. It's warm out. I need something to drink. I think I lost some weight just listening to you. And I must say, even though it was the same speech I've heard the last three times, I found it inspiring. You're getting better at this."

"Thanks, Mike, if you mean it. And as far as losing the weight, you've got to get ready for Dr. Eddie's second season. You'll be running in a month."

"Thanks for reminding me. You know, it will seem odd having you on Dr. Eddie's coaching staff. I might get envious watching you stand around instead of running." Enich knew it wouldn't be the same without Kinnick and Prasse on the field next year. But at least, he thought, Kinnick would still be at the practices. "I did hear a rumor you might run with us, though."

"I've got to tell you, Mike, I'll probably declare a coach's privilege and just run when I'm in the mood. I've always wanted to blow that whistle."

Tuesday, July 9, 1940. Frances and Nile Sr. sat next to each other on the back patio swing. Nile sat in a rattan chair across from them.

"Thank you, Mom, for a great dinner. I don't know how Dad stays so slim eating like that all the time. It's one of the things I missed in college. The quantity of food was always there at the training table, but it wasn't my mom's cooking."

"You are welcome. I just wish you were around more often."

"Mom and Dad, there is something I want to talk to you about. The Young Republicans have asked me to speak at a rally for Wendell Wilkie when he comes to Iowa next week. In fact, they asked if I would introduce Mr. Wilkie at the rally."

"Interesting," said Nile Sr. "His win at the Republican convention two weeks ago was quite a surprise. I thought Thomas Dewey would get the nod."

"Even though we haven't discussed your future in great detail, I know you've given politics a strong consideration," Frances said. "I've always thought your speaking engagements, to a certain extent, have been to groom yourself for a public career. But are you sure you are ready to endorse someone? We don't know very much about Wendell Wilkie, yet."

"I understand your concerns. It might seem I am declaring a party affiliation. But I feel very strongly that we need to get involved to combat the oppression in Europe, and that's why I'm in favor of Wilkie. Franklin Roosevelt can't sit back any longer. The world's freedom is at stake."

"I agree with you, Son," said Nile Sr. "I think we will eventually be involved. Tonight, I guess, we are discussing whether or not you are comfortable declaring partisanship."

"I am."

"What is the plan?" Frances asked.

"I am to meet Governor Wilson in Des Moines and then I'll ride with him to Iowa Falls. Governor Wilson will introduce me and then I'll introduce Mr. Wilkie from the back of the train."

Nile Sr. laughed. "I'm sure there will be several news organizations there. I suppose they would have Governor Wilson introduce him, but Wilson is only well-known in Iowa, while your name has national recognition. And I'm sure it will appeal to the younger voter."

Nile Jr. smiled. "Sounds like politics, Dad."

Saturday, July 13, 1940. Governor Wilson reiterated the qualifications of Wendell Wilkie to the gathered audience, asking the citizens of Iowa to support him in the Presidential election. Nile knew he would be introduced momentarily. As he looked out at the people, he was filled with a surreal sensation standing with the Governor of Iowa, and possibly, the next President of the United States.

Governor Wilson was finishing his remarks. "Thank you for joining us today. It is wonderful to see this immense turnout and interest in our country's future.

"Next, I have the privilege of introducing a young gentleman we are all very proud to call our own. He is Iowa's

Heisman Trophy winner, Maxwell Award winner, Walter Camp Award winner, and the Associated Press' Athlete of the Year, Mr. Nile Kinnick."

Mike Enich stood to the side of the train. The back of the caboose served as the temporary stage. He watched his ex-teammate stand before a crowd once again. Nile Kinnick, he thought, is no longer the leader of the Hawkeyes. He has moved on. He wondered what the future held for his friend.

Thank you. Thank you.

Kinnick waited patiently for the applause to end.

How lucky we are to live in Iowa. This beautiful, warm weather today is only matched by the warmth of the people in this great state. We are lucky to be here in the heartland of our nation. The University of Iowa has been a magnificent experience for me. It provided me the opportunity to be challenged intellectually. It is my belief that the essential experience to be gained from college is to learn to think, to think for yourself, to develop an active, alert, inquiring mind. In truth, we all must educate ourselves, and college presents an engaging environment for this learning process.

I have often been asked what my intentions are for the future. I believe my ultimate destiny will be imbued with a desire to benefit society in some type of service. And I believe my path to those goals will be best served by, first, attending law school.

I see a need for closing the gaps of inequities in human relationships. We tragically leave some people by the wayside as we move forward with our lives. The black people are too often permitted no sense of human dignity. It seems to be a problem especially in the southern states. And it's not right. We are all equal.

It seems religion bitterly divides people, not so much in our own country as in other places around the world. This is the twentieth century and we can no longer tolerate these injustices and bigotries.

Across the ocean civil rights of innocent people are being violated. And so far, our country still proclaims neutrality and I don't believe we can continue down that road. I believe we must jump into this mess strongly, regardless of the risk, or refuse to take our rightful place in the world. More than at any time since the Napoleonic period, Western Civilization is at stake. I think of Abraham Lincoln who was a moral and upright man. He was a pacifist at heart. But when there was no other alternative, he did not equivocate or fictitiously talk of peace when there was no peace. Realizing the country could not endure half-slave and half-free, he threw down the gauntlet and eradicated the evil. We are faced with somewhat the same dilemma in Europe now, and the longer we wait the worse it becomes. We must act to help our great ally, Britain.

We are not a people apart. We must view all the nations in this world as neighbors on this beautiful planet. Boundaries, beliefs, religions, and philosophies should not separate us or give us cause to quarrel. We must rise above to greater understanding of each other, here at home and worldwide.

In the past few months, Holland and Belgium have surrendered to the Germans. And more recently, the Germans entered Paris. Personally, I hope Britain's new Prime Minister, Winston Churchill, can become a voice for freedom and a voice of reason. The free world is in dire need of a leader.

If the tyranny is not eliminated, then what will become of our world, our world's economies, or our freedom to travel? Will the Nazis next want to conquer the oil-rich lands of Western Asia? And if so, what will become of our industrialized nation that relies so heavily on oil?

Too many of our good citizens have become comfortable and view our country as nothing more than the plot of ground on which they reside, and their government as a mere organization providing laws, and police, and contracting treaties. I am concerned that if we do not entertain warmer feelings for one another, and our worldwide neighbors, then the moral dissolution of our nation is at hand.

I feel it's time our administration changes its approach. And so, with this in mind, I have the great honor of introducing the man chosen at the Republican National Convention, just eight days ago in Philadelphia, to take over as President of these United States.

From the great state of Indiana, Wendell Wilkie.

The audience loudly applauded Mr. Wilkie. But they were also applauding their own football hero. They were startled by Nile Kinnick's political speech, but they were proud to hear their favorite son speak boldly and passionately.

Wendell Wilkie walked next to Kinnick. He put his arm around the All-American and said something to Nile. Then he turned to the citizens of Iowa Falls.

If Nile Kinnick were old enough, I'd vote for him. I know he just turned twenty-two years old last week, but I think there may be a place for him in politics in the future. Iowa can certainly be proud of this Heisman winner. Thank you, Nile.

Friday, August 30, 1940. Arch Ward, sports editor for the Chicago Tribune, sat across the table from Dr. Eddie Anderson and Nile Kinnick. Ward had asked if they could join him for breakfast at the Morrison Hotel where the College All-Stars were residing this past week, a hotel the two Hawkeyes knew well.

"Coach Anderson, first of all, congratulations on coaching the All-Stars last night. I was so glad you were voted to coach the team after the season you had last year. And, Nile, congratulations to you as well for being voted captain of the team and playing as well as you did.

"I wanted to do a follow up story to last night's game. Almost eighty-six thousand people were there, the largest attendance yet for the annual NFL/College All-Star game. I think the readers of the Chicago Tribune would like to hear more from the two of you."

"Thank you, Arch," answered Dr. Eddie. "It was much more thrilling than the final score indicates. The Green Bay Packers played quite well for this early in the season."

"And so did the All-Stars," added Arch Ward. "Losing 45 to 28 to the Packers can hardly be considered a loss. It was an exciting game. The crowd always backs the college players, but I've never seen the crowd so involved." Arch Ward turned to Kinnick. "Nile, what you did was nothing short of brilliant. You scored two touchdowns of your own. You played a major role in two other touchdowns. You made all four extra point attempts. But the most amazing statistic I heard from last night's game was that the All-Stars only had one first down while you were on the bench. That's incredible."

Kinnick smiled sheepishly. "I appreciate the compliment, Mr. Ward. We gave it everything we had. The Packers are formidable."

"Are you definitely walking away from football for law school?" inquired Mr. Ward.

"I am now certain of it. Yesterday was my last game." Nile leaned forward for emphasis as he spoke. "Nothing will deter me from my immediate goal of law school."

"After what I saw you do to the world champions, with a group of teammates you hardly knew, I must believe that pro football is missing out on something special."

"Pro football will do just fine without me. It was a difficult decision. But I know it's the right decision."

"I must say, Nile, the large attendance last night was, in part, due to you. You've captured the nation. They came to see a real All-American, not just a football player. I know some came because they had heard the rumors that it was the last time you would be on the gridiron. I think, someday, a team owner will probably make you an exorbitant offer to get you on the field again, maybe an offer you won't be able to refuse."

"Maybe," said Nile. "But for now, law school starts on Monday. Coach Anderson has asked me to help out with the team, especially the freshmen footballers, and also do some scouting. I couldn't say 'no' to Coach. So I'll have a nice transition out of football.

"But I must admit, Mr. Ward, I felt a tinge of remorse taking off my cleats yesterday."

Arch Ward looked over at Dr. Eddie. "Coach, what's next for you?"

"Next, I need to get a group of young men in Iowa City ready for the upcoming season. The nucleus is there to have another good year, but something magical will be missing." He paused and looked over at Kinnick while still talking to Arch Ward. "I may coach another twenty years, but what we had last year will never be duplicated. So we move forward, and do our best."

CHAPTER THIRTY

Friday, May 30, 1941. "Enich, Tollefson, and I will be at The Academy about eight o'clock if you want to join us." Couppee had phoned Kinnick at his Law Commons apartment. He knew Kinnick's final test was yesterday.

"I'll be there." Kinnick looked forward to an evening without studying. That's all he had done for three weeks. His first year of law school was finished. For once, he had no plans for the weekend.

Nile decided to walk across campus to the Hawkeye hangout. The walk conjured up five years of memories: The emotional strain of losing so many games his sophomore and junior seasons - baseball and basketball early in his college career before he decided they were taking too much time - the physical pain of the ankle injury his junior year - questioning his Christian Science faith when he started wondering if it would be best to receive medical treatment - Dr. Eddie arriving - his new coach being a Catholic doctor which seemed so foreign to his religious upbringing - Era Haupert - Barbara Miller - Couppee's carefree lifestyle and the way he just enjoyed life - the always easygoing and humorous Prasse who's now playing minor league baseball - Mike Enich, the gentle giant - Chuck Tollefson, the hobo turned football star, riding in railroad boxcars one year and the Rocket passenger train to Chicago the next - Red Frye who had a completely different childhood than his own - the Heisman - beating out Joe DiMaggio, Joe Louis, and Byron Nelson for the Associated Press' Athlete of the Year - instant fame - pro football offers with a chance of being a New York Yankee - the vibrating, ear-shattering roars from the Iowa Stadium bleachers after touchdowns against Notre Dame and Minnesota - the celebrations downtown after those victories - the train rides back to Iowa City after road wins - the sound of the wind blowing through the oak trees as he strolled across the campus towards The Academy tonight.

He would never forget this Midwestern town and how much it meant to him. He wondered what was in his future, both near and distant. He reflected on law school being his stepping stone to politics but Europe, he supposed, could change all that very quickly.

He thought about his parents and his younger brothers. He remembered those glorious evenings on his grandparents' porch reciting a poem or a chapter, learning to stand before an audience and deliver. Adel, Iowa - the farm - riding the tractor in complete solitude with no one in sight from horizon to horizon - his senior year of high school in Omaha. So much had happened in five years.

He wondered what his old college coach, Irl Tubbs, was doing tonight. Was Era Haupert happily married? Should he see Barbara Miller? Should he call Virginia Eskridge? Would he reach his goals, or be stopped in his tracks by an unforeseen obstacle he won't be able to overcome? Then he chuckled. Life's uncertainties, he mused, never allow one to rest on past laurels. Change is inevitable.

His mind continued taking in everything imaginable. Spring always felt, smelled, and looked so beautiful. His thoughts drifted toward God. Was there a specific purpose for his life? Was he being molded for something he hadn't yet envisioned? Did goodness beget goodness? Or, was he just lucky? Was he just at the right place at the right time? How could God allow such a great person like Chuck Tollefson to live in obscurity while barely existing? How could God permit the bigotry and unfairness occurring to the blacks in the United States? How could God tolerate the tyranny in Europe? Was there no Divine Intervention? Do we genuinely possess free will?

Then he laughed again to himself as he drew nearer to downtown. These questions weren't new. The answers are never handed to us, he thought. He surmised it was about having faith in something we don't understand, and possessing love for the others experiencing the same ride through life right now. No matter what is real or not, he thought, he wanted to live rightfully.

He crossed Madison Street as he approached the Old Capitol where the colossal pep rallies took on their own life in 1939. He wondered why they were so enormously important, or the football games for that matter - momentous one weekend, and then, a few months later in the dead of winter, people just bustling by the same areas trying to stay warm on their way to classes. Then he remembered the hope, the unity, and the common cause those weekends brought to everyone.

As Kinnick approached The Academy his pace slowed to a stop. He looked through the front window and viewed his teammates and friends engaging one another with friendly banter. Al Couppee was at the jukebox with a coed discussing what songs to play. Mike Enich was taking his shot at the billiards table. Bruno Andruska was his partner against Chuck Tollefson and Jens Norgaard in a game of Eight Ball. It was a sentimental moment standing outside The Academy, viewing his past through the window. He missed those moments, already. The 1939 football season was almost two years ago. But he also knew it meant his destination was that much closer. No one inside knew of his recent decision. He hadn't even told his parents, yet.

Nile thought about Erv Prasse who had just finished his first year with Oshkosh of the National Basketball Association. He was spending the spring with the Cardinals' farm club in Asheville, North Carolina, to give baseball one more try. Kinnick wondered what Prasse was doing this very minute. Whatever it was, he knew Prasse was having fun.

He wished he could just stand outside awhile longer and remember, but it was time to go inside and greet his friends. Soon he would tell his parents about his new plans, but tonight was a moment to share with the former Ironmen. He pushed the door open. Heads turned to greet him.

Tuesday, June 3, 1941. "Hi, Mom," Nile responded to his mother answering the phone.

"Hello, Nile. It's good to hear from you. How were finals?" asked Frances.

"They went well. In fact, it all went better than I had anticipated. I finished third in my class with a 3.8 average."

"Third in your class! That's wonderful. Your father will be so proud to hear the news."

"Is Dad home?"

"Yes. I can get him if you'd like."

"Can you hold the phone between the two of you so I can talk to both of you at the same time? I have some news I want to share."

Frances noticed slight apprehension in her son's voice. "Is everything okay, Nile?"

"Yes. Yes, everything is fine."

Nile Sr. joined the conversation while Frances held the phone between their heads. "What's this I heard your mother say about third in your class? Nile, this is the most disappointed I have ever been with you. Not first?" Nile Sr. laughed. "That is great news, Son. Congratulations."

"Thanks, Dad.

"I need to tell you of my recent decision." Nile paused. "It's been almost a year since I registered for the draft. I was speaking to a friend the other day, and based on what is occurring with him, there is a good chance I'll be drafted sometime around September. I'd rather enlist in the officer candidate school and become a Navy pilot."

Frances and Nile Sr. were momentarily silent.

"And put law school on hold for now?" asked Nile Sr.

"Yes, sir." Nile had rehearsed what he wanted to say next. "It is very sobering to realize just what the future holds for me. I don't feel I would be worthy of my background and heritage if I acquiesce to tyranny in order to cling to temporary safety and comfort. I feel that a man who talks but is afraid to act, who sacrifices principle in exchange for expediency when real danger threatens, is not worthy to keep and enjoy what he has been given. So, I have decided to enlist in the United States Naval Reserve Air Corps. I trust I will have the courage to act as I speak when the moment of bravery confronts me."

Frances responded, "We have wondered how soon the draft might affect you. I know you make this decision because you feel it is right."

"When are you enlisting?" asked Nile's father.

"Next week. I can only hope that Winston Churchill can convince FDR to join the war.

"Speaking of Churchill, I bought his most recent book, 'Blood, Sweat, and Tears,' which is a collection of speeches. Some of the passages in those speeches are beyond description. My favorites are speeches he gave last year after becoming Prime Minister. 'Blood, toil, tears, and sweat'; 'This was their finest hour'; 'Never was so much owed by so many to so few'; 'We shall fight on the beaches.' They are marvelous. It makes my spine tingle just to read those lines.

"Well, I need to make one more phone call. I hope you can understand my decision. I'll talk to both of you soon. Good night."

"Good night, Nile."

Nile wanted to talk to Dr. Eddie before ending the day. Transitioning from hearing the applause to studying in law school was cushioned by Dr. Eddie's desire to have Nile help coach the 1940 team. It gave Nile an opportunity to be around football. He was still part of the team - at practices, in the locker room, and on the sidelines. He still felt the roar of the crowd, the ecstasy of a good play, and the agony of a loss.

"Hello." Dr. Eddie answered the phone.

"Hello, Dr. Eddie. This is Nile."

"I don't usually get late night calls from you, Nile. So to what do I owe this pleasure?"

"Dr. Eddie, this fall I may not be able to help with the team. I have decided to enlist in the Naval Reserve Air Corps. It's likely I would otherwise be drafted sometime this fall, and that certainly prompted my decision."

"Does that mean no law school in the fall?" inquired Dr. Eddie.

"Yes. If I'm accepted into the pilot training program it's undetermined when exactly I'd be called to duty because those classes are full right now. So, law school is on hold, but I'd like to help you with the team as long as I'm around. I might be in Iowa City for one or two months or I could be around until December or January. But in any event, I'd like to help you until I leave."

"I'll take a Nile Kinnick as long as I can. Consider yourself hired." Dr. Eddie knew the war was imminent. The thought of losing his best player and other Ironmen to the war was sobering. "The '41 team will need an assistant backfield coach. Interested in a step up from the freshman team?"

"Yes, sir. I can't tell you how much it means to continue being part of the Hawkeyes. When we beat Notre Dame for the second straight time last year, I felt like I was in the ball game."

Dr. Eddie let out a laugh. "Maybe you'll end up like me, never able to let football be part of your past. Let's talk soon about the assistant backfield spot.

"By the way, Nile, I heard Ken Pettit signed up for the Navy Air Corps, also. You should give him a call."

"I will, Coach. And thank you." Nile hung up the phone and realized his days even on the sideline were limited. The battles on the gridiron, he hoped, had prepared him well for his next step.

CHAPTER THIRTY-ONE

Sunday, January 11, 1942. "Ken, I'm doing my first solo tomorrow morning. I can't believe I'll finally be up there by myself, especially since it's only been a month and a half since you and I drove down here. It's all happened very quickly." Kinnick met his old Hawkeye teammate, Ken Pettit, at the airfield's commissary for dinner. The food was not gourmet, but it was satisfying for two hungry young men in the Naval Air Corps. Coincidentally, they had driven together to Fairfax Airfield outside Kansas City three days before the attack on Pearl Harbor. They sat together in the barracks the night of December 7, 1941, listening to the news of the devastating Japanese attack. No one in the barracks had heard of Pearl Harbor before that day. The development of young pilots throughout the country had suddenly become a top priority.

"If I can get my radio down as well as my trigonometry, I should be up there soon." Ken Pettit was also one of the leading students in the pilot class.

"Don't be in a big rush, Ken. The temperature is expected to be ten degrees Fahrenheit tomorrow. If it's that cold down here, I can't imagine how cold it will be up there. I'll be bundled up like an Eskimo. You know, when we see live action I am hoping it's in the tropics." Kinnick smiled at Pettit, joking about the location. The seriousness of what they were preparing to do was being validated every day in the newspapers. Pettit and Kinnick both knew this wasn't a game. No longer were they preparing for the gridiron where thousands watched in the stands. Their next battle would most likely be seen by a handful of comrades, at most. It would be a fight with much more at stake.

"I just hope it's not long-lasting," said Pettit. "And I hope Churchill and Roosevelt will have a good plan when the time comes."

"And it will come, Kenny. It will come." Kinnick looked out into the dark cold winter evening. "Let's head into town. I talked to Merle McKay yesterday. She lives in Kansas City. She was a Pi Beta Phi at Iowa. She told me her sister, Mary Alice, is at home, too. Let's see if they would join us for a movie. We could see *Citizen Kane* or *Dumbo*. Frankly, I could use the light-hearted animation tonight."

Captain Wright was preparing some notes for class as the pilots took their seats. "Good morning, men. The ten of you have been asked to come in this morning to prepare for your first solo. Lieutenant Commander Swanson will be flying next to you. The Grumman F4F-4 will become your second home over the next several months. And you will become very proficient at flying it. Very soon, you will be flying with a hood over the cockpit's bubble so you will rely solely on your instruments. But for now, let's just get you up, do some maneuvers on your own, and get you back down.

"I need the ten of you, plus fifteen others, to get this down quickly because the USS Lexington will be christened soon, and you'll be assigned to her. Once you can fly by instruments, you will be sent to Pensacola for radio code, and then to Miami to practice takeoffs and landings on an aircraft carrier."

As the Captain paused, Kinnick thought about the quick learning curve. He was only twenty-three years old. Last week he learned about the six Browning machine guns on the 'Wildcat,' the Grumman's nickname. The week before that, he learned how and when to release the two 100-pound bombs it carried. The call to arms, he thought, involved heroism and learning what to do in that moment of truth. One involved chivalry, which he proudly felt lying in bed at night in the barracks when his thoughts were kept to himself. The other was about the harsh reality and intent of these fast-paced lessons, learning to destroy and kill.

Captain Wright continued. "Our advantage is well-trained pilots with good tactical knowledge. Also, the F4F is made of rugged construction and superior armament compared to the Japanese 'Zero.' But the 'Zero' has greater speed and maneuverability. We will win this war, partly because of how well-trained our boys are in the air. Ascent and descent will be critical in fighting the 'Zero.' Rolls have not proven to be strategically successful moves.

"The Grumman F4F-4 is the plane you will be flying on aircraft carriers. With the new folding wing version, it provides the ability to get more aircraft onto the carrier decks. Grumman is producing 3,000 of these planes this year for Britain and the United States. We need to train pilots as fast as we produce planes.

"You will be taking off with a gross weight of 7,975 pounds. This is the maximum weight when fully loaded with fuel, bombs, and ammunition. You will take the 1,200 horsepower Pratt & Whitney engine to its maximum speed of 320 miles per hour and to an elevation of 19,800 feet. Any questions?"

In unison ten young men shouted, "No, sir."

"Ensign Kinnick, you're the celebrity. You're first."

Thursday, May 14, 1942. Lieutenant Akery and Ensign Kinnick stood between two Grumman 'Wildcats' while the ground crew made final inspections.

"Okay, Kinnick, you've flown well these past few months. If you get a passing grade on today's flight, you're off to Pensacola. Do you have any questions?"

"No, sir, I'm ready."

"Again, Kinnick, as soon as you reach five hundred feet, I want you to pull the hood up in the cockpit so you can't see the horizon. You will be flying blind. I'll take off first. At one thousand feet, bank left. Remember, as soon as you bank, your lift decreases. Always keep in mind the cosine of the bank angle; rate of turn is greatest at low velocity and high bank angle. So apply back pressure to your stick while banking. That will keep you in level flight. I'm telling you this because many pilots start descending immediately and have to pull the hood back down. And that means failing. Remember, too, the airspeed will decrease slightly so increase the power to keep up with me. Got it?"

"Yes, sir."

Akery and Kinnick climbed into their Grummans. The pilots closed their bubbles. The propellers' revolutions increased as the ground crew backed away. Akery lead the way to runway twenty-seven. A fifteen mile an hour wind blew from the south so runway twenty seven, at two hundred seventy degrees from north, would have a crosswind as the planes took off headed west.

Kinnick quickly reached five hundred feet and pulled the hood up. The horizon was gone. The instrument panel and stick were all he could see. Soon he would be at five thousand feet.

"How are you doing, Heisman?" Kinnick acquired the nickname as soon as he reached the naval base.

"Okay, sir."

"How do you feel?"

"A little apprehensive, sir."

"Good. You should. You're an honest man, Heisman."

"Honest and a little scared, sir."

"Okay, Kinnick, let's head to two hundred twenty-five degrees, altitude six thousand. Lots of power as you turn. Nose up. Your focus should be on the rudder, then the bank angle with ailerons. You've got to feel it! And keep a close eye on the Attitude Indicator."

Nile made the left turn heading south-southwest.

"Kinnick, you've got some yaw to your left. Straighten out the nose. That wind is pushing from the side."

Kinnick checked his gauges. Altimeter read six thousand feet. The vertical speed indicator read 'zero,' meaning he was done ascending and in level flight. "What speed, sir?" Nile couldn't remember if he had been instructed on the speed.

"Good question. I hadn't told you. Let's take it to three hundred." Akery could tell from the sound of the young pilot's voice that he was processing the data. "Your yaw looks good. You got rid of the slip. I think you've got it. Let's just relax a moment and stay at level flight. It's a beautiful day. Too bad you can't see it."

"Ten four, sir." Nile knew he was doing well.

"You just need to have faith in the instruments, Heisman."

A few minutes passed. Nile listened to the loud roar of his 1,200 horsepower engine. He listened for his instructor's voice, too. "How are you doing, Heisman?"

"Good, sir."

"Okay, we're going to turn around and head back. You'll do a descent based on what I tell you. At five hundred feet you can pull the hood back down and do a visual flight landing, and catch a glimpse of this marvelous day."

"Can't wait, sir."

"But always remember, Kinnick, a flight is only as good as its landing."

Friday, May 15, 1942. Nile sat alone in the commissary. Private moments of solitude were rare, and appreciated. He decided to write his family and update them on his flight progress. The letters had become fewer and farther between. Free time was not part of a new pilot's life.

> *Dear Family,*
> *Training continues to move along very quickly. Our stay in New Orleans was short-lived. We are headed to Pensacola in two days.*
> *I must tell you, there is nothing quite as exciting as flying in and around the clouds on a beautiful day. Some clouds rise up like the Alpine mountains. 'Excelsior!' Remember the poem grandpa asked me to read? Exhilaration and peacefulness occur at the same time. You look down at the planet, with all its wonders and sorrows. A feeling of loneliness engulfs you while, at the same time, the meditative moment invigorates.*
> *I have mastered flying upside down. Most of our flying, of late, has been geared towards instrument flying. It entails flying without being able to see the horizon. Just imagine driving down the highway on a foggy day and all you can see is your dashboard. It's an odd feeling at first, but once you learn to trust your instruments, and senses, it becomes easier.*

Much of our time in Pensacola will be spent learning radio code and then I'll be moving to Miami to do takeoffs and landings from an aircraft carrier.

The Navy doesn't waste a moment as they prepare us for battle. I must admit I haven't thought about the old football days very often, but it is comforting to have my good friend and fellow Ironman, Ken Pettit, along as we constantly learn new tactics.

The stark reality of what is ahead is disturbing. The gruesomeness of war will soon be part of daily activity. May God grant me the strength to face my challenges. Let Ben know his older brother congratulates him on graduating from Iowa State. I wish I could have been there. And also let Ben know how proud I am of his decision to be a pilot in the Marines. Someday, he and I will have much to talk about while sitting on a porch after a Sunday dinner, listening to our children read poems. I yearn for those moments.

Love,
Nile

Wednesday, September 16, 1942. Twenty-five pilots were flown from Miami to Quonset Point, Rhode Island. Ken Pettit was not one of them. Pettit had been assigned to a ship in California.

Kinnick and his twenty-four classmates stood in awe looking out at the bay. The Naval harbor was much larger than he had imagined. In the distance, the USS Lexington, the reason they had come to Rhode Island, rose five stories above the other battleships and destroyers docked nearby. The Lexington was painted Navy blue in contrast to the battleship gray of its neighboring ships. It had already acquired the nickname 'The Blue Ghost.' It would be, when fully loaded, a thirty-six thousand ton miracle. The Lexington was an entire city, a mobile city. Kinnick marveled at its brilliance. He had studied about his new home while flying to New England. It was an engineer's masterpiece. Standing ninety-three feet above sea level, its total beam was one hundred forty-seven feet from side to side. Nine hundred ten feet separated the bow from the stern. It was over three football fields in length, thought Kinnick.

The steam turbines allowed it to cruise at thirty-three knots with a range of twenty thousand nautical miles before restocking. The deck and hangars below could house one hundred ten aircraft. Two thousand six hundred officers and enlisted men would occupy this transportable city.

Only the best of the best pilots would be asked to take off and land from the short, narrow decks serving as movable airport runways. Even though Kinnick had done takeoffs and landings on a similar ship in Miami the past few months, the idea of going out to sea on this ship sent shivers up and down his spine. One more rehearsal in the Caribbean and then they would proceed to the Panama Canal with Pearl Harbor as their first destination. Each of the men on board would earn the Navy's unofficial certificates of "Plank Owner" for being part of the first commissioned crew, and "Order of the Ditch" for passing through the Panama Canal.

Captain Felix Budwell Stump was on board to greet the new additions to his rapidly growing pilot crew. "Welcome, men. Welcome to your new home, the USS Lexington. First, I want everyone to find their bunk and unload belongings. You will then join the rest of the crew on deck at eighteen hundred hours.

"One other item. Which one of you is Ensign Kinnick?"

Nile stepped forward and answered, "I'm Ensign Kinnick, sir."

"I want you to stop by the Captain's quarters at seventeen hundred hours."

"Yes, sir."

Kinnick looked at his watch. It was the watch he received the night he won the Heisman. Though he had no belief in good luck charms, he discovered a personal need to always wear it in flight. It was sixteen forty-five. He had fifteen minutes to find the Captain's cabin.

His mind briefly drifted to Iowa. With Iowa in a different time zone, he realized football practice started fifteen minutes ago. He smiled knowing Dr. Eddie had them running sprints this very moment.

After asking a sailor for directions, he finally stood outside Captain Stump's door. He knocked briskly three times.

"Come in, Ensign."

Kinnick entered and saluted. Captain Stump stood next to another officer.

"Ensign Nile Kinnick, this is Lieutenant John Kennedy. He has a special assignment for you this weekend before we get this ship launched to sea next week. Lieutenant."

"Thank you, Captain. First of all, it is an honor to meet you, Ensign. I followed your football career, and I might add enviously. I tried playing football at Harvard before a back injury in practice ended those plans. I also graduated in '40, and can tell you we were all following the Ironmen story closely. It was quite exciting."

"Thank you, Lieutenant," Kinnick responded.

"And I am also aware of your political interests, giving the introduction speech for Wendell Wilkie, and speaking to the Young Republicans. Very impressive. But I must say, my father in Massachusetts was slightly dismayed at your Republican alignment, at least until he discovered that your grandfather was a Republican Governor." Lieutenant Kennedy showed a warm, wide smile. "Then he forgave you."

"Maybe we're all just born into party affiliation, sir." Kinnick returned the smile.

"Quite possibly, Kinnick. Anyway, I should address the purpose of this meeting. First, I want to stress the importance of this weekend's event. There is a large contingency of Marines on the base. And they have challenged the Navy to a game of football, full contact without pads. They want to prove their toughness, and virility. We want you to help us win this game. And as the appointed coach, when I heard you were headed for the Lexington, I had to make sure we could count on your services, and loyalty, to the Navy."

"It's an intriguing offer, Lieutenant Kennedy. But I must tell you I haven't played since the All-Star game against the Packers two years ago."

"Well, Ensign, there will be some players with college experience on both teams, but I think I can safely say, you will be the most talented person on the field, even if rusty." Kennedy grinned, and then looked at Captain Stump.

"Okay, I'm in. But I don't know the offensive or defensive sets." Kinnick knew he wasn't really being asked to play as much as being told to play. Navy pride was on the line.

"Well, Ensign Kinnick, I've put a great deal of thought into this, being the coach and recruiter. And I've decided on a very simple and effective offensive scheme. We will be hiking the ball directly to you in your usual halfback position on every offensive play, and then you will either be passing or running. I think it's a good plan. We'll huddle. You tell the wide receivers what routes to run. And then tell the line which way to block, left or right, so you can roll out, whether it's a run or pass play. Basic, but effective. I think, if we can get the ball in the hands of a Heisman winner every play, we'll do well."

"When and where should I be for the game?" Kinnick asked.

"It's Saturday, fourteen hundred hours. We'll have someone here to pick you up, and you, too, if you'd like, Captain. I know you're planning on attending. There will be three Admirals in attendance, Kinnick."

"I have one question, Lieutenant." Kinnick again gave a wry smile. "You mentioned full contact without pads."

"That's correct," answered Lieutenant Kennedy.

"Are cleats allowed? Change of direction would certainly aid our cause." Again Kinnick beamed.

"I like the way you think, Kinnick. I heard you were a Phi Beta Kappa." Kennedy looked up toward the ceiling, scratching his chin, recalling the rules that had been established. "I don't remember any mention of shoes, so I think we need to make sure we're not the team showing up without cleats. It could make all the difference in the world, especially given that we are relying on your cutting ability."

"Maybe we could make a deal with someone at Providence College to let us borrow a few pairs of football shoes," Kinnick replied. He could tell Kennedy and Stump were impressed with his idea.

"As I said, Kinnick, I like the way you think. If I wasn't planning on giving you the ball every down, I'd appoint you to be my assistant on the sideline. I think I'll take a ride up to Providence tomorrow." Kennedy shook Kinnick's hand and then turned and saluted Captain Stump.

"I believe this was a productive meeting, gentlemen." Captain Stump looked at Kinnick and then Kennedy. "You're both dismissed."

CHAPTER THIRTY-TWO

Saturday, September 19, 1942, thirteen hundred hours. Nile Kinnick stood at the base of the USS Lexington's gangplank waiting for his ride to the football field. A Navy jeep pulled up with an enlisted driver and Lieutenant Kennedy in the front passenger seat. "Come aboard, Ensign Kinnick." Kennedy was dressed in Navy khakis. "You might look in the box beside you and pick out a pair of shoes that fit."

"Very good, sir," Kinnick replied.

"Today, forget the 'sir.' Call me Jack."

"It appears you have shoes for the whole team," Kinnick said.

"It turns out the Providence coach was a Navy man in the last war. He'll be in the stands today cheering on his cleats." Kennedy looked at the driver. "Let's go sailor. We have one hour to kickoff."

Sixteen hundred hours. Kinnick was standing in the middle of the huddle at the Navy thirty yard line. The line of scrimmage was at the forty. The Navy players listened intently to their star athlete. "Jackson and Bell out wide left and right. Both streak for the end zone corners to get the cornerbacks and

419

safety away from the line of scrimmage. Linemen, I want to roll out right, so block the man lining up against you to your left. I'm faking a pass and running around right end, on the count of two." The players broke from the huddle.

"Hike, one, two." The center snapped the ball to Kinnick. The linemen blocked as Kinnick had told them. Kinnick took two steps to his right, stopped, and pump-faked a throw down the field. The cornerbacks were already running stride for stride with Jackson and Bell. The fake caused the linebackers to step back for just a moment, enough to stop their forward surge. Kinnick tucked the ball under his right arm and headed around the right side of the line following his quarterback and right halfback. The quarterback made a nice block on the outside linebacker, pushing the defender toward the sideline. It was vintage Al Couppee, Kinnick thought for the briefest moment. Kinnick cut back to his left and up the field. No Marine touched him as he ran past the line of scrimmage. He cut again, this time to his right. He raced toward the sideline as two Marines narrowed their angle on him. Kinnick stepped out of bounds at the Marines' twenty-five yard line after the thirty-five yard gain.

"Let's huddle quick," shouted Kinnick. "Let's score before the quarter ends. Same play but the receivers do a crossing route at the ten yard line. Linemen, just hold your blocks straight. I'm passing out of the pocket, on three."

Kinnick took the snap and dropped straight back. Bell and Jackson ran their pass patterns. Both had played college football, but not with someone of Kinnick's stature. They basked in the opportunity to catch his passes. As the two receivers ran past each other, Bell distanced himself from his defender. Kinnick threw a bullet pass directly into his chest and Bell sprinted the final ten yards for the touchdown. Kinnick jogged toward his coach on the sideline.

"Nile, the end of the third quarter and we're up 56 to 7. I think you've scored eight times in twelve possessions. You can take the rest of the day off. I need to give some other guys the chance to say they played in this game." Kennedy shook Kinnick's hand. "Thank you, Nile. It's been a pleasure. You made me look very good and all I did was recruit you and pick up some shoes."

"I guess that's why you're a lieutenant, Jack, and ready to captain a PT boat. You make good decisions."

"You know, Kinnick, I think we will meet again in the future, maybe in the Senate once this war is over. However, I'll be on the other side of the chamber floor."

"I can't think of a better place to meet, Lieutenant."

Wednesday, June 2, 1943, seven hundred hours. Venezuela was forty miles to the west. The island of Trinidad was twenty miles to the east. Both shores could be seen at the same time, but only from the bridge and flight control tower rising perpendicularly as a tall, majestic sentinel atop the Lexington's flight deck. The bright blue waters reflected the cloudless sky. The Gulf of Paria's three foot swells were too weak to sway the mammoth aircraft carrier.

Captain Stump met with the pilots in the hangar bay below. Kinnick stood five feet from the large deck elevators moving the fighter planes from the hangars to the flight deck. Two planes fit side by side on the elevator with their wings folded up. He looked at the designated area where his Grumman F4F-4 'Wildcat' was usually stowed. It was already on the flight deck for takeoff. The empty space contained only the chains usually anchoring his number '7' plane in place in case the ship pitched and rolled at sea.

"Gentlemen, this will be our final run-through before we head for the Canal." Captain Stump was referring to the Panama Canal. The Japanese seemed to be everywhere: the British Hong Kong, the Gilbert Islands, Guam, Wake Island, British Burma, Malaya, Borneo, and the Philippines. Japan's attempts to take over the petroleum and other natural resources of Southeast Asia had been successful, at least until the Battle of Midway one year ago. "The winds are calm today so we will be sailing at thirty knots directly into the wind to give you more lift, and obviously, we'll still be headed the same direction for your landings.

"As I said, this is the final run. The next time will be the real thing. We will be heading for Pearl Harbor immediately after this last practice. We have not been told, yet, the plan beyond Pearl Harbor, but I can guarantee it will involve dogfights against the Japanese 'Zero.' You are about to become part of the greatest Naval war in history. Churchill and Roosevelt have declared that the Allied fight against Japan will rest squarely on the shoulders of the United States while all other Allied forces, including the United States, will concentrate on the European theatre. I want all of you tonight to ponder the reality of what you will soon face. Your training will be officially over after today. Your courage will win the battles. Be prepared. Be proud. God be with you.

"Lieutenant Commander Buie. Take over."

"Squadron Sixteen, you will commence takeoff at eight thirty hours." Lieutenant Commander Buie hollered loudly. "Planes '1' through '20' will go first."

Nile Kinnick stood next to Lieutenant Bill Reiter, Ensign Robert Cotton, and Lieutenant Ardis Durham Jr. They comprised a four man fighter team, planes '5' through '8.' "It looks like a nice day for a flight, Lieutenant." Kinnick grinned at Reiter. "Let's see what Trinidad looks like from the air."

"Today's a long flight. We can check that out and Venezuela." Bill Reiter and Nile Kinnick had become close friends since the Lexington had been launched nine months ago. "Time for the flight suits."

"Maybe we should put our swim suits on just in case we find a landing strip far from everyone's sight," said Ardis Durham.

Kinnick suddenly realized how much Durham's personality paralleled Erv Prasse's. "You remind me of a guy I played football with at Iowa. He was the most unserious person I ever knew. Someday, when the Ironmen meet up again, I want you three to join me."

"We can be the second edition, Ironmen II!" added Cotton.

Eight thirty hours. The sound of twenty 'Wildcat' engines was deafening for the deck crew. Hand signals were the only form of communication.

The first four Grummans took off. Reiter, Durham, Kinnick, and Cotton moved into position. One by one they lifted off over the ship's bow, simultaneously rolled left, and then rapidly climbed to ten thousand feet. The four flew in unison, practicing various maneuvers before searching for the mark.

"Our target is an old ship. We should have visual contact in fifteen minutes." Reiter was the lead pilot.

Five minutes later, Kinnick radioed Reiter. "Lieutenant, oil pressure is dropping."

After a short moment, Reiter radioed back. "Number 7, you've got major oil leaking out of the engine!" An uncomfortable silence followed. The solemnity of the situation crept across the minds of the four pilots. All were mentally processing the next step. "You've got to head back immediately, number 7. I'll accompany you. Durham and Cotton, continue with the practice mission. There will be too much air traffic by the ship, anyway."

"Lieutenant, Lexington is in takeoff mode. There won't be any place to land," Kinnick said, sounding calm while flying over the vastness of blue. The ship was the only possible landing area other than the sea. "I'll radio Lex.

"Lexington, this is Ensign Kinnick, number 7. I have a problem. The engine is leaking oil badly."

The ship's traffic controller in the tower responded instantly. "Can you give us ten minutes?"

"I'm not sure but I'll try."

"Who's with you, number 7?"

"Lieutenant Reiter is on my right." Kinnick anticipated what the controller would tell him next. It would be impossible to clear the runway for a landing. Kinnick knew the only alternative. "I'll keep my landing gear up."

Sixty seconds of radio silence preceded the tower's instructions. "Landing should be off the bow, possibly four miles ahead. That should give you time to get out before the rescue boat reaches you."

"Nile, keep the nose positive to avoid a somersault," hollered Lieutenant Reiter.

The engine was overheating. Kinnick could feel the heat in the cockpit. He saw the last plane that took off before the tower was notified of his emergency. But several planes still remained on the crowded flight deck.

The engine sputtered several times. Suddenly, there were no sounds emanating from the engine compartment. Nile had lost power, but he held tightly to the stick. There was no yaw. The 'Wildcat' was aimed straight ahead, nose to tail. He knew he had to keep the wings level to avoid any roll, otherwise the uneven force on his wings would cause too rapid of a descent. He fought to apply back pressure to the stick, trying to stay level.

The outcome was up to Kinnick, a feeling he had experienced many times on the gridiron. Over two thousand Navy personnel were on the ship headed directly toward him. Reiter was next to him, but no one could help. He was alone. It was fourth down and long, and he had to make one more great play.

The fuselage lowered nearer to the sea. The pitch looked good with the nose slightly up. Then the Grumman settled down, the speed reduced sharply by the water's resistance. The plane glided to a stop, then floated motionlessly.

Reiter flew over and radioed the ship. "I see Kinnick. He's clear of the plane but I'm not getting any hand signals from him." Reiter banked to his left and circled back. On his subsequent flyover, neither Kinnick nor the plane could be seen. An oil slick was all that remained on the Gulf of Paria's surface. Reiter circled again, but still nothing. The Lieutenant stayed above the crash site to assist the oncoming rescue boat to the oil slick. A futile search ensued.

At twenty-four years of age, Nile Kinnick was gone.

Mr. and Mrs. N. C. Kinnick
1114 South 79th Street
Omaha, Nebraska

My dear Mr. and Mrs. Kinnick,

It is with deepest regret and sympathy that I inform you of the loss of your son, Nile, in an airplane crash on the second of June 1943. Nile was engaged in a practice flight that took off from the USS Lexington about eight thirty on the morning of the second of June and remained with his flight until he was forced to land in the water about an hour and twenty minutes later. His plane developed a serious oil leak about ten minutes before he landed. Having lost all oil, the engine, without lubrication, failed, forcing Nile to land in the water. Nile made a normal unhurried water landing in calm water about four miles ahead and in full view of the ship. He was seen by one of his teammates to get clear of the plane. Both the Lexington and the plane guard boat proceeded directly to the scene of the landing, which had been kept under constant observation, both from the air and from the ship, and was further definitely identified as being the exact location by gasoline and paint chips in the water, arriving at the spot about eight minutes later. A diligent and immediate search of the exact location of the landing and the adjacent water, by both planes and ships, failed to reveal any trace whatever of Nile. Since Nile was definitely not on the surface of the water eight minutes after he landed and at no time for the next hour and a half, it must be assumed that he drowned. Knowing Nile to be a very good swimmer, an excellent athlete, and in wonderful physical condition, it is inconceivable that he could have failed to remain afloat for the short period of time required for the crash boat to arrive unless he had been seriously hurt in the landing itself.

I would like to emphasize the fact that there can be no doubt, whatever, that the exact spot of Nile's landing was very thoroughly searched both by ships and planes immediately following the landing. A water landing is normally a relatively safe landing, especially under conditions of calm water. There is small probability of serious physical injury in such a landing. It is very difficult to understand just what could have gone wrong. The best guess, and it is nothing more than a guess, is that his safety belt broke on landing allowing Nile to lurch forward upon impact, probably striking his head on the structure of the airplane and injuring him to the extent that he could neither maintain himself afloat nor remember to inflate his life jacket.

Nile was an outstanding man in every respect. His calm and determined manner, his quick grin, his sound common sense, and his outstanding all-around abilities made him a wonderful asset to the squadron and a man that we were all proud to call our friend. His loss was a terrible blow to all of us and a serious loss to the country he so ably served.

Again let me extend my deepest sympathy to you for your great loss. Should there be any service that I can render, either now or later, please do not hesitate to call on me.

Sincerely,
Paul Buie
Lieutenant Commander, U.S. Navy
Fighting Squadron Sixteen

EPILOGUE

Most of the Iowa Hawkeye Ironmen joined the military to serve their country during World War II.

Lieutenant Wally Bergstrom

Lieutenant Ray Murphy

Major Ed McLain

Chief Specialist Henry Vollenweider served in the Coast Guard.

Sergeant Ham Snyder

Burdell "Oops" Gilleard and his football roommate, Bill Gallagher, both enlisted in the Army. Gilleard died in action in New Guinea.

Chuck Tollefson enlisted in the Marines but was discharged due to bad vision. He went on to play for the Green Bay Packers.

Dick Evans joined the Marines after playing for the Green Bay Packers and Chicago Cardinals. He later coached under legends Paul Brown and Vince Lombardi.

Lieutenant Al Couppee served in the South Pacific before playing for the Washington Redskins. He was later the broadcasting 'voice' for the San Diego Padres and San Diego Chargers.

Jim Walker enlisted in the Marines and was discharged as an officer. He later was the head football coach for several years at Central State University in Wilberforce, Ohio. The school's gymnasium is named the 'James J. Walker Gymnasium.' The football team's Most Valuable Player Trophy is the 'James J. Walker Award.'

Bill Green trained pilots in the Navy Air Corps.

Buzz Dean made the military a career.

Lieutenant Commander Max Hawkins, after the war, spent much time lobbying for Iowa's three state universities, and also schools for the deaf and blind. Hawkins Boulevard now runs along the east side of the stadium where the Ironmen played.

Lieutenant Colonel Jens Norgaard flew the lead plane, a B-26 Marauder, on a bombing mission over Utah Beach during the Normandy Invasion. He concealed his neck injury, sustained in the Wisconsin game, in order to become a pilot.

Captain Erwin Prasse signed with the St. Louis Cardinals to play baseball and also played for Oshkosh in the National Basketball Association before joining the Army. He later led his platoon in a boat crossing of the Roer River in Germany. Shrapnel in his right arm ended his professional sports careers. He was awarded a Purple Heart.

Captain Red Frye won the Air Medal for meritorious achievement in aerial flight during operations against Japanese forces in the Palau Islands.

Colonel Bruno Andruska was awarded a Bronze Star in World War II and, later, the Korean Medal for Bravery.

Jerry Ankeny earned five battle stars flying for the Navy Air Corps in the South Pacific and Africa.

Major Mike Enich was seriously injured at Okinawa. He later attended law school at the University of Iowa and eventually became a District Court Judge.

Captain Ken Pettit was awarded the Distinguished Flying Cross and an Air Medal. He also attended law school at the University of Iowa.

Dr. Eddie Anderson served as a Major in the Army medical corps and then returned to the University of Iowa, after the war, to resume coaching.

Lieutenant Reiter, the pilot flying alongside when Nile Kinnick attempted to land in the Gulf of Paria, was killed in action during a night battle at Wake Island three months after Kinnick's death.

Ben Kinnick, a Marine bomber pilot, was killed in action over the Kavieng Peninsula on New Ireland fifteen months after his older brother's death.

Following World War II, there was a strong movement to re-name Iowa Stadium after Nile Kinnick. Nile's parents refused the honor because they did not want their son singled out among all the Iowans who died in the war. Instead, they suggested it be named Veterans Stadium.

Years later, Nile Sr. agreed to the stadium being re-named Kinnick Stadium. He participated in a pre-game ceremony September 23, 1972, before the Oregon State game, when the stadium was officially named after his son.

Since 1965, a coin bearing the image of Nile Kinnick has been used for the coin flip in every Big Ten stadium before every Big Ten conference football game.

Nile Kinnick still holds six football records at the University of Iowa.

Interceptions in one season: (8) 1939.
                          Tied by Lou King, 1981

Interceptions in a career: (18) 1937 to 1939.
                          Tied by Devon Mitchell, 1982 to 1985

Punt returns in one game: (9) October 7, 1939, Indiana.

Punt return yards in one game: (201) October 7, 1939, Indiana.

Punts in one game: (16)   November 11, 1939,
                                      Notre Dame.

Punting yards in one game: (731) November 11, 1939,
                                      Notre Dame.

REFERENCES:

Papers of Nile Kinnick, Special Collections Department, University of Iowa Libraries, Iowa City, Iowa.

Couppee, Albert W. *ONE MAGIC YEAR - 1939 An Ironman Remembers.* 1989.

Baender, Paul. *A Hero Perished - The Diary & Selected Letters of NILE KINNICK.* University of Iowa Press. 1991.

Stump, D. W. *KINNICK The Man and the Legend.* The University of Iowa. 1975.

Fisher, Scott M. *THE IRONMEN The 1939 Hawkeyes.* Xlibris. 2003

Des Moines Register, 715 Locust St, Des Moines, IA 50309

WOW! Hawkeyes Defeat Minnesota, 13 to 9 by Bert McGrane, November 19, 1939. Copyright 1939, printed with permission by The Des Moines Register.*

Excerpts from miscellaneous Bert McGrane articles, 1939.

Two images, 1939, reprinted with permission from the Des Moines Register.

Omaha World-Herald, Omaha World-Herald Building, Omaha, NE 68102-1138

Two images, 1939, reprinted with permission from the Omaha World-Herald.

Chicago Sun Times, 350 N. Orleans Street, 10th Floor, Chicago, IL 60654

Excerpt from James Kearns' article, Chicago Daily News, Nov 19, 1939, as published in the Chicago Daily News. Reprinted with permission.

*Bert McGrane's November 19, 1939 Des Moines Register article follows in its entirety.

WOW! HAWKEYES DEFEAT MINNESOTA, 13 TO 9
2 Kinnick Passes Net Victory
50,000 Go Wild As Prasse, Green Snag Fourth-Period Aerials to Win.
By Bert McGrane
IOWA CITY, IA. – A grizzled observer wiped a tear of admiration off his leathery cheek. Writers hardened to emotion in many a year in the pressbox fumbled for words. Mad, milling thousands hauled an all-American halfback off the field on their shoulders. Pandemonium everywhere.

Iowa, probably the most astounding football team ever to cross the tawny turf of a gridiron, had just written another glorious chapter in its book of hair-raising, breath-taking finishes.

The Iron Hawks, underdogs as usual, had blasted Minnesota off the gridiron with another of their torrid, story book onslaughts that brought them an unbelievable 13 to 9 triumph over a team that had all but smashed them into submission through three bruising periods.

Here was another amazing victory against colossal odds. Outweighed, overpowered at times, outmanned as usual, the invincible Hawks went into the fourth quarter trailing, 9 to 0, moved the length of the field twice on passess and whirled on in the national spotlight with a thundering climax that 50,000 spectators still can't believe.

With the echo of the timekeeper's gun still in the air and thousands swarming onto the field in wild acclaim, fans hoisted Nile Kinnick onto their shoulders and hauled him away to the dressing room. Kinnick, the lad who had kept the Hawks together when it seemed fate was against them at the start, had just put the clinching touch on his all-American reputation.

It was Kinnick who fired the two touchdown passes that beat Minnesota. First to Erwin Prasse, later to Bill Green, the Comet of the Cornbelt shot home the winning throws. But it wasn't entirely Kinnick's triumph. His role was to dish up the dynamite that left a stunned, unbelieving Minnesota team the victim at the finish.

You had to have an eye-witness view of the terrific Minnesota power that had shackled Iowa through three periods to appreciate the spot Iowa was in when the final quarter opened.

Trailing, battered, worn, theirs was a Herculean task as they moved into their smashing climax. Minnesota had literally butted them aside, pulverized them, for 45 minutes. Only the indomitable courage, the iron determination of this Iowa team kept the Gophers in check at all, but that handful of heroes up front fought their hearts out and Minnesota, for all its physical advantage, had only a touchdown and a field goal to show for its 45-minute superiority.

Then Iowa, weakened all the way by an injury to Al Couppee on the very first play of the game, but keeping its feet in the face of Minnesota's irresistible power, launched a counter attack.

The fourth quarter was on. A Gopher punt rolled into the end zone and the Hawks took the ball a long 80 yards from the Minnesota goal.

In four plays they had a touchdown and a moment later they had the point that Kinnick's dropkick added. But Minnesota had 9 points to Iowa's 7.

Something like 11 minutes remained. Minnesota received the kickoff, fumbled early in a threatening drive and Iowa recovered in Gopher territory. But that threat failed when a pass was intercepted and Minnesota had the ball again.

They never can count this Iowa team out. After four minutes or so of maneuvering, Iowa got the ball again, this time when Kinnick hauled down a punt on his own 10-yard line and ran it back to his 21. Then lightning struck again.

Starting 79 yards away from the Minnesota goal, the Hawkeyes thundered through the air, covered that long stretch to the goal in just five plays and changed the scoreboard to read Iowa 13, Minnesota 9. Kinnick's dropkick was blocked, but only three and one-half minutes of battle remained and the Hawks fought off the ensuing Gopher blasts.

So that's how it happened and the mighty throng that witnessed this titanic duel still can't believe it.

It was a babbling, incoherent array of observers on the Iowa side of the pressbox who attempted to tell the story. This Iowa team, with its fiction-like thrillers over Indiana, Wicsonsin, Purdue, Notre Dame, had simply left observers at a loss for words. Some of them choked back tears in those mad, heart-stopping minutes at the finish. They groped for ways to describe this triumph over favored Minnesota.

After all, it was the same old Iowa story, a bunch of kids with iron physiques who recognize no odds. They don't care how many men the opposition calls upon to face them. They're not impressed by the enemy if they happen to trail near the finish. They believe they're the best team in football, and darned if they haven't almost convinced the football nation.

They lack a lot of things. Brute strength, replacements, smashing power, for instance. But no team in football history ever demonstrated more heart. And considering the limited manpower available I doubt if ever a team accomplished what this Iowa team has accomplished, against some of the strongest foes on the gridiron.

Things looked bleak for Iowa in this ball game. Al Couppee, a great quarterback, jammed his bad shoulder on the opening kickoff. He stuck it out for a while with that Spartan spirit that characterized the entire Hawk array. But even Couppee had to come out after three consecutive 60 minute games, and Iowa, robbed of his spark, his ferocious line-backing, his smart leadership on offense, looked ready to fall without Couppee.

Through three white-hot quarters they seemed a beaten team. Early in the first period the Gophers whirled through to Iowa's 12, where a penalty stopped them. They came right back, this time attempting a field goal that missed its mark.

In the second quarter, they hammered down to Iowa's 10-yard stripe again. Their power stopped momentarily by the fighting Hawkeye line, the Gophers turned to Joe Mernik who sent a placekick spinning through the uprights from the 16-yard line for three points.

Minnesota, for all its evident superiority, had only a narrow three-point lead at the half, but the Gophers quickly widened the gap in the third period. Backed into a hole when one of Harold Van Every's kicks bounded over the sideline at Iowa's 4-yard stripe, the Hawks couldn't shake off the Gophers.

Kinnick punted out from his end zone and Van Every raced back to Iowa's 27 with the kick. In four plays, the Gophers were on the 7-yard line. Then Iowa's fighting front dug in and on fourth down Minnesota still was five yards away.

The Gophers tried new tactics. George Franck, handicapped by an ailing leg, burst away on a long, slanting run around Iowa's right end. The Hawks made a desperate attempt to head him off but the driving Davenporter shot across the goal in the very corner of the field. Mernik's placekick was blocked by Wallie Bergstrom of Iowa and the Minnesota lead was 9 to 0.

The stage was set for a typical whirlwind finish by Iowa.

Nile Kinnick, the kid who was stopped cold on his runs, playing in a jersey ripped wide open by fiercely clutching enemy hands through the first half, returned again to the hero's role he had filled so often in the past.

Kinnick of Iowa. There's a name they know wherever football is played. The most durable back in football. Through six consecutive battles now, all of them against big-name teams of the gridiron, Kinnick has fought his way without replacement. Through 360 consecutive minutes of bitter, slamming action, this 170-pound dynamo has never had relief, never taken time out.

It was Kinnick who moved Iowa's scoring machinery into action. Early in the fourth quarter, with the cards apparently stacked against him, he set the stage. He was calling signals in the absence of Al Couppee.

He called a first down pass on his own 20-yard line, rifled the ball to Buzz Dean for an 18-yard advance. He slammed another to the racing Dean for 15 yards more and a first down on Minnesota's 47. Then he smashed for two yards.

Iowa was on Minnesota's 45-yard line. Kinnick faded back, just out of reach of crashing Gophers, as Capt. Erwin Prasse streaked down the field. With Prasse on Minnesota's 8, Kinnick fired. The racing Hawkeye took the ball in stride behind Bob Paffrath and Harold Van Every, and sprinted into the end zone. Iowa had six points and Kinnick made it seven with his dropkick.

It couldn't have been two minutes after the ensuing kickoff that Minnesota, booming up the field, ran into a jolt of its own making. The Hawks never could consistently stop Minnesota's power, although they did succeed in limiting it to the old fashioned smashing gains of from two to five yards a crack.

Surging upfield, the Gophers sent Bog Sweiger ramming into the Hawkeyes. Sweiger fumbled and Mike Enich and Ken Pettit of the Iowa line were all over that ball in no time at all. Iowa, whose fourth-quarter punch has been a feature of virtually every battle, bounded in with a menacing threat. That threat died when Kinnick rushed by harassing Gophers, shot a wobbly pass that Sweiger intercepted for Minnesota on his 25-yard line.

The Hawks lost the ball but they never quit. After reeling off two first downs, Van Every punted deep into Iowa territory. Kinnick fielded the ball on his own 10-yard line and recovered

11 yards before the Gophers slammed him into the sod on his 21-yard line.

Then Kinnick roared again. Setting up a drive that was almost a dead ringer for the first Hawkeye advance, Kinnick fired a pass to Bill Gallagher. It slid off Bill's fingers. Next Kinnick tried Buzz Dean again and racked up a 17-yard gain when Dean reached Iowa's 38 before they nailed him. Kinnick fired again, this time overshooting Prasse far down the field but an eagle-eyed official had detected a Gopher interfering with a Hawkeye and Iowa drew a first down by penalty on Minnesota's 45.

Kinnick varied his tactics. He sent Bill Green careening through the Gophers for seven yards. Then he carried the ball himself on a 10-yard wallop at Minnesota's left end. Next he sent Green scurrying wide as a decoy, with Buzz Dean apparently circling in a reverse to get the ball.

But Dean never intended to get that ball. As he whirled around, with Gopher attention on him momentarily, Bill Green's fleet feet took him into the end zone. Kinnick, drifting back with the ball, eluded the oncoming Gophers, turned and fired a pass to Green, who was in behind two Minnesota defenders in the end zone. Green tucked that football to his bosom for the points that won the battle and was all but mobbed by frenzied Iowa fans who swarmed out from the seats at the south end.

So that was the ball game. Kinnick's dropkick was blocked, but it didn't matter. During the three and one-half minutes remaining, Iowa had no thought of losing. Minnesota received the kickoff and took to the air immediately. Franck dropped one pass and the others missed their mark. Van Every ran with all the fury in his makeup, but it was no use. He passed once more, Kinnick intercepted, and Iowa shot line plays at the Gophers to use up that last precious minute.

It was the first Iowa victory over Minnesota since 1929 and the fourth triumph in five Big Ten battles for the Hawkeyes.

They enter their final battle against Northwestern Saturday with a chance to share the Big Ten championship providing Michigan can topple Ohio State.

This like all others, was a team triumph for Iowa. Six of the seven men in the line played 60 minutes, as usual. Kinnick went the route again to make it seven 60-minute men for the Iron Hawks.

Because of Couppee's injury, Iowa used four quarterbacks starting with the rugged Council Bluffs sophomore and using Gerald Ankeny and Bill Gallagher as replacements. In the closing minutes, when speed was vital in covering Gopher passes, Henry Vollenweider was rushed into the battle.

Once again, Iowa's honors were spread across the entire team. Kinnick, Prasse, and Green had a hand in the scoring, but the story might have had a different ending had it not been for the heroic 60-minute performances of Mike Enich, Bruno Andruska, Ken Pettit, Dick Evans, Wallie Bergstrom and Prasse in the line, and the valiant, inestimable services of Ray Murphy, Ed McLain, Buzz Dean, Bill Green, Ham Snider, and Charley Tollefson, who didn't fight the full distance, but earned an even part in the triumph.

ABOUT THE AUTHOR:

Tom Lidd lives in Cedar Rapids, Iowa, and is an avid, lifelong follower of Iowa Hawkeye sports.

LaVergne, TN USA
10 July 2010
189014LV00001B/1/P